400 DAYS

Get in touch with Chetan Bhagat and access content created by him here:

Instagram

X

Facebook

YouTube

Threads

LinkedIn

Spotify

Moj

Website

CHETAN
BHAGAT

400 DAYS

HarperCollins *Publishers* India

First published in 2021

This edition published in India by HarperCollins *Publishers* 2022
HarperCollins *Publishers* India, Cyber City,
Building 10-A, Gurugram, Haryana – 122002, India
www.harpercollins.co.in

2 4 6 8 10 9 7 5 3 1

P-ISBN: 978-93-5629-114-0
E-ISBN: 978-93-5629-137-9

Printed and bound at
Nutech Print Services Pvt. Ltd.

FSC
www.fsc.org
MIX
Paper | Supporting responsible forestry
FSC® C195953

This book is printed on FSC® certified paper which ensures responsible forest management.

*

HarperCollins *Publishers*, Macken House, 39/40 Mayor Street Upper, Dublin 1, D01 C9W8, Ireland

To my mother,
and all the other mothers in the world

Acknowledgements and A Note to Readers

Hi all,

Ever since my first book, I have had tremendous support from my readers. Even today, you have chosen to read my book. I thank you from the bottom of my heart.

To be read in a world flooded with social media, video content and other digital distractions is a real privilege and you have made it possible. Thank you!

Several people helped me with this book. These include:

Shinie Antony, my editor and friend for nearly two decades. Her guidance and support are invaluable.

The group of early readers who gave wonderful feedback on the manuscript. (Alphabetically) Ameeta Chebbi, Anjli Khurana, Anusha Bhagat, Ayesha Khan, Bhakti Bhat, Ishaan Bhagat, Mahua Roy, Melody Toh, Nandini Mehra, Prateek Dhawan, Ranodeb Roy, Santhosh M.V., Shalini Raghavan, Shameeli Sinha, Sinjini Das, Trisha Vasudeva, Virali Panchamia and Zitin Dhawan. Thank you all for your help and suggestions for the book. Thank you all also for being there for me whenever I needed you.

The editors at HarperCollins India. The entire marketing, sales and production teams at HarperCollins India. To all the online delivery boys and girls who put the book in my readers' hands. Thank you for all your hard work, particularly in these testing times.

My social media followers, including those on Facebook, Instagram, Twitter and YouTube. Those who love me. Even those who don't. I am thankful to all of you.

My family—a pillar of support in my life. My mother Rekha Bhagat, my wife Anusha Bhagat, and my children Shyam and Ishaan. My brother Ketan and nephew Rian. My in-laws Suryanarayan Annaswamy and Kalpana Suryanarayan. My brother-in-law Anand, my sister-in-law Poornima, and their children Ananya and Karan. Thank you all for being there.

With that, you are invited to *400 Days*!

Chapter 1

'I hate this stupid UPSC exam,' I said, tossing my pen onto the table. I read the exam question from a previous year's General Studies paper again.

Locate the following places on a map of India and write about their significance:

a) Karakoram Range
b) Gadchiroli
c) Tawang
d) Malkangiri
e) Jaitapur

While I couldn't locate any of the places on the map of India, I could definitely locate a niggling feeling in my stomach. It told me my IPS preparations were crap. I only had two attempts left before I reached the upper age limit of thirty-two years for the exam. My dream of becoming an IPS officer was going to be flushed down the Karakoram Range and get lost somewhere between Malkangiri and Jaitapur, wherever the hell those places were.

'Tea's ready,' my mother called out from the living room. I ignored her.

I wanted to be an IPS officer instead of running a tiny detective agency like I was doing at present. As a senior cop, I could solve a lot more crimes and help society. Noble, right? The problem is, the tough UPSC exam for civil services doesn't give a damn about nobility. Over a million people apply. Among those, a general category student like me has to achieve a top-500 rank if they want an IPS seat.

'This is insane,' I said, shoving away my textbook.

'Keshav, tea. Come now.' My father's explosive voice made me stand up in reflex. There's something about Indian fathers. When they call you, it's always urgent.

'I called you earlier,' my mother said, pouring me a cup of tea.

'Sorry,' I said, pulling up a chair.

I leaned forward to pick up a Parle-G biscuit from the plate on the dining table.

'How is the preparation going?' Papa said.

'Good,' I said, taking the biscuit to my mouth in slow motion.

'Good is not enough,' he said. 'It is a tough exam. Work harder.'

Wow, thanks for the deep insight, I wanted to say, but didn't. The rule of staying peacefully with parents is to keep the sarcasm minimal.

I only nodded.

'Say something,' Papa said.

'Leave him alone, Rajpurohitji. He's doing his best,' Ma said. She refilled my father's cup and stirred a spoonful of sugar into it. She handed it to him and my father grunted in response, his usual way of saying thanks to my mother.

'Is he?' Papa said.

'He is twenty-nine,' she said. 'He can decide his own career. If we must interfere, we should help him get married.'

No, thanks, I wanted to blurt out, but didn't. When Papa retired, my parents had moved to Gurugram to live with me. *Maybe my life is a total mess,* I thought, *and fixing it is their life's biggest passion.* My father wasn't happy with my career. My mother wasn't happy with my marital status. I had managed to disappoint both of them in different ways at the same time.

'Who will marry him?' my father said. 'No job. Sitting around the house all day. Doing his silly detective business while pretending to prepare for the toughest exam ...'

'Rajpurohitji, again you started,' my mother said.

'So you can tell him anything, but I can't?'

While my parents played their tennis match of hurling insults at me, I ate six biscuits. I checked the time. It was 5.30, time for their evening walk. I would get a break soon.

'Rajpurohitji, he went to IIT,' my mother was saying. 'Don't think so little of your son. And he has solved some good cases. His name came in the newspaper also. Many girls will want to marry him.'

'But he needs to get settled, right? Become responsible. Have a good, regular source of income.'

'He's trying hard for IPS, aren't you, beta?' Ma said.

'Huh?' I said, pausing mid-bite. 'Yes, I am. Ma, it's 5.30.'

'Oh, yes,' she said.

My parents stood up. 'We'll go now. Tell Saurabh not to snack when he gets home. I have made aloo-matar for dinner. Come, Rajpurohitji.'

I heaved a sigh of relief as I heard the front door shut.

Hi, I am Keshav Rajpurohit and I am a disappointment to everyone around me. I live in Gurgaon, or Gurugram, or whatever new name they may give this place next week. My best friend Saurabh stays with me. He works at Cybersafe, a computer security company.

I grew up in Alwar, where my father was a lawyer by profession and a dedicated RSS functionary by passion. We now live in my parents' three-bedroom apartment in a residential building complex called Icon, near the DLF Golf Course. My parents and I moved here after my father retired and purchased this flat. I asked Saurabh, my best friend and partner in our detective agency, Z Detectives, to move in with us as well.

Home-cooked food and a rent-free life had their benefits, but they came with an 'LFK' or 'Let's Fix Keshav' package.

My parents keep telling me how I should a) get married, b) get a job, c) meet more people, d) close this detective agency business (not that we have much business anyway), e) keep my room clean, f) talk more (when I don't talk to them), g) talk less (when I talk back to them), or whatever else they feel is wrong with me that day. Saurabh, a sell-out, always agrees with my parents. My mother would make kheer or halwa for him, and he'd join the LFK tirade, telling me to get serious about life.

Trrrring!

The doorbell signalled the sell-out's arrival.

'So tired, man,' Saurabh said, throwing his laptop case on the dining table. He loosened his tie.

'You're back early,' I said.

'Nothing happening in office,' Saurabh said. He went to the kitchen to get water.

'Ma said don't eat any junk. She's made aloo-matar for dinner,' I said.

'I am not hungry anyway,' he said between big gulps of water.

I stared at him.

'What? You okay?'

'Yeah.'

'Tea?' I said.

'A quarter cup,' he said.

I poured him a little bit of tea and we both sat at the dining table.

'Where are Uncle and Aunty?' Saurabh said.

'They went down for a walk. Let me have some peace.'

'What happened?' Saurabh said.

'Another lecture, what else? Marriage. Career. Close the agency.'

'They are not completely wrong.'

'Fine, join them.'

'The agency doesn't have cases. The last one was that small burglary two months ago.'

'After this coronavirus lockdown, the economy will take a while to get back to normal.'

'Even crime will take a while to get back to normal?' Saurabh said. I ignored his question.

'Anyway, I am doing my IPS prep in my free time.'

'How is that going?'

I didn't respond.

'You did a mock paper today, right? How did it go?'

'I haven't marked it yet,' I said in a sheepish voice.

'I think you know the marks won't be great,' Saurabh said in a firm tone.

I stood up with a jerk and the chair almost fell.

'Why is everyone after my life? I am trying, okay?' I said.

Saurabh finished his tea and put the cup on the table. Before he could respond, my phone rang. It was my mother.

'Why is she calling me?' I said.

Saurabh shrugged. I took the call.

'Yeah, Ma?'

'Could you come downstairs? To the garden area?'

'Why?' I said, puzzled.

'Someone wants to meet you,' Ma said.

'Who?'

'Just come down,' she said.

'But meet who? I am not even dressed properly.'

I was in gym shorts and a sleeveless T-shirt, my usual clothes for home.

'If your mother said come down, come down. Is it that difficult?' My father's voice startled me. He had taken the phone from my mother.

'No, Papa, I just ...' I said, but he disconnected.

Chapter 2

The sprawling gardens of the Icon were half the size of a football field. I went past the evening walkers trying to finish their daily step-count targets to the play area with its swings, slides, seesaws and a sandpit where children were building sandcastles. Maids and doting mothers were keeping an eye on their little ones.

My parents sat on a bench near the play area. As I came closer, I saw someone sitting with them. It was a woman, probably in her twenties. I noticed her striking looks first. She had a fair complexion, smooth skin and a cascade of brown curls. Her high cheekbones and full lips were visible even from a distance. She wore a white salwar kameez with blue embroidery on it. Were my desperate parents trying to set me up? Were they going to suggest a match?

'Keshav, come.' My father had noticed me.

'Meet Alia,' my mother beamed. 'She stays in Tower B, right opposite our Tower C.'

'Hello.' Alia extended her hand.

'Hi,' I said, shaking hands with her.

I felt like an idiot in my bathroom slippers and an old college vest. Alia wasn't just beautiful, she was stunning. She was might-be-a-model-level gorgeous. Her hazel eyes, a mix of light brown and green, were her most electric feature.

'Aunty was just telling me about you,' Alia said.

I wondered what my mother had said about me. Had she told her what a loser I was, or had she marketed me a bit? For once I liked my parents' choice.

'Oh, really?' I said.

'Sit with us, Keshav beta,' my mother said in an unusually sweet tone.

The four of us sat in a row on the bench. I wondered what my parents expected me to do. Chat her up?

'Which flat in Tower B is yours?' I said, forcing myself to make conversation.

'Sixteenth floor. Apartment 1602. How about you?'

'We are in Tower C, unit 1703. One floor above you.'

I pointed to our apartment, high above us, to our left. My parents continued to stare at both of us. I couldn't talk under this pressure. Fortunately, she could.

'Aunty told me you are a detective?' Alia said, brushing a lock of hair away from her forehead.

'Yes. I've helped the police with a couple of cases,' I said.

'He also went to IIT Delhi,' my mother said in a non sequitur, to pad up my resume.

'Nice,' she said. 'Tell me about your detective business. What exactly do you do?'

'All kinds of cases. Though the more serious the crime, the better it is. More fun,' I said and smiled.

'Fun?' She looked surprised.

'Sorry, I meant those are the ones I look forward to the most.'

'This detective stuff is just a hobby,' my father said. 'He is preparing for the IPS. He also worked in a software company before. Tell her properly no, Keshav.'

I smiled and remained silent.

She took out a small box from her handbag and opened it. There were laddoos inside.

'Would you like one?' she said.

'Thanks,' I said, taking a tiny piece of one. 'Ma?'

'We already took. She made them herself. They are amazing,' Ma said. A pretty girl who talks politely to elders and makes laddoos. Doesn't get more perfect than that for Indian parents.

I nodded my appreciation after tasting the little crumb.

'Take more, I have plenty,' Alia said. She handed me a full laddoo.

'Delicious,' I said, taking a bite.

'They are Kerala's brown rice laddoos. Not as unhealthy as you think,' she said.

'You are from Kerala?' my father said. Somehow, he is always deeply interested in people's hometown or state or religion or caste.

'On my mother's side. My father was a Rajput from Rajasthan. I am an army kid though. Grew up all over India.'

My parents' eyes lit up at the mention of the words Rajput and Rajasthan. If it were up to them, they would give her a sagan right there.

'So, you stay with your parents here?' my mother said. Before Alia could answer, a small girl came running towards her from the play area.

'Mummyyy,' she sang and jumped into Alia's lap. My parents' faces fell. Their disappointed expressions were so funny, you could turn them into memes. I wanted to burst out laughing but controlled myself.

'I brought the laddoos you like. Would you like one?' Alia said.

The little girl nodded vigorously.

'Okay, Suhana. Wish everybody first. That's Rajpurohit uncle and aunty. And that's their son, Keshav.'

'Good evening, Raj-pulo-hil uncle and aunty. Good evening, Keshav uncle,' Suhana said.

I had gone from prospective groom to uncle in five seconds flat.

'Hello, beti,' my mother said in a deflated voice.

'This is Suhana, my daughter,' Alia said.

My father grunted and stood up. He signalled to my mother to get up as well.

'I have to arrange dinner. Nice meeting you, Alia beta. Thanks for the laddoos,' my mother said.

Alia looked surprised at their abrupt departure.

'You are welcome, Aunty. I will bring some more Kerala sweets when I make them.'

My mother only smiled in response.

'Is Daddy home?' Suhana said.

'He's on his way. He messaged me,' Alia said.

'You are coming or not, Lalita?' my father said to my mother in a semi-stern voice.

I stood up to leave.

'Bye, Keshav uncle,' Suhana said in a cheerful voice.

'You should have seen your faces, Ma—both yours and Dad's,' I said, laughing as I put some aloo-matar sabzi on my plate.

'What nonsense!' Ma said.

My father didn't say a word. He just continued to eat.

I recounted the story to Saurabh, who didn't seem amused, going by his sullen face. I passed him the sabzi. He declined. I handed him the chapati box. He shook his head.

'No food?' I said, keeping the chapati box back on the table.

'Why?' my mother said.

'Not hungry,' Saurabh said.

'Did you eat junk again? Chips? Maggi?' my mother said.

'No. Excuse me, please,' Saurabh said and stood up. 'I'm tired. I'll go rest in my room.'

I noticed Saurabh's droopy shoulders as he walked to his bedroom. I sent him a message.

'Everything okay?'

My mother said, 'She's married. But by the grace of God, she is so beautiful. Isn't she, Keshav?'

'Huh?' I said, looking up from my phone.

'Stop checking your phone during dinner. It's rude,' Papa said.

'Sorry,' I said, and turned to my mother. 'What did you say, Ma?'

'Her eyes. Her skin. Her hair. So pretty,' Ma said.

'I didn't notice,' I said.

'Didn't notice!' my mother said.

'This sir here is above everyone else. Why did you come down in this old vest? Don't you have any shame? What impression will it create?' Papa said.

'How does it matter, Papa? She's married.'

'We still have to create a good impression as neighbours. Marriage, ha, what a joke! She would be way beyond you even if she were single. She won't look at you twice.'

'Golu, are you unwell?' I had come to Saurabh's room after dinner. He was sitting on his bed in a T-shirt and shorts, playing Candy Crush Saga on his phone.

'I am fine,' he said, without looking up from his game.

'You are not.' I jumped onto the bed next to him and snatched his phone.

'Hey, stop it. I almost cleared that level,' Saurabh said.

'Tell me what's wrong.'

'Nothing is wrong. I just didn't want to eat.'

'Golu, you and food are like inseparable lovers.'

Saurabh got off the bed. He pointed at the door.

'Keshav, can you please leave my room?'

'What?' I said, surprised. 'I was joking.'

'Lovers, is it? That's it? That's your idea of humour?'

'Why are you acting so touchy, Golu?'

'I am sick of it,' Saurabh screamed, loud enough for my parents watching TV in the living room to hear.

'Sick of my jokes about you and food? Sorry, Golu. I will stop.'

'No. I am sick of being fat.'

Saurabh plonked himself on the bed and it creaked loudly. The irony of him landing with a thud versus his delicate emotion about being fat was funny. However, I forced myself not to laugh.

'Has something happened, Saurabh?' I said in a soft voice.

Saurabh looked at me.

'I had a lunch date today,' he said.

'Date during office hours? With whom?'

'Well, with Rashmi. She works with Vodafone, ex-client of Cybersafe.'

'And?'

'She was amazing. Smart and attractive. A one-hour lunch at Pizza Express stretched to three hours. I made her laugh so much.'

'Great—what happened then?'

'I sent her a message later. Told her I had enjoyed meeting her and asked her out again.'

Saurabh took his phone and opened WhatsApp.

'Here, read this long message she sent me.'

I read Rashmi's message out loud.

'Saurabh, I enjoyed meeting you as well. You are good fun, intelligent and kind. However, relationships are about being honest. To be honest, I don't think I could be physically attracted to you. Your big frame, yes, some girls may find it cuddly and cute, but I see only future heart attacks. I could try to ignore the lack of fitness, but it will always bother me. Also, I used to be overweight once. It took me huge pains to lose weight. If my partner doesn't eat healthy, I'd be tempted and lose my resolve again. Hence it's better we remain just friends. No hard feelings.'

I kept the phone aside and remained silent.

'Bad, isn't it?' Saurabh said.

'Sucks. Friend-zoned. It's over. Full marks for honesty, though.'

'What do I do, bhai?' Saurabh said. He sounded like he was going to cry.

'This is brutal. But maybe you needed this.'

'I need Rashmi.'

I smiled.

'Will you help me get thin, bhai? Be my trainer? You are so fit and disciplined. I want to be that way.'

'I have tried in the past, Golu. You always find excuses and quit.'

'I won't this time, promise,' Saurabh said, pinching his neck like little children do.

I did not want to be trapped again. Making Saurabh stick to a diet was like trying to turn an alcoholic gambler into a monk.

'Say something, bhai?'

'I am not sure. Let me think about it,' I said before leaving his room.

Chapter 3

'Hello, Aunty.' I heard a female voice say. My mother had just answered the doorbell.

I was sitting at my desk, reading a chapter on major Constitutional amendments in a book that could compete for the most boring textbook in the world and win hands down. Saurabh had left for work. Papa had gone out to meet a friend. I checked the time: 11 o'clock.

I opened my bedroom door a little to peek at the unexpected guest.

'Alia beta, what a nice surprise! Come in,' Ma said.

I shut my bedroom door quickly. She must not see me in a vest and shorts again.

'Keshav!' my mother shouted. I ran to my closet and pulled out a pair of jeans and a shirt.

My mother opened the bedroom door. She found me buttoning up my shirt.

'What are you doing?' my mother said.

'Nothing.'

'That girl we met from Tower B has brought us payasam.'

'Is she still here?' I said, tucking my shirt in.

'I can't send her away from the door, no? She's not some delivery boy.'

'Of course not.'

My mother came close to me. She sniffed my neck.

'What are you doing?' I said.

'Checking if you smell. Should have taken a bath before wearing a fresh shirt.'

'It's fine, Ma,' I said.

'Come and talk to her. I will make tea.'

'What do I talk about?' I said.

'I don't know. She asked for you.'

'Really? Why?'

'How do I know? Go now.'

'Hi, Keshav. Sorry to disturb you,' Alia said, standing up to greet me. Black Lululemon yoga pants, a lavender sports top and a pair of hazel eyes.

'Happy to be disturbed while studying. Ma said you brought payasam.'

'Yes, elaneer payasam. Coconut kheer with jaggery.'

'You shouldn't have ... but thank you. Please sit,' I said.

We sat across each other on the living room sofas. Alia scanned the Rajasthani artefacts in the room.

'Nice place,' she said. 'You live here with your parents?'

'With my parents and Saurabh, my friend and partner in the agency.'

Her eyes had taken on a searching quality. I didn't want to be caught staring back, so I looked down at her pink and white sneakers.

'Your mom said I need not remove them.'

I brought my eyes back to her face. 'There's no need ...'

'Your partner is around?'

'No, he has a day job.'

'Actually, I wanted to see you. Regarding your detective work.'

My mother came in from the kitchen. I took the tray with tea and mithai from her.

'Aunty, you are being too formal. And all this mithai. I have to go to the gym now and burn calories.'

'You are so skinny already,' my mother said. 'You can't be the only one feeding us. Here, try the gujiya. I made it myself.'

Alia took a bite of the crescent-shaped sweet. 'Oh, it is delicious,' she said.

'You wanted to talk about something related to my detective work?' I said.

My mother looked at Alia and me with her mouth slightly open.

'Do you have many cases right now?' Alia said.

'Not really. Ever since the lockdown, business is slow.'

'I keep telling him not to do all this detective stuff,' my mother said. 'Such a waste of time!'

I gave my mother a firm look.

'I need your help, Keshav,' Alia said.

I turned to Alia, surprised.

'What kind of help?' I said.

'I have a case for you. In fact, that is why I asked your parents to call you downstairs that day.'

My mother put her cup of tea down and looked at Alia.

'Aunty, I've seen you and Uncle take a walk downstairs several times. Someone told me your son is a detective. That's why I approached you, actually.'

'Oh,' my mother said.

'What kind of case exactly?' I said. I didn't want another 'my maid stole my necklace' type of case.

'My daughter,' she said in a serious tone.

'The one we met? Suhana?' I said.

Alia shook her head.

'I have another one, Siya,' Alia said. 'Manish and I have two kids.'

'Manish is your husband?' Ma said.

'Yes, Manish Arora.'

'What does he do?' Ma said.

'He's a jeweller, family business. He runs the online part of it,' Alia said.

I didn't like my mother being a part of this conversation. Alia was now a prospective client. Could my mother please let me conduct my own business meetings?

'Sorry, Alia, what about Siya?' I said.

'Siya was taken away. Someone took her away nine months ago.'

'What?' I said. 'Like a kidnapping?'

She looked back steadily.

'You haven't heard of the Siya Arora case? I am Alia Arora, Siya's mother.'

I shook my head.

'I've heard about it. Something about a girl missing from a kothi,' my mother said.

'Yes, from my in-laws' bungalow two kilometres from here,' Alia said.

'It came on the local news channel. It was long ago so I don't fully remember it. Police suspected someone in the family, I think.'

'The police don't know anything. Just theories floating around,' Alia said. Her eyes had become sad and had lost their sparkle.

'How old is Siya?' I said.

'She was taken away a month before her thirteenth birthday.'

'You have a teenage daughter?' my mother burst out.

'I was only eighteen when I had her, Aunty. I am thirty-two now.'

'You don't look it,' my mother said.

I wished my mother would leave us alone and let me work.

'Excuse me for a second. I need to take notes,' I said. I went to my bedroom. I collected a notebook, a pen and my laptop from the table.

'Ma,' I called from the bedroom.

'Why are you shouting?' she said, coming in.

'May I talk to Alia alone about the case? Please,' I said.

'Why? What is the harm if I am there?'

'It's work. She's a client now. Not a neighbour you can feed gujiyas.'

My mother's chin went up a little. 'She's a guest in my house.'

'Fine, you met her. But now please give me and my client some privacy.'

'Privacy?' my mother said.

'Yes, client–detective privacy. Leave us alone.'

'You have the guts to throw me out of my own living room. Will you try this with your father?'

'I am not throwing—' Before I could complete my sentence, she stormed out of the bedroom to the kitchen, where she banged pots together to register her protest. I ignored her and returned to the living room.

'Found my laptop. Mind if I take notes?'

'I actually appreciate you taking so much interest.'

'You obviously went to the police?' I said.

'Of course. Police, media, neighbourhood appeals. We tried our best.'

'What happened then?'

'We couldn't find her. Or even find out what happened to her.'

'So, the police are still looking?'

Alia shook her head.

'It's become a cold case for them. Even my family feels it is best to move on.'

'And what about you?' I said.

'I will never stop looking. And I can never move on,' Alia said.

'I am sorry,' I said.

A tear escaped her eye. I handed her a tissue.

The pressure cooker whistle from the kitchen broke the silence. I went up to the kitchen door and gently shut it, ignoring my sulking mother.

I came back and sat down on the sofa again.

'What happened? What was done to find her? Tell me everything,' I said.

Alia looked at me, puzzled.

'What?' I said.

'Sure, I will tell you. But don't you want to negotiate first? Like your fee and advance? Don't I have to pay you for this meeting, too?'

'Oh,' I said. 'I didn't even think of all that.'

Maybe that's why my detective business sucked. I might be okay as a detective, but I was terrible at the commercial part of it. Alia had a small purse in her hand. She pulled out a wad of 2,000-rupee notes from it. I needed the money. I had no real income or savings. Yet, I could not get myself to take it. Not like this at least.

'Please, stop,' I said. 'You are our guest.'

'But I want to hire you.'

'We will figure all that out later. Tell me more about Siya. Tell me what happened.'

'You sure?' she said.

I nodded. She put the money back in her purse.

She closed her eyes to compose herself. I opened a new Word document on my laptop to type in my notes.

She opened her eyes.

'It happened last year on 17 September. The worst night of my life,' she said.

Chapter 4

Alia Speaks – I

9 months ago

'Hey, this is not right, kids. It is 10.30 already. You should be asleep,' I said.

'But we don't want to sleep,' five-year-old Sanjay, Manish's brother's son, said in his cute baby voice.

Siya, Suhana and Rohit burst out laughing. The four cousins were all in bed in the guest room on the first floor, peering into an iPad.

'Sanjay, it's past your bedtime,' I said.

'No. Big people not allowed here. Go away,' he said, not looking up from the iPad. I laughed as I mock-spanked my nephew. Rohit, his eight-year-old brother, looked up at me.

'Please, Alia chaachi. We are having a sleepover after so long. Ten more minutes? We just want to finish our game.'

'You said "ten minutes more" thirty minutes ago. Come on, everybody has to sleep now. Sanjay, Rohit, go to your rooms.'

'Mom! Please, leave,' Suhana said, eyes on the iPad screen.

'What are you guys playing anyway?' I said.

'Ludo,' Siya said.

'Ludo? On a screen? When we were kids we played Ludo on an actual board.'

'Oh, Mom, you are so primitive. Did dinosaurs roam the streets when you did that?' Siya said. She checked the messages on her phone in between playing the game on the iPad.

How can this generation work on different screens simultaneously, I wondered.

'Very funny. Siya, be responsible. You are the eldest.'

'Seven minutes more, Chaachi,' Sanjay screamed.

'Fine. Seven minutes. I will wait here. Then everyone goes to their room and to bed, okay?'

'Can we all sleep in the same room, Mommy?' Suhana said. She stood up and kissed me on the cheek. 'Please, Mommy.'

Even though I scolded them, to see the four of them jump around in the bed filled me with joy. I loved Suhana and Siya spending time with their cousins. This was the only thing I missed about my in-laws' house since we'd moved to Icon two years ago.

I smiled as I saw the kids huddle together, arms around each other's shoulders as they moved their electronic counters around the screen.

I sat down on a tiny chair near the bed.

'What?' Siya said.

'I am waiting. The game will finish and you will all go to sleep like good children,' I said.

'But same room, please, Chaachi,' Sanjay squealed.

'How can you all sleep here? There's four of you.'

'We can, Chaachi. Please,' Rohit said.

I looked at the innocent faces of Sanjay and Rohit, the two brothers who no longer lived with my daughters. Sanjay yawned. Clearly he was finding it hard to keep his eyes open.

'Fine, same room. But iPad gone, and lights off in ten ... nine ... eight ...' I said and grabbed the iPad from the centre of the bed.

'Last person tucked in is a stinky potato,' I said. The two boys and Suhana leaped to their pillows, giggling and scrambling to grab a sheet.

Siya was too old for such games. She continued to browse through Instagram on her phone.

'Young lady, you too,' I said to her and continued the countdown, 'seven ... six ...'

'I'm in,' Rohit said. 'I am not a stinky potato.'

'Everyone brushed their teeth already?' I said. 'Five ... four ...'

Suhana, Sanjay and Rohit nodded. Siya shut her phone and plugged it in to charge. Lying closest to the window, she pulled up the sheet to cover herself. Suhana lay next to her, and then Rohit and Sanjay. The four kids looked like adorable bunnies about to take a nap.

'Three, two, one, gone.' I switched off the lights.

'Too dark. Monsters will come,' Rohit said, trying to scare his younger cousins.

'There are no monsters in this world, okay?' Suhana said.

'Who told you?' Rohit said.

'My teacher did,' Suhana said.

'Maybe your teacher is a monster,' Rohit said.

'No,' Suhana screamed.

'Shh ... quiet, kids,' I said. 'I will leave the bathroom light on.'

I went to the bathroom and turned on the light switch, leaving the door ajar. Light came into the bedroom through a ventilation window on top as well.

'That's too bright,' Siya groaned.

I ignored her. 'Is this okay, kids?'

'Yes, Chaachi. Thank you,' Sanjay said.

'Scaredy poop,' Rohit said.

'You are the poop,' Suhana said.

'Shut up, guys,' Sanjay yelled.

'It's sleep time, not fight time,' I said. 'Come on, shut your eyes. I am watching.'

The three younger kids closed their eyes. Suhana wrapped an arm around her big sister.

'Siya, you too. Eyes closed. And why are you sleeping with your phone next to you?'

'It's charging. I won't check it, I promise,' Siya said in a pretend sleepy voice.

'So let me charge it downstairs,' I said.

'No,' Siya said.

'Why not? You are sleeping now, right?'

'Fine, whatever,' Siya said. She pulled out the charger from the plug and handed me the phone with the charger attached to it.

'Good night, guys. Love you,' I said.

'Good night, Chaachi,' Sanjay and Rohit said.

'Good night, Mommy,' Suhana said.

'Siya?' I said, when she didn't reply.

'Good night, Mom, love you,' she said in a somewhat disinterested voice, pulling the sheet over her head. I ignored her routine pre-teen indifference, smiled and left the guest room.

I went downstairs. Timmy, Manish, Mummyji and Papaji sat on the plush oversized living room chairs that resembled thrones you see in period TV shows. The bottle of Scotch had gone down a couple of inches since I had left. The surround sound music system played a Jagjit Singh ghazal, *Hoshwalon ko khabar kya*, Mummyji's favourite. My mother-in-law's large frame took up an entire chair. She held a drink in her hand and, with eyes closed, was moving her head gently to the music. She wore a gold-embroidered maroon silk salwar kameez. A chunky, uncut diamond necklace covered her neck. It was a signature piece from Navratna Jewels, our family-run store.

'Are they asleep?' Manish said.

'With a lot of protesting. And all in the same room,' I said.

'All four fit in one bed?' Manish said.

'Squished together like little puppies,' I said.

Timmy laughed. His big belly jiggled along with the Scotch glass in his hand.

'They used to sleep like that, remember, when they were little?' Timmy said.

'That was two years ago, Bhaiya, when everyone was tiny. They are all big now. Must be uncomfortable,' Manish said.

'I know. Try explaining that to them,' I said.

'How sweet,' Papaji said. 'They must miss each other a lot.'

'If only we lived as one family, they wouldn't have to miss each other ...' my mother-in-law's strong, raspy voice startled all of us. Was she listening to the ghazal or to our conversation?

'Drink, beta?' Papaji said to me, changing the topic. My father-in-law, Shamsher Arora, avoided controversial subjects at all costs and knew better than to take his wife's bait. I didn't want to fight either. We were only there for the weekend.

'No, Papaji,' I said. 'It is late. I will sleep too.'

Papaji leaned forward to refill his glass. Even at sixty-eight, my father-in-law had a fit, upright frame. He had left the Indian Air Force to start his own business thirty years ago and still retained some of his military attributes, including a bushy silver moustache. Even though it was just a gathering of immediate family that day, he was dressed in a grey suit and tie. 'Our business is about making people look and feel good. We must start with ourselves,' was what he used to tell us often.

'Pour me another drink as well, Shamsher,' said my mother-in-law, Durga Arora.

'Good night, Timmy bhaiya, Mummyji, Papaji,' I said.

Papaji stood up. He walked over to me and placed his hand on my head.

'God bless you, beta. Good night,' he said.

'Is it okay if I come after a bit? I'll finish my drink,' Manish said to me.

'Of course,' I said. 'Whenever. Good night.'

I turned around and walked towards the steps leading back up to the first floor.

'Manish, teacher has given you permission. Now enjoy one more drink,' my mother-in-law said with a laugh. I wanted to turn around and retort that I had never tried to control her son. In fact, Manish didn't even have to ask me just now. I clenched my fists and took a deep breath. I had promised Manish I would ignore his mother's nasty barbs. If only he realised how difficult that could be sometimes.

I heard the bedroom door open.

'Hey, are you asleep?' Manish said as he walked in.

'Hey,' I said in a sleepy voice.

I switched on the bedside lamp. Manish changed into his pyjamas with his back to me.

'This used to be our kids' room,' he said, 'with little beds. Now it is a proper guest room. Feels strange, doesn't it?'

'Yes,' I said.

'Are you okay?'

'Hmm.'

'Alia's famous one-word answers. I can sense something is not okay.'

'I am sleepy.'

'Okay, I know. My mother's comment about teacher and permission. Sorry, quite unnecessary.'

'Why are you sorry? She's the one who said it.'

'Because you felt bad.'

'She also said "If only we lived as one family". Another jab at me.'

'She said "we". Not directed at you. Don't get too touchy now, Alia.'

'Oh, really? I am touchy? You know what, forget it. Good night.'

I switched off the lamp. He switched on the one on his side. He turned towards me.

'Oh, come on. The kids are having fun. They need their cousins. Can we all please be pleasant for one weekend?'

'Ask your mother if she knows what being pleasant means. What did I even do? I only kept quiet and smiled.'

'But now you are complaining.'

'You asked me. I didn't—' I stopped mid-sentence. I turned to lie on my stomach and shut my eyes. I didn't see the point of this argument. Some things never changed.

Manish switched off his lamp and put an arm around me.

'I am sorry,' he said.

'It's not your fault.'

'I just want this weekend to be perfect.'

'I didn't react, right? Don't think I am this uncontrollable hysterical fool.'

'I never said you are.'

'But it would be nice if you acknowledged the effort I make to keep peace.'

'She can be annoying.'

'Not just annoying. She's hurtful.'

'She doesn't mean it. And thank you for staying calm despite her caustic remarks.'

He kissed the back of my head.

'You are welcome,' I said.

He came and lay down facing me.

'I had too much to drink. Papa and Timmy have a lot more capacity,' Manish said.

I turned sideways to face him.

'You are a fake Punjabi,' I said and giggled.

'Maybe. That's why I married you, my Malayali.'

'Half-Malayali,' I said. 'What time is it?'

'Eleven.'

'You checked on the kids when you came upstairs?'

'Yeah. All four of them fast asleep.'

'They could be acting. When a parent goes in, they pretend to sleep. Then the chattering starts again.'

'I love them, Alia. Too much. So much, it hurts sometimes,' Manish said. 'Just seeing all four cousins sleeping like that. Really, there's nothing more precious than these little ones.'

'Yes,' I said.

'And I am sorry about Mummyji.'

I patted Manish's cheek.

'It's okay,' I said. 'Good night, Manish.'

'Good night, love,' Manish said as he drifted off to sleep.

Chapter 5

'Manohar, get more rusks,' Mummyji said to the cook.

'And make the filling for the paranthas. I will come and check soon,' Rachna said.

Manohar placed the tea tray on the garden table and headed back into the house. Rachna picked up the kettle and poured tea into three cups. I added a spoonful of sugar into mine. I was about to do the same for Mummyji when Rachna stopped me.

'Stevia for Mummyji,' Rachna said.

'Oh, sorry. I didn't realise,' I said.

'I have to manage my sugar now. Stupid doctor,' Mummyji said.

My in-laws have a seven-hundred-square-yard bungalow in Phase V of Gurugram. It's a sprawling house spread over two floors. The ground floor has a garden, a huge living room, a kitchen and a massive master bedroom. The first floor has four bedrooms. Manish and I occupied two of them when we lived there. These are now guest rooms. The other two bedrooms belonged to Timmy and Rachna, who have a room each for themselves and their kids.

Manohar returned with homemade elaichi rusks and placed them on the table next to the tea tray. The table was an eight-seater, with cast iron chairs painted white.

'It's almost eight. When will the men wake up?' Rachna said. 'Shall I go wake Timmy?'

'Let them sleep. They drank too much. They miss being together, the two brothers, with their father,' Mummyji said.

Okay, the first crisp taunt of the day had arrived, along with the crisp rusks. Then I remembered what Manish had said the previous night. Perhaps I was being too sensitive. I dug my feet in the dewy morning grass and stayed quiet.

'And the kids?' Rachna said. 'Not good to sleep so late. It will be difficult to wake them up for school tomorrow.'

'I'll wake them up in a few minutes if they don't get up on their own,' I said.

Just then Sanjay and Rohit walked into the garden. Sanjay rubbed his eyes and held a small teddy bear in his hand.

'Good morning, Daadi. Good morning, Chaachi. Good morning, Mommy,' the boys sang.

'Hello, beta, good morning,' I said. 'Did you sleep well?'

Sanjay nodded. Rohit sat next to me and picked up a rusk.

'Where are your sisters?' Rachna said.

'Sleeping,' Sanjay said, sitting next to my mother-in-law.

'I'll go wake them up,' I said.

I left the garden and walked up to the first floor.

I knocked on the door of the children's room.

'Good morning,' I said in a sing-song voice. I entered the room and saw Suhana fast asleep clutching her pillow tight. I did not see Siya in the room.

'Wake up, little princess,' I said to Suhana.

Suhana moved a little. I went to the bathroom door.

'Siya, are you in there?' I said loudly. No response. I knocked on the bathroom door. Again, no answer. I pushed down on the handle and saw the door was unlocked. I entered the bathroom. It was empty. The light was on, same as I had left it the night before.

'Beta, where's Siya didi?' I said, shaking Suhana's leg.

Suhana didn't answer. I tugged at her sheet.

'Wake up, beta. Where's Siya didi?' I said again.

I noticed then that Suhana had wet the bed. She had not done this in a long while. She had smudges under her eyes.

'Suhana, wake up,' I said, gently tapping her cheek.

She opened her eyes.

'Mommy,' she said. Suhana sat up on the bed, her eyes red. She grabbed my arm and pulled me towards her. I hugged her tight as she buried her face in my shoulder.

'Good morning, darling,' I said. 'Why do you look tired?'

'Mommy,' she said.

I decided not to bring up the wet patch on the sheet to avoid embarrassing her.

'Come on, you need to change,' I said. 'And where is Siya didi? Is she sleeping with Daddy?'

'Mommy,' Suhana said again and held me tighter. I extracted myself from her. I pulled out another set of Suhana's night clothes from my weekend stroller bag. The last thing I wanted was my mother-in-law to comment on Suhana's wet pyjamas.

I made Suhana stand on the bed as I changed her into a fresh set of clothes.

'Go to the garden. Wish everyone good morning. Daadu, Daadi, Rachna taayi and Timmy taaya. All separately, okay?'

'Mommy,' Suhana said again and began to cry.

'What happened, beta?' I said. She held me tight again. I wondered if she had realised she wet the bed. I stroked her long hair as she cried. I swept her dark brown curls from her forehead and wiped her eyes.

'Bad man,' she said, pointing to the pillows.

'What?' I said, confused.

'Bad man with knife,' she said.

'Beta, you had a bad dream?' I said. *That explains the bed-wetting,* I thought.

'Bad man, Mommy,' she said and continued to cry.

'Okay, beta, it's over. Bad dream gone. Now let's wash your face. Don't go downstairs like this.'

I washed her face in the bathroom and combed her hair. She refused to let go of me. I walked out of the room with her, her hand in mine. I knocked on the other guest room door, right opposite the room the children had slept in.

'Manish,' I said. 'Wake up now. Everybody is downstairs.'

He didn't answer. I opened the door. Manish was on his stomach, mouth slightly open, snoring lightly. No Siya next to him. I checked the bathroom of this room too. Nobody was inside.

'Manish?' I said. 'It's past eight. Get up. And where's Siya?'

'Huh?' Manish said, rubbing his face as he woke up. 'What?'

'Where's Siya? She came to sleep with you?'

'No.'

Manish sat up on the bed. He stretched his arms and twisted from side to side.

'Sure?'

'Do you see her here?' Manish said, slightly irritated. 'Hi, Suhana dear. Good morning.'

He leaned forward to give Suhana a hug. I left her with him.

I went down to the garden again.

My father-in-law and Timmy had come downstairs by then and were laughing about Timmy's rusk breaking in his teacup as soon as he dipped it.

'Good morning, Bhabhiji. Welcome,' Timmy said. He stood up and pulled out a chair for me.

'Let's go to Sagar Ratna and have dosas for lunch. What say? Punjabis become Madrasis for a day,' Timmy said, and everyone laughed again.

'Where's Siya?' I said.

'What?' Timmy said, surprised at my serious tone.

'You went to wake them up, no?' Mummyji said, placing her cup on the table.

'She's not there. Suhana was still sleeping in the room, but I couldn't find Siya.'

'Bathroom?' Rachna said.

'No. I checked our room too. She didn't go to Manish. And she's not in our bathroom either. Papaji, did she come to your room?'

'No, beta,' Papaji said. Timmy and Papaji got up and walked back into the house.

'Manohar,' Timmy shouted. Manohar came from the kitchen, hands specked with flour.

'You saw Siya beti?' Papaji said.

'No, sirji,' Manohar said. 'I was preparing paranthas in the kitchen.'

I checked my in-laws' bedroom on the ground floor. I couldn't find Siya either in the bedroom or in the en-suite bathroom.

'When did you see her last, beta?' Papaji said as he entered his room.

'Last night, Papaji, when I put all the kids to bed. Manish checked on them later too, right before he came to sleep,' I said. I checked the bathroom again, even though I knew there was no point.

'Nobody saw her in the morning?' Papaji said.

I shook my head.

'Ask the other kids. Maybe they will know something.'

We returned to the garden. Sanjay and Rohit were eating frosted cornflakes with milk.

'Beta, you saw Siya didi this morning?' I said. They shook their heads. Timmy joined us in the garden.

'She's not upstairs, I checked all the rooms, including our bedrooms,' Timmy said. 'In case she walked in there and dozed off ...'

'Bathrooms?' I said.

Timmy shook his head.

Manish came to the garden.

'What's going on? Where is Siya?' Manish said.

Something did not seem right. My hands began to tremble.

'Where's my daughter?' I said. I was starting to panic.

'Could she have gone for a morning walk or something?' Timmy said.

'She never does,' I said. 'She goes to the Icon garden sometimes in the evening. Never in the morning. And never without telling me. Manish, I've got a bad feeling.'

'She must be around. Maybe went out to meet a friend. Or to get something from the market,' Mummyji said.

'What friend? Get what?' I said.

'Sit down, everyone. Beta, you sound too tense. Relax,' Papaji said. He signalled to all of us to move inside.

We went into the living room and sat on the sofas.

'She is the mother, she will be tense. Let the rest of us think in a calm manner,' Papaji said. 'Manish, what do you think?'

'I don't know what to think, Papaji. I just woke up.'

'Did you see her asleep at night?'

'I took a peek. The kids were there. Either asleep or about to sleep. But, yes, I did see all four of them,' Manish said.

'Okay,' Papaji said. 'So she was at home safe at that time. If she's not around, it is likely she went out on her own.'

'She has her phone. Alia, call her, no, instead of freaking out,' Manish said.

'I am not freaking out,' I said, my voice hysterical.

I called her from my phone and I heard it ring upstairs. Manish ran up the steps. He came back after a minute. He held Siya's phone in his hand.

'It was charging in our room,' Manish said.

'Oh, then she should be around,' Rachna said, 'if her phone is here.'

'I forgot … I kept her phone there to charge. Otherwise she keeps checking it at night and doesn't sleep,' I said.

'Oh,' Rachna said. Everyone fell silent.

'She hasn't left on her own,' I said. 'She never leaves without her phone. Anyway, she couldn't she have made a plan with a friend without her phone.'

'You have the phone password?' Manish said.

'I do,' I said. I unlocked her phone. No new calls. She had a couple of Snapchat messages from her various friends' groups, most of them memes and funny forwards.

'Nothing here suggests she had to go somewhere,' I said, scrolling through her messages.

'Let's check the house again. We looked into the bedrooms.

There's the terrace, backyard and servants' room,' Timmy said.

For the next half hour, Timmy, Rachna, Manish, Papaji and I scanned every square inch of Navratna House.

I went to the terrace. No Siya.

I checked the servants' room and the toilet on the terrace as well. Nothing.

'She must be here only, having fun seeing us searching for her,' Mummyji said.

The adults in the family had gathered in the living room again.

'The side gate is not locked. Isn't that supposed to be locked?' Timmy said.

'I don't know. Manohar checks it usually,' Rachna said. 'Though we seldom open it. So how could it be unlocked?'

'She didn't leave through the front gate. That's still locked,' Timmy said.

'Who the hell opened the side gate? And when? That's dangerous,' Papaji said.

'That idiot Manohar must not have shut it. He opens it sometimes for deliveries. I always lock it,' Mummyji said.

'Where is Siya?' I said to no one in particular. I couldn't stop trembling.

The three kids in the house were at the dining table. Suhana stared at the wall as her two cousins fumbled with the iPad.

'Manish?' I said. 'What do we do?'

'Did anyone ask the kids?' he said in a soft voice. Nobody responded.

Manish walked to the dining table.

'Hey guys, good morning,' Manish said.

'Good morning, Chaachu,' Rohit said. Sanjay remained busy with the game on the iPad.

'Do you know where Siya didi is?'

The two boys shook their heads.

'Suhana beta,' Manish said. 'Do you know where Siya didi is?'

Suhana shook her head. She did not make eye contact with Manish.

'Where could she have gone?' Manish said.

'Bad man,' Suhana said.

I jumped up from the sofa. Did she know something?

I went to the dining table and sat on a chair next to Suhana.

'Bad man was not just a dream?' I said.

Suhana shook her head.

'Bad man knows about Siya didi?' I said.

Suhana nodded.

My in-laws gathered around the dining table as well, intrigued.

'What happened, beta?' I said in a gentle voice.

'Bad man came with knife. He took Siya didi,' Suhana said, finding it hard to put the words together.

'Took?' Manish said. His loud voice caused Suhana to tremble in fear. Papaji kept a finger on his lips, signalling to everyone to be quiet.

He stood next to his granddaughter.

'Tell Daadu, don't be scared. You saw something?'

Suhana nodded.

'Tell me,' Papaji said.

'We were all lying down. Sanjay and Rohit bhaiya had gone to sleep. Didi and I were chatting. Daddy came to check, so we pretended to be asleep.'

'What happened then?' Manish said.

'We slept. Then a noise woke me up. I saw a bad man. He had a knife that he kept on Didi's neck like this,' Suhana said, placing her hand sideways on her neck to show the position.

'Oh!' I gasped.

Papaji said, 'And then, beta?'

'Bad man said to Didi, get up and come with me. Don't make a sound. If you do, I will kill all your brothers and sisters. And your whole family.'

'You heard that? For sure?' I said.

Suhana nodded, staring at the wall.

'How come? Weren't you asleep?' Manish said.

'I was pretending to sleep. Like I did when you came to check.'

'What happened afterwards?' I said.

'Didi left with him. I stayed in bed, scared. I stayed quiet because I didn't want the bad man to kill any of you.'

Suhana burst into tears. I picked her up and held her, resting her head on my shoulder.

As I consoled my younger daughter, my heart pounded fast, worried sick about my elder one.

'Papaji,' I said. 'What do we do now?'

'Beta, I think this is beyond us. We need to call the police.'

Chapter 6

If Inspector Ratan Chautala hadn't worn the Haryana Police uniform, you would not have guessed he was a cop. In his mid-forties, he sported a bald patch, a thin moustache and a pot belly. It made him look like a neighbourhood uncle who could be a friendly RWA president. He stood in the living room, scanning the expensive yet gaudy decorations of my in-laws' house. The two constables who accompanied him searched the house again. Rachna took the kids upstairs to keep them from seeing the cops. The rest of us remained in the living room.

'She isn't here, sir. We checked multiple times before calling you,' Manish said.

'Hmm,' Chautala said. He stared at the art on the walls and the several Buddha heads on the side table. He walked up and lifted one of them.

'You are Buddhists?'

'No. We are Hindus only. But I am really into spirituality, so these heads,' Mummyji said. Three diamond rings sparkled on her spiritual fingers.

'Sir, we are very worried,' I said in a tense voice.

Chautala nodded.

'Let's all sit down and remain calm, like the Buddha,' Chautala said, replacing the Buddha head on the side table.

We settled down on the sofas.

One of his constables came into the living room.

'Nothing, sir. We checked the garage, the toilets and the terrace,' he said.

'Found anything else? Any blood anywhere?' Chautala said, his tone casual, like he was asking if they'd found soap in the bathroom.

The constable shook his head.

Chautala listened as I narrated the events of the previous night. I also told him what Suhana had told me.

'Who could have taken her, sir?' Timmy said.

Chautala looked at his wrist watch. 'It's only 11 o'clock. Maybe we should wait before jumping to any conclusions.'

'What do you mean, sir?' Manish said.

'She's twelve, almost thirteen. Girls these days age quite fast. What we normally find in such situations is the child goes and comes back on their own.'

'Goes where, sir?' I said. 'My younger daughter said "bad man took her"'.

'How old is your younger one, madam?' Chautala said.

'Six,' I said.

Chautala smiled.

'Madam, you want me to take a six-year-old seriously? Register a kidnapping? Launch a manhunt?'

'I want you to take some action, sir. My daughter went missing in the middle of the night.'

'Any boyfriends?' Chautala said.

'What? What are you even saying, sir?' I screamed.

Chautala did not like my tone. He turned to my father-in-law.

'Aroraji, you are a respected member of the community. Ex-serviceman too. I came running on a Sunday only because you called. But your family will not speak to me like this.'

Chautala stood up and folded his hands as if to leave.

'But, sir,' Papaji said.

'My suggestion is you wait a while. If you want, come to the police station and file a report. I don't need to personally be here at your service. Especially when I am going to be insulted.'

'Chautala sir, come on. We have known each other for years,' Papaji said. 'Durga, get some tea for sir.'

Mummyji stood up.

'Alia, can you please help Mummyji in the kitchen.'

I nodded, standing up.

'Alia, first say sorry to sir,' Mummyji said. She would never miss an opportunity to publicly humiliate me.

I took a deep breath. I needed the police's help to find Siya. I couldn't annoy them.

'I am sorry, sir. I am quite disturbed.'

'Of course, madam. You are the mother,' Chautala said. 'But often parents don't realise when their kids grow up. I have had cases in my village. Twelve-year-old girls running away with grown-up men.'

'What!' I said.

'They think they are in love. Watching too many movies on cheap Jio data, what else?' Chautala said.

'Siya isn't like that,' I said. 'I assure you.'

I left for the kitchen with my mother-in-law. Mummyji instructed Manohar to prepare tea. I arranged plates full of cookies, chutney sandwiches and chips to ensure the police felt we cared for them.

'No need for formality,' Chautala said even as he loaded a quarter plate with all the snacks on the tray.

'Please, sir, you came all the way,' Mummyji said as she passed him a cup. He took slow, noisy sips. Papaji and Mummyji had tea as well. Every passing second seemed like a waste of time.

We should find Siya, not slurp tea, I thought.

I checked the time: 11.30 a.m. It was over twelve hours since Manish had seen her. Chautala sensed my unease. He placed his cup on the table and stood up. Everyone else followed.

'Anything missing from the house? Cash, jewellery?'

'No, sir,' Papaji said. 'Everything is in the safe as before.'

'Are any of Siya's items missing? Clothes? Did she have money with her?' Chautala said.

'Her phone and purse are still here. Four hundred rupees in it, like before,' I said.

'You have the phone password?' Chautala said.

I nodded.

'We will get the phone checked. In case there's something helpful,' one of the cops said.

'Was she wearing any jewellery?' Chautala said.

'Small diamond studs, that's all,' Manish said.

'Twelve-year-old girl wearing diamonds?' Chautala said.

'We are jewellers, sir. Just tiny solitaires,' Manish said.

Chautala shrugged.

'Let's go upstairs,' he said.

'Be careful,' Chautala said. 'We may need to check for fingerprints or other clues.'

The rest of us remained outside the children's room as Chautala went in to scan it. Rachna and the kids heard the commotion on the first floor corridor and came out.

'Police, police,' Sanjay said.

'Go inside, Sanjay and Suhana. Rohit, take everyone inside. Watch TV,' Rachna said.

'No, wait,' Chautala said. 'May I speak to the little girl?'

Inspector Chautala, Suhana and I sat at the dining table. The others stayed upstairs with the other kids. I got two soft toys from the kids' room, a teddy bear and a baby elephant, both Suhana's favourites, to make her feel comfortable.

'Wish uncle, beta,' I said.

'Good afternoon, Police uncle,' Suhana said. She squeezed the teddy bear in her hand.

'Good afternoon, beta. I am here to help find your sister,' Chautala said in a soft voice.

'Bad man took her,' Suhana said.

'Yes, beta. Can you tell me exactly what happened?' Chautala said.

Suhana did not answer. She took the soft baby elephant and squished it next to the teddy bear. The inspector opened his mouth to ask again, but I stopped him. I let her play for a few minutes.

'Beta, you saw the bad man?' I said finally.

Suhana nodded, eyes still on the elephant.

'Can you tell us what he looked like?' Chautala said.

She glanced at the police officer.

'Answer him, beta,' I said. 'Mommy will be quiet now. Answer Police uncle, so he can find Didi. Okay?'

Suhana nodded.

'Tell me, Suhana, can you recognise him?' Chautala said.

She shook her head. 'There wasn't so much light. But it was a man.'

'You were awake?'

'Yes, but I kept my eyes only a little bit open and pretended to sleep.'

'Could you hear him? Did he say anything?'

'He said, "Shh, shh. Come with me. Be quiet. I won't do anything, chalo." Like that.'

'Anything else that you noticed?'

'He had a big knife. Like the one Daadu uses to cut watermelons. He kept it on Siya's neck.'

'Did your didi say anything?'

'No. He told her, "Make any sound and I will chop your sister and brothers into little pieces." Then he told Siya didi to go with him.'

'Oh my God,' I said, placing my hand on my mouth.

'Shh, Alia ma'am, please. Don't make the child tense.'

I found it hard to fight back tears. The inspector stared at me and shook his head. I had to keep my composure.

Chautala continued.

'Suhana beti, how did they leave the room?'

'He walked behind her. He covered her mouth with one hand. He held the knife in the other.'

'This bad man, was he old, young, tall, short, fat, thin? Anything you can tell me, beti?'

'He was normal,' Suhana said.

Inspector Chautala sighed.

'He spoke in English or Hindi?'

'He spoke both.'

'Both how?'

'Like he said, "Chalo chalo." But he also said, "Quiet. Shh."'

'What hair colour?'

'Black, I think.'

'Long? Short?'

'Normal.'

'What was he wearing?'

'Normal clothes.'

'Shirt? T-shirt? Kurta?'

'Shirt or kurta. Not T-shirt.'

'How can you tell, beta?'

'Because I saw buttons.'

'That's good, beta. That's very clever of you,' I said. 'Tell Police uncle everything.'

Chautala smiled at Suhana.

'Okay, so a normal man with black hair who wore a shirt. A grown-up, right? Not a teenager or someone near your didi's age?'

'No, all grown up.'

'Good,' Chautala said. He took down some quick notes on his phone.

'Anything else, beta?' I said.

'He had a watch. I saw his wrist as it was close to me.'

'Good. What kind of watch?'

'Normal,' Suhana said.

'Okay, that's fine,' Chautala said. 'Anything else you saw on his hand or arm?'

'Yes, he wore friendship bands.'

'What is that?' Chautala said.

'Friendship bands,' Suhana said and turned to me.

'You mean like the friendship bands Siya didi used to make at home?' I said.

Suhana nodded.

'What are these friendship bands, Aliaji?' Chautala said.

'They're handmade bracelets made of string or colourful thread. Children make them and give them to their friends. Siya did too. We have many at home.'

'This is not your home?'

'It was. I mean, it is. It is my in-laws' home. We lived here until a few years ago. Now we are at the Icon, near the golf course.'

'Oh. Why did you move there?'

'More space.'

'This is a huge house. Five bedrooms, right?'

'I didn't mean space in that way, sir.'

'Joint family issues?'

I didn't respond.

'Sorry, not my business. But it is happening everywhere. Everyone wants independence, or space, as you say it.'

I wanted to shake the inspector and tell him to focus on Siya. However, I simply nodded.

Chautala turned to Suhana. 'Is that your elephant?' he said.

'Yes, but I let Sanjay borrow it sometimes,' Suhana said.

'I have a daughter too. She's fifteen now.'

Suhana did not respond.

'What colour were these bands? Can you remember the design? Or draw it maybe?'

'It was too dark to see,' Suhana said, looking down at the elephant on her lap.

'Okay, anything else, beti? Anything at all about the bad man?'

She shook her head.

'What did you do after they left?'

'I lay in bed. I was scared. I thought didi will come back soon. But then sleep actually came and I slept off.'

'Why didn't you go wake up your mother?'

'I was scared,' Suhana said and turned to me. 'Mommy, I don't want to talk. I want to go upstairs and play with Rohit and Sanjay.'

'Sure, go, beta. If you remember anything else, tell your mummy,' Chautala said.

Suhana didn't respond. She hugged me and hid her face in my neck. I carried her up the steps. As I went, I heard Chautala speak to someone on the phone.

'Hello, Viren? File an FIR. Kidnapping. Twelve-year-old girl.'

Chapter 7

The Sushant Lok Police Station in Gurugram is a ten-minute drive from my in-laws' place as well as the Icon.

The leafy compound with a yellowing low-rise sarkari building stood in sharp contrast to the swanky skyscrapers of Gurugram. It felt like things moved at their own pace at the station, with various cops carrying files from one room to the other in slow motion.

There were a lot of people, either to complain about something or answer the police's questions. Most were there for routine work, to sort out passport verification issues or register their domestic help. In between such mundane jobs, I wondered how these cops could switch to handling serious crimes.

My father-in-law's clout and our arrival in two Mercedes cars meant we received more attention than other visitors. I was in a daze. I had checked Siya's recently dialled numbers and the friends she had messaged on WhatsApp. I'd called all of them. Nobody had any idea about where she might be.

Inspector Chautala had arranged for extra chairs in his office, and my in-laws, Manish and I sat there surrounded by files. He had a computer on his desk as well as two landline phones on which he constantly made calls for two hours.

'Yes, I am sending you the pictures,' Chautala said on a call to another station in Gurugram. 'Yes, circulate it to Delhi Police and to Manesar district too. Spread it on the walkie to all Gypsies. Siya Arora, twelve years, very fair, greenish-grey eyes, curly hair. Could be with a man wearing a watch and friendship bands. Yes, inform Noida Police too. Good idea. Faridabad also.'

Inspector Chautala ended the call and turned to us.

'I've informed as much of the police force as possible,' he said. 'You gave me some pictures, but please share more. Always helpful.'

'Sure, thank you, sir,' Manish said.

'Any information … at all … yet … inspector … sir?' I said, finding it difficult to construct a sentence.

Inspector Chautala shook his head.

'The first twenty-four hours are crucial. We have told the police in the entire National Capital Region. If someone spots anything, they will inform us immediately.'

I bit my lip. I couldn't control myself anymore. I broke down.

'No, beta, stay strong,' Papaji said.

'My Siya, what has happened to her?' I cried.

Manish held my hand. Mummyji looked away.

'It's four o'clock,' Chautala said. 'Assuming that the earliest the abduction could have happened was midnight, it's still eight hours more to twenty-four hours.'

'What is so special about twenty-four hours?' Manish said.

'In kidnapping cases, we usually find out something within a day. If not, chances drop.'

'Chances of what drop?' I said, hysteria in my voice.

'Nothing, madam. These are mere statistics. Let's focus on the important decision. What do we do now about informing the media?'

'Are you sure about the media at this stage, sir? Everyone we know will find out then that someone has taken our girl,' Mummyji said.

Chautala swivelled on his creaky chair towards her.

'It can speed things up, madam. Alert the common man. Increases chances of a sighting. It also has disadvantages. It's completely your call.'

'What disadvantages?' Manish said.

'The kidnapper gets alerted. He could get scared and panic. And of course, like madam said, it will bring a lot of unwanted attention. Also, the media moves in its own unpredictable ways.'

'We shouldn't tell the media yet. It hasn't even been a day. Alia, you sure she didn't run off on her own?' Mummyji said.

'No, Mummyji. Why would she run away? She was a happy kid.'

'With a boy?' Mummyji said. 'Inspector sir said these things happen.'

'No, Mummyji, Siya is not like that. Siya didn't take any money or her phone. What are you people even talking about?'

'How could she vanish in the middle of the night?'

'Suhana told us what happened.'

'She's six,' Mummyji said.

'Can you two please not argue? Let us remain one for God's sake,' Manish said. 'We have to decide something here. Media or no media?'

'Not so soon. People just watch the tamasha, nobody helps. Let the police do their job,' Mummyji said.

'I think we should,' I said, glaring at Mummyji. 'Whatever can help, let's do it.'

Mummyji stood up abruptly and waved her hands in the air.

'Then do what you feel like. Shamsher, why are we even here? Let's go. It's claustrophobic here. Nobody in my entire khandaan ever came to the police station.'

'Sit, Durga ...' Papaji said.

'Why? My grandsons are alone in the house. Let me be there for them. In our home, we take care of our kids.'

That hit me hard. Maybe it was her toxic tone or the implication that I hadn't taken care of Siya, leading to her abduction. Perhaps it was my current state of mind and I needed to vent. I forgot Manish's 'keep the peace' principle.

'She was taken from *your* house. Where we trusted we would be safe. Nothing like this could have ever happened at the Icon.'

'Alia,' Papaji spoke in an undertone. 'We can't quarrel in public.'

'Shamsher, are you coming? Or should I go back alone?' Mummyji said. Papaji looked at his wife.

'It's okay,' Manish said. 'Papaji, you take Mummyji home. We will call if we need anything.'

My in-laws left. Manish and I remained in the inspector's office. I felt dizzy. I had had nothing to eat or drink all day, apart from half a cup of tea. Chautala offered me a glass of water. I refused it. His phone rang. A ray of hope lit up in me. However, it was just a routine work call for Chautala on some other issue.

'Who were the important people in your daughter's life?' Chautala said, after ending his phone conversation.

'Friends. Family,' I said.

'School friends?'

'Mostly. A couple of building friends.'

'All her age?'

'Yes, more or less.'

'Boys? Girls?'

'Majority of them girls. Parvathy Ravi and Mahima Sharma are her closest friends. Most of her calls and messages are to them.'

Chautala noted down their names and numbers from Siya's phone.

'They are her school friends?'

'Yes. Class VII, Ambience Valley School.'

'It's in Phase V?'

'Yes, one kilometre from the Icon.'

The inspector nodded, taking frantic notes.

'Any boys she spoke to?' Chautala said.

I looked at the inspector.

'Please, madam, don't get me wrong. I am being thorough.'

'There's a boy—Aryan Sinha. I have heard his name sometimes. He and Siya are friends.'

'Any messages with him on the phone?'

'I saw some chats. Jokes about teachers. Making fun of other classmates. That sort of stuff.'

Chautala took Siya's phone. He opened the chats between her and Aryan.

'There are hugs and kisses emojis,' Chautala said. 'Would you say they were close?'

'No, sir. Kids talk like that these days.'

'Not all kids,' Chautala said, handing Siya's phone back to me.

Will the world stop judging my child and help find her?

'I have called up all her friends. Spoken to their parents too. They have no clue,' I said, feeling nauseous.

'You told them your daughter is missing?'

'No, I just said that she went somewhere and left her phone behind.'

'Good. Any grown-ups she interacted with?'

'Anybody?' Manish said.

'Anybody on a regular basis. In such cases, there's a good chance the victim and the abductor know each other.'

'Family. My in-laws who you met,' I said.

'Yes, I have known Manishji's parents since long.'

'Our family is our entire world. We have a family business. We are all very close.'

'Hmm,' Chautala said, biting the pen. He looked unconvinced. Maybe the saas-bahu showdown he had just seen didn't make us seem so close.

'Your family, Alia madam?' Chautala said.

'No siblings. Only my mother, who lives in Kochi.'

'Your father?'

'My father was in the army. He died on duty in Kashmir when I was sixteen.'

'Sorry to hear that,' Chautala said. 'Any other grown-ups in Siya's life? Teachers, servants, drivers? Anybody your child mentioned?'

'Their class teacher is Mrs Gupta.'

'All her teachers are female?' Chautala said.

'Yes, but why is that important, inspector?' I said.

Inspector Chautala let out a sigh.

'Aliaji, there is no ransom demand call or note so far, right?'

'None,' Manish said.

'No financial motive. Then what is the motive? We cannot

rule out another angle. Especially when the abducted child is a young female.'

'What angle?'

'A sexual motive.'

I gasped. I felt I would faint. Manish held me so I could sit upright.

'Madam, please have something to eat,' Chautala said.

I shook my head. I would not eat until I found Siya. My child was twelve, a baby. How could anyone think of her, even remotely, in a sexual way?

'I am not saying that's what happened. I am just saying we cannot rule that out. Any men she interacted with?' Chautala said.

I looked at Manish.

'We have a cook, Manohar, at my parents' place. Been with us for five years at least,' Manish said.

'Anything shady about him?'

'Not that I know of. Alia, what is he like?'

'He is a good cook, hardworking. But he keeps complaining about his salary and his obligations back in his village. My mother-in-law says he may be stealing groceries . Nothing more than that.'

'Any other men employed by you?'

'No. Our full-time help at Icon is a woman, Neelu. My parents have Manohar. They also have two drivers, Manoj and Daljeet. Both been working with the family for over ten years.'

'You have a driver?'

'No, my office is five minutes from home, so I drive. If we need a driver, we call him from Papaji's place,' Manish said.

'Okay. We will talk to all your support staff. I'll need everyone's names and numbers.'

Manish noted down the details of our support staff in the inspector's notebook.

'Anyone else?' Chautala said.

'Dharmesh? Her tutor? He's like twenty-one,' I said.

'Oh,' Chautala said, looking interested. 'What kind of tutor?'

'Maths. He is a maths graduate and a full-time tutor for many students in their school. Teaches Siya twice a week, two hours at a time.'

'Where?'

'At home usually. Once or twice at my in-laws' house, if we are there for the weekend and Siya has a test on Monday.'

'Good, we definitely have to talk to him,' Chautala said. Manish and I nodded.

I checked the time. It was 5.30.

'Sir, let's inform the media,' I said.

'Wait,' Manish said. 'Inspector sir, what do you think?'

'They will find out sooner or later anyway,' Chautala said. 'And we don't have any information yet. No harm sending out a "missing girl" press release with a photo. What if someone recognises her?'

Manish looked at me.

'The kidnapper could hurt Siya if he sees the news being flashed on TV,' he said.

'He could take her very far away if we don't catch him soon,' I said.

'Twelve-year-old girl kidnapped from Gurugram jeweller's house

The headline flashed on the local news channel. Other national channels displayed the news on the ticker at the bottom of the screen.

High-profile kidnapping from Gurugram bungalow

Siya Arora, 12, abducted from grandparents' house

The anchor showed Siya's pictures we had given to the police. In one she held a trophy. She had won it at an inter-school dance competition. She had performed a Kuchipudi dance, re-enacting the mythological story of Menaka who was sent by Indra to break

Vishwamitra's meditation. The crowd had given her a standing ovation. She had later told me that was the happiest day of her life. I bit my lip as I saw her smiling picture on TV.

The anchor spoke briskly.

'Last night, a twelve-year-old girl, Siya Arora, a student of Ambience Valley School, was kidnapped from her grandparents' house in Gurugram. The parents say they had gone to the house for the weekend. Siya's younger sister, six-year-old Suhana, was apparently awake and saw an intruder walk Siya out of the children's room at knife-point.'

The channel flashed a police helpline number.

'That's our phone number,' Chautala said. 'We will be the first to know if anyone has any information.'

My phone rang: Papaji.

'You saw?' he said.

'Yes.'

'You informed the media?'

'No choice, Papaji. Time is running out.'

'Beta, it's not even been a day. Kids leave home sometimes, right? If they are upset over something ...'

'She wasn't upset.'

'You were quite strict with her. Are you sure she wasn't angry with you about something?' my mother-in-law's voice on the other side surprised me. I realised Papaji had me on speaker.

'Mummyji, please, don't start this again,' I said. I stepped out of Chautala's office and whispered on the phone, 'And please don't give the police such theories. They will stop looking. I am standing on their head so they do their work.'

'We are only trying to help,' Mummyji said. I heard their home landline ring. She continued, 'We are getting non-stop calls because you broadcast our family problem on TV.'

She ended the call. I went back into Chautala's office.

Manish noticed my frazzled expression. He raised his eyebrow. I shook my head slightly.

No time to get distracted.

Inspector Chautala was eating his dinner.

'Did anyone call on the helpline yet?' I said.

'No, madam,' Chautala said, taking a spoon of curd to his mouth.

'The news just came on TV. Be patient, Alia. Sir is trying his best,' Manish said.

I watched the inspector tear a roti. He noticed me looking at him.

'Madam, please eat something. You cannot go on like this,' he said.

I shook my head and looked away.

4 hours later

The dusty wall clock in the police station struck midnight. Chautala yawned as he ended a call to his wife.

'Madam, it's late. Let's continue tomorrow,' Chautala said to me. 'I had told my wife this morning I was just going to Mr Arora's house for a few minutes. I haven't gone home since.'

'Of course, sir,' Manish said, standing up. 'I can't even tell you how thankful we are for all the effort you put in today.'

Chautala stood up as well.

'Every NCR police station is on high alert. All traffic police Gypsies know about it. They have pictures. We have checkpoints. TV channels are flashing the helpline number. Someone somewhere ought to see her.'

'Thank you, sir. You must go home and rest,' I said.

'Come, Alia,' Manish said.

I shook my head as I continued to sit in Chautala's office.

'What?' Manish said.

'I will wait here. You guys go home and sleep. I will see you here in the morning.'

'Are you crazy? You have to come home,' Manish said.

I shook my head hard.

'I am not leaving until I find my daughter,' I said and burst into tears.

I don't exactly recollect what happened then. Exhaustion came over me. Manish grabbed my hand and pulled me out of the office. I reached home in a daze. Manish gave me a sleeping pill with a glass of orange juice. He ensured I finished the juice. I went to the hall and switched on the TV. Local channels were still running the news about Siya. Manish paced around the bedroom, distraught, dealing with his own pain even as he maintained his composure in front of me. I don't know when my eyes shut. Siya's smiling face flashed before my eyes before the sleeping pills knocked me out.

Chapter 8

2 days missing

'It's okay, madam. Don't be so formal,' Chautala said.

I served idlis and chutney to Chautala and two other cops. They had come to my apartment in the afternoon to interview the domestic help and the tutor.

We had no information on Siya yet. The hotline number had had five calls so far. Three were spam calls from automated bots, selling insurance. One call came from a psychic who said he could see Siya's future but needed money to gaze into it some more. The fifth call came from a person who had seen a young and fair girl with a seedy-looking man in Punjabi Bagh market.

'We sent a Gypsy within minutes. Turned out to be a neighbourhood girl who was there with her domestic help to buy groceries,' Chautala said.

I nodded, disappointed.

'This will happen, madam,' Chautala said. 'Once it is in the media, all sorts of calls come, from crackpots to well-meaning individuals. Rest assured, we will still attend to all of them seriously.'

Manish and I sat with the police as we waited for Dharmesh, Siya's tutor, to arrive.

'Newspapers have covered the story, too,' Chautala said.

He displayed a bunch of newspapers. They had all carried the story of Siya's abduction along with her picture.

The three cops ate in silence.

'Will my Siya be okay?' I said.

'It's only been forty-eight hours. No dead body yet. No reason to think she is not okay,' Chautala said.

'Body?' I said. My heart stopped for a moment and my legs felt weak.

'Sorry, madam,' Chautala said, dabbing chutney on his idli.

'I shouldn't have said it like that. But that's how we look for a person. Any evidence of them, dead or alive.'

'But who could hurt her? Or want her dead?' I said, now unable to stop the tears.

'Not saying she is, madam,' Chautala said, his mouth full of idli.

The doorbell rang, interrupting our conversation.

'Hello, Alia didi,' Dharmesh said as he walked in. Skinny and six feet tall, he looked younger than his twenty-two years. Perhaps because he had little facial hair. The sight of cops at the dining table, where he normally taught Siya, made his body stiffen.

I told him to sit with the policemen. The three uniformed cops gave him a penetrating gaze. Dharmesh squirmed in his seat.

I cleared the empty plates.

'Didi, I heard about Siya,' Dharmesh said, breaking the awkward silence. 'What really happened?'

'You tell me.' Chautala's firm and powerful voice contrasted with his portly uncle frame.

'What?' Dharmesh cleared his throat.

'What's your full name?' a cop said, pulling out a notepad.

'Dharmesh Yadav.'

'You are Siya's tutor?' Chautala said.

'I … I taught her maths … I teach maths to several students at Ambience Valley.'

'How many students?' Chautala said.

'Six, seven … eight, I think.'

'Six, seven or eight?' Chautala said.

'Eight, sir.'

'Where do you teach them?'

'Private tuitions at their houses. Sometimes two or three students gather at one child's house. I take a group class there.'

'Hmm,' Chautala said.

'Is everything okay, Alia didi?' Dharmesh said.

'Answer Inspector sir's questions, Dharmesh.'

Dharmesh nodded as he swallowed.

'When did you last speak to Siya?' Chautala said.

'Last Thursday. I came here to teach her about square roots. She had a test on Friday.'

'Did she say anything to you?'

'As in, sir?'

'Anything out of the ordinary? Like something that would indicate what has happened?'

'No, sir.'

'Did she ever talk about anything personal, apart from maths?'

'She and I would chat sometimes, yes. She talked about her friends in school. How they get jealous because she does well in class and at dance.'

'Okay, who gets jealous?' Chautala said, taking out his notebook.

'Her best friends. Parvathy, Mahima and Aryan. She loves them a lot, though.'

'Okay, Rajan,' Chautala said, turning to one of the cops. 'Speak to them. Their parents too.'

'Yes, sir,' Rajan said.

'And? Anything else?' Chautala said.

Dharmesh looked at me.

'What? Tell me,' Chautala said, slamming his palm on the table.

'She said sometimes her mother pushes her too much. She has to come first in class. Win at whatever she participates in.'

'Oh,' Chautala said, taking down notes.

'That's not true,' I said, but the inspector interrupted me.

'It's okay, madam,' Chautala said and turned to Dharmesh. 'Who do you live with and where?'

'I live alone in a one-bedroom rented flat in Manesar.'

'Manesar is far from here.'

'Rents are low there. I have a bike—it takes me forty minutes to come to my students in Gurugram.'

'Parents?'

'In Patna. My father works in a factory there.'

'Where were you on the weekend? Especially that night when Siya was abducted.'

'I was in Goa, sir.'

'Really? Goa?' Chautala said.

'Yes, sir. I went with my college friends.'

'Is it?'

'You can check, sir. We stayed in a small guesthouse in Calangute. Four other boys went with me.'

The inspector nodded and turned silent. Dharmesh shifted in his seat. The other cops continued to stare at him.

'You have a girlfriend?' Chautala said.

'No, sir,' Dharmesh said.

'Why not?'

'I don't get time, sir. I am working all the time.'

'All the time?'

'I mean, I remain quite busy, sir.'

'May I check your phone?' Chautala said.

'What? Why, sir?' Dharmesh said. 'I haven't done anything.'

'Hand me your phone. Or I will take you to the station and take it there.'

Dharmesh's face turned blank. He pulled out his mobile phone and placed it on the table with shaking hands.

'Open it, hero,' Chautala said.

Dharmesh looked like he was going to cry.

He unlocked his phone, which Chautala passed to the other cop.

'This is sub-inspector Viren Hooda from the cyber cell. He will check your phone and give it back to you.'

Tears rolled down Dharmesh's cheeks.

'If you did nothing wrong, no need to worry. If you did, tell us now,' Chautala said.

'I don't know anything about Siya going missing, sir,' Dharmesh said.

Viren hooked up Dharmesh's phone to his laptop. He downloaded some files and returned the phone to Dharmesh.

'You are free for now. If we need you, we will come to you. If you hear anything, you will come to us. Clear?' Chautala said.

'Absolutely, sir. Thank you, sir.' Dharmesh stood up. 'Bye, Alia didi. Bye, sir. Jai Hind, sir.'

'Check this fellow thoroughly,' Chautala said after Dharmesh left. 'Rajan, go and meet the parents of Siya's friends. Viren, you talk to the cook and drivers.'

'What happened to your eye?' I said to Manohar as he served me a hot phulka.

'Nothing, didi,' he said, turning his head to hide the black eye.

The intricately carved ten-seater table at Navratna House had just enough chairs to fit our entire family. Now Siya's chair was empty. The three younger kids sat silently, eating dal and rice.

'Will the police find Siya didi?' Rohit said after a couple of minutes.

'Yes, beta,' Timmy said. 'Don't spill your dal. Be careful.'

'Could Siya didi be dead?' Sanjay said.

'Shh, Sanjay. Don't talk like that,' Rachna said.

'It's okay. He's a little kid,' Manish said and turned to Sanjay. 'No, beta, Siya didi is just lost. We will find her.'

'She's not lost, Daddy. Bad man took her,' Suhana said.

'Eat your food, beta. It's getting cold,' Manish said.

Mummyji and Papaji ate in silence. The kids finished their meal and went to watch TV.

'The police have hit Manohar,' Mummyji said. 'Whoever this sub-inspector Viren is, this is not the way.'

'Why did he hit him?' Manish said.

'Because he is from a lower class,' Mummyji said.

'What did he tell the police?' I said.

'Nothing,' Papaji said. 'He slept on the terrace like every night. He woke up as clueless as the rest of us.'

'He's not a straight guy. Remember when Mummy realised he stole from the grocery money?' Manish said.

'He's greedy, yes,' Mummyji said. 'But he's still with us. If he had kidnapped her, he would have vanished too.'

'What about the drivers?' I said.

'One of them, Manoj, is on leave. He's been in his village in Saharanpur for the last two weeks. They checked there. He's there only. Nothing wrong with his story.'

'The other one? Daljeet was on duty that day, no?' I said.

'Yes, he finished his duty at 7 o'clock and went home to his basti two kilometres away from here. The police checked. He was sitting outside his house playing carrom with his friends until late. Sunday was an off for him,' Papaji said.

'So, nothing of value from our support staff?' Manish said.

'Our workers are good people,' Mummyji said. She stood up to clear the table. Rachna and I sprang up to help her.

Manohar was wiping the counter in the kitchen.

'Did they hit you a lot?' I said.

Manohar sniffled but did not respond.

'I am sorry. I will talk to them,' I said.

'Kasam se, Alia didi, I don't know anything,' Manohar said, fighting his sobs.

'We are all really worried, Manohar, that's all,' I said.

I went to the living room. Everyone had moved to the sofas. Rachna took the children upstairs.

'Thank you for dinner, Mummyji, Papaji. Shall we leave, Manish? It's late,' I said.

'Stay for a while. You guys being here helps with our anxiety,' Papaji said.

I walked to a chair and sat down.

'I've asked for an appointment with the commissioner. It should happen in a day or two,' Papaji said.

'Thanks,' I said.

My phone vibrated in my hand. I had an SMS. It was from an unknown spam-like number.

'Five lakhs. If you want her back.'

Along with the text was a picture of a black hairclip with a tiny pink butterfly on it. Siya's.

I jumped up from the chair.

'Manish! Look at this.' I handed him my phone.

Manish read the message and stood up.

'Oh my God. Who sent this?' he said.

'What happened?' Papaji said. We showed the message and the photo to everyone in the room. My heart beat fast. This was the first sign of hope since Siya had vanished. Five lakhs? Money wasn't a problem in our house. A paltry five lakhs for my girl?

Take ten and give her back right now, I thought.

'Should we call this number?' Timmy said, returning my phone.

'It's a gibberish number. Not real. Like the messages you get about buying car insurance,' Manish said.

'We will give the five lakhs, right?' I said.

'Of course, but how, when, where?' Manish said.

'We should tell Inspector Chautala,' Papaji said.

'No,' I said, raising my hand. 'Please. Let's not annoy the kidnappers. It's just five lakhs.'

'But, Alia beta ...' Papaji said as my phone buzzed again. This time I had four more messages.

'Thursday. 5 p.m. Sultanpur National Park.'

'Leave tiffin box under Important Local Birds signboard.'

'2000-rupee notes only. No police.'

'Collect her at entry gate, after we have received tiffin.'

Everyone read the messages.

'Papaji, we have to give them the money. Quietly. Please, please,' I said, desperate.

'Yes, beta,' Papaji said. 'Don't take tension.'

'She's fine. My daughter is fine. They just want some money,' I said to myself, even as I tried to catch my breath.

Chapter 9

5 days missing

'If they find out the police is with us, they will hurt her,' I said.

'They won't,' Manish said. 'Even you won't be able to tell they are here.'

My father-in-law's Mercedes reached Sultanpur National Park. The three-hundred-acre-plus forest reserve, with a lake spanning a hundred acres, is famous for housing dozens of species of rare exotic birds. Just twenty kilometres from the concrete jungle of Gurugram, the abundance of nature and peace was a complete contrast to the city we had left behind. The desolateness of the park made it an excellent location to trade a kidnapped child.

Despite my protests, Papaji and Manish had informed Chautala about the ransom demand. Papaji felt the police had gone the extra distance to help us so far. If we did things without informing them, they could get upset and lose interest. Chautala insisted on sending undercover cops.

'Sir, if I get Siya, let them take the money,' I had said.

'Don't worry, madam, we won't interfere. But trust me, you will be safer this way. Let me separately send two cops in plainclothes—one male, one female—dressed as tourists, that's it.'

The security guard scanned Manish's backpack at the park entrance.

'What's in the tiffin box?'

'My lunch. Didn't get a chance to eat it,' Manish said.

'Please don't feed the birds,' the guard said.

'Of course not,' Manish said.

I did not see any police at the entrance. Had Chautala even sent anyone?

Papaji decided to stay by the entrance, the designated place to collect Siya.

We followed the walking trail and, five minutes later, I saw a metal board with chipped-off paint. 'Important Local Birds', it said. The sign described cranes and pelicans found in the park. Manish and I couldn't see anyone around. He took out the tiffin box with the cash in it and kept it under the sign.

'What do we do now?' I said. My phone vibrated after two minutes as I received a message.

'Leave.'

But where is my Siya? I wanted to scream. I couldn't. Manish and I had no choice but to comply.

We walked back to the park entrance.

'Dropped it off?' Papaji said as he stood up from the bench near the ticket counter.

I nodded.

'Where's Siya?' he said.

'Supposed to be released here,' I said.

I checked the time. It was 5.30 p.m. No sign of Siya.

The man at the ticket counter downed the window shutters.

'Nobody's around. The park is closing soon,' Papaji said.

'Maybe they released her in the park,' I said. 'Maybe we need to search the park.'

'How can we search hundreds of acres? We will have to call,' Papaji paused, 'our friends, right?'

We continued to sit at the park entrance, nervous and anxious. Half an hour later, a member of the park staff came to us.

'The park closes at sunset. You will have to leave now.'

'My daughter might be inside,' I said.

'What? Where?' the staff member said. 'She's lost in the park?'

'Might be,' I said.

'I can inform the rangers inside. But how did you lose her?' he said.

Before I could answer, a lady in a blue salwar kameez with binoculars around her neck came running to us from the parking lot.

'Are you Alia Arora?' she said, trying to catch her breath.

'Yes,' I said. 'What happened?' My hopes skyrocketed. Had someone spotted Siya?

'I work with Inspector Chautala. My colleague caught someone. Come with us.'

'Caught who?' I said.

'Follow me.'

All of us rushed to the parking area.

A man in a Hawaiian shirt and shorts stood near a private taxi, holding on to a skinny man by his collar. I went close and realised the man in the Hawaiian shirt was sub-inspector Rajan Saini.

'He's your kidnapper,' Rajan said.

'And Siya?' I said.

Rajan didn't answer me. He turned to my father-in-law. 'Hello, Mr Arora, Chautala sir sent me. I caught this guy picking up the tiffin box.'

'But where's Siya?' I thought I had screamed, but I was barely audible.

'He'll tell us. Real soon,' Rajan said, slapping the kidnapper hard across his face.

6 days missing

Manish and I reached the police station. We found several media OB vans parked outside. Chautala had called early morning and told us to come there.

For 8 in the morning, the place looked really busy. I saw my in-laws' black Mercedes parked at the station as well.

A barrage of reporters came towards me. A constable

signalled to Manish and me to remain quiet and whisked us into Inspector Chautala's office. My in-laws were already there with Chautala and sub-inspector Viren Hooda.

'The person we caught at Sultanpur National Park is Sonu. He's a distant cousin of your cook Manohar. They belong to the same village in eastern UP,' Chautala said.

My mother-in-law looked at Chautala, shocked.

'Sonu has a history of petty theft cases. Spent six months in an Allahabad jail five years ago,' Chautala said.

'We are sorry, Mrs Arora. We came unannounced early morning today to get Manohar. He could have escaped,' Viren said.

Chautala took out a tiffin box from his desk drawer.

'Here is your money,' Chautala said, sliding the box towards me. I didn't care about the money. I wanted Siya.

'Sonu used a fake phone number-generating app to send texts to you. His phone records show he was in touch with Manohar.'

'Sir, but Siya?' I said.

'Sonu is tough. He still maintains he didn't kidnap your daughter. But we have the messages between him and Manohar, planning the ransom.'

'Looked so innocent, this Manohar. Stayed in our house for five years,' Mummyji said.

'You can't tell, Mrs Arora. The most innocent-looking men commit the worst crimes,' Chautala said. 'And both of them are seasoned. Not scared of the police or their beatings.'

'Chautala sir, what about Siya?' I said again.

'Calm down, madam. We are getting close. Please take a seat.'

He pointed to the empty chairs at one side of his desk. I sat down and tried to stay still.

'We have planned a small press conference to announce the arrests of Sonu and Manohar. It's big news,' Chautala said.

'Sir, we haven't found Siya and we are doing a press conference? For what?' I said, flustered. 'To celebrate?'

'Madam, nobody is celebrating. We just want to use this as a chance to get some more publicity for the case. Keep the public aware. Improves the chances of someone spotting her.'

'Spot her? Haven't you caught the kidnappers? They know where she is,' I said.

'They are not accepting it yet. Sonu isn't talking. We just took Manohar into custody.'

I stood up again and threw my hands in the air. 'But these guys have Siya.'

'The UP police have sent a team to their village. Madam, please relax.' Chautala turned to Manish. 'We want the family with us at the press conference.'

Manish signalled to me to sit down. He spoke to Chautala in a calm voice.

'Sir, Sonu and Manohar could have another partner. If news of their arrest gets out, they could hurt her.'

'News of their arrest will get out anyway. If we do a press conference, we control the narrative. We show we are one. The family says the police is working hard and has caught the kidnappers. We say the family is cooperating really well. It's a win-win.'

'There is no winning until Siya is found,' I said.

'She will be. Relax, madam. Someone from Sonu's or Manohar's family will know. They will reveal it once they see it all on TV. These village people get scared.'

'Can't we just beat them up and make them tell us?' Papaji said in a stern voice.

'Oh, we will be doing a lot of that too. But first, let's go. It's time for the conference.'

Chapter 10

The Sushant Lok Police Station had arranged a makeshift press conference room. Chautala, Viren, Manish and I sat in the centre, while my in-laws took chairs adjacent to us. We faced a group of twenty reporters. A pile of mikes on a table separated us from the journalists.

'Thank you all for coming so early in the morning,' Chautala said. 'We called you here to give updates on the Siya Arora case. With us today are Siya's parents, Manish Arora and Alia Arora. We also have Siya's grandparents.'

A dozen flashlights blinded me as photographers took close-ups of my face. I took a deep breath and kept a neutral expression. If this was what it would take to find my daughter, so be it.

Chautala continued.

'A few days back, Mrs Alia received an anonymous message, asking for five lakh rupees in return for Siya. The family immediately informed Gurugram Police. We caught the person who sent the message at Sultanpur National Park. His name is Sonu Lal and he is from Champakpur, near Prayagraj. Sonu has a criminal history and is a relative of Manohar Lal, the cook at Siya's grandparents' house, from where Siya was abducted. We have arrested both Sonu and Manohar and are interrogating them. We are working with UP Police to conduct searches in Champakpur. Do note we have done this within five days of the kidnapping. Our teams have worked non-stop—'

A cacophony ensued amongst the journalists as they scrambled to ask questions.

'Sir, where is Siya Arora?' said one reporter. Exactly the question I wanted to ask.

'We are investigating her whereabouts. We have the two culprits. We should be able to find out soon,' Chautala said.

'Have the two arrested people admitted to the crime?' another reporter said.

'We caught them red-handed. One picked up the cash, and they both exchanged messages about the ransom plot. We should have a confession soon,' Chautala said.

'Could Siya Arora be dead?' one journalist said.

'We don't have the body, so we can't presume that,' Viren said. The mention of the word 'body' ran like an electric shock down the room and caused a commotion. A reporter turned to me.

'Aliaji, as Siya's mother, are you satisfied with the performance of the police?'

I looked at Chautala.

'Well, they are working really hard,' I said.

'But are you happy with their performance?'

'I will only be happy when I see my daughter,' I said.

'So you are not happy?' said the reporter.

'I didn't say—' Before I could finish, a barrage of questions went to Chautala. His expression told me he was upset at what I had just said.

'Inspector Chautala, when can we hope to find Siya?' said one reporter.

'Is your job even done if you haven't found her?' said another.

'We are working on it. In six days, we made two arrests. We are not magicians.'

'Your responsibility ends with the arrests?' a reporter said.

'No. We also have the responsibility of finding her. But you have to understand, the family could have been more responsible too. In what sort of house does a child get abducted while sleeping in her own bed? In fact, we want to use this platform to tell viewers this—please be careful and keep your kids safe in the house. The cook, who is under arrest, was hired without a police verification. Please, viewers, get your domestic help verified at the police station.'

My in-laws' faces fell. Chautala, miffed at my lack of enthusiastic praise for him, had struck back. The reporters turned to my in-laws.

'Mrs Arora, do you feel you had adequate safeguards in your house?' said a reporter.

My mother-in-law froze as she faced blinding camera lights for the first time in her life.

'Why did you not have twenty-four hour security?' said a journalist.

'We have lived in that house for over ten years as a joint family. We never had an issue,' Papaji said, wiping his forehead.

'Did you screen the cook before hiring him? Why wasn't the police verification done?' someone screamed at my mother-in-law.

'He worked with us for five years. Never had a problem,' my mother-in-law said.

'How could you have been more careful, Mrs Durga Arora? What could have prevented your granddaughter from being kidnapped?' another reporter said, shoving a mike in front of Mummyji. She was close to tears. The cameras were loving it. More camerapersons gathered around her, hoping to catch the exact moment when she would start to cry.

'Okay, enough, let's maintain order,' Viren said. The reporters ignored the cop and huddled around Mummyji.

My mother-in-law broke down. Photographers went into a frenzy. Nobody wanted to miss the 'diamond-laden grandma in tears' shot. Rich people suffering made for great TV.

'Would you like to say anything to other parents?' one reporter said.

'What can I say? Who listens to elders these days anyway?' Mummyji said, as her humiliation turned to anger.

Reporters clicked more photographs as my mother-in-law's expression became more aggressive.

'You were saying, madam?' said one.

'This is some strange new modern parenting thing, making little kids sleep in their own room. Not right next to their parents. We were not brought up like this.'

My father-in-law gave her a warning pat on the back, signalling to her to be quiet. He folded his hands in a namaste to the reporters. He held his wife's hand and walked out of the room.

'Aliaji? Anything you would like to say in response to your mother-in-law?' a young reporter said.

'All I want to say is, I want to find my Siya. Please, please, if anyone watching this has any information, let us know,' I said to a bunch of mikes before leaving the room.

'Chautala sir, we appreciate your help, but you should not have said the family could have been more responsible,' Papaji said.

'Enough, Shamsherji. It isn't fair for us to get the entire blame either. Did you hear what your daughter-in-law said?'

'What?' I said.

'What do you mean you are not happy with us, madam?' Chautala said. 'My officers have not slept for four days. We ignored all other cases to help you.'

'I never said I am not happy with your work. I only said I will be happy when I see Siya. I didn't blame the police.'

'You saw how they twisted it,' Chautala said.

'Alia shouldn't have said that,' Mummyji said.

I wanted to pick a pile of dusty brown files from Chautala's desk and smack it on my mother-in-law's big head. What about the nonsense she had said about modern parenting?

'Leave it now, Durga. This is not about the media. This is about Siya. What's the next step, Chautalaji?' Papaji said.

'Beat the hell out of Sonu and Manohar so they talk. But the media will roast us if they find out we hit them. They will say the police is harsh on them as they are lower class people. So yes, media does matter.'

'I don't care. Beat them if you have to, sir,' I said.

'Easy for you to say,' Chautala said. 'You don't have your job on the line. But fine, I will do what it takes.'

Chautala stood up from his chair to signal the end of the meeting.

Everyone stood up to leave as well.

'Sir, one request before we go?' I said. 'May I meet Manohar once?'

Manohar lay on his back in the lockup, his arm covering his eyes.

'Madamji?' he said when he saw me enter the lockup with two constables.

'I want to talk to you. Not as "madam", but as a mother.'

The two constables moved away to give us privacy.

'Madamji,' Manohar said. He sat on his haunches, hands folded and eyes on the floor. 'Madamji, please. Forgive me.'

'Look at me,' I said.

He turned his gaze towards me.

'They said they will beat me at night,' he said and broke down. 'The police beats people like us a lot.'

The two constables looked up when they heard Manohar cry and then went back to their phones.

'Where's Siya?' I said.

'Maa kasam, I don't know.'

'Listen, Manohar. The police might just beat you. But if you hurt Siya, I will kill you.'

'Madamji, Sonu and I didn't take Siya. Maa kasam, madamji,' Manohar said.

'What about the messages? The five lakh rupees?'

'I did ask Sonu to send the ransom message, yes. I sent the hairclip photo too. But we did not kidnap Siya.'

'What?' I said, confused.

'We thought we could make quick money. Five lakh rupees won't be a big amount for the family. They will give it without telling anyone. We will simply take the cash and vanish, that's what we thought.'

He broke into loud sobs. Two prisoners in the adjacent lockup peeked to see what was going on. A constable forced them back into their cell with his bamboo stick.

'Sonu and I wanted to open a catering business with the money. That's all our plan was, Alia madamji. Please forgive me.'

He folded his hands and touched my feet.

'Manohar. Where is Siya?' I said.

Chautala entered the lockup, just in time to see Manohar begging me for mercy.

'Don't be fooled by his tears. Sonu is crying in the other lockup,' Chautala said.

I winced as he kicked Manohar in the stomach.

'Please, Inspector sahib, don't hit me,' Manohar said, rolling on the floor in pain as I left the cell.

Chapter 11

My phone buzzed as multiple 'Siya Arora' news alerts popped up in my notifications.

Cook at Siya Arora's grandparents' house arrested, said one.

I switched on the TV. One channel was showing visuals of the press conference. Manish looked up from his phone to watch as well.

An anchor was speaking. 'The Gurugram police made two arrests in the Siya Arora kidnapping case. Siya is the daughter of Manish Arora, who runs an online jewellery business, and Alia Arora, an ex-model.'

Ex-model? I'd done six fashion shows and two print ads over a decade ago.

Why mention that, I wondered.

The anchor continued. 'The two arrested are Manohar, the family cook, and his cousin, Sonu. Despite these arrests, the police have been unable to locate Siya or get any information about her whereabouts. Tensions ran high at the press conference today with the family disagreeing with the police on the arrests being a major breakthrough. Each side seemed to blame the other, and Siya's grandmother even seemed to suggest that modern parenting was to blame.'

The TV showed a clip of the press conference. I was looking straight into a camera and saying in a grim tone, 'I will only be happy when I see my daughter.'

Chautala came on the screen.

'In what sort of house does a child get abducted while sleeping in their own bed?' he said.

The visuals changed.

'This is some strange new modern parenting thing, making little kids sleep in their own room,' my mother-in-law said.

The anchor came back on the screen.

'As the blame game between the police and the family, and even within the family continues, Siya remains missing even after a week,' she said, before going into a break.

An advertisement of a private MBA college promising students international jobs started.

Manish switched off the TV.

'Not good,' Manish said, 'the way they are twisting it. You could have avoided the "will only be happy when I see my daughter" statement.'

'And what are your views on your mother's "strange new modern parenting" comment? Targeted at me, of course, that too on TV.'

'Mummyji was stressed. You saw how the journos hounded her?' he said.

A surge of anger rushed through me.

'And I wasn't fucking stressed, Manish? Only your mother was? I made a simple and general comment. Your mother insulted me and held me guilty on national TV. And you pick on me?'

'She's old, traditional. Maybe even a little foolish. You have to be sensible, keep it together.'

'Why the fuck, Manish?' I screamed, 'why do I have to be sensible always?'

'Alia, you are not getting the point,' Manish said, waving his hand in front of me.

'No, damn it, I am not. It is my daughter who is out there. God knows what is happening to her. But I must keep it together? Really?'

I picked up the remote to turn on the TV again. The news was back on. The anchor was now discussing Siya's case with a lady who claimed to be a 'vedic psychologist'.

'What do you have to say about the "modern parenting" point?' the anchor said.

The vedic expert responded with full enthusiasm.

'Well, you see, many of our traditional Indian systems were great. Modern generation concepts like the need for privacy for parents and creating an independent space for children were never there. Nuclear families are a fairly new phenomenon. You see, in Indian culture we had big joint families, which helped kids grow up safe. They would sleep in their parents' room, or with their grandparents, feeling secure. So, yes, Siya's grandmother has a point that modern parenting has a part—'

Manish took the remote from me and switched off the TV.

'This will kill you,' Manish said. 'It will kill us. Our relationship. We need to be together.'

'Let me watch it,' I said, staring at the black screen.

'No,' Manish said. 'Please, no.'

I heard the wobble in his voice and then the sound of the remote falling as it slipped from his hand. His whole body shaking, he sobbed uncontrollably. I had never seen him like this in my entire life.

'Manish,' I said and embraced him.

'Where is our Siya?' he said. 'Where is our Siya? Our little Siya?'

'I don't know,' I said, my voice faltering.

'I am sorry for what my mother said,' he said.

Suhana walked into the bedroom. Manish turned to look away from her to hide his tears.

'Mommy, can you come cuddle me? I am scared.'

15 days missing

'Sonu and Manohar don't have your daughter. They only did this for a quick buck. They didn't kidnap Siya. Sorry it took so long to find out,' Chautala said, lifting his cup of tea. He had come home to apologise.

I nodded.

'Manohar and Sonu had to be hospitalised last night,' Chautala said.

'Really? What happened to them?'

'Nothing much. A couple of stitches and they will be back in lockup.'

'You won't release them?'

'They did commit a crime. Demanded ransom and tried to cheat you. They have to be punished.'

We sat in silence as Chautala sipped his tea.

'I heard Siya's school is assisting you,' Chautala said.

'Yes, the school community is trying to help,' I said. Siya's school principal had got the students to make posters about her. The younger kids had made missing-person posters with crayons and the older students had made them on computers. All the posters had Siya's picture and our contact details. The students helped paste the posters in the neighbourhood as well as other parts of Gurugram.

'School aside, what do we do next to find Siya?' I said.

'Keep the media attention going somehow, madam. It increases the chances of finding her.'

'That's it? We depend on the media, which has already created a rift in our family? Not to mention blamed us, with your help, of course.'

'Madam,' Chautala said, keeping his empty tea cup on the table, 'as I said, let's forget about that press conference. We were all inexperienced. The media is nobody's friend.'

'And you want to depend on them?

'Unfortunately, yes. The story stays alive, the public remembers it and other police stations remain focused on it.'

I sighed.

'What else can we do, though?' I said.

'We will review the report on the contents of Siya's phone again. We may get some leads from there. And we are going to talk to people again. That tutor, for instance. Anyone else you think we should talk to?'

'Navratna Jewels. People who work there,' I said.

'We will interview all the staff,' Chautala said and stood up to leave. 'Give us time.'

'She's out there somewhere, sir. The longer we take, the more she suffers.'

'Five-crore-rupees reward? What are you even saying, Shamsher,' Mummyji said.

'I am serious. The police are telling us to retain media attention. A big reward will do it,' Papaji said, sipping his Scotch from a crystal glass. The rest of the adults sat around him in the living room. 'What say, Timmy? Rachna?'

Timmy and Rachna looked at each other but remained silent.

'Papaji, it could create complications. Random people will call us with fake sightings,' Manish said.

'We will give the police's contact number. Nobody will mess with them,' Papaji said.

Manish did not respond. Papaji took a big sip of his drink and continued.

'Have you seen how the country goes crazy over KBC? Why? Because of the seven-crore-rupees top prize. You know what, let's make our reward seven crore rupees. We'll get the attention, and hopefully Siya too.'

'Seven crores?' Mummyji said, eyebrows raised in disapproval.

'What do you think, Alia beta?' Papaji said to me in a soft voice.

'It's a lot of money, Papaji,' I said. 'How can I ask you to do this?'

'Are you crazy? She is my granddaughter. What else is money for? To put diamonds on our graves?'

'Shamsher, you are getting too emotional,' Mummyji said.

'Shh,' Shamsher said to his wife.

Tears rolled down my cheeks.

'Thank you, Papaji,' I said, folding my hands.

'What thanks? We are family. Let's set up the press conference.'

Chapter 12

20 days missing

Manish and I were watching TV in our bedroom at night. The evening news was playing snippets of the press conference we'd held that afternoon. The seven-crore-rupees reward was flashed multiple times on the screen.

'The police came to my office today,' Manish said.

He sat on the other side of the bed, with Suhana sleeping between us.

'They did?' I said, eyes still on the TV.

'Spent the whole day interviewing all the employees. Anyway, switch off the television. Let's sleep.'

I turned off the TV. I slipped under the blanket and stared at the darkness above me. I knew I wouldn't sleep for another four hours. That had been the pattern every night since Siya had gone. I had to try, though.

'I love you, Alia,' Manish said, more out of habit than genuine feeling.

'Love you too,' I said in reflex.

Thoughts raced through my head. Would the reward offer work? Would someone call that night itself, saying he had seen my girl in the window of the house opposite his? It could happen, right? Seven crore rupees is an insane amount of money. Maybe the kidnapper himself would offer to release her. He could pretend to be a hero, collect the reward and go scot-free. I didn't care. I just wanted my daughter back.

Oh God, just give me back my daughter, and I won't ask you for a thing ever again till I die.

As the night progressed, I became more anxious. What if the kidnapper freaked out though? What if he felt the world would be after him because of the reward? What if he realised he would never get the reward, as Siya would identify him? What if he decided to kill Siya?

I sat up. I couldn't breathe. Perspiration covered my entire body. I turned towards Manish and Suhana, but both of them were fast asleep.

I picked up my phone to distract myself. Of course, the first thing I did was open Siya's photos. I saw pictures from her third birthday, which we had celebrated in the Navratna House garden. We'd decided on a circus theme, hired two clowns to play games with the kids. Siya had been dressed as an acrobat. I flipped through photos of various family vacations. We had gone to Paris four years ago and Sydney the year before that.

My phone pinged with a notification. A news alert on Siya Arora flashed on my screen.

'Is Siya Arora's family as straight as they seem to be?' said the headline. I clicked on the link. The article had appeared on an independent news website called SpiceNews, unaffiliated with any of the major media houses.

I read the opening lines of the article.

> Twenty days after the disappearance of her daughter, the once-upon-a-time-model Alia Arora walked into her second press conference for her daughter. She was dressed in an off-white chikan salwar kameez, impeccable and elegant despite the sombre colour chosen for the occasion. She sat with her in-laws and remained quiet throughout. Her father-in-law pleaded with the public, promising a staggering seven-crore-rupees reward to anyone who finds Siya, his granddaughter. For a mother with a missing child, Alia Arora seemed extraordinarily composed. There were no uncontrollable tears. Not even a hair was out of place. Her hazel eyes simply gazed into infinity.

My hazel eyes opened wide in shock as I read the rest of the bizarre article.

> If the lack of Alia Arora's maternal emotion isn't enough to lift eyebrows, one look at Alia's mother-in-law, Durga Arora, may also make you question the absurdity of it all. She wore two diamond necklaces, each worth at least thirty lakh rupees. Durga looked at Alia with disdain throughout the conference. At the last press-con, she had accused Alia Arora of being negligent as well.

I took a deep breath.

> The big question is, why the grand 'seven-crore-rupees-reward' announcement? Surely designed to catch media attention, is this KBC top prize-level amount also an attempt at distraction? To establish the narrative that 'someone else' took their granddaughter? Thus, to imply there is no chance of the family being involved in the abduction? After all, didn't Siya Arora disappear from her own house with all these people present? Why isn't that angle being investigated? Is it because just as the family can afford this prize, they can also 'pay' the police and the mainstream media to look the other way?

> These are tough questions nobody is asking, but SpiceNews dares to. Neighbours and previous part-time maids of the Aroras confirm that all is not well within Navratna House. After all, why else did Alia Arora leave her big happy joint family? As a website seeking the truth, all we want to say is nothing should be kept off the table, nothing at all.

It's just a stupid clickbait website, I said to myself, trying to calm myself down. It didn't help. I read the article five more times. I checked the time: 3 a.m. I took the strip of sleeping pills from my bedside table drawer and popped two.

This nonsensical article is not going to be read, I told myself.

We needed to focus, focus on Siya. My mind continued to bubble with thoughts as the pills made me drift off to sleep.

24 days missing

'It's trending on Twitter,' Ashwin, the lead anchor of a TV channel, said on the phone. 'I wanted your statement.'

'What kind of statement?' I said.

'Come to my studio. Rebut the article. I am giving you a chance on national TV,' he said.

'Let me think about it,' I said and ended the call.

I brought the bowl of dal and aloo sabzi to the dining table.

'Who was it?' Manish said.

'Ashwin, TV anchor.'

'Oh, what happened?' he said, serving himself.

'There's this article about the case that's trending. Absolute nonsense.'

'Show me,' Manish said.

I searched for the link on my phone and passed it on to him.

'Fuck!' Manish said. 'What the hell is this!'

'SpiceNews is notorious for its clickbait stuff,' I said.

'They are accusing the family.'

He pushed his plate away.

'Is it trending on Twitter?' Manish said.

I nodded.

'Holy fuck! Now this Ashwin will pounce on it,' Manish said.

'He invited me for an interview to counter the article.'

Manish shook his head vigorously.

'Don't do it. It will only fan the flames further.'

'He said I should come and talk. Be emotional. Like if I cried on TV, I could get sympathy.'

'What crap!' Manish said.

'He said the general public thinks that, as the mother, I am not sad enough, given the situation.'

'Nonsense, Alia. You are not going to that vulture's show,' Manish said. He strode off to the bedroom. Tears rolled down my cheeks as I texted Ashwin, politely declining his offer. Then I checked Twitter. #SiyaAroraFamilyInvolved was trending in the fifth position in India, sandwiched between the two constant pro- and anti-BJP trends.

I read some of the tweets related to the hashtag.

Rich people feel they can buy justice. Don't spare them #SiyaAroraFamilyInvolved

Stone-cold mother hides a lot behind her pretty face. #SiyaAroraFamilyInvolved

Pervert grandfather hurt the poor girl. Now announcing reward to hide. #SiyaAroraFamilyInvolved

Twelve-year-old girl just vanishes from her family home at night. And the family should not be questioned? #SiyaAroraFamilyInvolved

How many carats of diamonds did the Aroras pay to hide their dirty secrets? #SiyaAroraFamilyInvolved

Why is the evil green-eyed mother wearing fashionable clothes to press conferences? Kuch toh hai #SiyaAroraFamilyInvolved

I clenched my jaw to stop myself from screaming.

Who were these people? Why were they talking like this?

My phone pinged with a message from Ashwin.

'Disappointed you won't come. Carrying the story anyway, sometime in the next few days. Just FYI.'

I had three missed calls from my mother-in-law. I called her back.

'Sorry Mummyji,' I said. 'I was in the other room giving Suhana her dinner.'

'You really are a curse on our family, aren't you?'

'What!' I said, surprised.

'You aren't watching TV?'

'No, why?'

'They are accusing us, Shamsher and me, of kidnapping your daughter.'

'It's nonsense, Mummyji, just a stupid article ...'

'It's on TV. On the most popular news channel. Everyone we know watches this.'

I switched on the TV while still on the phone. Manish looked up from his laptop as he saw me search for the right channel.

'It was your idea, right? To go to the media?' Mummyji said on the phone.

'One minute, Mummyji, I'm finding the channel.'

My mother-in-law ignored me and continued to talk.

'They are ruining everything Shamsher ever worked for. Now you know why I call you a curse? That's why I did that puja, to get rid of your evil eye. Kameeni, why did you even come to our house?'

I gulped hard to fight back my tears. The phone fell from my hands onto the carpet. Manish picked it up.

'Mummyji?' Manish said. She continued to scream on the other side.

'Calm down, Mummyji,' Manish said. 'Okay, okay, we'll come over.'

Manish ended the call and returned my phone.

'Alia,' he said.

'Yeah?' I said, my voice breaking. Was he going to say something supportive to me at last?

'Increase the volume, no?' Manish said as Ashwin came on the screen.

I exhaled and threw the remote towards him. Manish increased the volume.

'Ladies and gentlemen, I have three burning questions. One, are the rich in this country above the law? Two, can money matter more than the life of a twelve-year-old child? Three, is the police of this country scared to take on the powerful? Let's look at the latest explosive revelations in the murky Siya Arora case.'

The TV visuals switched to a reporter who spoke to the camera from outside Navratna House.

'This is the posh seven-hundred-yard bungalow owned by leading city jeweller Shamsher Arora. Siya Arora was abducted at night from here. The family claims she was taken away when six adults were sleeping in this house. Three other children were also sleeping in the same room as Siya. The police have questioned a number of people, but so far have not raised a finger at the most obvious—perhaps because it would be uncomfortable—suspects of them all, the Arora family.'

'Fuck,' Manish smacked his forehead.

The news report went on to show clips of our past press conferences. They added ominous, horror movie background music, making us all look like villains.

Ashwin came back on the screen.

'Let me tell you viewers, I invited Alia Arora, the mother of Siya Arora, on this show tonight. Guess what happened? She refused. Why? What is she afraid of? We did manage to reach Inspector Chautala, the investigating officer on the case, on the phone. Let's patch him in.'

An old picture of Chautala, probably taken twenty years and twenty kilos ago, surfaced on the screen.

'Good evening, sir,' Ashwin said. 'The people of India are clamouring for justice. #SiyaAroraFamilyInvolved is trending on social media. What do you have to say?'

'We have made arrests, questioned a lot of people. We are working hard. Investigations are still on—' Chautala said before Ashwin interrupted him.

'Sir, six adult family members were in the house when the girl vanished. The mother doesn't show enough emotion. All this is not fishy to you?'

Show enough emotion? What constituted showing enough emotion?

Ashwin continued. 'The grandparents announce this KBC-style award and turn this kidnapping into a reality show. And, sir, you do nothing?'

'Who said we did nothing?' Chautala's livid voice crackled down the phone line.

'But you have ruled the family out.'

'Who said we have?'

'So you have not?'

'Nothing and no one is ruled out. However, the family is cooperative and there is no reason to believe—'

Ashwin began to shout, drowning out Chautala's words.

'Okay, viewers, this is breaking news right here, first heard on your channel. The Gurugram police confirm that nothing is ruled out, no one is ruled out. The family angle could well be there. Before I go to a break, let me just say this tonight about the Aroras, who deal in jewellery—all that glitters is not gold.'

Everyone in Navratna House sat with a sullen face, like someone had died. I hadn't seen such sadness even on the day Siya was abducted. Papaji clasped his hands and kept his gaze down.

'Never expected Chautala to talk like that,' Timmy said. 'Papaji has known him for years.'

'The media trapped him. He had no choice,' Papaji said and shook his head. 'We are ruined.'

'Papaji, it's all noise,' I said. 'It will pass.'

'Enough, Alia,' Papaji said. 'I supported you so far. God knows I did everything to get my granddaughter back.'

'Yes, Papaji,' I said.

'But this is too much,' he said. 'They are calling me a criminal. A pervert. A murderer. Of my little granddaughter! I worked all my life for this?'

Papaji put his head in his hands. For the first time in my life I saw him cry. Mummyji went behind his sofa and put a hand on his back.

'Barbaad. We are ruined,' she said.

I looked at Manish. He sat frozen, unable to react, like a mute statue.

'They suspect us?' Timmy said. 'On what basis? Why would we hurt our own child?'

'It's just noise. If we haven't done anything wrong, there's no need to worry,' I said.

'Who the hell are you to tell us there's no need to worry?' Mummyji's thunderous voice filled the room.

'Mummyji, please,' I said in a soft voice. 'Sit down.'

'Why should I sit down? It's almost a month since your girl ran away from this house. Look for her and worry for her, that's all we have done since that day. Seven crore rupees Shamsher offered. Do you even know what is seven crores? Has anyone in your khandaan ever seen that much money in their life?'

I clasped both ends of my dupatta to keep my composure as I took in the insults. I turned to Manish, my husband, the man who had once begged me to marry him. He remained quiet as he let his wife be humiliated one more time.

'Siya did not run away, Mummyji,' I said in a measured voice.

'How do you know she didn't? And you wanted this media, no? See how they are painting us. Like we chopped her into pieces and buried her or something. All because of you. The family curse.'

'Mummyji, please,' Rachna said.

'What please? The police will now come after us. All of Shamsher's and Timmy's customers will run away. Even if we prove our innocence, our business will be ruined. All because of this curse and her manhoos daughter,' Mummyji said.

I glared at her. I could take a million insults but I could not hear anything against my child.

I stood up to level with my mother-in-law. I wagged a finger at her. 'Not my daughter, Mummyji.'

She looked back at me, shocked at my defiance. Manish stood up too. But I signalled to him to stay put.

'There is no need to overreact like this. We all know media drama ends in a day or two. If nobody here has done anything wrong, this stupid theory of family involvement will pass. But you know my real fear, Mummyji? Given what you think of me and my daughters, Ashwin might be right—nothing can be ruled out.'

Chapter 13

40 days missing

'Ten hours again today,' Timmy said. 'I don't see what Chautala is trying to achieve.'

Timmy, Rachna and my in-laws had spent the entire day at the station. The police let Rachna leave when it was time for Rohit and Sanjay to come back from school, but the rest of them had been made to sit in the interrogation room. This had become a daily ritual for the last ten days.

'Sorry, bhaiya,' Manish said. 'Because of us you have to go through all this.'

Timmy was at our house for dinner on his way back from the police station. Manish had called their parents too. However, my mother-in-law had told Manish she could not bear to see my face.

'Ditto,' I told Manish.

I had made lemon rice with curd for dinner, something Suhana loved. Manish had asked me to make a sabzi and chapatis for Timmy bhaiya as well. I had agreed. A part of me had never given up trying to win his family's approval. I heard the two brothers talk at the dining table as I made chapatis in the kitchen.

'When will Chautala stop bothering you guys?' Manish said.

'When they find the culprit. Or when they find Siya. Or when something makes it clear the family had nothing to do with any of it.'

'Of course we had nothing to do with it,' Manish said, banging his fist on the table. 'Chautala is mad. Does he want money? Should we try that route?'

'No, no, Manish. That's the charge, right? Guilty family wants to buy the police. Don't do that. Chautala is just under media pressure.'

I entered the dining room with a large tray carrying various dishes for dinner.

The three of us ate in silence.

'How's Papaji?' I said to Timmy after a few minutes.

'Tired,' Timmy said.

I nodded as I served him some more matar-paneer and raita.

'For the first time, I feel my father is old. Otherwise, with his energy and drive, could you ever tell he's sixty-eight?'

'He's going to the factory?' Manish said.

'When will he go? He is at the police station most of the day.'

Manish nodded as Timmy continued. 'Even Rachna is so sick of it all. Neighbours talk nonsense about us. Kids are getting neglected. It is too much.'

'Anything we can do to help?' Manish said.

'I just want this drama to end,' Timmy said.

Drama. That's what they were calling the search for my daughter now.

'They took the tutor into custody,' Manish said. He had called me from his office, where he spent most of his day. It helped him forget the pain was what he told me.

'What happened?' I said. I didn't have much hope from the police interrogating Dharmesh. After meeting the police at my house, Dharmesh had gone home to Patna and stayed there with his parents. If he had Siya, why would he have gone home? Another interrogation seemed like a wasted exercise, just like all the other ones the police had conducted so far. No evidence whatsoever, was the standard conclusion the cops had reached after all those meetings. However, if the police had taken him into custody, they must have had some basis for it.

'He had pictures of Siya on his phone. The police did a scrub of his phone hard drive. He had pictures of Siya in his secret folders.'

'What? What kind of pictures?'

'I don't know. Chautala said he wants to meet us.'

'Station?' I said.

'No, outside. I'll pick you up in ten minutes.'

The Le Meridien hotel in Gurugram is a short drive from my house. Chautala called us to the club lounge on the top floor, where he sat with Dharmesh on a couch. He was in a white shirt and his khaki police pants. He had a fizzy drink in his hand. Dharmesh wore a tense expression.

'Too many people at the station. Hope you don't mind coming here?'

'Not at all, sir,' Manish said courteously.

'You never know who leaks what. "Chautala made the family meet another suspect, even when the family itself is suspect". You know how the media will twist it.'

Manish and I nodded, sipping the water served to us.

'I am not trying to harass you or your family. I am under a lot of pressure.'

'We understand, Chautala sir,' Manish said.

'He might finally end your misery,' Chautala said, pointing to Dharmesh.

'Does he know anything about Siya?' I said.

Chautala grinned at Dharmesh, who spoke in a rush.

'I don't know anything, Manish bhaiya, Alia didi. The police just kept me at the station. I did nothing.'

Chautala took out a set of colour printouts from his briefcase and slid them towards us.

There were pictures of Siya during her tuitions with Dharmesh. I saw two selfies of Dharmesh, with an unaware Siya solving math problems in the background. In one picture, she smiled at the camera with her tongue out. In another, she had a pencil in her mouth.

'Sir is quite a photographer,' Chautala said and winked.

Manish flipped through the pictures again.

'Where's Siya?' I said to Dharmesh. 'I don't care about anything else.'

'I don't know, didi,' Dharmesh said, almost in tears.

'Why the fuck did you take her pictures when she was studying?' Manish said menacingly.

'Just like that, bhaiya. Sorry.'

'You teach your students or take pictures with them?' Manish said, loud enough for the waiters in the club lounge to look at our table.

'Manishji, you don't need to raise your volume. He will talk. If not in this five-star hotel, maybe at our seven-star lock-up. We will give him room service,' Chautala said.

Dharmesh was crying by now. The police wouldn't have to beat him up. He would crack the moment they tossed him into the lock-up.

Chautala took out a small plastic packet from his briefcase. The packet contained three friendship bands.

'We found these at his apartment,' Chautala said.

'Suhana mentioned these,' I screamed. 'Yes, she said the kidnapper wore these.'

'No, Alia didi, I swear, I wasn't even in town that night.'

'Relax, madam, we will ensure he talks,' Chautala said and chuckled.

'Alia didi, Siya made these bands. She herself gifted them to me when she got an A in an algebra test.'

'Oh, hero, we will give you some gifts too,' Chautala said. He grabbed Dharmesh's collar from the back in a mock playful manner.

'Just tell me where my daughter is,' I said with folded hands.

'Madam, what are you doing?' Chautala tut-tutted. 'Don't beg in front of this lowlife. This is my job. I will find out.'

I continued to talk. 'Please, Dharmesh. If you did something by mistake, tell me. I just want my little girl back.'

'I took the photos, yes. But that's it. She was my prettiest student. I just took the pictures to show my friends, that's all, mother promise.'

'She's twelve, haraami,' Chautala said. 'Prettiest student? You will rot in jail for the rest of your life.'

'I showed them to my mother also,' Dharmesh said, 'not in any bad way. It's just her unusual eye colour ...'

I shuddered. I had let this creepy man into my house for over a year.

'Chutiya, she is a bachchi,' Chautala said, and continued to curse Dharmesh with the choicest of Haryanvi abuses. I shifted uncomfortably.

'Sorry, madam,' Chautala said and stood up to leave. 'I'll keep you updated on him.'

'Okay, sir,' Manish said.

'For now I won't be needing your family to come to the station. I have this new suspect. Let me focus on him.'

'Thank you, sir, thank you so much,' Manish said, looking overjoyed. 'I will inform my parents.'

Chautala nodded and turned to Dharmesh.

'Come, let's move to the seven-star.'

Chapter 14

70 days missing

'Amazon delivery, madam,' the guard at the Icon entrance told me on the building intercom. I checked the time: 11 a.m. Suhana was in school, Manish in his office.

'Can you send him up to my apartment?' I said.

'He dropped a packet for you and left. Didn't even wait for a signature,' the guard said.

I sent my maid, Neelu, to the main gate to bring it up.

Neelu came back with a brown cardboard box large enough to fit a basketball. The package had the Amazon logo and our address printed on it. However, it did not have any invoice or receipt.

I kept it on the dining table and WhatsApped Manish.

'Hey, you there?'

'Yeah, sitting with the new app developers. Anything urgent?' he replied.

'Did you order anything from Amazon?'

'No,' Manish said. 'Chat later. Bit busy.'

I brought a knife from the kitchen and slit open one of the edges of the box. I found a big transparent plastic bag inside. I saw the contents and screamed so loud, Neelu came running from the kitchen.

'What happened, didi?' Neelu said.

My head was swimming. I dropped the knife, which narrowly missed my foot.

'Didi?' Neelu said. She forced me to sit down.

'I have to call Manish,' I said unsteadily, as I tried to hold my phone.

I dialled Manish's number twice. He cut my call each time. Neelu went back to the kitchen.

'Busy. I didn't order anything, told you,' Manish sent me a message.

'Please call, Manish. Urgent.'

He called me back.

'What is it, Alia? These developers have come from Bangalore and—'

'Manish, can you come home? Now?'

'Now? I told you, I am with people.'

'Come home, Manish,' I said, my voice tense.

'What happened?'

I was finding it difficult to talk, to breathe.

'Manish, I think I am having a panic attack. Please come,' I said and ended the call.

I stared at the packet and the packet stared back at me. Neither of us blinked.

The doorbell rang fifteen minutes later. Neelu answered the door.

'This better be important,' Manish said, entering the house.

I pointed to the dining table.

'What? What's in that box?' He picked it up.

'Oh my God,' he said, when he saw the contents. Siya's night suit, the one she had worn the night she disappeared, lay crumpled inside. The baby blue T-shirt and pyjamas had pink and white snowflakes printed all over them. The T-shirt had a picture of Elsa, from the movie *Frozen*. Manish had bought this night suit from a Disney store in London while on a work trip two years ago.

'Who sent this?' Manish said in a shaky voice.

'Somebody dropped it at the main gate and left.'

'What else is in the packet?' he said.

I shrugged. I hadn't summoned up the courage to look at the rest of the contents yet.

'Should we check?' Manish said. 'Or call the police first?'

'I don't know, Manish. My mind is not working right now.'

What was Siya wearing if her night suit was with us? What must my daughter be going through? Seventy days since she had left us. I had been learning to somehow survive the days without losing my balance. This box had unsettled it all. I could neither move my body nor use my brain. I simply kept staring at the printed snowflakes inside the transparent packet.

'There could be fingerprints,' Manish said. 'I'll call Chautala.'

Chautala and Viren arrived soon after Manish called them. I hadn't moved from the dining table.

'Where is the evidence?' Viren said.

The little belongings of my daughter were now being called evidence. I pointed at the plastic packet. Viren, who carried a forensic tool kit with him, took out a pair of rubber gloves, calipers and a powder to help find fingerprints. He slipped on the gloves before he began examining the parcel.

'It's an Amazon box, but recycled,' Viren said, opening the cardboard box.

He used his calipers to pry open the plastic packet. He pulled out the top of the night suit first, followed by the pants.

'Anything else inside?' Chautala said.

Viren carefully took out a lock of light brown, curly hair from inside the packet.

'Siya's?' Chautala said.

I nodded, paralysed. Viren took out a pair of diamond ear studs.

'Siya's,' Manish said.

'What's this?' Viren took out a tiny ceramic box. He opened the lid. It had a black ash-like substance in it. He kept it on the table.

Viren spread out Siya's night suit on the dining table. Princess Elsa smiled up at us, even though her face had brown stains on it. *Frozen*, the story about two sisters in a palace, was a favourite of both my daughters. The pyjamas had brown marks all over them too.

'All this belongs to Siya?' Chautala said.

'Yes,' I said. 'She was wearing this that night. But I don't recognise the box with the black powder.'

'It's ash, madam. Seems like ash after you burn a body,' Viren said. 'We'll get it checked, though, to see if it contains human remains.'

I gripped the table hard as I absorbed what he had said.

Viren took pictures of all the items laid on the table. Afterwards, he collected each item and placed it in a separate plastic packet to be marked as evidence.

'We'll get the clothes analysed too,' Viren said.

'What will you be checking for?' Manish said.

'The brown stains look like dried blood. We'll confirm if it belongs to Siya,' Viren said.

'We can compare the DNA with the hair sample. Madam, you sure that's Siya's hair, right?' Chautala said.

I held on to the table, unable to speak.

'Madam?' Chautala said. 'You're sure this is Siya's hair, right?'

'Yes,' Manish answered for me.

'What does this mean, Chautala sir?' he said as the inspector and Viren began walking out of the room.

'I don't want to jump to conclusions,' Chautala said. 'Let's wait for the reports.'

'But aren't these clues? Can't all this help us find Siya?'

'We'll see,' Chautala said. He was almost out of the door when I ran after him.

'The person who has Siya sent it,' I said. 'And he's out there. He's out there with Siya and sending couriers to us. We have to catch him.'

Chautala looked beyond me.

'What, sir? Say something,' I said.

'He is out there, yes. But I am not sure Siya is there with him now.'

'What do you mean, sir?' I said.

'Ashes. Blood. Victim's dress. No ransom note. The only valuable item— the diamond earrings—even those have been returned. I am fearing the worst.'

'What worst? Nothing. We have to find Siya.'

Chautala sighed and shook his head.

'Are you sure, sir? How can that be?' Manish said.

'Looks like the kidnapper ended up hurting Siya. Maybe he didn't intend to. She died. He cremated her and sent you the package.'

'Why would he send the package?' I yelled.

'Many reasons. To get rid of the evidence. To make you stop looking. To help you get some closure.'

'Closure?' I looked straight at Chautala.

'Not the closure you wanted, madam. Sorry,' Chautala said as he and Viren left my house.

83 days missing

'The police are doing a press conference? Without informing us?' I said.

'Yeah,' Manish said, removing his shoes. 'They did inform us though. Told us to watch the coverage on TV tonight. They just didn't invite us.'

Manish had just returned from work at 9 p.m. He had left at 7 in the morning, saying the new app development required a lot of work. He removed his socks, sat on the sofa and stretched his legs.

'I have a midnight call as well. With a potential partner in San Francisco,' Manish said.

'Did you have to start such a big project in the middle of what we are going through?' I said.

'I told you, it helps take my mind off Siya. Plus, the business needs the money.'

'What do you mean?'

'I am trying to find an investor from abroad.'

'But you are not helping find Siya.'

'What can I do anyway?' Manish said. He went to the bar and poured himself half a glass of Scotch. He came back and sat on the sofa.

'Where's the TV remote? Let's see if Chautala's press conference came on the news.'

I tossed him the remote.

'Do you want to talk?' Manish said.

'No, thanks. Let's watch TV. Then do your call. Do business.'

'Alia, the business needs attention. First, the lockdown. Then our family reputation dragged through the mud. It has hurt our brand.'

'I am sorry my kidnapped daughter affected your brand and marketing, Manish.'

I took the remote back from Manish and switched on the TV. I flipped through the news channels. One was showing old footage from the PM's trip to Europe. He was telling NRIs how India was the best place. The NRIs cheered loudly, wholeheartedly agreeing, even though they were choosing not to live in India themselves.

Finally, I found a channel that was showing the press conference.

'The Gurugram police today gave another briefing on the Siya Arora case,' a reporter said on screen.

The visuals changed to Chautala, flanked by Viren and Rajan, in the station conference room. Chautala addressed the reporters.

'Around two weeks ago, the Arora family received a parcel. It had Siya's diamond earrings, hair and blood-stained clothes. DNA testing confirmed Siya's blood and hair. There was also a small box with ash, which, although hard to analyse, could be her remains after cremation. The ash samples had traces of Siya's blood DNA in them.'

'What the hell!' Manish said. 'Shouldn't he tell us this first?'

I ignored Manish and raised the volume of the TV.

'An unidentified man on a bike dropped off the box outside the building where Manish and Alia Arora live. He was wearing a full helmet so the CCTV footage at the building gate doesn't reveal his identity,' Chautala said. 'Anyway, we are sad to say this, but we now believe the victim, Siya Arora, may be dead.'

Journalists scrambled to ask questions.

'What about catching the kidnapper, sir?' said one.

'The kidnapper is still at large. However, with the victim deceased and no further leads, it is difficult to pursue this case.'

'What about the family, sir?' another reporter said.

'We have investigated the family thoroughly. There is no evidence to suggest their involvement. They have been interrogated enough. Police records can be checked.'

'Any other suspects, sir?' one reporter said.

'The cook is still in custody for cheating and fraud. We have spoken to some other people. However, there's no evidence against anyone.'

'Is this a murder case too now, sir?' a reporter said.

'Possibly,' Chautala said.

Manish turned off the TV.

'Talk?' he said, turning towards me.

I stalked into the bedroom and slammed the door shut.

'It's not reasonable. It's nonsense,' I shouted.

'Stop screaming. The kids will hear,' said Mummyji, with the frown she reserved just for me.

'Beta, I understand your feelings. But you saw the package. She's not with us anymore,' Papaji said. He closed his eyes and folded his hands up to the sky.

We were all sitting at the dining table in Navratna House.

'Don't say that,' I said. 'We haven't caught the kidnapper, have we?'

'It will be difficult to find him. It could be anyone. Anyone. And even if we do, will it bring Siya back?' Timmy said.

Chautala had called my in-laws post the press conference. He had convinced them to stop pursuing the case.

'So Chautala said close the case?' I said.

'No, Alia, not exactly that,' Timmy said. 'He said to reclassify it as a cold case.'

'What's that? A dead case?' I said.

'No. It means the case is out of leads or direction at the moment. If something new is found, it could be revived.'

'It means a dead case, Timmy bhaiya,' I said, frustrated.

'Again this girl is shouting. Is this how you speak to your jeth?' Mummyji said.

'I am not shouting, Mummyji. I am only making my point.'

'Disrespectful girl,' Mummyji said. I looked at Manish. He remained silent.

'Chautala plans to retire in a year,' Papaji said. 'In his last year, he doesn't want a blemish on his career. Wait, let me read out what he sent me.'

Papaji picked up his phone. He wore his reading glasses and read out the message.

'Aroraji, police will say that we remain open to further investigation if we get more leads. However, for now we will pause investigation on the case as we don't have leads and Siya may not even be alive. However, the police will also confirm that the Arora family is absolutely innocent and not involved. On your part, you put out that you will go with what the police says as you trust them, and that the family thanks the police for their sincere efforts.'

Papaji kept the phone back on the dining table and removed his glasses.

'They don't want to work on the case anymore,' I said in a flat voice. 'That's all.'

'He is also offering to clear our name. Do you realise the value of that?' Timmy said.

'Manish?' I said, turning to him. 'What do you think?'

Goddammit, say something, is what I really wanted to say to my husband.

'Papaji lost ten big clients. A statement like this from the police, clearing the family, will really help. There's value in it.'

'Manish, seriously?' I said, stunned.

'What?' He looked puzzled.

'What about Siya?' I said.

'The police will stop working on the case anyway, Alia,' Manish said, 'whether we agree to this or not. This way, we make them look good and they clear our name. That's the deal.'

'Deal? Is this about a deal or about our daughter?' I said.

Manish fell silent.

My mother-in-law's diamond-encrusted gold bangles made a hard thud as she banged her hands on the table.

'Are we done?' she said. 'I have to go do my meditation.'

Chapter 15

104 days missing

Manish walked into our bedroom and came over to the desk where I sat, towering over me.

'What is Suhana doing?' he said.

I looked up from the computer screen.

'She's drawing posters,' I said.

'What posters exactly, Alia?'

'To find Siya. She's helping me.'

'What will you do with these posters made by a seven-year-old with crayons?'

'Put them up all over Gurugram, wherever I can. Lamp posts, bookshops, cafés ... Why are you interrogating me like this?'

'You can't make Suhana do this.'

'Excuse me? Why can't Suhana help her mother search for her sister? Not all of us are blessed with a convenient memory!'

'She's seven, for God's sake, Alia. This will mess her up.'

'How?'

'I want her to move on. If she keeps thinking about Siya, makes posters about her, how will that happen?'

'Why should she move on?' I said, my voice loud.

'Because Siya is dead,' Manish said.

'Shut up, Manish,' I screamed, so loud that Suhana must have heard in the other room. She ran into our bedroom, a poster in her hand.

'Mommy, why are you fighting with Daddy?' she said, making a puppy face with her eyes wide.

'I am not, beta. I shouted by mistake, sorry.'

'I'll make one more poster for Didi?'

'No,' Manish said. 'Go to your room and play with your Barbie.'

'I only like playing with Barbie with Siya didi.'

I didn't want Suhana to see me cry or get upset. I gently held her shoulders, turned her around and nudged her to leave the room.

'Watch TV or something,' Manish called out after her. I shut the door and collapsed on the bed. Manish came and sat next to me.

'I have to keep looking for her, Manish. Even if I have to do it alone. Don't ask me to stop. I beg you,' I said in between sobs.

'Calm down, Alia,' he said. 'I miss her too, you know. It is a continuous hammering in my heart. But this won't help.'

He had tears in his eyes as well. For the first time, both of us had acknowledged Siya's loss and cried together.

'Let us cry as much as we want today,' Manish said, his voice choked. 'But let us also try to move on. And maybe accept that Siya is gone forever.'

The last line echoed in my head a few times. I cried the most I ever had in my life.

Ten minutes later, I heard a knock on the bedroom door.

'I'll lay out the lunch?' Neelu said.

145 days missing

'Sorry ma'am, we can't allow posters of missing children. It upsets our customers,' the café barista at Locomotion Café in Gurugram said.

'You have a picture of a missing kitten on your noticeboard.'

'We like to project a fun vibe. A missing kitten flyer is cute. A missing child poster is serious,' he said, working the levers of his coffee machine.

I nodded. I took a seat at one of the tables. Since morning, only six out of the forty places I had visited had allowed me to put up Siya's poster.

I checked my phone. I'd made a special email account for information on Siya and mentioned it on all the posters and on all online forums and posts I had for Siya. I had two new emails in this account. I opened them one at a time.

From: WellWisher
Dear Mother of Siya,
I am sorry for the loss of your child. I know the maternal instinct wants you to keep looking, but fact is Siya is dead, as they showed on TV. Look after your other daughter, the one still alive. Life has to go on.
Regards,
Wellwisher

I opened the next email.

From: RescueTeam
Dear Parents/Guardian,
We can help you find your missing child. If you want us to work on it, please send an advance of Rs 50,000 to the PayPal account mentioned below.

I deleted both the emails and kept my phone aside.

The barista arrived with my black coffee.

'Is this your daughter?' he said, glancing at the poster.

I nodded.

'I saw her on TV. She went missing a few months ago, right?'

'Four months, twenty-two days and twelve hours ago,' I said.

260 days missing

'I am so glad you started coming downstairs again,' said Anita, who lived on the tenth floor of Tower B. We were sitting on one of the benches by the playground in Icon.

I smiled, my eyes on Suhana, who was playing with Yukti, Anita's daughter, in the sandpit.

'What happened is terrible,' Anita said. 'I can't even imagine what you are going through. If something happened to Yukti, I would just die.'

'I thought of dying too,' I said, my eyes still on Suhana.

'Really?' Anita said.

'Yes, but I can't.'

'Because of Suhana?'

'That, and one more reason.'

'What?'

'If I am gone, nobody will look for Siya. I am the only one still trying to find her.'

Anita squeezed my hand in support.

'Manish knows you are still looking?'

'Sort of.'

'As in?'

'He has an idea when he sees me busy on my computer. We don't really discuss it.'

In fact, we don't really discuss anything these days, I thought.

'I am just happy you're coming down to the garden again.'

'I don't want to. I don't want to be out, go to the gym, cook or do the things I used to. But I have to. For Suhana. I have to give her a semblance of normalcy. Suhana asked Manish, "Why is Mommy always sad?"'

'Oh,' Anita said in a soft voice.

'All I really want to do is look for Siya. No real purpose to life otherwise.'

'You should get help,' Anita said.

'From whom?'

'I don't know. Maybe hire someone professional. Oh, do you know the people on the seventeenth floor, Tower C?'

I shook my head.

'There's a Rajasthani uncle and aunty living in one of the flats there. Sweet people. They come to the garden every evening.'

'What about them?'

'I heard their son is some private detective. Say hello to them next time they come to the garden.'

I nodded, looking up at the seventeenth floor of Tower C.

Chapter 16

I offered Alia a tissue to wipe her tears.

'I am sorry,' I said. 'You have been through a lot.'

Alia nodded, wiping her eyes with the edge of the tissue. I kept my laptop aside.

My mother came out of the kitchen. She kept a bowl of dal on the dining table and looked curiously at us.

'Oh, it's already lunchtime. I'm sorry I took so much of your time,' Alia said.

'It's okay,' I said. 'You needed to give me all the details.'

My mother made another trip to the kitchen. She returned with the chapati box and a bowl of sabzi.

'Aunty, let me help you,' Alia said as she walked quickly to the dining table.

'It's okay, I am almost done,' my mother said.

I went to the kitchen and brought back three plates.

'Please have lunch,' I said.

'Oh,' Alia said, looking at the plates. 'I should go. I am already ...'

'I have made for you also, so sit,' Ma said in that scolding-yet-caring Indian mother tone.

Alia smiled and sat down on one of the dining chairs. My mother had made the Rajasthani panchmel dal, a blend of five different lentils, along with carrot and peas sabzi and rotis.

'Can you help me in any way?' Alia said.

'I still have to process it. Also, it is a cold case. Never done one before,' I said.

'Money won't be an issue.'

'It's not about the money, ma'am,' I said.

'Alia is fine. Please, no "ma'am" business, Keshav.'

'Okay,' I said.

'And let me know your fees.'

'I told you, ma'am, I mean, Alia. It's not about the fees.'

'How about I give you an advance of one lakh rupees? Rest as and when you figure out your quote.'

My mother's eyes had opened wide at 'one lakh'.

I remained quiet.

'Or two lakhs?' Alia said.

Ma offered Alia desi ghee for her rotis and looked at me, wondering why I wasn't saying yes to this golden goose.

'Relax about the money, Alia. My concern is that it is a cold case. The police, the media and your family—everyone has already tried.'

'Have they really?' Alia said and shook her head.

We ate in silence for a few minutes. Then Alia folded her hands and said, 'Can you please help me, Keshav?'

'I could help, but I need you to understand a few things. First, I have not done a kidnapping case before. Murder yes, kidnapping no. Of course, it could be both here.'

'Don't say that,' Alia said.

'Sorry. Anyway, my point is, my help will be on best efforts basis. No guarantees.'

'I understand that.'

'Frankly, chances are low. Anything could have happened. Anyone could have done it. It's not like we have a finite list of suspects.'

'I am aware of that. Do whatever you can.'

'Also, I will need to talk to and meet with people again. Will they cooperate?'

'Who?'

'The family, for instance.'

'I'll convince them.'

'What about the police? I need access to whatever they have done so far.'

'Meet Inspector Chautala, the main investigating officer. If I request him, I am sure he will agree to meet you.'

'I have a senior contact in the police too.'

'Does this mean you are taking my case?'

I nodded after a pause.

'Thank you so much!' Alia smiled. 'Thank you, Aunty, for introducing me to Keshav. And for this wonderful lunch.'

My mother smiled. Alia stood up to leave.

'Keshav, don't forget to give her your bank details, so she can send you the advance,' my mother said before Alia left.

'Case?' Saurabh said.

I was in his room. He was changing out of his office wear into a T-shirt and shorts.

'From Icon only,' I said. 'The client stays in the opposite tower.'

'What kind of case? Maid stealing milk?'

'No. Kidnapping. Maybe murder.'

'What?' Saurabh said, and stopped pulling on his T-shirt midway. I gave him all the details of the Siya Arora case.

'They lost their child nine months ago? They are coming to us now? What are we? Magicians?'

'It's a cold case, yes,' I said.

'It will go nowhere. It will make your IPS preparation go nowhere as well.'

'It will pay well.'

I told him the advance amount. Saurabh let out a mini gasp.

I sat down on his bed.

'I miss working on a case,' I said.

'I do too. But we decided. Your IPS studies first, agency later,' he said.

'I can't do it without you,' I said.

'I don't know if I can spare the time. I have the Cybersafe job. Plus, my new fitness routine, which is really hard.'

Saurabh collapsed on the bed.

'I wish you would agree,' I said. 'I'll have to say no to her, and the two lakh rupees advance.'

I stood up to leave his room. He placed an elbow on a pillow to lift his head up.

'You didn't agree to become my fitness trainer either,' Saurabh said.

'What?'

'You said you would think about it. You were not sure. But you never reverted.'

'Okay, how about I agree to be your fitness trainer?'

Saurabh sprang up.

'Really? You would?'

'Yes.'

'Thank you. I can't do this fitness-diet nonsense alone.'

'And neither can I do the case alone. I will help you with fitness. You help me on the case. Deal?'

Saurabh looked at me.

'I am not sure,' he said.

I turned to leave his room.

'Fine,' he said from behind me. I turned towards him again.

'Yeah?'

'I better get a six pack like yours in return,' Saurabh said, covering his face with his quilt to go to sleep.

275 days missing

'It's still dark,' Saurabh said, rubbing his fat thighs with his hands.

'Start running. The sun will rise soon,' I said.

I had woken him up at 6.15 a.m. and brought him to the jogging track which ran around the perimeter of the building garden.

'Five rounds,' I said. 'Keep a steady pace.'

'Five?' Saurabh said, looking at me like I had asked him to cut off five fingers.

'That's just two kilometres. You have to build stamina so you can run ten kilometres.'

'This is torture,' Saurabh said.

'This is health. Come, I will run with you,' I said.

Saurabh jogged at the lowest speed possible for a human being, like the hero of a movie running in slow motion towards the heroine in the climax scene.

'Faster, Golu. Your heart rate needs to go up.'

'It's up, bhai. I can feel it. This is my natural jogging speed.'

'Okay, stop,' I shouted.

'What?' he said, freezing mid-jog like we were playing statue.

'Do not argue with or answer back to your trainer. I am not "bhai". I am your teacher. Understood?' I said in a tough, military sergeant voice.

Saurabh looked at me, surprised.

'Okay,' he said meekly.

'Good, let's finish this fast. We have to go back and watch videos,' I said.

'Fitness videos?' Saurabh said.

'No. All past media coverage related to the Siya Arora case. We will watch some every day. Now let's run,' I said, prodding his back to get him moving again.

Chapter 17

283 days missing

'You tell me,' Ashwin screamed in the video. 'Six adults sleep in the same house. Three other children are sleeping in same room. One child vanishes in the middle of the night. The family has no clue? Were they drunk? Under the influence of drugs?'

Saurabh lowered the volume on my laptop.

He wrote down the title of the YouTube video we had just watched in his notebook. This was the thirty-sixth media clip we had seen on the case.

'I think we have seen enough coverage on this. I'd like to meet the mother now,' Saurabh said.

'I have already set up a meeting for next week. You will finally meet her,' I said.

'Good. I'd like to see Navratna House. Meet the extended family too.'

'Of course. One step at a time.'

'We are not ruling the family out, right?' Saurabh said.

I looked at Saurabh.

'We never rule anyone out, Golu,' I said.

'Good. Any headway with the police? Will they share whatever they have?' Saurabh said.

'They will. If we go to them with some influence,' I said.

'ACP Rana?' Saurabh said.

'Who else. He's the only senior officer who owes us favours,' I said.

'Keshav!' My mother's scream from the living room startled me.

'What, Ma?'

'It's 4 in the afternoon. You two have been watching videos all day. Stop behaving like pigs and take a shower.'

'Look who's here. The hotshot detectives who forgot me,' Rana said and stood up to greet us.

We knew ACP Rana as we had worked with him on two cases. He had recently shifted to the Delhi Police headquarters near the Bangla Sahib Gurudwara in central Delhi.

'Sir, the real hotshot is you,' Saurabh said. 'Look at your new office.'

Unlike his usual office in a dusty police station, Rana's new air-conditioned office now had paintings on the wall and sofas with lace covers.

'Let's sit on the sofas,' he said and grinned, happy to show off his new space.

He pinged a wireless bell and a peon came in.

'Three masala teas. If it's not hot, I will send it back,' Rana said to the peon. He turned to us after the peon left.

'So, what brings you here?'

'We have a case,' I said.

'Ah, kameeno, you only think of me when you have work,' Rana said and laughed.

'It is not that, sir,' Saurabh said. 'We don't want to disturb a senior officer like you.'

'Arrey, where senior?'

The peon brought us three cups of tea on a tray. Alongside, there were biscuits, sandwiches, samosas and kaju barfi.

Saurabh's hand reached for a samosa in reflex.

I cleared my throat. Saurabh's hand froze while still holding a samosa.

'What?' Rana said, surprised.

'He is not supposed to have it,' I said.

'Why?' Rana said.

'Samosa down, Golu,' I said.

I stared at him till he put the samosa back on the tray.

'One biscuit?' Saurabh said, with the feeble air of a famine victim.

'No. Just tea. Without sugar,' I said.

Saurabh began to sip his tea as if it was malaria medicine.

'What the hell just happened?' Rana said.

'No, he is right, sir. I am on a diet,' Saurabh said. 'He's my fitness trainer.'

Rana burst out laughing.

'Good, good. I have put on too.'

'You look great, sir,' Saurabh said.

'Stop buttering me up. Tell me about your case. And how can I help?'

I gave him a briefing about Siya's case and our need to meet Chautala.

'Inspector Ratan Chautala? Really?' Rana grinned. He kept his empty cup back on the table.

'You know him?' I said.

'Yes. He joined the police force the same year as me. He's from my hometown Hisar too.'

'We wanted his cooperation. If they can share whatever they did so far on the Siya Arora case …' I said.

'I'll try. He doesn't like me much,' Rana said.

'Why, sir?' Saurabh said.

'I am ACP going on DCP. He will retire as an inspector. Think about it.'

Saurabh and I nodded. Rana picked up his phone.

'I have his number. Let me call Chautala while you guys are here.' Rana dialled a number and placed the call on speaker mode.

'Chautala sir,' Rana said when he answered. 'How are you, sir? This is your old Hisar wala Vijender Rana.'

'Oh, Rana sir,' Chautala said. 'Good to hear from you. Tell me, of what service can I be to you?'

'I have these two friends, more like brothers to me, like you are,' Rana said. He went on to tell him about us and what we wanted.

Chautala remained silent after Rana finished briefing him.

'Chautala sir, you there?' Rana said.

'Yes, sir. But Siya Arora case, sir? That's a cold case.'

'I know. But these boys want to work on it. They are a little stupid, but are like my brothers.'

'Okay, sir. Private detectives, you said?'

'Not hard-core. It's their hobby. Like we used to play kabaddi in Hisar, they like working on cases.'

'Strange hobby.'

'They are strange. But they helped me. Your brother became ACP because they helped me solve a high-profile case.'

'Really, sir?'

'Well, it was mostly me, but they helped a bit.'

Rana winked at me. Chautala remained silent on the other side.

'So, will you take some time out for my younger brothers?' Rana said.

'ACP sir, I can't say no to you, my elder brother, right?'

**

'ACP Rana's contacts?' Chautala said, looking up from a file.

'Yes, sir. Working on the Siya Arora case,' I said.

'Working?' Chautala was sarcastic. 'I thought we were working on it, but sit please. Let us learn from you.'

Saurabh and I sat across from him.

'Mrs Alia Arora has hired us. We are just trying to help. I am Keshav Rajpurohit and this is my partner, Saurabh Maheshwari.'

I held out my hand to shake his. Chautala didn't reciprocate.

'Hired you for what?' he said.

'To see if we can find anything new. Best efforts, that's all,' I said.

Chautala turned to Saurabh.

'Is all this just a way for you to get money from her? She is rich, I know.'

'No, sir,' Saurabh said, his voice nervous.

Chautala smirked.

'I wish I could send her a bill for all the head-breaking I did on her case,' he said.

I ignored his comment.

'Sir, we wanted to find out whatever you know so far. Not go by media reports.'

'The media is a brothel. They will say anything to sell their crap news.'

'I know, sir,' I said.

'Anything on file will be helpful,' Saurabh said.

'Oh, you will check my work now? You think we didn't do it properly?'

'Not at all, sir,' I said. 'I just want to see if there's even anything to be done here. If not, I'd rather return the money to Alia Arora.'

Chautala shrugged. 'Fine. ACP Rana sent you, so I'll let you have a look.' He tore a slip of paper from his notebook and scribbled in it.

'Show this to my junior sitting in the next room. They will let you access the files.'

'Thank you so much, sir,' I said.

'No copies, no photos,' he said.

'Understood, sir,' said Saurabh.

'And if this leaks out to the media, that you have been hired to work on this case or were snooping around the police station, I will not just kick you out, I will get you locked up. Clear?' Chautala said.

'Clear, sir,' Saurabh said.

'Anything else?' Chautala said.

We shook our heads and stood up to leave. Chautala looked down at his files again.

'One thing, sir,' Saurabh said.

'Yes?' Chautala said, looking irritated.

'Is it possible to get sugar-free tea in that room?'

'It all ties up,' I said.

I placed the various testimonies in neat piles on the desk in front of us. Saurabh and I had spent three hours going through the police files. Manohar and Sonu's story added up. They were still in custody for the cheating case. The police had spoken to Siya's friends and their parents. There was no useful information there. Aryan, Siya's crush, had mentioned constant fights between Siya's parents, which would disturb Siya. Parvathy, Siya's best friend, had corroborated this in her testimony.

'Siya would cry in school every time her parents fought the previous night. She said there would be loud arguments late into the night. They affected Siya a lot. But she never discussed it much,' read one of Parvathy's statements.

'Problems in the marriage,' Saurabh said. 'Did you know?'

'Sort of,' I said. 'I know Manish and Alia had fights after Siya disappeared. I didn't know there were issues before the kidnapping.'

The testimonies of the family members didn't reveal much either. I went back to Shamsher's statement.

Shamsher Arora's testimony
Taken by Inspector Ratan Chautala

Mr Shamsher Arora, what exact business do you do?

My company is called Navratna Jewels. We are wholesalers of diamond and gold jewellery, with a factory in Manesar. We supply to various jewellery retail shops and export ornaments worldwide. My younger son, Manish, also has a direct online retail jewellery business, with the brand name Nava.

Who owns Navratna Jewels and Nava?

Navratna Jewels is owned by me. My son Tanmay Arora, or Timmy, runs it with me. Nava is owned by my son Manish and some private equity investors.

So Timmy Arora does not own any share in Nava?

No. But all this is on paper only. We are one family. Everything belongs to everyone. After me, Navratna Jewels will be split between both my sons only, who else?

How are the relationships within the family?

Excellent. Timmy and Manish love each other. There has never been an issue between them, even though they work together. I have two wonderful daughters-in-law. My wife is a bit bossy, but she is a God-fearing spiritual person and wonderful at heart.

Bossy?

That was a joke, obviously.

Is it true that your wife and your daughter-in-law, Alia, do not get along?

It's the standard saas-bahu relationship.

Isn't that the reason why Manish moved with his family to the Icon?

(Pause) That's not the only reason. Alia wanted a play area and community for her children, which you get in an apartment complex.

But it was one of the reasons?

Yes ... Alia's not Punjabi. Half-Keralite, half-Rajasthani. Doesn't understand our culture sometimes, that's all.

Can you elaborate further?

My wife expects her daughters-in-law to listen to her. Alia belongs to the modern, independent category of women. Durga is also modern, actually. She is fine with her bahus drinking, for instance. However, she can be a bit traditional in other ways. Some clashes are unavoidable. Like I said, normal conflict. Nothing that doesn't happen in other homes.

'We have to meet them,' Saurabh said. 'There's more to this "normal conflict".'

'Working on it. First you meet Alia day after tomorrow,' I said.

Saurabh nodded. He pointed to a black plastic folder that seemed different from the brown cardboard police files.

'What's that?' Saurabh said.

'What?' I said and picked up the black folder.

I read the title on the cover.

Cyber investigation report: Siya Arora case

I opened the file. It had details of cellphone tower locations of all the people the police had considered relevant to the case. They had done a thorough job. The people were divided into categories.

1. Siya Arora's family and Manohar (all were found in the same tower as Shamsher Arora's house)
2. The Arora family's domestic staff—drivers, maid Neelu (all cell towers found in the respective places of residence)
3. Siya Arora's friends and parents of friends (all cell tower locations found near their respective homes)
4. Miscellaneous people associated with the Arora family—Navratna Jewels staff, Nava staff. Family doctor, plumber, electrician, gardener, priest, massage lady (used by Durga Arora)—all at their respective homes or work locations, corroborated by witnesses
5. Siya's tutor Dharmesh Arora (suspect)—tower location found in Goa

'They have done a good job. They even tracked the cell tower location of the massage lady?' Saurabh said.

Before I could answer, Chautala entered the room.

'We left no stone unturned in this case,' he said.

'Hello, sir,' I said and stood up.

'Are you studying for an exam?' Chautala said and checked the time. 'It's 6 in the evening. I am going home. You will be here a while?'

'Not much longer, sir,' I said. 'Just going over the cyber file.'

'I don't even fully understand all this cyber stuff. Sub-inspector Viren did a fabulous job with it, though. The media never acknowledged all this great work.'

Chautala signalled to his constable, Joginder, to keep an eye on us and left us to it.

Saurabh and I went back to the cyber investigation report.

'They scrubbed Siya's phone,' Saurabh said, flipping through the pages. 'This has a list of all the apps she had and what they found there.'

I took the file from him and read through the pages.

'They did it for the tutor's phone too,' I said. I saw a small sealed envelope stapled to the last sheet of the cyber investigation report. It had a hard plastic object inside.

'What is it?'

'Pen drive,' I guessed, tracing the outline.

'We need this,' Saurabh whispered.

'How?' I whispered. Joginder sat ten feet away from us, filling in a register.

Saurabh took out the pen drive from the envelope and slipped it into his pocket.

'Joginder sir, where is the toilet?' Saurabh said.

'Outside, on the left,' he said, without looking up at us.

Saurabh stood up, picked up his backpack and went to the toilet.

When he returned from the washroom, he put his backpack on the floor and slid the pen drive back into the envelope.

'You guys are private detectives?' Joginder said.

'Yes,' I said.

'This is a dead case.'

'Yeah,' I said with an amiable smile. 'I can see that. Anyway, we are done here.' I stood up to leave.

'You realise we just stole from a police station?' I said to Saurabh after we came out of the building.

'I stole nothing. I kept the pen drive back. Only made a copy on my laptop,' Saurabh said and winked at me, pointing to his backpack.

Chapter 18

'You fixed a meeting with the client here?' Saurabh said. He panted as he clutched his stomach.

We had come for his morning workout in the Icon garden.

'She drops her daughter to school every morning. She said she'd join us here afterwards.'

'Okay, fine, let's just sit and wait,' Saurabh said and sank into one of the garden benches.

'No, let's do ab crunches. Give me twenty.'

'Bhai, I hate abs.'

'On the floor. Now,' I said in a stern voice.

He lay down on the grass as I counted.

'One, two ... come on, three.'

With every sit-up, he made an agonized face like someone was stabbing him with a knife.

'My stomach will burst,' he said, groaning in pain.

'It didn't all these years when you filled it up, right?'

His T-shirt lifted, exposing his big belly and navel. His fat thighs trembled as he did his set.

'Imagine that six pack. Come on, Hrithik Roshan, seven, eight, nine ...'

'Hi, Keshav,' Alia's voice came from behind me.

'Hi, Alia,' I said as she came up to us. She was wearing pink track pants and a black T-shirt, and her hair was tied in a bun.

She saw Saurabh on the ground, and looked somewhat surprised.

'This is Saurabh Maheshwari, my partner,' I said.

'Oh, good to meet you. Good morning,' Alia said.

'Good morning,' Saurabh said, his cheeks red, and sounding flustered.

I gave Saurabh a hand to help him up from the ground. He stood up and straightened his T-shirt.

'Shall we sit there?' Alia said, pointing to two benches that faced each other.

We sat down and updated her on our progress.

'We have Siya and Dharmesh's phone data. We are analysing it,' Saurabh said.

'That's great.'

'We obtained it unofficially. Please don't mention it to anyone,' I said.

'Understood,' Alia said.

'Would it be possible for us to meet the rest of your family?' Saurabh said.

She took a deep breath.

'I'm working on it. Give me some time. I'll convince them.'

'Alia, you are here?' a slightly overweight man in his early forties said as he walked up to us. He was wearing a formal pinstriped shirt and trousers. His wavy hair had obviously been dyed black, and he had a clean-shaven baby face. He wore a Rolex watch and his car keys were in his hand.

Alia stood up, somewhat startled. 'Hi, Manish.'

'I was waiting for you upstairs,' he said.

'Sorry, I'm just coming up,' Alia said.

Saurabh and I stood up.

'Meet Keshav, and this is Saurabh,' Alia said. 'And guys, this is Manish, my husband.'

'Hello,' Manish said. He eyed Saurabh and me from top to bottom.

'They stay in Tower C, seventeenth floor,' Alia said.

'Okay, okay. I wanted to say I am leaving early for work. I have some conference calls.'

'But what about breakfast?' Alia said.

'That's why I was waiting for you,' Manish said in a sarcastic voice.

'Come up for a few minutes. It's ready,' Alia said.

'Too late. I have to go. Bye, guys,' Manish said and turned to leave.

'Manish, one minute,' Alia said.

'What?' Manish turned around.

'Keshav and Saurabh will be helping us.'

'Helping us?' Manish said, puzzled.

'To find Siya,' Alia said.

Manish's face froze. He squinted at me.

'They have a detective agency which they operate out of home,' Alia said.

'Wait, what?' Manish said, surprised.

'Completely independent and private investigations. No police or media involved. Right, guys?'

'Well, yes—' I started, but Manish interrupted me.

'Alia, let's chat about this in private? I was not aware of this,' he said.

'I was going to tell you,' Alia said. 'I thought I should meet them first.'

Manish looked at Saurabh, pink and sweaty from his workout.

'You are a detective?' Manish said.

'Yes, sir,' Saurabh said. I don't know why he addressed him as sir.

Manish smirked.

'They are good,' Alia said as she stepped up to Manish. They walked a few steps away and I tried not to look at them as they had a little argument. A few minutes later, from the corner of my eye, I noticed Manish clench his lips to fight back his tears. Perhaps to hide his emotional state, he spoke loudly.

'I don't have time for this right now. I have to go to work,' he said, turned around and left.

'I am sorry about Manish,' Alia sent me a WhatsApp message.

I was at my study table, reading a book called *The Short-cut Subject Guide to Ethics, Integrity and Aptitude*, one of the compulsory subjects for the Civil Services mains. I don't think the authors realised the inherent irony of creating a shortcut guide to ethics and integrity.

'Don't worry about it,' I replied.

'Are you home? May I come over for a bit?' she messaged back.

Be good, Keshav. Finish a chapter first, I told myself.

'Sure, come now,' I messaged.

The doorbell rang after five minutes. I heard my father answer the door. I walked up to the living room as well.

'Hello, Uncle,' Alia said. 'Is Keshav home?'

My father looked at her, surprised.

'I am Alia, Uncle. Remember me? From the garden?'

'Yes, of course,' my father said. 'Please come in.'

'Hi, Alia,' I said.

She and I sat down on the sofas. My father looked at both of us with a puzzled expression.

I cleared my throat to signal that he should leave.

My father ambled back to his bedroom with reluctance.

'All okay?' Alia said after my father left.

'Yes,' I said.

Alia was wearing a navy blue Western-style dress, with a small diamond pendant as the only accessory. She had showered recently, and droplets of water were still in her hair. Her eyes had dark circles around them. One of her cheeks was more pink than the other.

'I wanted to apologise personally. For Manish's behaviour.'

'No big deal.' I shrugged.

'He had no business being so rude and obnoxious. You and Saurabh must have felt so bad.'

'We didn't, actually. We were worried about something else.'

'What?'

'With that attitude, how will we get cooperation from the family? How will we do any investigation?'

'Don't worry. I will get all of them to agree. I just need some time.'

'Okay,' I said.

'You have everything from the police files?'

'Yes. Saurabh is checking everything thoroughly, especially the phone contents. Even deleted items.'

'Great,' Alia said. 'Anyway, that's all I came for.'

She stood up to leave.

'Did you get hurt?' I said.

'What?'

'Sorry, as a detective, I notice such things. Your cheek.'

She touched her right cheek.

'Oh, this?' she said and smiled. 'Nothing. I have sensitive skin. Must have slept the wrong way.'

I looked at her, unconvinced. The dark circles told me she had not slept at all.

'You don't believe me?' Alia said.

'No,' I said.

'It's Manish,' Alia said, a tremor in her voice.

'Are you okay?' I said.

'He's not like this normally. He's not a bad guy.'

'What?' I said, confused.

She tried to compose herself.

I went to the kitchen and came back with a glass of water.

'Thanks,' Alia said as she took the glass from me.

'Manish slapped me,' Alia said, after drinking the water.

'I'm listening,' I said.

'He's no wife-beater. I don't want you thinking of him that way. This was the first time.'

'He slapped you out of love? Kabir Singh style?'

'He's stressed.'

'Go on.'

'As a father, he feels guilty if he doesn't keep looking for Siya. As a son, he feels guilty if he does. He promised his family he would move on.'

'He wants you to fire us?' I said.

'He didn't say that.'

'Why did he slap you?'

Alia looked away towards the balcony of my house. I waited for her to respond. She spoke after a minute.

'He asked me to choose between him and the search.'

'As in?'

'He said, "I will divorce you if you keep looking for Siya. Choose now".'

'What did you choose?'

'What do you think? You can see the mark on my cheek.'

'Of course,' I said.

'I'll never stop looking,' she said. 'Even if I am all alone in this world.'

She began to weep.

'Relax, Alia.' I placed my hand on her arm. 'Please don't cry. You are not alone. I am with you. I will do my best.'

Okay, why did I say it like that? Had I become a detective-cum-friend now?

'I meant Saurabh and I are both with you,' I said.

She nodded. I gently withdrew my hand from her arm. She composed herself.

'I am sorry. I am such a loser. Crying away in front of anyone who lends an ear.'

'It's okay,' I said.

She turned towards the front door.

'Thank you for listening to me,' she said, and, after a brief hesitation, reached out to hug me. She smelled of fresh shampoo and soap.

Right at that moment, my father walked out of his room. I stepped back from her automatically.

'Bye, Uncle,' Alia said, folding her hands in a namaste.

'That girl Alia Arora is married. You are aware, right?' Papa said.

'What? Yes. To Manish,' I said.

We were having dinner.

My father grunted, his preferred method of communication to express his disapproval.

'What happened?' Saurabh said, spooning dal into his mouth.

'Why aren't you eating any chapatis? And the fried bhindi? Don't you like my cooking?' my mother said.

'I love your cooking, Aunty,' Saurabh said morosely. 'Just watching my carbs.'

'Carbs means?' Ma added ghee to her dal.

'Diet thing. Anyway, Keshav, what happened with Alia? She came here, right?'

'Nothing happened. We talked about the case.'

'Why were you hugging her then?' my father said.

'You hugged her? Why?' Saurabh said.

'How backward are you, Saurabh?' I said. 'It was just a greeting as she left.'

'See,' my father said, 'even Saurabh thinks it is odd.'

'What's odd?' I said.

'Better to be careful, Keshav. No need to call her home,' Ma said.

'She's a client. Our agency doesn't have an office yet, so we operate from home.'

'Call her when Saurabh is also there then,' Ma said.

'Saurabh comes back late from work. It is difficult for her to meet then.'

'Why difficult?'

'Her daughter is back from school by then, and she doesn't want to leave her alone. You know what happened to her other daughter. She's extra careful.'

My mother fell silent. My father spoke after a pause.

'Do you have to take this case? What about your IPS preparation?'

'I can do both.'

'You spent two hours of your study time with her today.'

'It won't be every day,' I said. I pushed my plate away. I had lost my appetite.

My mother turned to my father.

'Rajpurohitji, what are your friends doing? They can't recommend one nice girl for our Keshav?'

Chapter 19

Saurabh sat on a chair and bent to remove his shoes. I had come to his room after dinner and made myself comfortable on his bed.

'We hug clients now?' Saurabh said.

'Seriously, Golu?' I said.

'What happened?'

'When she was leaving, she gave me a hug. Dad entered the living room right then. Now he acts like I have committed some mortal sin and I should be stoned to death.'

'Hmmm ...' He sat down on the other side of the bed.

'What hmmm? Tell me what you found in the phone data.'

'I am hungry.'

'What?'

'Do you have any idea how hungry I am these days? I am starving when I go to bed. Sometimes I feel like eating my pillow.'

'Gross,' I said, removing my hand from the pillow on his bed.

'I am following your diet. It's so hard.'

'No pain, no gain. Open your laptop. Show me what you have found so far.'

'Can't I eat something first?'

'No.'

'I hate you,' he said as he switched on his laptop. 'You are a sadist.'

'Thanks,' I said.

Saurabh opened the files from the tutor Dharmesh's phone first.

'He had over fifty pictures of Siya,' Saurabh said. 'He deleted them before meeting the police.'

I looked at the photos. He had taken them during class.

'Pictures of her tying her hair?' I said. 'We should meet him.'

Saurabh nodded. He double-clicked on another file.

'Now these are what I found on Siya's phone. The police had noted most things but they missed one thing.'

'What?'

'Siya was on Telegram.'

'What's that?'

'A chatting app. Allows anonymity. You can set it so messages vanish after some time.'

'Why would she be on that?'

'For secret chats, I am guessing. Maybe her mother checked her WhatsApp.'

'She's twelve. What secrets?'

Saurabh shrugged.

'She definitely used it. Her phone CPU usage data confirms she was active on it.'

'Wow,' I said.

'That's all for now. I am trying to figure out who she spoke to on Telegram.'

'Good.'

'Now if I could eat something, my mind would get sharper and I might be able to figure out things faster,' Saurabh said.

'Good night, Golu,' I said and slid off his bed.

'But, bhai, not even a snack?'

'6.15 tomorrow morning. Ten rounds,' I said, switching off the light.

302 days missing

'Yeah, we can meet outside,' Alia said on the phone. 'What happened? Uncle didn't like my coming to your house?'

'Nothing like that,' I said.

She had called to fix a meeting to discuss updates on the case.

'Uncle didn't seem happy to see me,' Alia said.

'My parents are a bit ...' I paused for the right word, '... old-fashioned.'

'As in?'

'Nothing. I could come to your house too. Simpler.'

'Yeah, but there's an issue. You will have to sign in at the Tower B entrance before coming up.'

'So?'

'When Manish comes in, he might check. And he will know. He's still not fully on board with me hiring you guys.'

'Oh,' I said.

'I am trying to convince him. I just want to give him the time he needs to agree to it. It won't help if he finds out I called you home.'

'I understand. You want to wait until Manish is okay with us?'

'No, of course not. This is about finding my daughter. Why should I wait until he comes around? Let's meet anyway.'

'Okay,' I said. 'At a café?'

'Even a café in Gurugram is not safe. One of Papaji's customers or even a neighbour might see us. Or Manish might call me and I will have to lie about my location.'

'Fine. So where?' I said, somewhat perplexed.

'I am going to Marco Aldany. Come there?'

'What's that?'

'A salon in South Point Mall.'

South Point Mall is relatively small compared to the other Gurugram malls.

Marco Aldany, a Spanish salon franchise, is located on the upper ground floor of the mall. I walked in a little uncertain, but soon found Alia sitting on a reclining chair in the pedicure section. In a white sleeveless top and brown palazzo pants pulled up to her knees, she was resting her feet on a cushioned stool.

'Thank you for agreeing to come here. Odd place for a meeting, I know,' Alia said, gesturing to me to sit by her side.

I looked around the salon, empty at 11 in the morning.

I sat down on the black recliner chair next to her. She turned sideways to face me.

I said, 'Dharmesh had some sort of obsession with Siya. We found over fifty more photos of Siya on his phone.'

'What? Why? That's so strange.'

'It is.'

'But the police said he had no role in the abduction. He was in Goa that night.'

'Saurabh and I still want to meet him.'

'Okay. Anything on Siya's phone?'

Before I could answer, a girl, with 'Nancy' written on the pocket of her white overcoat, came up to us holding a tub of water with flower petals in it. She kept it on the floor and gently put Alia's feet into it.

'Pedicure for sir too?' Nancy said.

Before I could answer, Alia responded. 'Thanks, Nancy. Sir will get one too.'

I looked at Alia even as Nancy left to fetch another staff member for my treatment.

'Looks more natural if we are both getting it,' Alia said.

'I have never had a pedicure.'

'Try it,' Alia said. 'You were telling me about Siya's phone.'

'Yes, we found that she used Telegram,' I said.

Alia frowned. 'What's that?' she said.

'An app that can be used for secret chats.'

'Really? That is strange.'

'Did Siya tell you things? Like personal stuff.'

'I think so. She would tell me about her crushes. We were close. As close as a mother can be to a pre-teen.'

Nancy returned with her colleague, Sara.

'May I roll up your pants, sir?' Sara said.

I nodded. Sara rolled up my jeans till my knees and soon my feet too were in a tub with warm water and flower petals.

'This feels funny,' I said, shifting in my seat.

'Relax, try to enjoy it,' Alia said and smiled.

She moved her face closer to mine and spoke in a low voice so the pedicurists could not hear us.

'Who did she talk to on Telegram?' Alia said.

'It's difficult to figure out. Saurabh is trying to hack it.'

Alia nodded.

'Ouch!' I screamed as Sara poked a sharp object along my cuticles.

'Sorry,' Sara said. 'Sir has not done a pedicure for a long time.'

'Not a long time. This is the first time I am getting one,' I said, shifting left and right in my seat.

Sara and Nancy laughed.

'Bring your husband more often, madam. Can't believe he's never had a pedicure,' Nancy said.

I looked at Alia, shocked.

Alia's face turned red, like someone had applied a rose filter on it.

'Oh, he's not my husband. He's a ...,' Alia searched for the right word, 'colleague. On a project.'

'Ah,' Nancy said, somewhat unconvinced, even as she scraped diligently at Alia's feet.

'Sorry,' Alia whispered and tapped my upper arm. The touch of her fingers resonated through my entire body.

'It's okay,' I said. 'How is Manish? Any closer to cooperating with us?'

'Better. I talked to him about you guys again. This time he listened without losing his head. That's progress.'

'Good.'

'I assured him you will not go to the media.'

'Of course,' I said.

'He seemed more amenable after that. There's one thing though.'

'What?'

'He prefers to keep his parents out of it. They have already been through the trauma of being suspected and investigated once.'

I remained quiet. The sound of nail clippers as Sara clipped my toenails could be heard in the silence.

'That's a problem?' Alia said.

I tilted my head towards her.

'I don't understand this. How are we supposed to investigate if the family itself is divided and won't cooperate?' I said.

'I see your point.'

'Is it a surprise people suspected the family? If they act so cagey, anyone would. I would.'

'True,' Alia said.

'You think your in-laws could be involved in this?'

Alia stared intently at her feet and didn't respond.

'Nail colour, madam?' Nancy said, breaking the awkward silence. She brought out a tray full of little nail polish bottles. Alia selected a maroon one and a red one.

'I like both of these,' Alia said.

'Whichever you say, madam,' Nancy said.

Alia turned towards me.

'Red or maroon?' she said.

'Alia, I asked if you feel your in-laws could actually be involved in the crime,' I whispered.

Alia and I made eye contact.

She handed the red bottle to Nancy. As the pedicurist painted her nails, Alia spoke softly without looking at me.

'I don't think Papaji could be involved. But anything is possible with my lunatic mother-in-law.'

'Pedicure done, sir,' Sara's cheerful voice interrupted our conversation. She applied moisturiser on my feet as the final step. My toes had not looked this pink since I was a baby.

'Yours is done too, madam,' Nancy said. 'But wait for a few minutes until the nail polish dries off.'

Nancy had placed a rubber contraption called a toe separator between Alia's toes to keep them apart as the nail polish dried. I didn't even know such products existed.

'Sure, Nancy,' Alia said. 'May we both wait here for a while?'

'Of course,' Nancy said.

Alia tipped Nancy and Sara a hundred rupees each. The two girls thanked us and left.

I spoke when Alia and I were alone in the treatment area.

'What could be your mother-in-law's motive to make your daughter disappear or harm her?'

'I need to tell you more, Keshav. I told you what happened since Siya disappeared. I will have to tell you what happened before. Right from how I entered the Arora household.'

'I am listening,' I said.

'I was just seventeen,' Alia said, 'when I met Manish for the first time.'

Chapter 20

Alia Speaks – II

13 years ago
India Jewellery & Fashion Week ITC Maurya Hotel, Delhi

'What do you mean I can keep this?' I said. My fingers ran over the sharp diamonds on the necklace.

'It's for you,' Dhruv, my agent for the fashion show, said.

I was sitting at the dressing table in the green room. Light bulbs framing the vanity mirror made my reflection glow.

My feet hurt—I had worn heels the entire evening—yet my excitement outweighed any aches. I had walked the ramp six times in tonight's show, each time wearing a different diamond set. The most expensive one cost sixty lakh rupees. That was more than the cost of Amma's house in Kochi.

I kept the necklace back in its box.

'How can this be for me?' I said.

Before Dhruv could answer, my phone rang.

'Amma,' I said excitedly, 'I just got done. Oh my God, I wish you'd been here. Sushmita Sen was sitting in the audience.'

My mother congratulated me and said how proud my dad would have been to see me on stage.

'A year since he passed away in Siachen. Everyone said we would be ruined after he was gone. But look, my daughter stands tall, working independently in Delhi. You are a brave soldier and survivor, just like your father.'

'Amma, don't get senti. By the way, I was literally standing tall today. Four-inch heels. And they hurt so much.'

'I will massage them with karpuradhi thailam when you come here, vaava. When are you coming back?'

'In two days. I'll do some sightseeing and shopping in Delhi.'

'Sorry,' I said to Dhruv as I ended the call. 'My mother.'

I lifted the box again.

'Who said I could keep this? This must be very expensive.'

'It costs two lakh rupees,' Dhruv said. 'Manish sir told me this personally. He said it looked nice on you on stage, so it is for you. You are damn lucky.'

'Manish sir who?'

'Manish Arora, the owner of Navratna Jewels, one of the show sponsors. Remember seeing their logo on stage?'

I noticed the necklace box had an 'NJ' logo on it as well.

'I can't take this. It's too expensive a gift. Where's Manish sir?'

'He has invited everyone to the after-party at the hotel bar.'

'I am seventeen. Will they let me in the bar?'

Dhruv laughed.

'No bar ever denied entry to a model.'

'What a pleasure to meet you finally, Miss Alia Singh.'

At thirty years of age, Manish Arora was six feet tall and handsome. In a well-fitted black suit and white shirt, he stood confidently at the bar, elbows on the counter, smiling. I flashed him a nervous smile.

Loud music blared. I spoke loudly to be audible.

'Nice to meet you too, Manish sir,' I shouted.

'Drink?' he said, lifting up his glass of whisky.

'I'm seventeen,' I said and shook my head.

'Oh. Fresh orange juice?' he said.

I was soon sipping my juice.

'You are a natural on the ramp,' he said.

I put the necklace box on the bar counter. He pretended not to see it.

'Thank you,' I said. 'Sir, I wanted to return this.'

'You didn't like it?'

'I love it. That's not the point ...'

Manish shook his head and smiled. He pushed the box towards me.

'It will never look as beautiful in my warehouse as it does around your neck. Please, accept it with my compliments.'

Is this how the high-class world works? I wondered. *Do rich people toss around gifts that cost as much as a car at random?*

He lifted my hand, picked up the box and placed it in my palm. He folded my fingers around the box with his other hand.

'Don't worry about it. You are going to be a top model for sure. Consider this as my company's investment in you. Once you become big, give us a discount for being our showstopper. Okay?'

I blushed.

'Sir, thank you so much, but I am a beginner. This is my first show.'

'First? Wow, couldn't tell. You had so much confidence on stage.'

He took out the necklace from the box and gestured to me to turn around.

'Allow me,' he said.

'I am not sure if I am accepting this, sir.'

'Manish, not sir. And turn around. At least wear it this evening.'

I smiled and complied, disoriented by his aftershave as he came up close behind me to hook the necklace. He held my shoulders to turn me around again.

More than his perfume, his self-confidence and his hundred percent attention on me had an intoxicating effect. The after-party had the high society of Delhi in attendance, yet he was choosing to talk only to me.

'Shall we move someplace quieter?' he said. 'Too noisy here, isn't it?'

'Where?'

'Hungry? You haven't had dinner, right?'

'The models didn't even get time to have lunch.'

'They have Bukhara here, one of Delhi's best restaurants. The chef is a friend. Let's go.'

'You mean leave this party? What about your guests?'

'I am with the guest who matters the most to me.'

'I love the lack of pretence at this restaurant,' Manish said. He removed his jacket and tied the Bukhara-supplied apron over his impeccable white shirt. We sat on wooden stools at a small table facing each other. The restaurant had a roadside dhaba theme, despite being in a five-star hotel. I lifted the menu, printed on a wooden plate. My eyes popped wide open as I saw that the black dal was priced at five hundred rupees.

Manish asked me if I ate non-vegetarian food. I nodded. He ordered black dal, butter chicken and naan.

'It's classic Punjabi fare here,' Manish said. 'That's why I love it. My entire family does, actually.'

'Who else is there in your family?'

'Dad, Mom, my brother Timmy and his wife Rachna. That's all,' he said.

'Oh,' I said.

'What? You thought I am married as well? I look that old?'

'No, not at all,' I said and smiled.

'I should be married. I'm thirty. What to do! I work so much to build our brand ... Let me know if you can recommend a bride.'

'Me?' I said. 'How can I recommend someone, sir! I mean, Manish.'

We both burst into laughter. The waiter arrived with our order.

'This is the best, best dal I have ever had,' I said.

Manish smiled as I picked up a second naan.

'I bet you are thinking I won't stay a model for long. I am going to get so fat,' I said.

Manish laughed. 'As a Punjabi, I am happy you are enjoying the food.'

'More than any necklace, thank you for feeding me. Nobody bothered to ask me about food all day,' I said.

'You're welcome. Please eat well,' he said and patted my hand.

He told me about his business. His father, an ex-Air Force officer, had taken voluntary retirement several years ago and started a diamond-polishing business with a partner. Later, Manish's dad had branched out on his own and created Navratna Jewels. They had a factory to manufacture jewellery, selling wholesale to top retail stores in Delhi.

'Even though we are wholesalers, we want to have a brand,' Manish said.

'Makes sense. A brand will create demand. Better margins too,' I said.

'Wow, you are really smart too, apart from being extremely pretty,' Manish said.

'I ... I ... sorry, I am not good with compliments,' I said.

Manish laughed with delight as I blushed.

'Okay, enough boring shop talk. Tell me about you,' he said. 'Where in Delhi do you stay?'

'I live in Kochi. I am in Delhi only for a few days.'

'Kochi? In Kerala?'

I told him more about myself. My father, a Rajasthani, had served in the army as a colonel. I had lived all over India while growing up. Dad's last posting had been in Siachen. A year ago, he and six jawans had been trapped in an avalanche in the mountains. All of them had died.

'I am so sorry,' he said. He lightly placed his hand on mine.

I wouldn't cry. Not in Bukhara. Not in front of him.

'He was brave. And taught us to be the same. My mother belongs to Kochi. That's why we live there now.'

'Wow, behind all the modelling glamour, there is such a tough story.'

'I started modelling part-time this year. Last year I was busy with my Class XII boards.'

'Class XII?' Manish said.

'Yes, I told you. I am seventeen. I'll be eighteen in three months, though.'

'Would you like to be the brand ambassador for Navratna Jewels?' Manish said.

'What?'

'We are a small brand, I know.'

'What, seriously? It would be such an honour.'

'You can stay back in Delhi a few more days then to do some photo shoots?'

'Yes, of course.'

'And would that justify me giving you the necklace? The brand ambassador has to wear the brand, right?'

Flabbergasted, I thought of a gracious response.

Instead, I did the unclassiest thing ever: I burped. Two garlic naans, black dal and half a butter chicken will do that to anyone.

'Oops,' he said.

I wanted to bury myself in the floor of Bukhara. I hid my face with my napkin. He laughed out loud.

'I like a girl who is real,' he said.

I had come to Delhi for a couple of days. I ended up staying three weeks.

'This is nice,' he said after the shoot. 'We make a good team.'

I smiled. We had remained work-focused for most of my stay. We did photo shoots, planned looks together and met various jewellery designers.

'I like you, Alia,' Manish said one evening after work.

I was sitting next to him in his Mercedes, and we were stuck at a traffic light. I looked at him, surprised by his timing but not by what he had said. Things had been sweet between us for the last few weeks.

'I think I do too,' I said and smiled.

'You are so beautiful,' he said. He leaned forward to kiss me. I did not stop him. It only lasted a second before the lights turned green. Delhi traffic wailed behind us with loud horns. The honking was meant to abuse us, but to me it sounded like a celebration. I had never had a boyfriend, nor had I been kissed. I sat in a car surrounded by traffic, but in my head I was floating in the sky surrounded by clouds.

'Please don't go,' Manish said, not releasing me from a hug.

'I have to. Amma is alone,' I said.

We were at the departure lounge of the Delhi airport. My flight to Kochi was in two hours.

'But I will be alone here,' Manish said.

'You have your family. Aunty and Uncle are with you.'

'Promise me you will come back soon.'

'I will,' I said. I started to remove my necklace.

'Are you crazy? Keep wearing it. Never take it off,' he said, pulling my hands down.

I smiled, even though my eyes had turned moist.

'This is real, right?' Manish said. 'The last three weeks. It wasn't just a fling, right?'

I nodded.

'Thank you for everything,' I said.

'Thank you for coming into my life,' Manish said.

I turned to leave.

'One more thing, Alia,' Manish said.

'What?' I said.

'I love you.'

Chapter 21

6 months later

'Are you sure your mother won't mind?' I said, adjusting my peacock-blue dupatta over a white chikan salwar kameez. We were on our way to Manish's house. He had rented an apartment for me in Defence Colony in Delhi. It gave us a chance to spend time alone whenever I came down. Six months into our relationship, he felt I should meet his mother.

'Of course, isn't your Amma fine with me?' he said.

'She's sort of fine now. You remember at the start, she was shocked her young daughter was dating an older Punjabi man.'

'But she's quite fond of her daughter's Punjabi man now,' Manish said and smiled.

Despite her initial reluctance, Amma had come to like Manish. She had expressed reservations, but they were more about our age difference than the fact that we were from different communities. However, Manish had made a real effort. He had come to Kochi several times. He had managed to charm her, just as he had charmed her daughter. He had even worn a Kerala mundu to impress her. Manish's military connection also reassured Amma, which somewhat superseded her other concerns.

Manish and I reached Navratna House and I saw that the plot size was four times my house in Kochi.

An overweight Punjabi lady wearing a maroon velvet salwar kameez waddled out, along with a man in his thirties. The man was wearing a saffron kurta and white pyjamas. He had beads around his neck and a big tilak on his forehead. The lady folded her hands to him as she had come out to see him off.

Manish and I walked up to them.

'Just adjust the living room sofas ninety degrees. And plant tulsi in the front garden and at the back of the house. Otherwise, the energy is perfect,' the priest was saying.

'Pranaam, Panditji. Alia, this is Pandit Shastri,' Manish said and brought his palms together. I did the same.

'God bless you, beta,' he said to Manish and raised a palm in blessing at me.

'Hello, Mummyji,' Manish said. The priest spoke before Manish's mother could respond.

'Okay, Durgaji. I will leave now. Any problems, call me. Manishji, give Shamsherji my regards,' Pandit Shastri said before turning to leave.

Manish led me into the house. I entered the giant living room with huge sofas. The room resembled a Mughal dynasty TV serial set.

'Mummyji, this is Alia,' Manish said. Upon his signal, I lunged forward to touch her feet.

'What is the need for this?' she said and smiled, lifting me up by my shoulders. 'Wow, you are so beautiful. Kinni soni hai.'

'Isn't she? I told you,' Manish said with pride.

'I had seen your pictures in the company brochure,' she said. 'You are even prettier in real life. Most beautiful girlfriend either of my sons have ever had,' she said and laughed.

Was that a compliment? A joke? I couldn't tell.

I smiled to be polite.

We proceeded to have lunch together. She laid out an array of Punjabi dishes, ranging from chole to kadhi to shahi paneer. I had to stop her from over-feeding me. She told me to drop my modelling diet for a day.

'So, you are South Indian?' she said midway through the meal.

'Half-Keralite and half-Rajasthani. But I live in Kerala, yes.'

'Not for long. You will be moving to Gurgaon soon,' Manish said and winked at me. His mother smiled even as she looked somewhat confused.

'What do you think, Mummyji?'

'About what?' she said with a puzzled expression.

'About Alia?'

'What about her?'

Manish looked at me and smiled, oblivious to his mother's reaction.

'Excuse me, I have to read this so I don't get this speech wrong,' Manish said.

I looked at Manish, surprised.

He took out a slip of paper from his pocket. He read out the lines written on it.

'I am here today, in front of the two most important women in my life. One who gave me birth, made me who I am and means so much to me. The second is the girl who swept me off my feet. I know that abroad people propose to their girlfriends in private. But I am an Indian and a Punjabi. We take the family along, always. Mummyji, see, your son is finally ready to settle down. Hence, in the presence of my mother, I ask: Alia, will you marry me? And Mummyji, will you give us your blessings?'

Manish kneeled down on the floor. My mouth fell open. He took out a small box from his pocket with the letters NJ engraved on it. He opened it and I saw a massive solitaire diamond ring inside. He held up the ring towards me. Was this really happening? His parents had known he was dating me and I thought today was just about me meeting his mother. I hadn't expected him to propose. Was this all a big sweet surprise? Was his entire family in on the plan and already on board?

I looked at Manish's earnest face. My eyes turned moist.

'Alia, is that a yes?' he said in a soft voice.

Mummyji's dining chair creaked as she shifted her position. Her elbow hit the bowl of kadhi. The yellow yogurt-based curry spilled all over the dining table. A rivulet of kadhi flowed towards me and fell on my white salwar kameez. I suppressed a scream as I stood up. Manish looked up at the table.

'Oh, no,' he said, standing up. He pulled out napkins from a tissue box and started wiping the table and my kurta.

'It fell on your mother too,' his mother said in a sarcastic, authoritarian voice.

No, this wasn't pre-planned. Her tone told me she was not only unaware of Manish's unique proposal plan but she also hated it.

'Oh, okay, Mummyji,' Manish said. He handed a bunch of tissues to his mother.

Manish finished wiping my kurta and kept the soiled tissues aside.

'One day, after many years, we will all remember this incident and laugh about it,' Manish said and smiled.

Clueless Manish had not sensed the tension in the air yet. For a jeweller who literally manufactured and sold engagement rings, he should have known better than to spring a surprise proposal. Every girl wants her proposal to be special. But special doesn't mean a heart attack. Hell, I would have been okay if he had proposed to me in the neighbourhood park, his car, at the airport or even at the bus stop. Anywhere other than in front of my future mother-in-law and a spilt bowl of kadhi.

Unfazed, Manish went back on his knees. He extended the ring to me again.

'Manish, what is this nonsense? Get up,' his mother said.

Manish looked at his mother, surprised, but obediently stood up. His mother loudly called for her domestic help to clean the table. Manish, his mother and I moved to the Mughal-era sofas.

'Is this one of your pranks, Manish?' Mummyji said.

'What? No, Mummyji. You know Alia is my girlfriend. I told you I am bringing her to meet you.'

'Girlfriends-virlfriends when did I stop you and Timmy from having? But what is this? Proposing like this? Offering a two-carat ring? Are you a kid, Manish?'

She was talking about me like I wasn't in the room. I tried

to zone out. I looked down at the Italian marble floor. I tried to find unusual patterns in the black streaks in the white Statuario marble below me. I could make out a goat, an angel and an apple. Unfortunately, no matter how much I tried to distract myself, I caught a few words between mother and son.

'But Mummyji—' Manish started, but Mummyji shut him up.

'Who is she? Some small-time model you picked up? So many like her roaming around in Delhi.'

'Mummyji, stop talking like that. She's my girlfriend.'

'So? Marriage is not a joke. What's her background?'

'I just need to use the toilet,' I said.

Manish nodded and pointed to a door in the corner of the living room. I should have simply locked myself in the washroom and waited for the drama to get over. However, I couldn't. I wanted to hear this conversation. I left the door slightly ajar as I looked at myself in the bathroom mirror. I heard Manish speak.

'She's a decorated army officer's daughter, Mummyji. He gave his life for the country. Forces background, just like Papaji. What's the issue?'

'Really? Have you seen Shamsher's status now? Don't you see the house you live in? The diamonds you carry around in your pocket? Is she of that class?'

'What class? I have visited her house. Met her mother.'

'Oh, really? That's what you went to Kochi for? Not just to have fun with your girlfriend but to meet her mother?'

'Her mother is a very nice person, Mummyji.'

'And your mother is not?'

'When did I say that?'

'So my approval doesn't matter? What about her horoscope? You met Pandit Shastri on the way out. Did you show him her patri?'

'What horoscope and all, Mummyji—' Manish said as Mummyji interrupted him.

'You are an idiot, Manish. You don't realise your value. You are a catch. She and her mother both must have planned to trap you.'

I could take pointless insults aimed at me. I could not take a word against my mother.

I charged out of the bathroom.

'Aunty, there is no plan. I am as surprised by this proposal as you are.'

She looked up at me, surprised by my firm voice. Then she turned away without responding.

'Manish, I'd like to leave. Aunty?'

Mummyji turned to look at me.

'Thanks for lunch,' I said and stormed out.

'I fucked up, didn't I?' Manish said, hands on the steering wheel.

I kept my eyes on the road ahead and did not respond.

'Anything I can do to make it up to you?'

'Yes, bring my flight forward please. I'd like to leave for Kochi tonight.'

'Alia, stop. She's a Punjabi mom. She's supposed to kick up a fuss when her son finds the woman he wants to marry. Territorial thing, you know. Like lions and tigers.'

'I have never heard a lioness or tigress insult a prospective daughter-in-law. Don't insult the poor animals please.'

Manish shook his head and grinned.

'I am not giving up on this. This makes it more exciting. Parental opposition. Love winning against all odds.'

'This isn't a movie, Manish,' I said.

'I know. It's better than that. It's our life. Don't worry. I will fix it.'

'How?'

'God will show us a way. For now, let me bring your flight forward. And let me also escape to Kochi with you.'

Chapter 22

2 months later

'Aunty, your appams are perfect. Light like fluffy clouds. Out of the world, really,' Manish said.

We were sitting on the floor in the courtyard of my tiny two-bedroom house in Kochi. I had never described my house as tiny earlier. However, after seeing Manish's palace, everything about my life felt small. My mother smiled as she added more stew to his banana leaf. Manish had been coming to Kochi every fortnight. A part of me wanted to end our relationship after the fiasco with his mother. Another part of me didn't, and frankly, couldn't. Manish showered me with even more love after that episode. Once he made a short daytrip to Kochi only to see me for a few hours. He did it because I had told him I was feeling low. He listened to whatever I said. I had told him to stop spending money on me or giving me expensive gifts. He had agreed. I had told him to stop pushing for marriage. He never brought up the topic again.

Except that day. Everything would change that day.

I had done the test for a third time in the bathroom. The two small lines that indicated a positive result confirmed what I knew already.

'Manish, can I speak to you for a second?' I said.

'Sure,' Manish said, dipping his appam in the stew.

'Alone,' I said, my tone serious. I signalled to him to step outside.

Amma was upset that I was interrupting his meal but Manish washed his hands and came running after me as I left the house.

'How can you be pregnant?' Manish said.

'Because we had sex. Seriously, Manish?'

We had come to Kashi Art Café, a quaint, bohemian place with an open-air veranda, wooden tables and brass vessels. It was popular with foreign tourists who came to visit Fort Kochi, a heritage town where Amma lived.

'Sorry. I meant, since when?' Manish said.

'Not sure. I did the test today. I have missed my cycle twice.'

I stirred jaggery into my coffee, waiting for him to absorb the news. He wasn't freaking out as I had expected. He simply nodded as he took a couple of deep breaths.

Maybe him being older than me made him that much more mature. He clasped my hands.

'Whatever happens, we are in this together, okay?'

I nodded. 'But what will happen?'

'I am thinking,' Manish said, biting his lip. The homemade vanilla cake slice we had ordered remained untouched.

'It happened to another model I know. She has a doctor who fixed it,' I said.

'Are you crazy? What do you mean fixed it?'

'I mean ab—'

'Don't even say that word,' Manish said, scoldingly. 'Just hang on. Let me think for a minute, will you?'

I looked around. Some Europeans with long hair and printed kurtas occupied the adjacent table. Manish spoke after two minutes.

'This is good. This is really, really good,' he said. He held my hands again.

'What will happen?' I said in a weak voice. I didn't want to cry in public.

'Only good things will happen. This is a gift from God, Alia. God is telling us something.'

'What?'

'That we need to be together. As husband and wife. So we can be a good mum and dad for our baby.'

I looked up at him.

'What about your mother?'

'She's not important now. This is about another life,' Manish said. He had a twinkle in his eye.

'You sure? I just turned eighteen. Will I even be a good mother?'

'You will be an amazing mom. Meanwhile, I thought of something. That could help convince my mother.'

'What?'

'Mummyji has someone she believes in more than anyone else. We have to get Pandit Shastri's blessings first.'

'Griha pravesh, vaastu, dhanteras puja in the factory. You do everything for my parents. Now, for the first time, I am asking you to do something for me,' Manish said.

'That's fine, Manishji, but this?' Pandit Shastri said. He scratched his head. He shouted out after a pause, 'Balan, come here. Get the computer.'

Manish and I had come to Hauz Khas Village, a semi-rural area in South Delhi. Now famous for high-end fashion boutiques and trendy cafés, the prior inhabitants of the area still lived in the original village. The village had transformed into two-storey-high pucca houses. Pandit Shastri had his house, and if you could call it an office, here as well. A huge sign outside advertised the services he offered. They ranged from horoscopes to weddings to vaastu advice.

We sat on mattresses laid out on the marble floor in the main puja hall that occupied the entire ground floor. Images of Hindu gods and goddesses adorned all four walls.

Balan, a twenty-year-old boy who was one of Panditji's staff members and disciples, entered the room. He wore a dhoti–kurta and was carrying a laptop. He sat down next to Panditji.

'What is the time and birthdate of Aliaji? And where was she born?' Pandit Shastri said. 'Balan will take out the patri in minutes. We already have yours, Manishji. We can match them then.'

'Leave all that, Panditji.' Manish grinned, sitting cross-legged in front of the priest.

'What do you mean?' Panditji said.

'Let's do it the other way round for a change.'

'Which way?'

'Instead of us telling you the time and place of birth, you tell us the time and place needed to match our horoscopes perfectly. Make us look like a jodi made in heaven.'

Shastri and Balan looked at Manish, surprised. They turned to me. I looked away.

'You are asking me to lie? In the house of God? Look all around you,' Shastri said.

'Who's asking you to lie?' Manish said, somewhat taken aback. 'It is me who will tell you the wrong time, if at all. You are simply telling me what will match. The lying is all on me.'

'Clever, Manishji. But you are involving me in your plan to deceive your mother.' Pandit Shastri shook his head.

'Please, Panditji,' Manish said and folded his hands. 'This is for our love. My mother will not refuse if it comes from you. If you say our horoscopes match and Alia will bring immense fame and fortune to the family, Mummyji will agree.'

'Manishji,' Panditji said and folded his hands in return. 'I won't be able to do this. Sorry.'

'Balan,' Manish said, 'can you give us a moment?'

Balan looked surprised. Panditji nodded, signalling to him to leave.

'I will give you anything to make this happen,' Manish said. He took out a thick paper packet from his pocket and slid it towards Panditji.

'This is two,' he said, referring to the amount in lakhs. 'More when we get married. You will only make Alia and me do our seven pheras, of course.'

Panditji touched his left and right ear, to seek forgiveness.

'Please, Manishji. I am not like this. Please take this back.'

'I can give more,' Manish said.

'I have known your family for decades. My guruji used to be your grandfather's priest. When he passed away, your mother gave me a chance. She and your father introduced me to so many of their friends who gave me work. I had just finished my vaastu course. They invited me to sit in meetings with the architects to do vaastu for Navratna House. You are asking me to betray them?'

Manish sat with a sheepish expression. Panditji moved the envelope back to him.

'Not at any price. If the horoscopes match on their own, I will be happy to communicate that. Shall I call Balan again to make her patri?'

'She is pregnant,' Manish blurted out. 'Please, Panditji, help us. My mother is against this marriage.'

Panditji looked at me and Manish in quick succession with a shocked expression on his face.

'It's true,' I said.

Panditji threw his hands in the air.

'Then this is God's sign, isn't it? Who am I then to make horoscopes and judge this?'

'What do we do, Panditji? Mummyji is dead against this match,' Manish said.

'We will make honest horoscopes. But whatever it is, I will recommend Aliaji to your mother.'

'What if our patris don't match?'

'I'll recommend some solutions to mitigate the effects,' Panditji said.

'Thank you, Panditji,' Manish said. We stood up. Manish and I bent forward to touch his feet. He blessed us by putting a hand on our heads.

'Close your eyes, Alia beti,' Panditji said to me.

I stood with my eyes closed. Panditji removed his hand from my head and spoke again.

'Open your eyes. Whatever male or female god you see first will be the child's name, depending on whether it's a boy or girl.'

I opened my eyes. I saw an image of Ram and Sita on the wall in front of me.

'Ram if it is a boy. Siya if it is a girl,' I said to Manish and smiled for the first time in weeks.

'Panditji, but ...' Mummyji said.

'Calm down, Durgaji. Stress is never good. See this as God's blessing.'

Manish's mother glared at him, as if her eyes had lasers and she was trying to skewer her son. He had not only got this random lower-status girl pregnant, but also had the audacity to ask the family priest to intervene and make his case. This time, Manish ensured that Papaji, Timmy and Rachna were also present. Of course, in the great Durga's presence, nobody else spoke a word.

'How far along is she?' she said.

'Three months,' Manish said.

'And how long have you known?'

'A couple of weeks,' Manish said. 'Mummyji, I already made you meet Alia. I told you I want to get married to her.'

'When did all this happen?' Papaji said. 'Nobody tells me anything.'

'There was nothing to tell, ji. He just brings anyone home and says he wants to marry her.'

That anyone is bearing your grandchild, I wanted to retort, but didn't.

'Panditji, who is she? We don't know her family. We have to see our standing. There's societal perception, there are horoscopes—' Mummyji said and Panditji interrupted her.

'Other things I don't know, but I already checked the horoscopes.'

'And?' she said.

'They somewhat matched. I see one issue in the girl's kundali. Sun, Rahu, Jupiter and Venus are in conjunction with each other in the eighth house. This can cause problems.'

'What kind of problems, Panditji?' Papaji said.

'This causes Guru Chandal Yog.'

'See, there is a problem. I knew it,' Mummyji said.

'But there is a solution. I can recommend some stones,' Panditji said.

'Which stones?' Papaji said.

'Aliaji can wear a four-carat yellow sapphire on her index finger and a half-cent diamond on her middle finger.'

'And then all will be fine, Panditji?' Papaji said.

'Yes. There will be ups and downs, but mostly okay. You will sail through. In fact, if handled right, the stones combined with her horoscope may bring a lot of prosperity in new ventures.'

'My online venture. Which I am going to start soon,' Manish said, excited.

'Don't worry, Durgaji. Things will be okay,' Panditji said and smiled. 'God came in my dreams. He told me everything will be okay. Everything happens for a reason.'

Mummyji seemed unconvinced.

'Where are your parents, beta?' Papaji said.

'My mother is in Kochi, Uncle. Dad died in Siachen two years ago.'

His eyes lit up. 'Siachen? Army?'

I nodded. I missed my father. I needed him here with me, to protect me from these Punjabi elders, some of them double my size and age.

'Infantry. 19 Kumaon. Colonel V.S. Singh,' I said with pride in my voice.

'I know Unnis,' Papaji said and smiled, referring to the Hindi nickname for my dad's battalion. 'They won more medals than anyone else. I did some sorties with them in my time. Much before your father's days.'

I knew I had won Papaji over at that moment. He told me later how he had always wanted a daughter-in-law from a defence background. Rachna, who Timmy had married a year ago, came from a family of gold traders in Ludhiana. Mummyji had handpicked her after scanning hundreds of proposals. She had wanted the same kind of match for her younger son, someone rich and docile.

Papaji continued to talk to me.

'I miss my defence days ...'

'Will you stop it, Shamsher?' roared his wife and the ex-Air Force officer shut up in an instant.

'Durga, I am just—' he began after a second.

'You save your defence nostalgia for when you go to DSOI. We are dealing with a situation here. Your son got this eighteen-year-old girl pregnant. We have to find a solution.'

'I have a solution, Mummyji. Alia and I want to get married. We love each other. We just want your blessings.'

'One slap I will give you as blessing,' she shouted.

'Enough, Durga,' Papaji said. 'Manish is right. There's nothing else to do here. At least the kids have come to us instead of running away. Let's go to Kochi and meet Alia's mother.'

'*Main nahi jaana kiddan koi Madrasi nu milan*,' Mummyji said and stormed out of the living room.

I didn't understand Punjabi, but I figured she hadn't rushed out to buy a ticket to Kochi.

'I'll take your leave, Shamsherji. Let me know if you need anything,' said Panditji, seeing the escalating family tensions. Papaji left the living room to see off the family priest.

'Don't worry, Alia,' Timmy said and smiled reassuringly. 'Papaji knows how to handle Mummyji. She will come around.'

Timmy and Manish left to soothe their mother.

Rachna came and sat next to me.

'Treat me like your sister. Not bhabhi. Ever,' she said and gave me a hug. My eyes became moist at the unexpected affection after the public humiliation.

'Why are you crying? Don't cry. You should be happy,' Rachna said, wiping my tears.

'I am so scared.'

'Why? Papaji has agreed, no? Now wait and watch, everything will fall into place.'

'Manish's mother seems so ...' I said and turned silent, avoiding any negative word.

'She has an acid tongue, that's all. You'll get used to it. In Ludhiana, all my cousins' mothers-in-law talk like this. Don't worry, okay? I am here, your sister.'

'Thank you,' I said and nodded.

'How are you so slim and trim? Give your fat elder sister some tips too.'

'Durgaji, I must say, this is the grandest wedding we have ever attended,' said Mrs Mehrotra, one of Manish's family friends. For the Arora family, comments like these made the one-and-a-half crore rupees blown on the wedding worth it.

'It's nothing, ji. Everything happened so fast. Luckily Shamsher knew the GM here, else you never get Taj at such short notice,' my mother-in-law said. Manish and I had our wedding reception at the Taj Palace in Dhaula Kuan, New Delhi, with two thousand guests. Only twenty people attended from my side.

Manish and I had our pheras in the hotel garden, under the sky, with a canopy of flowers above us. Pandit Shastri chanted prayers as we sat around the holy fire.

'Promise that you will always be there for each other, in good times and bad,' Panditji said, translating one of the Sanskrit mantras.

'I do,' both Manish and I said in unison. Manish clasped my hand as we stood up for the pheras. I looked up at the sky and saw the flowers and stars above me. For a moment, my life felt like a fairy tale. Fairy tales don't have Punjabi mothers-in-law, of course.

'She is Madrasi?' I heard Manish's aunt Shilpa ask Mummyji during one of the seven rounds around the fire.

'Half-Madrasi. Father is from Rajasthan,' Mummyji said.

Pandit Shastri chanted mantras as Manish and I continued to walk around the fire.

'How come she is so fair? And those light eyes?' Shilpa aunty said. 'She isn't a Muslim or something, right?'

'They said half-Kerala, half-Rajasthani. But who knows? All I know is she did some magic on Manish.'

'I could have got you the best of rishtas. On my husband's side, we have a big builder family. Full pure Punjabi.'

'My fate, what to do?' Mummyji said.

Chapter 23

6 months later

I heard the maternity ward nurse speak excitedly to my in-laws in the corridor outside the delivery room.

'It's a beautiful baby girl,' she was saying.

'Hmm, okay. Never mind, koi gal nahi,' Mummyji said after a long pause.

Did I hear her wrong? Did she actually say 'never mind' on the birth of her first grandchild? I looked at Manish. He pretended he hadn't heard his mother. He beamed as he held little Siya for the first time.

'She has your eyes,' Manish said. 'Gorgeous.'

I looked at my daughter. Two years ago I was wearing a school uniform. Now I had to take care of another human being for the rest of my life. Would I be able to do it?

I clasped Manish's hand tight. He released it as his parents entered the room. He bent forward to touch their feet. I propped myself up a bit on the hospital bed as well.

'Don't move, beta. You rest,' Papaji said. Manish offered Siya to him. I saw the delight in Papaji's eyes as a little child had come into the family after decades. I also saw the indifference on my mother-in-law's face. She hardly spoke to me at home anyway. But couldn't she just pretend to care for one day?

Papaji passed Siya to her. Mummyji rocked her for precisely two seconds before handing her back to Manish.

'*Hun sambhal ik aur billi ankh wali nu*,' she said in Punjabi. It translated to 'now take care of another cat-eyed one'.

She laughed at her own comment. I didn't think it was funny. Nobody in the fucking world would think it was funny. But I didn't want anger to seethe through me right after delivering a child. It would only make my already weak body hurt more.

'She's beautiful, Mummyji. Please don't talk like this,' Manish said, in a rare act of standing up to his mother.

'She's come just minutes ago and you are already ticking off your mother for her!'

'No, Mummyji ...'

'Listen, don't be in a rush to tell people,' she said next. 'They will calculate the wedding date and figure out something is fishy.'

Answer her back, I mentally implored Manish. *Say Alia and I are married. I am proud of my daughter and I don't care. I can't wait to tell the world.*

'Yes, Mummyji,' Manish said instead.

'Anything you want, beta?' Papaji said.

'Could I be left alone? I want to rest,' I said.

9 years later

Papaji rubbed his face. The electric fireplace in the living room flickered, creating an orange glow in the room. Papaji sat alone in front of the heat, holding his brandy glass.

'Enough, Shamsher. You said one drink to feel warm, but you are half a bottle down,' Mummyji said.

'Let me be,' he said, staring into the fake flames.

Mummyji picked up the brandy bottle.

'Leave that where it is.'

Mummyji sat down on the couch next to him.

I could hear them talk as I lay the table. Papaji sounded concerned.

'If it stays like this, I will have to fire everyone from the factory and close it down.'

'Someone cursed us, I am convinced,' Mummyji said.

'Everything will be over, Durga. All I ever worked for.'

'How bad is it?'

'Business has dropped ninety per cent to almost nothing. I

am stuck with twenty crore rupees worth of inventory and dues from retailers. The moneylenders want their money back. How do I return it?'

I went to the kitchen and came back with plates and glasses. My in-laws continued to talk.

'You are wearing the panna?' she said.

My father-in-law nodded. He lifted his right index finger to show her his green emerald stone ring.

'Wear a ruby as well.'

'Already am.' Papaji raised his wrist to show her the red stones in his bracelet. 'These stones are not helping, Durga.'

He refilled his glass with brandy.

'It's a shraap. Someone has cast an evil eye on us. Hundred per cent. Else, how come none of the stones work?'

'My dhanda is stones only, Durga. Nobody is buying them, that's the problem. Modi also had to do this demonetisation now. Is this the way? Will black money go away like this?'

He gulped his brandy like water and slammed the glass on the table. Papaji normally sipped on one drink through an entire evening. Ever since demonetisation four months ago, this had become his daily ritual.

'Now demonetisation is over. Why isn't business back now?' Mummyji said.

'I don't know. Jewellery is entirely a cash business. They sucked cash out of the system. Everything is at a standstill.'

'No, ji. Demonetisation is gone now. Someone is jealous of us, wants to harm us. This is an evil eye.'

Papaji shook his head, unconvinced.

'Let's do a puja at home to get rid of the bad nazar. Change the furniture around for better vaastu,' she said.

'Nonsense, Durga,' Papaji said in a rare bold tone, thanks to the brandy.

'What do you mean nonsense?' Mummyji said, upset at his unexpected defiance of her authority in the house.

'What will all these pujas and stones do? I have to fire my people. They have families to support.'

'You were nothing in business, Shamsher. I did so many prayers for you, designed the vaastu of the factory, put in the reception lounge facing east and ensured that all negative vibrations were killed. That's how you made Navratna Jewels. You forgot all that?' Mummyji said.

'Okay, fine. Don't scream in my ear.' He took a sip of brandy. 'Do whatever.'

I went upstairs to call everyone down for dinner. As I climbed the steps, I heard Papaji say, 'Who will cast an evil eye on this house or wish us bad luck? We have done good to everyone, Durga. We just have to pray that business recovers soon.'

'You think this cat-eyed bahu wishes well for us?' Mummyji said. I froze in the middle of the staircase.

'I heard her bitch about me to her mother on the phone. She talks in Malayalam, but doesn't realise how much English she ends up using.'

'You also talk badly about her to your relatives. You taunt her. You are rude to her all the time.'

'No, I don't.'

'In the last nine years, have you ever been genuinely nice to her? Or even to her daughters? They are your granddaughters.'

'So? Why should I be nice to them? The elder one is the reason her mother even entered this house. Then the younger one followed. Two girls she dumped on us, apart from invading our house herself.'

'They are all our family.'

'Says who? She inserted herself. Shamsher, you have a soft spot for her, but I am telling you, it is this green-eyed woman casting the evil eye on this house.'

'Alia? You are here? We were just coming down for dinner,' Rachna said, as the four kids scurried down the steps.

6 months later

'What? Another puja?' Manish laughed, leaning back on the bed in our room on the first floor of Navratna House.

'It's so not fucking funny, Manish,' I said, livid. I had tolerated ten jibes a day for ten years. I had learnt to live as a second-grade citizen in this house. I accepted that my mother-in-law would never love my daughters the way she loved Timmy's sons. I had even accepted a husband who managed an internet company with forty people but turned into a wimp when he had to deal with his own mother. However, today I'd reached my limit. I needed my husband. I wanted him to man up and not hide his cowardice by turning everything into a joke.

'I am sorry, okay?' he said. He sat up straighter and looked serious. 'I am listening,' he said.

'Pishachini nazar utaar puja,' I said.

I could see him suppress his laughter.

'Don't trivialise it, Manish. Enough is enough.'

'It is a little funny. Sounds right out of those TV serials. One second, I will change and come back.'

Manish went into the bathroom to wear his nightclothes. Yes, my life had become like a bad saas-bahu TV serial. Except that in those the bahu tormented the saas. In my life, it was the other way round, always.

He came out of the bathroom and plopped himself back on the bed.

'Do you even know what pishachini means?' I said.

'Demon?'

'Female demon,' I said. 'A witch.'

'Okay, but why does it hassle you? Mummyji does pujas all the time. She is addicted to them.'

'Because that female demon is me.'

'Don't be silly. My mother is just trying to help Papaji deal with the stress from work. He's drinking every night now.'

'Manish, come here.'

I opened the bedroom door and pointed to the corridor ceiling right outside our room.

'What's that? Lemons? Chillies?' Manish said, looking up.

'Yes, to ward off the evil eye or buri nazar. It's only outside our room.'

'Really?'

'Don't you get it? The pishachini is me. Her bahu who slept her way into her house and now wants to bleed everyone dry. That's how she thinks about it.'

'No way. Business is horrible. That's why they are doing this.'

'Will these pujas bring customers back? Or should all of you be figuring out how to make things work in the post-demonetisation environment?'

'My mother can be crazy sometimes. I never denied it.'

'She's not crazy in a silly, innocent or cute sort of way. She is doing this to hurt me and show me my place.'

Manish shrugged.

I began to cry. I felt helpless and alone.

'Oh, come on, Alia. Don't be so sensitive. It's not about you.'

'Have you ever seen her hug Siya or Suhana? She pats Rohit and Sanjay to sleep every night. Have you ever seen her do the same for your kids?'

Manish came forward and gave me a hug.

'You are too sensitive, my little Alia. Really, listen to a Punjabi mother-in-law from one ear and let it immediately go out of the other.'

'It's not just her words. She's actually doing that puja. Placing superstitious totems around me. Neglecting my daughters and favouring Timmy bhaiya's kids.'

'That's only because they are boys.'

'What does that mean?'

'It's just how she thinks. I am not saying it is right. But it's not about you or your kids.'

'Stop justifying it.'

'What do you want me to do?'

'Stop this puja. It's making me feel uneasy. I don't know what all they will say in it about me and my daughters.'

'They won't.'

'Stop the puja, Manish.'

'Fine. I will tell Pandit Shastri not to do it. I'll tell him to suggest another one to Mummyji.'

'No. You tell your mother it is wrong to do it. Don't be a coward and go sideways to Panditji.'

'Okay, fine,' Manish said after a pause. 'Anything else?'

'Can we move to our own place?'

'What?'

'You bought a flat in the Icon, right?'

'Yes, I did, as an investment. It's ready. I have to find a tenant.'

'No, let's move there instead. Lots of kids and sports facilities, which will be great for Siya and Suhana. Good security too.'

'Leave my parents' house? Are you kidding me, Alia?'

'We will be five minutes away. Everyone gets more space. Trust me, it will improve all our relationships.'

Manish shook his head.

'No, Alia, that won't happen here. We are one family, one business. I told you. I will stop the puja. She will listen.'

'What if she doesn't? Or does another one later? Is this the environment you want your kids to be brought up in?'

I heard a knock on the door.

'Mommy, can you please come and tuck me into bed?' Suhana said.

Chapter 24

'Nail polish is dry, madam?' Nancy's voice brought us back to the present moment.

'Yes, Nancy,' Alia said, wiggling her newly painted toes. 'All dry now.'

She turned to me.

'So, yeah, that's it. Soon after that, we moved to the Icon,' Alia said.

'Let me guess. She did the puja,' I said.

Alia nodded.

'She did the puja. I left home in anger. I took the kids and went to Kochi for a few days.'

'What happened then?'

'Manish came down to get me back. I placed only one condition—we move out of Navratna House or I stay with my mother in Kochi. He agreed to shift to the Icon.'

Alia's phone rang.

'Hi, Manish, I am not at home. Came to South Point for a pedicure ... Fine ... I am done, I will come now.' She ended the call.

'Manish isn't feeling well. Came home early. I have to go,' she said to me.

'Sure.'

We walked outside the mall. She called for her driver and turned to me.

'I'd take you back in my car, but not sure what the driver will say to Manish.'

'It's a short walk home. Not an issue,' I said.

'Still, it is rude to leave you here like this. As it is, I made you get a pedicure.'

'Felt good, actually.'

'Did you like it?' she said, smiling after a long time. She looked beautiful when she smiled.

Why am I thinking this way, I thought to myself.

'Yes, I did. Anyway, I will keep you updated if we find anything else on Siya's phone.'

'Sure,' she said.

Her black Mercedes arrived at the pick-up point.

'Thank you, Keshav, for listening to me,' she said.

'It's my job,' I said.

'I never even told my mother my marital issues. Didn't want to stress her out. You are literally the first person I ever shared this with. I feel so much better after talking to you. Thank you.'

She came forward and gave me a long, somewhat tight hug before walking to her car.

I walked back home. Her perfume and the sensation of her hug still lingered. Somehow, I felt light on my feet now. Was it the pedicure? Or was it something else?

'What are these? Cotton balls?' I said.

'Yes,' Saurabh said.

A pile of cotton balls lay on his table. Next to it were two glasses of orange juice.

I raised an eyebrow.

'It's time for drastic measures. I am going on a cotton ball diet,' he said.

'Cotton what?' I said, lifting a puffy ball in my hand.

'I only eat these balls. I dip them in orange juice so it's easier to swallow.'

'What the actual fuck? You can't be serious.'

'This is an actual diet, bhai. Models do it. Google it.'

He picked up a cotton ball and soaked it in orange juice. He popped it in his mouth but struggled to swallow it.

'That's disgusting, Golu. See, it's not even going down. Humans are not supposed to eat cotton.'

Saurabh swallowed hard to force the ball down. He picked up another one.

'It's fine. This is my dinner,' he said.

I slapped my forehead.

'Saurabh,' I said, 'that's cellulose. You studied chemistry and biology, right? Humans can't digest cellulose.'

'Some animals and insects can.'

'Yes, but you are not a cow. Or a termite.'

'I am not supposed to digest it. It goes in my stomach and expands. Makes me feel full. I won't feel hungry.'

He popped two more balls into his mouth. I felt nauseous.

'As your trainer, I do not approve. It can clog your digestive system. It is seriously bad for you.'

I picked up the cotton balls and went to the bathroom. I returned after flushing them down the toilet.

'Why did you throw them? I want fast results,' Saurabh said, sounding frustrated.

'Not this way. Anyway, you said you found something in Siya's phone?'

Saurabh opened his laptop.

'Fine, let's just discuss the case,' Saurabh said. 'Yes, I found something interesting in her phone.'

'Good, but first tell me what happened. Why did you decide to go on this horrible cotton-ball diet that would classify as an eating disorder?'

'Leave it. You met Alia Arora today, right? Anything worthwhile she told you?'

'No,' I said, pushing down his laptop screen. 'I want to listen to my best friend first. Case later.'

Saurabh kept his laptop aside and dramatically waved his hands as he spoke to me.

'I can't get a date. Everyone chickens out at the last minute, or friend zones me, or calls me a teddy bear and never phones back. Because. I am. Fat,' Saurabh said.

'Who now?'

'Forget that. Why am I not getting thin?'

'Saurabh, give it time. Six to nine months. You will get in shape. Don't—'

Before I could finish my sentence, Saurabh ran to the bathroom. I heard the sound of retching as he puked out strands of cotton mixed with orange juice.

'It came out. All the cotton,' Saurabh said.

'See,' I said, 'fitness is patience.'

'I hate patience. Anyway, let's talk about Siya. Or rather, who Siya was talking to,' Saurabh said and opened his laptop again.

'Yes, who?' I said.

'She chatted on Telegram with someone called Roy,' Saurabh said.

'Roy?'

'Did we see that name anywhere in the police files? Friend, parent of friend, acquaintance, anyone?'

'No,' I said.

'Did Alia Arora mention anyone called Roy?'

'No. But I'll ask her. What kind of chats did Siya have with Roy?'

'Strange and creepy stuff. See for yourself.'

'Really?'

Saurabh turned his laptop screen towards me.

'I only found some screenshots that Siya took and deleted later. I also managed to retrieve one archived chat.'

'Good work,' I said as I flipped through the screenshots on Saurabh's laptop screen. I read the chat.

Roy: Do you miss me?

Siya: No! Haha.

Roy: C'mon, a little?

Siya: Dunno. Maybe.

Roy: How was school?

Siya: Normal. Aryan still behaving like an ass.

Roy: How?

Siya: Talks to Parvathy all the time. In front of me. Deliberately, of course.

Roy: He's an idiot. Doesn't realise how special you are.

Siya: Am not ☹

Roy: Of course you are. You are my favourite.

Siya: Yeah, right. How have you been?

Roy: Just busy with work.

I looked up at Saurabh.

'Work? Is this guy all grown up?'

'Keep reading, bhai.'

I flipped to the next screenshot.

Roy: We haven't done our secret naughty chats for a long while.

Siya: Don't feel like it.

Roy: Why, baby?

Siya: I hate my parents.

Roy: What happened?

Siya: They fight all the time.

Roy: And ignore you?

Siya: Yes. It's like I don't exist. Or they don't care if I do.

Roy: What do they fight about?

Siya: My grandmother. Oh, and I think my father has a girlfriend in office.

Roy: Really? Your mother knows?

Siya: Yes. They had a big blowout last night. Gosh, I feel like running away.

I looked up from the chat at Saurabh. I tapped the screen where it said 'running away'.

'You saw this?'

'I am literally scrolling through these with you. I downloaded them and then that Rohini busted my mood. Didn't get a chance to see them.'

'Rohini?'

'The girl I had fixed a date with. Before she cancelled, of course.'

'Oh,' I said.

'Forget it. Let's get back to Roy.'

'Okay, when did Siya have these chats with Roy?'

Saurabh checked the meta file of the screenshots.

'Three months before she disappeared.'

'We need to find out who this Roy is.'

'Yes. Let me open that archive chat. It is a much longer one.'

Saurabh took the laptop from me. I heard frantic keystrokes as he retrieved the archived file and dumped the output to a readable text format.

Roy: Send me a picture of your cute feet.

Siya: You are weird!

Roy: Just one. Please!

Siya: Really, my feet? Why?

Roy: They are beautiful. Like the rest of you.

Siya: What do I get?

Roy: I'll order your favourite hairbands for you.

Siya: Really?

Roy: Ya. Like last time, I'll mail them to your school. Which ones do you like?

Siya: The pink butterfly ones. And the one with the ladybirds.

Roy: Done!

Siya: Thank you!

Roy: Welcome. I wish you were older. I would marry you.

Siya: I don't want to get married. Marriage sucks. Seen my parents.

Roy: We would be different. Anyway, my pic?

Siya: Okay, wait.

After Siya sent a picture of her feet, the chat continued. Roy asked for some more pictures. He promised to buy her a new dress in exchange for a swimsuit picture.

'He's sick, whoever he is,' I said.

'I also retrieved permanently deleted pictures on Siya's phone. The police could not find them. I did. Have a look.' Saurabh clicked some keys to reveal a set of photos. I saw

Siya's selfies, in which she pouted in an unusually sexy manner, especially for her age. In one, she wore a towel, and her shoulders and legs were bare. I also saw a dozen photos of just her legs and feet.

'Disturbing,' I said.

'And sick,' Saurabh said. 'This Roy is definitely our suspect, whoever he is.'

'You can't find out anything about his identity from the chats?'

'Telegram allows one to be anonymous. I couldn't locate his phone number, email or IP address.'

'Alia knows nothing about all this. She never mentioned it today.'

'Oh, how did it go with Alia today?'

I paused, wondering what to tell him. I decided to tell him the truth and recounted my entire meeting.

'Pedicures? With your client?' Saurabh said.

'I told you. That's the only place that made sense.'

'Show me your feet,' he said, pulling up my left calf.

'No,' I said, kicking his stomach. 'Don't be a creep like Roy.'

'Hmm, your feet do look nice. Be careful, bhai.'

'About what?'

'Alia is married.'

'What? Me and Alia? Are you mad?'

'No, but feelings can drive us mad.'

'I don't have feelings for Alia.'

'You heard her personal problems when she came home. Today you spent two hours in a beauty salon together. You had a pedicure for the first time in your life. All this for her. Would you do it for any other client?'

'Shut up, Saurabh,' I said, agitated.

'Bhai, I have lived with you for five years. I am a detective too. Give me some credit.'

I shook my head and stood up to leave his room.

'Swear on your mother you are not attracted to her,' he said.

'What are we? Primary school kids?'

'Do it then. Mother swear?'

'I swear I want to solve this case more than anything else. So let's find Roy, okay?' I said and shut the door hard behind me as I exited his room.

I ran my newly smooth feet against the bedsheet. Questions shot through my head: *Who is Roy? Who are these creepy people who ask twelve-year-old girls for pictures?*

I tossed and turned in bed, unable to sleep. I thought of Alia.

I remembered how she looked that afternoon, beautiful yet vulnerable. I remembered how she had leaned over to talk to me. She had opened up to me so much.

I could still smell the waft of perfume that came from her hair. Was Saurabh right? Did I have some feelings or some kind of an attraction for her?

No, Keshav. This will be completely wrong, a loud voice said in my head. What was this voice? My conscience?

I turned on my side.

Keshav, calm down. You have a good-looking client. Learn to deal with it. Be professional, my conscience knocked sense into my head.

Of course, I am professional, I told myself.

How dare Golu insinuate I had feelings for a married client? And why the hell did he have to say it? Now it wouldn't stop playing in my head.

Sleep evaded me. I got out of bed and went out to the balcony. I looked at the midnight skyline of Gurugram, its residential towers all around me. I could see the garden below, pitch dark at this time. I leaned against the ledge of the balcony and took a deep breath of the relatively less polluted air at this time of the night. My eyes went to the tower opposite mine, about twenty metres away. I could identify Alia's apartment, exactly one floor below ours. One of the rooms had its lights on. Questions formed in my head again. Was it her bedroom? Were she and Manish talking? Were they fighting? Or were they making love?

Keshav, it doesn't concern you, my Mr Do-good Conscience scolded me again. I nodded. It didn't matter. Still, I checked WhatsApp on my phone. I saw that Alia was online. Why the hell had I checked that? I looked at her display picture. She had Siya's 'Missing Child' poster as her DP. She had put this poster up all over Gurugram and also on the internet.

'Hi.' It was a message from Alia. I jumped back. Why had she messaged me right then? Did she know I was stalking her?

I looked at her apartment. I didn't see her at the balcony or near a window.

'Hi,' I replied. My heart beat fast.

'Sorry to message so late. I saw you online so thought of taking a chance,' she messaged.

I was checking if you were online, I wanted to say. Of course I didn't.

'What's up?' I replied.

'Having my usual insomniac night.'

'Oh, okay,' I said.

'Found something else on Siya's phone?'

'Yes. Need to talk to you about that.'

'What?'

I didn't want to break the news of a grown-up man chatting up her daughter over WhatsApp.

'I'll tell you in person. Hard to do it over the phone.'

'Sure, tomorrow?'

'Yes.'

'All good otherwise with you?'

'Yes.'

See, I can be professional. I can reply to her messages with a simple 'yes'.

'You were really supportive today. Thanks for coming to the salon. And being an amazing listener. Meant a lot.'

'You are welcome.'

Again I had given a formal reply, just like one would to a client.

'How are your feet?' Alia messaged.

This isn't connected to the case, I wanted to tell her.

'Smooth,' I said instead.

She replied with a smiley emoji.

'I better let you sleep now,' she typed after a pause.

'Good night,' I typed back a client-appropriate response.

'Good night, Keshav. Sweet dreams,' she replied. She followed it up with several hug and zzz emojis.

I kept staring at the hug emojis and wondered why she had sent them to me. I was overthinking the emojis, perhaps even more than the people who invented emojis.

'Keshav? Is that you?' My mother's voice startled me.

'Ma?' I said. 'You scared me.'

'You scared me! Standing in the balcony in the middle of the night.'

My mother had woken up to fill her water bottle.

'Why aren't you sleeping?' she said.

'Nothing,' I said. 'I woke up for water too.'

'And you thought you will find it in the balcony?'

'No,' I said and smiled. 'I will go sleep.'

'These phones have become like a disease. You are addicted to your mobile.'

'I am not, Ma. I just checked it for a second.'

'I saw you typing and chatting on the phone. Who are you talking to so late?'

'Just replying to some work messages,' I said.

'Work? The only work you have is your studies.'

'I have the case too. It's okay, Ma,' I said. 'You go sleep now.'

I walked back to my bedroom.

'Oh, is it that Tower B girl? Were you chatting with Alia Arora?' she said, following me.

'Goodnight, Ma. Sweet dreams,' I said and shut the door behind me.

Chapter 25

'Only scrambled egg whites? Is this breakfast? You serious?' Saurabh said.

'Better than cotton balls and far more nutritious,' I said.

'They taste like used condoms.'

'You have tasted used condoms?'

'Disgusting,' he said. 'Please, at least let me have brown toast.'

'You said you want faster results,' I said.

He reach out for the ketchup bottle on the dining table. I pulled it away.

That's what you get for planting weird thoughts in my head about Alia.

'Ketchup has sugar,' I said.

'Come on, bhai. Ketchup calories don't count.'

'They do. Now do you want the egg whites or would you like to skip breakfast?'

He ate with a disgusted expression.

I transferred the contents of Siya's phone from Saurabh's computer to my own laptop.

'I have a meeting with Alia today. I'll talk to her about Roy,' I said.

'When did that meeting get fixed?'

'Last night,' I said, 'after you showed me Roy's chats.'

'You messaged her that late?'

'She messaged me first, Saurabh. Now leave. You will get late for work.'

After Saurabh left, I sat at my study table in my room. I had to read about Central Asian and Greco-Bactrian elements in Gandhara art. Why did future cops need to learn all this?

My phone pinged.

'Good morning!' Alia messaged, along with a smiley emoji.

I shut my boring textbook and picked up my phone.

'Good morning,' I replied.

'What's the plan? We meeting today?' she messaged.

'Yes.'

'We can't meet at your place, right?'

I bit my lip as I wondered what to reply.

'Ideally, no. Parents are at home. Don't want another lecture from my father.'

'What happened?'

'Nothing. His default mode is grumpy. He needs any excuse to take off. My being aimless in life. Marriage. My studies. Same old.'

'I am sorry.'

'Don't be. Anyway, I have all the information on my laptop. We need a quiet place to meet, that's all.'

'Listen, come to my place. Silly to keep going out when we live in the same complex.'

'How? You said I have to register downstairs. Manish won't like it.'

'Can you sign in as some random repairman? Like you came to fix something in my place?'

'Really? Like an electrician or a plumber?'

'No!' she said and sent two laugh emojis.

'Then?'

'Wi-Fi.'

'What?'

'Say you have come to check the Wi-Fi. You can definitely pass off as a good IT guy.'

'But how? They will ask me to put in my details in the register.'

'Scribble something illegible in it. Add a computer company name. They won't care. I'll anyway inform them I am expecting the Wi-Fi guy.'

'Oh, okay,' I said, unsure about her request.

'Sorry, am I asking too much?'

'What about your maid?'

'Neelu's gone to Khari Baoli with my mother-in-law.'

'Old Delhi?'

'To buy fresh spices. My in-laws are particular about their food.'

Chapter 26

'Heard your Wi-Fi is slow, madam?' I said when Alia opened the door of her apartment. She wore a peach sleeveless T-shirt and black three-quarter fitted yoga pants. A guard from the Tower B entrance had accompanied me to the sixteenth floor.

'Huh? Oh, yes, thank you, guard bhaiya,' Alia said.

The building guard smiled and left. I walked into the apartment and she shut the door behind me.

'Oh my God,' she said. 'I almost couldn't tell it's you. What is all this? Cap? Cables?'

I had worn Saurabh's Cybersafe company cap, which had the company logo of a computer with a stethoscope surrounding it. It helped me look like a computer repair guy. I had also carried as many spare cables I could find in my house.

'Might as well play the part,' I said and smiled.

I kept my laptop on her granite dining table and looked around. Alia's apartment was nearly double the size of my parents' home. Her living room was filled with plush, expensive furnishings. We had simple light fixtures in our living room ceiling. Alia's living room had a false ceiling, concealed lighting and two crystal chandeliers. Persian rugs covered the floor. Long minimalist grey sofas ran along two walls, with a long, all-glass coffee table in between.

Alia picked up a blue yoga mat spread out on the Persian rug.

'Sorry, I just finished an online yoga class,' she said, deftly rolling up the mat. 'Coffee?'

'No, it's okay,' I said, as I took in the expensive surroundings.

'I am making one for myself anyway. Try it, it's good.'

'Fine,' I said.

I watched her as she walked back to the kitchen. The black of her fitted pants contrasted with the fair complexion of her calves. She had a fit body, which made her look younger than her age.

Why doesn't Saurabh look like this in fitness clothes, I wondered. *Why does he look like a baby hippo in diapers instead?*

'Sugar?' she said from the kitchen.

'One spoon,' I said.

I heard the automatic coffee machine whirr for a while as it ground fresh beans. Rich people don't make instant coffee. They grind the beans fresh for every cup.

She returned with two mugs of coffee and handed one to me.

We sat next to each other on the dining chairs. She sipped her coffee, holding the mug in both hands, and leaned forward to have a better look at my laptop. I avoided looking at her legs and turned my eyes to the screen.

'Heard of anyone called Roy?' I said.

'Roy who?'

'Anyone you know? Or Siya mentioned?'

Alia shook her head.

'Okay, I am going to show you some disturbing stuff.'

'Go ahead,' Alia said, taking a deep breath.

I went through Siya's chats with Roy. Alia kept her coffee mug down and placed a hand over her mouth as she read the contents on the screen.

'What is all this? I had no idea,' Alia said.

'We need to find Roy,' I said.

'Who the fuck is this Roy? Is he the one who took Siya?'

'We are trying to figure it all out,' I said, folding my laptop shut.

Alia paced around the living room. I remained silent.

She sat down on one of the sofas. She spoke out loud, mostly to herself, 'We neglected her. Manish did. I did.'

I left the dining table and sat opposite her. Alia continued to talk.

'Our fights took a toll on her.'

I remained silent. She looked out towards the balcony and mumbled, 'It's hard. To think of the past. The regrets. If only I had done this differently, maybe she would still be here. It's hard being in the present. Am I doing enough to find her? Am I being too normal if I do a yoga class to keep me sane? Should I feel guilty if I eat lunch? It's hard to think about the future. What am I living for? They all tell me to stop looking, but seriously, what the hell do I do with my life otherwise?'

I passed her coffee mug to her.

'Thanks,' she said as she took a sip. 'I need to stop crying.'

'It's okay,' I said.

'No, it's not. I just need to fucking stop crying. I need to be strong to fight them all. The media. My family. This creepy Roy. Everyone.'

Alia paused and spoke after she had composed herself.

'Anyway, what else are you thinking about for the case?'

'Siya mentioned Manish and his colleague.'

'Manish's affair? With that girl Yamini in his sales department? Yeah, he was fucking her.'

'Oh,' I said, keeping a straight face.

'Is that important?'

'Just wondering if she could be involved. If it's a serious relationship, she could be jealous of you and your family.'

'It was not serious. And I suspect there are more.'

I tried to look neutral.

She said, 'The Yamini one, I found out about. I lost my shit. I didn't realise Siya had heard us fight about it. I didn't realise it hurt her so much.'

'It's natural to feel angry if your partner is cheating on you.'

'Partner!' Alia said and smirked.

'These girls. Should we talk to them?' I said.

'You can. All simple, middle-class, small-town girls. I don't think any one of them is behind Siya's disappearance. The police spoke to all of his employees anyway.'

'We will still talk to these girls and double check their alibis, just in case.'

'Fine. Anyway, none of them is jealous of me because of Manish.'

'Why?'

'Because they all eventually find out. That he is a wimp. Not to mention bad in bed. That's the whole point of an affair, isn't it?'

I looked at her, shocked at her words. She smiled.

'Is my straight talk embarrassing you?'

'No,' I said. 'I'm just surprised.'

'You expect me to be this dainty Punjabi bahu always? I was a tomboy in school. This is the real me. Direct. Not politically correct. Is that okay?'

'Yeah,' I said, gulping.

'Good,' she said. She stood up and patted my shoulder. 'Come, let's have lunch.'

'It's delicious. Truly, you are a great cook,' I said.

'This is nothing. You have to try my amma's cooking,' she said.

She had made idiyappams, soft discs of steamed rice-flour noodles, and a coconut milk-based egg curry which had fennel, pepper, chillies, curry leaves and mustard seeds in it.

'Too good,' I said.

'Thank you. You know what is good with this?'

'Water?' I said, taking deep breaths. 'It's spicy.'

'Not water.' Alia laughed. 'Toddy. Wait.'

She went to the kitchen and came back with an earthen vessel with a thin, white translucent liquid that resembled buttermilk. She poured some out into two glasses.

'What's this?'

'Fermented coconut sap, or toddy. Kerala's superfood. I have a special supplier, known only in Malayali circles.'

I took a sip of the cold and slightly sour drink.

'Is this alcoholic?' I said.

'A little. Like it?'

'Does cool off the chilli,' I said.

We moved back to the sofas after lunch.

'Alia, you have to get us access to your family,' I said.

'Trust me, I am working on it. Fighting about it literally every day.'

'I understand.'

'I am taking Suhana and going to Kochi for a few days. That's the only way Manish will agree.'

'As in?'

'I leave the house whenever I am upset and want my way. Takes a trip to Kochi, always.'

'Really?' I said.

'Yeah,' she said.

'Alia, can I talk to your younger daughter? '

'Suhana?'

'Yes, she's the only real witness to what happened that night.'

'She spoke to the police.'

'I know what she said to the police. I feel if I can make her open up in a non-threatening, friendly way, maybe she will reveal something more.'

Alia spoke after a pause.

'She's seven. Kids that young don't open up easily. You have to spend a lot of time with them. Become friends with them. Win their trust.'

'I am ready to do that. I will do whatever it takes.'

'The problem is, without Manish's approval, it is difficult for you to spend a lot of time with her.'

'Yes.'

'She's also very sensitive. She needs to be in a totally calm environment.'

'True,' I said.

'You could always come to Kochi.'

'What?'

'Yeah, Suhana is most relaxed at Amma's place.'

I remained silent, unable to figure out a suitable response. She sensed my hesitation.

'Or maybe I can convince Manish soon. Then you can do it right here. Kind of silly for you to come to Kochi when all of us live here.'

'Yes, that will be best. Whenever possible,' I said.

'Okay. Anything else?'

'That's all for now on the case. We'll try to find Roy somehow.'

'Thank you so much, Keshav, for all the hard work. It's just nice to have someone on my side.'

'You are welcome,' I said and smiled.

'Listen, that toddy was too weak for me. I am going to have a real drink. Would you like one?'

I checked the time. It was 1 p.m.

'Now?'

'Are you the judgmental "oh god she drinks in the afternoon" types?'

'No, I have my parents for that.'

She laughed.

'You have to understand. Suhana finishes school at 3.30 p.m. After that I get no respite. Homework, answering the maid's questions, preparing dinner, Manish coming home, it never stops. This is my only window to enjoy a drink on my own time.'

'I get it. Totally,' I said.

'Am I being irresponsible if I have a drink? I don't drink to feel good, Keshav. It just helps lessen the pain, at least for a while.'

'It's okay, Alia. Please, stop explaining and badgering yourself.'

'Yes, I need to stop being morose again. Okay, vodka?'

'Sure,' I said.

She went up to the bar at the corner of her living room. From an antique wooden cabinet, she took out a bottle of Grey Goose.

'Need soda or Sprite or something?'

'Whatever you are having it with.'

'Me? Just ice and lemon.'

'Same,' I said.

She took the vodka to the kitchen and soon returned with two glasses with vodka, ice and lemon wedges in them. She handed me my drink.

'I don't do this every day, though. I have company today, so that's why,' Alia said.

'I told you. I am not judging.'

'Good, you better not. I am your client,' she said and grinned.

I nodded and smiled.

'I am kidding,' she said and tapped my shoulder. 'Please treat me like a friend. I need some real friends.'

'I am sure you have many,' I said.

'Nope. Everyone in my husband's high society circles is fake. The women in the Icon are gossipy. Bitching about me behind my back.'

'I don't have many friends either. Only Saurabh,' I said.

'He seems sweet,' Alia said.

She slipped off the sofa to sit cross-legged on the carpet.

'Mind if I sit like this? I am trying to improve my posture. Advised in my yoga practice.'

'No problem,' I said. 'I guess this advice also includes sipping vodka while doing your practice?'

'Shut up,' she said and laughed.

We finished one drink. She wanted a second. I offered to make it this time.

'I told you so much about me. I don't know anything about you,' Alia said, taking a sip of her next drink.

'What do you want to know?' I said.

'Anything. What's going on at home?'

'My parents,' I said and sighed. 'They are after me to sort out my professional and personal life.'

'Marriage is overrated. Career, of course, is important. I wish I hadn't given up modelling. Who quits at eighteen! Only idiots.'

'You got married. Became a mother.'

'Exactly, stupid me,' she said and fell silent, lost in her own thoughts.

'When do you leave for Kochi?' I said to break the awkward silence.

'In four days. Suhana's school has a mid-term break then.'

'Is going to Kochi the only way to get Manish on board?'

'The only way I know. Listen, Keshav, this is weird. You up on the sofa and me on the floor. I have to strain my neck to look at you.'

'Oh,' I said. 'Sorry.'

I slid down from the sofa to sit on the rug as well. The vodka had begun to take its effect. I found myself more at peace and less inhibited. She went to the bar again and came back with a third round of drinks for both of us.

'I should stop,' I said, even as I took the glass.

'Why? Are you driving back to your tower?' she said and laughed.

I checked the time on my watch. It was 2 p.m.

'Don't worry, I will myself kick you out at 3. I have to pick up Suhana at 3.30.'

'You can go to Suhana's school after three drinks?'

'Yeah, I only wait in the car outside. Suhana comes to the gate.'

'Cool,' I said and took a sip.

'I'll make sure none of the moms see me. The ones that go …' Alia began, switching to a high-pitched falsetto, '"… oh, that Alia Arora smelled of vodka in the afternoon. Her daughter went missing, no?"'

'I am sorry …' I said.

'Why are you sorry, Mr Detective? It's not your fault …' she said and smiled.

'That people talk like that.'

'People are assholes. I wish there were no people in this world,' Alia said.

I smiled at her statement. She spoke again.

'Okay, tell me more about you. Why are your parents trying to find you a girl? No girlfriends?'

'My parents are jobless. They need my marriage project for timepass. It's like this reality show for them.'

Alia laughed.

'You didn't answer my second question. Any girlfriends?'

I looked into her eyes a second longer than I should have.

'I am single.'

'Always have been?'

'No. But have been single for a while now,' I said. I looked at the condensation droplets on my glass to break eye contact with her.

Alia spoke after a pause.

'Someone broke your heart. Real bad.'

I looked at her, surprised.

'What?' Alia said and smiled. 'Am I right?'

'Are you the detective or me?'

'Ah, see,' Alia said and smiled. 'I knew it.'

'The name of my detective agency is Z Detectives. The Z stands for Zara, my first girlfriend.'

'Wow, someone has a story.'

'Indeed.'

'Want to share it?'

'Another time?'

'Sure,' she said and smiled.

I smiled back at her. I noticed how beautiful she looked, especially with her cheeks pink from the drinking.

'How do I give you updates on the case while you are in Kochi?' I said.

'Call me whenever. No restrictions there at all.'

'Have a good trip,' I said.

I had to leave. I didn't want to. I continued to look at her.

'I should go,' I said and reluctantly stood up. I picked up my laptop and the cables from the dining table and wore my cap again.

'Will you miss me?' Alia said.

'What?' I said and looked at her, surprised.

'Nothing,' Alia said and smiled. 'You look a little sad to have to leave.'

'Huh? No,' I said.

She walked up to stand close to me. Mere inches separated us.

'I will miss you, so try to miss me a little, okay?' she said.

We looked into each other's eyes.

I managed a coherent and sensible sentence despite my vodka-soaked brain.

'It's not right for us to have such feelings.'

'Do feelings always come based on what is right and wrong? In fact, do they ever?'

I would like to say she leaned towards me. It would help to deflect the moral blame for what happened next. However, it could well be that I moved towards her. Our lips touched. We just pecked. There was no smooching, wild kissing or frantic making out. But for exactly a quarter of a second, I felt her lips on mine.

'I better go,' I said as the realisation of what had happened dawned on me.

'What?' Alia said, surprised.

'Yes,' I said, adjusting my laptop bag.

'It's only 2.30.'

'Yeah, I want to leave while there is still time,' I said.

Chapter 27

'When is your flight?' I messaged Alia.

I had typed and deleted this question twenty times on my phone in the last three days. She had called me earlier. I had ignored her call. I had overlooked her messages too. Finally, I pressed 'send' on the message the night before she was to leave.

Saurabh was sitting in my room.

'Are you even listening to me?' he said.

I lay in bed, wondering when Alia would respond. I had avoided her for three days. Now I wanted a reply in three seconds.

'Huh? Yes, I am,' I said, tossing my phone aside.

'Who are you messaging so late anyway?'

'No one,' I said. 'What were you saying?'

'About Roy. If he's contacted her on Telegram, he is likely to be connected to her on another platform as well.'

'Like?'

'He could be following Siya on social media.'

'Siya only had Instagram. We analysed all her followers there, right?' I said.

'Yes. Almost all.'

'Almost?'

'Most are her friends. Some accounts seem fake. The usernames are fake names.'

'It is a private account, so Siya would have approved all followers. So even the fake usernames are likely to be her friends only. They are called FakeInstas or Finstas, fake Instagram accounts. Sometimes kids make them to avoid parents checking on them,' I said.

The chair creaked as Saurabh sat up straight.

'Okay, so you mean Roy could be using a FakeInsta to follow her too?' he said.

'Maybe. Worth checking out. We need to check these fake accounts following Siya.'

My phone pinged.

'Tomo evening. 6 p.m. Indigo. Why?' Alia messaged me.

'Nothing,' I replied.

'Where have you been? You didn't return my call.'

'Yeah, sorry. Busy working with Saurabh to locate Roy.'

'Any luck?'

'Trying,' I replied.

'Bhai? You listening?' Saurabh kicked my shin with his foot.

'Huh?' I said, looking up from my phone.

'Seriously, who are you chatting with?'

'No one. Sorry, repeat what you just said.'

'I said we need access to Siya's Instagram account. Her login and password.'

'Her mother should have it,' I said.

Right at that moment, Alia messaged me again. I read her message.

'You are being unresponsive and weird. Is this about that afternoon?'

'I am going to take that away from you,' Saurabh said. He climbed to the bed and snatched my phone.

'Saurabh,' I yelled out loud. 'Give me my phone back. Right now.'

'Who the hell are you messaging?'

He glanced at my screen. He saw the last few messages.

'You are talking to Alia?' Saurabh said, eyes on my phone screen. 'What afternoon is she talking about?'

'Nothing, Golu. Seriously, stop reading my private conversation. Not cool.'

Saurabh saw the anger on my face. He threw the phone back on the bed towards me.

Meanwhile, Alia had sent another message.

'See, again. You read my message but are not responding.'

'One sec, Alia. Be right back,' I replied. I kept my phone aside, on my bedside.

'Yes, sorry, Golu. Let's focus. Siya's Instagram login details, right?'

'Bhai, why did Alia say you were unresponsive and weird?'

'Because I didn't reply to her message.'

'She called you weird for that? That sounds more like a friend than a client.'

'It's okay, she talks like that. So we get into Siya's Instagram. Then check all her followers, right?'

'What happened that afternoon?' Saurabh said.

'I gave her an update. Showed her Roy's chats.'

'And?'

'Nothing. Can we get back to Siya's Instagram?'

Saurabh continued to stare at me.

I looked away.

'Bhai, how long have we been best friends?' Saurabh said.

'Five years?'

'Yes. Have we ever hidden anything from each other?'

'No, but some things are private, right?'

'I always tell you about every girl. Even when they friend zone or rakhi zone me.'

'Yes, you do, Golu.'

Saurabh shrugged and looked at me, waiting for a response.

'Nothing much happened,' I said, my head down.

'But something happened? Oh my God. I was right, wasn't I?'

I shrugged.

'You like her, don't you?'

I remained silent.

'What exactly happened?' Saurabh said.

I looked at Saurabh. I never hid anything from him. Although, for something like this he could be as judgmental as my seventeenth-century parents.

'If you tell my parents ...' I said.

'Mother promise, I won't,' he said, pinching his neck.

'And you won't judge?'

'Fine.'

'It was just a peck.'

'Peck?'

'Yes, just that. Honestly, one inconsequential half-a-second dry peck.'

'Like a kiss?'

'Like the start of a kiss. That's it.'

'On the lips?'

'No, on the elbow.'

'Elbow?'

'No, you idiot. Of course on the lips. Where else?'

'Oh my God. You kissed a married lady,' Saurabh said, like I had broken a temple or burnt the national flag.

'Fuck you, Saurabh. You said you won't judge.'

'But oh my God, she has two kids and a husband. She lives in the same building as us.'

I took a pillow from the bed and threw it hard across his face.

'Calm the fuck down,' I said, 'and speak softly. Papa and Ma will hear.'

'They are sleeping. And I am trying not to judge. I really am,' Saurabh said and counted on his fingers, 'Wife. Mother. Client. Neighbour. Parents disapprove. Bhai, this is wrong on so many levels, it will take a lot of work to unjudge.'

'You think I don't know all this? That is why I left immediately. Minimised communication. I know it is wrong too. Okay?'

'But did you start it or did she?'

'We both did.'

'But someone has to make the first—'

'Shut up and listen. I had a weak moment. Frankly, it is you who flooded me with thoughts like that.'

'I did? I caused the peck? What the heck!'

'Yes, you. My parents also hinted at that possibility. So I started thinking all that.'

'Oh, if I suggest you are attracted to the ninety-year-old

grandmother of my boss Jacob, you will just go kiss grandma in the afternoon, right?'

'That's a gross example.'

'Don't blame me. Or Uncle and Aunty. This is all you. And that Alia Arora.'

'I take the blame. Fine. Nothing else will happen now. From now on, we just work on the case.'

'Oh, we are still doing the case?'

'Yes, there is a missing child, Saurabh. She could be out there.'

'Yeah, I am sure that's the only reason you are doing this case.'

'Are you being sarcastic?'

Saurabh stood up from the study chair.

'I better go sleep. You get back to your phone. You don't want to be, what did she say, weird and unresponsive.'

'What about Siya's Instagram?' I said in a firm voice. 'Let's work, okay?'

'Ask Alia Arora for her daughter's account details. It'll give you another excuse to chat with her,' he said.

Before I could respond, he slammed the bedroom door behind him.

I decided to tackle Saurabh later. I picked up my phone.

I saw Alia was online.

'I'm sorry. Something came up,' I messaged.

'Hmmm. Are you avoiding me?'

'No, I am not. Listen, do you have Siya's Instagram login and password?'

'I do. Gave it to the police earlier too. Will send you.'

'Thanks. Good night. Have a good trip,' I replied.

'That's abrupt. But good night.'

'Sorry, didn't mean to be rude.'

'You are acting strange since that day.'

'I slipped that afternoon. I am sorry. It's completely my fault.'

'Why are you apologising? Nobody is at fault.'

'You are attractive, I admit it. I should control my feelings and myself.'

'Is it just that, Keshav? My being attractive?'

'What do you mean?'

'You are alone. You needed to feel close to someone. Someone who wouldn't judge you.'

'I don't know.'

'That's what it was for me. After a long time, I felt I could be myself with someone.'

'Same here. But all this is very difficult for me.'

'What's difficult? That I am married?'

'That, of course. But I know myself. I fall hard.'

'Fall?'

'If I catch feelings for someone, I catch them hard. If I care for the person, I get too involved.'

'Do you care for me, Keshav?'

I took a minute as I thought of an answer.

'I do. I care for the case, but yes, even for you.'

'Thank you.'

'It still doesn't make what happened right.'

'No, it doesn't. It doesn't have to happen again.'

'Yes, better that way,' I responded.

'Cool. Listen, I have to go. Manish is shouting at me for being on the phone.'

'Oh, all okay?'

'Yeah, yeah, he just woke up next to me. Good night.'

Somehow, I'd never visualised her chatting with me while her husband slept in the same bed.

'Good night,' I replied and tossed my phone aside.

'Tell me again why you are going to Chennai?' my father said, his eyes on a WhatsApp forward about how Hindus were the most advanced people in the world more than a thousand years ago. The video didn't explain what happened after that and why companies like Amazon and Microsoft weren't founded by brahmins.

'Not Chennai, Kochi,' I said.

'Same only. But why?' he said, removing his glasses as he finished watching the video.

'Kochi is in Kerala. Chennai is in Tamil Nadu. Two completely different states, like Rajasthan and UP.'

'Kerala?' my mother said. She was cutting up a huge cauliflower into little florets.

'Yes, Ma,' I said.

'Rajpurohitji, are you listening? Kerala. Who else is from Kerala?'

'Yes, it's Alia's hometown. I am going there to do some investigations for my case.'

Saurabh walked into the living room. He had kept his bedroom door open and had heard the conversation.

'What investigation exactly, Keshav?' Saurabh said.

I glared at him.

'I need to talk to the little girl, Suhana. But I have to get to know her first. Spend time with her.'

'Really?' Saurabh said. 'Spend time with whom?'

'Suhana. I told you.' I said in a firm voice. 'It's not possible to meet her in a relaxed setting here.'

I gestured to him to remain quiet.

'What about your studies?' my father said.

'I will study there too, Papa. I am taking my books.'

'Why do you have to do this case?'

'Five lakh rupees,' I said, bringing out what I knew would work with my parents.

'What!'

'That's the minimum we get paid for this case, whatever the outcome. If we do find out what happened to Siya, it goes up to twenty lakh rupees.'

'Twenty lakhs?' Ma said, her knife paused at the cauliflower.

'Yes,' I said.

'You negotiated with her? You never told me,' Saurabh said. I ignored him and continued.

'The money is good. The case is interesting. And I need a break anyway. I can bill the trip to the client. I can study there. Can you guys stop questioning my trip?'

'Twenty lakh rupees? Seriously? How rich are some people?' my mother said as she stood up to go to the kitchen.

'The Aroras are loaded. And this is about their daughter,' I said.

'Where will you stay?' Ma said.

'At a hotel. I can bill that to the client too,' I said.

'Banana chips are famous in Kerala. Get some back with you,' my mother said as she went into the kitchen.

I finished packing my suitcase by 1 a.m. Saurabh knocked on my bedroom door.

'You have office later today. Why aren't you sleeping?' I said, letting him in.

'Won't see you for a while, so thought will chat a bit.'

He plonked himself on my bed.

'Like you care,' I said, looking away from him. I removed my strolley from the bed and kept it on the floor. 'Also, I am not going to Mars. I will be one phone call away.'

'Anyway, you checked Siya's Instagram account? Checked her followers?' Saurabh said.

'Yes. Fifteen unknown username accounts are following her. The rest are all known friends.'

'What now?'

'We spoke about this, Golu. We have to explore these unknown ones without raising any suspicion. And see if one of them is Roy.'

'We can't message them from Siya's account. A missing girl's account suddenly becoming active will alert people.'

'Obviously. I will make a new account. For a fake girl called Daisy. Will send follow requests from this Daisy's account to the fifteen unknown ones following Siya. Again, we already discussed all this, Golu. Now go and sleep.'

'Yes, I'm leaving soon,' Saurabh said. He spoke after a pause. 'So Alia and Suhana are in Kochi?'

'Yes, of course. That's why I am going there. To spend time with Suhana.'

'Only Suhana or also her mother?'

I looked up at Saurabh and spoke to him slowly, one word at a time.

'There's nothing going on between Alia and me. We decided it is wrong. We will not go in that direction.'

'And yet you are heading in the direction of Kerala today morning.'

'Good night, Saurabh,' I said.

Saurabh smirked. He slid off the bed but continued to look at me.

'What?' I said.

'Bhai, remember chemistry in school? The lab experiments?' Saurabh said, standing at my bedroom door.

'What? Yes.'

'I recall this experiment. We dropped some potassium in water. Remember that?'

'No. Come to the damn point, please. It's late,' I said, looking at my watch.

'Both water and potassium are pretty harmless when kept apart. But you know what happens if you bring them close?'

'What?'

'Boom, it explodes. Watch some YouTube videos on it. They're fun.'

'And your point is?' I said.

'Be careful. Chemistry is real. Good night.'

Chapter 28

Kochi

316 days missing

'Hi, I am here,' I sent a message to Alia.

'Where?'

I took a picture of the Chinese fishing nets visible from my hotel room window. The nets hung off the fishing boats docked at the pier. The pinkish sunlight came in through their spider web patterns.

'What!' she messaged. 'Are you in Kochi?'

'Fishing boats are hard to find in Gurugram,' I typed back with a smiley.

She called me the next instant.

'You actually came!'

'You were right. This is the best place for me to talk to Suhana in peace.'

'Yes, of course,' Alia said. 'Where are you staying?'

'The Tower House.'

I had taken a room at a heritage hotel that was a restored seventeenth-century lighthouse. The white, low-rise colonial building had a brick-coloured tiled roof. The hotel only had fifteen rooms, each with their own names. My room, called Moens, had a royal four-poster bed, a high ceiling and huge windows with views of the waterfront and the Chinese net fishing boats.

'Oh, your hotel is walking distance from my house. Such a pretty heritage property.'

'You told me your mother lived in Fort Kochi, so I decided to stay here.'

'What a nice surprise. Come home for dinner.'

'You sure?'

'Yes. Meet Amma. Suhana too.'

'Who will you say I am?'

'A weirdo. Who gets unresponsive sometimes.'

'What?'

'I am kidding. I will say the truth. I will tell Amma you are helping me with Siya's case. I will tell Suhana you are Keshav uncle, a friend. Both are true, isn't it?'

'What if Manish finds out?'

'He won't. I hope he does, actually. I don't care. So see you soon?'

'Yes.'

'Will message you the location pin. We are right opposite the Delta Study School.'

'Please have some more, Keshav,' Alia's mother said.

She added more chicken stew to my plate. Alia's mother, Manju Singh had retained her husband's last name, according to the nameplate of her house. She lived in a small, traditional Kerala home with an open courtyard that merged into the living room. The single storey two-bedroom house had a coconut tree in one corner of the courtyard.

We sat on jute mats laid out on the courtyard floor.

'It's enough, ma'am,' I said. Manju added one more appam to Suhana's plate.

'Muthassi, I'm full,' Suhana said.

'You have become so thin! You should have at least two appams.'

'I did,' Suhana said.

'Suhana, come on, be a good girl. Don't waste,' Alia said.

'I hope this food is okay for you. Different from your North Indian cuisine,' Alia's mother said to me. She looked like an older version of Alia, with the same hazel eyes. She looked beautiful and graceful in a traditional white and gold mundum neriyathum.

'I love Kerala food,' I said.

'Alia's father was also from Rajasthan. He used to love our food as well.'

'Alia told me,' I said.

'Thank you for helping Alia. The police and the media messed it up totally,' Manju said.

'Yes, we will do our best,' I said.

'What happened to Siya, I wonder ...' Manju said, her voice wobbling. 'I miss her so much, my cherumakal.'

I looked at Suhana. She was playing with her third appam and seemed distracted. I spoke in a low volume so the little girl couldn't hear me.

'Ms Manju, Alia. I would really prefer if you don't discuss anything related to the case in front of Suhana.'

'Oh, njan kshama chodikkunu,' Manju said.

'She says sorry,' Alia said and turned to Suhana. 'Go wash your hands, vaava.'

'Chocolate?' Suhana said.

'In a little while. Now go read in your room. No TV, okay?'

Suhana skipped away, leaving Alia, Manju and me in the courtyard.

'I have come to Kochi to talk to Suhana. I will need your help for that,' I said.

Two pairs of hazel eyes stared at me.

'Sure,' Manju said. 'Anything we can do?'

'I don't want to talk to her like the police did. I don't want it to be traumatic.'

'What do you mean?' Manju said.

'Questioning her like adults would intimidate her. She won't reveal everything.'

'She did, quite a bit,' Alia said. 'She is a brave girl.'

'We don't know if she had more to say,' I said.

Alia and her mother looked at each other.

'How do you wish to proceed?' Alia said.

'I have to become friends with her. Get to know her well. Talk about several other things before approaching the topic of that night.'

'Will it work?' Manju said.

'Worth a shot,' Alia said. 'It's tough in Gurugram, with school, home and so many constraints. Here, in her grandmother's house, she feels safe and free.'

'I'm glad,' Manju nodded.

'I also feel safe and free here, Amma,' Alia said and gave her mother a hug.

Alia walked me out after dinner. The narrow moonlit cobblestone lane and the old houses of Fort Kochi made it look like a historical, colonial film set. Fort Kochi's quaint streets were the very opposite of Gurugram's crowded, claustrophobic roads.

'Any luck in finding Roy?' she said.

'Trying to find him on Instagram.'

'Let me know if you need anything else,' Alia said.

'Yeah. I just need to meet Suhana often.'

'Sure, have lunch at my place every day. Then spend time with her in the afternoon.'

'Thanks. She can't find out that I am a detective.'

'She doesn't know that.'

'Who does she think I am?'

'I don't think she's given it a thought. I'll tell her you are a neighbour from Delhi who is visiting Kochi for work.'

'Fine. What does she like to do? Something I can do with her?'

'She likes board games. Ludo or Uno.'

'Cool,' I said as we reached the end of the lane. 'I can walk from here. It's just five minutes.'

'I could walk you to your hotel,' Alia said.

'No, it's dark. You will have to walk back alone. I don't feel comfortable with that.'

She looked at me and smiled.

She leaned forward to hug me goodbye.

Stop, my brain shouted, so I extended my arm and offered a handshake instead. She looked at me, somewhat surprised.

I kept my hand outstretched. She smirked as she shook it.

'Thank you for offering your services, Detective Keshav Rajpurohit. Have a good night,' she said.

318 days missing

'Wow, look at that room! I see a four-poster bed behind you. Are you living in a palace?'

'No,' I said and laughed. 'It's a heritage hotel.'

I had video-called Saurabh at his office. I was at the antique study table in my room. My laptop and phone lay in front of me.

'Are those French fries?' I said, noticing the food next to him.

'I wish! Cucumber slices. Cut in long strips like fries,' he said. He lifted one and brought it close to the camera.

'Good,' I said. 'Stay on your diet.'

'Yes. What have you been up to in Kochi?'

'I made an account for a girl called Daisy on Instagram. Daisy220309 is the username.'

'And now Daisy will send follow requests to all the unknown accounts following Siya?'

'Yes. And if Roy likes them young, he will accept it.'

'Nice work,' Saurabh said, chomping on the cucumber.

'This is Daisy's bio. Thirteen, but mature. Aries. Born to spread sunshine. Kerala girl.'

'Don't use the word "mature". May raise suspicion.'

'Okay, how's this: Thirteen. Young but not dumb.'

'Perfect.'

'Display picture?'

'Will find an out of focus, hazy image of a young girl on the internet.'

'Good. But I have an issue,' I said.

'What?'

'Daisy's is a new account. It doesn't have any followers. Roy may get suspicious. In fact, that's why I called you. Need your help.'

'My help?'

'Make thirty more fake accounts. Of Daisy's "classmates".'

'What? Thirty?'

'Yes, make up names. Add cheesy bios. Find random DPs.'

'But thirty accounts? What for?' Saurabh said.

'These accounts will follow each other, including Daisy. We not only have to make a fake Daisy, we have to make an entire fake world for Daisy on Instagram. That's when she will look real.'

'Thirty will take a long time.'

'I'll do half. Done?'

'Okay. How are things otherwise?'

'Good. Yet to open my books.'

'You met Alia Arora?'

'Yes, I did. Went to her house for dinner and met her mother and daughter.'

'Oh. Interesting.'

'I am going to start meeting Suhana from today, for your information.'

'I didn't say anything,' Saurabh said and grinned.

'Say anything crap and I will cut the call.'

'Okay, relax. How was the food?'

'Amazing.'

'I miss food.'

'More than you miss me, I know. Okay, I have to go buy board games. Bye.'

Chapter 29

'Games?' Suhana said excitedly as she clapped her hands.

I pulled out the boxes from the brown paper bag.

'Let's see. I have Ludo, Scrabble, Uno, Cluedo,' I said, placing them in front of her.

She jumped up and down in her pattupavada, a traditional full skirt and blouse which was off-white with a golden border.

'So many games for me?' she squealed.

'For you,' I said.

'Mommy, can I accept the gifts?' Suhana said, looking at her mother. 'Is Uncle a stranger?'

'Yes, you can accept them. Uncle is a friend,' Alia said and smiled. In a maroon saree with a yellow border and jasmine flowers in her just-washed hair, she looked different, and yet, like always, beautiful.

'Yay,' Suhana said.

'What's the magic word?' Alia said.

'Thank you, Uncle. What's your name, Uncle?'

It felt strange to be addressed as uncle. Maybe my parents were right. I was getting old. I should get married soon before every girl in this world started calling me 'uncle'.

'This is Keshav uncle,' Alia said.

'Thank you, Keshav uncle,' Suhana said, hopping on one leg and then the other.

'Would you like to play something now?' I said.

Suhana looked at Alia for approval. Alia nodded.

'Can we play Uno?' Suhana said.

'Yes, I love Uno,' I said.

Suhana picked up the pack of Uno cards.

'I'll help Amma with lunch,' Alia said and left. Suhana and I sat cross-legged in the open courtyard. The mild afternoon sun fell on our faces. She knew the game well. She distributed seven cards each to both of us. We fanned them out in our hands.

The game involves throwing your cards down, subject to various rules like matching colours, wildcards, penalties and several other variations. The winner is the person who gets rid of all their cards first.

Suhana played the game much better than I did.

'Uno,' she screamed as per the game rules, when she had exactly one card left. I counted mine. I had eight.

'Yay! I won,' Suhana said, placing her final card down. She stood up from the floor and did a happy dance, her pigtails bouncing.

'Mommy,' Suhana shouted out to her mother, 'I won!'

'Smartypants,' I heard Alia say from the kitchen.

'Another game?' Suhana said. I nodded. She and I played Uno for the next one hour. She won every single time. Each time she danced, her pattupavada whirling around her, to express her joy.

'I am the winner. You are the loser,' Suhana said in a sing-song voice.

'Shh. No need to call anyone a loser,' Alia said, as she came with a tray carrying the lunch dishes.

'But Uncle lost,' Suhana said. I laughed.

I helped Alia arrange the food on the floor.

'I am horrible at Uno. You have to teach me, Suhana,' I said.

'No. I won't teach you,' Suhana said, wiggling a thumb at me.

'Why?' Alia said.

'How will I win then?' Suhana said, packing the Uno cards into the box.

'You are too good, Suhana,' I said.

'That's why I am the winner,' she said, swinging her arms.

'Ah, so this is the famous Kashi Art Café,' I said. We sat on a bench at one of the stone tables. An art installation, comprising eight steel pots of decreasing size, lay in the middle of the leafy courtyard. Paintings and sculptures adorned the walls and black wooden pillars. The café, set up in an old Dutch house, serves as an art gallery as well. It is also a place for tourists and artists to linger over coffee. 'You knew about this place?' Alia said, surprised.

'You told me. About meeting Manish here.'

'Ah,' Alia said. 'You are a good listener.'

'It's my job,' I said and smiled.

'Two fresh ground coffees. Homemade cake and a banana cream pie,' she ordered for us.

'Cakes and pies?'

'You have to try it. It's okay, you're on a break.'

Our food and coffee arrived.

'The pie is delicious,' I said.

'Told you it's great. Manish loves it. He has to have it every time he comes here.'

Her statement pinched me. Somehow, the pie didn't seem so special anymore.

Why the hell is the mention of Manish bothering me?

I decided to change the topic.

'Suhana is really smart,' I said.

'You didn't just let her win?'

'She beat me fair and square.'

'You have so much patience. You played with her for hours.'

'I enjoy her company. I never knew kids could be so much fun,' I said.

Alia smiled.

'Someone is definitely ready for marriage and family,' she said.

I smiled and looked at my coffee.

'We cool, right?' she said after a pause.

'Yes,' I said. In the sunlight her eyes were almost transparent.

Don't look at her lips next, I told myself.

'I made a fake account on Instagram. A girl called Daisy. We're going to use it to get to Roy,' I said.

'I still can't believe a paedophile was talking to my daughter,' Alia said.

'The internet makes it easy for anyone to contact anyone.'

'I should have been more careful. Kept an eye on her,' she said.

'Stop blaming yourself,' I said.

'You think he did something to Siya?' Alia said.

'One step at a time,' I said. 'Let us first find him.'

I added a line to Daisy's bio.

25% Portuguese by blood. 100% Indian by heart.

'Is she Goan?' Saurabh said when he saw her profile.

'Yes, Goan parents with a Portuguese grandmother. Her dad works at a shipping company. He was in Goa earlier but posted in Kochi now, where Daisy lives as well.'

'Nice. Tell me more about your Daisy. Let me quiz you more to see if it all adds up.'

'Daisy Fernandes. Goes to the Delta Study School in Kochi. Class VIII.'

'Favourite subject?'

'Loves geometry. Did you see the new geometry box she bought? I put up a post.'

'Yes, I did. Good. I saw some of her pictures too. She's a bit too fair.'

'Had to buy stock images. Most of them were of American or European girls. That's why I changed her bio to European mix.'

'Good, bhai, it all adds up. Daisy is up and running,' Saurabh said, after asking me a few more questions about my Daisy.

'Thanks,' I said.

'And you didn't show the full face in any of the posts. That's good too.'

'Yes. You made Daisy's fake friends? I made my fifteen.'

'Yes, sir. I did mine too. So, all thirty friends are ready,' Saurabh said.

'Let's make them all follow each other. Then Daisy looks like a real person.'

We worked till 2 a.m. to make Daisy's friends look real.

'You should sleep,' I said when I saw Saurabh yawn on the video call.

'Almost done now. We ready to send requests?'

'Doing it as we speak. Sent it to all the fifteen FakeInsta accounts following Siya,' I said.

'Let's see if he bites,' Saurabh said.

'Not *Charlie and the Chocolate Factory* again,' Suhana said.

Every afternoon after lunch, Suhana settled down on the mat in the courtyard with a cushion under her head for a nap. I would sit next to her and read her stories. We had followed this routine every day in Kochi for the past week.

'*Matilda*?' I said.

She nodded and placed her palm on her forehead to shade her eyes from the sun.

'Come into the shade,' I said.

She moved the cushion and repositioned herself. She opened her eyes and looked at me. Her eyes weren't hazel like her sister, mother and muthassi. Suhana had dark brown eyes like her father, whom she resembled a lot more than she did her mother.

'Come on, read, Keshav uncle,' she said.

I picked up the Roald Dahl book and read the opening lines.

'It's a funny thing about mothers and fathers. Even when their own child is the most disgusting little blister you could ever imagine, they still think that he or she is wonderful.'

Suhana laughed out loud.

'Say that again. It's so funny,' she said.

I read out the first line three more times, with an exaggerated expression. She dissolved into giggles each time.

'Disgusting little blister,' she repeated, laughing uncontrollably.

Alia stepped out from the kitchen to look at us, smiled and returned to the kitchen.

'You are too funny, Keshav uncle,' Suhana said. I ruffled her hair and opened the book to read again.

'What does "disgusting little blister" mean?' she said.

'You didn't know the meaning? And still laughed so much?'

'Yes, because you say it so funnily.'

'A blister is a small bubble on the skin filled with water. You get it after a burn, or when your shoes don't fit.'

'How can a child be a blister?' she said. 'A child is a person.'

'Yes, it is a figure of speech. Like a really annoying or misbehaving or bad child.'

Suhana nodded.

I opened the book again.

'Maybe that's why the bad man took Siya didi. He thought she was a blister,' Suhana said.

I took a quick look at her. She was looking up at the sky, talking to herself. I had to act calm, like she had said nothing unusual.

'Was she like a blister?' I said, eyes still on the book.

She shook her head.

'Never. Siya didi was very nice. Bad man made a mistake.'

'We should find him and tell him he made a mistake,' I said.

'Yes,' Suhana said, her voice low.

'You miss Siya didi?' I said.

'A lot,' she said.

'How did she go away?'

'Bad man took her at night,' she said. She turned to her side and kept her head on my knee. I spoke after a pause.

'You remember that night, Suhana?'

I felt her nod.

'What did bad man look like?'

'I couldn't see. It was too dark.'

'Okay, no problem. What did you see?'

'His knife. His hand.'

'What kind of knife?'

'Like muthassi uses in the kitchen.'

'Big one?'

'Big one.'

I kept my body language and tone relaxed as I spoke in short, simple sentences.

'What about his hand?'

'He had a watch.'

'What kind of watch?'

'Normal.'

'Round or square face?'

'Round.'

'Colour?'

'Don't know.'

'It's okay. Did he have anything else on his hand?'

'Yeah.'

'What?'

'I am sleepy. I want to take a nap.'

'Sure. I will read to you later,' I said. I kept the book aside.

She placed her hands between her head and my knee. Her eyes started to shut. I rocked my knee gently to make her fall asleep.

'Many friendship bands,' she said, looking at the pattern on the jute mat.

'What?'

'Bad man wore many friendship bands.'

'You saw them?'

She nodded. She seemed too sleepy to talk.

'What colour?'

She shrugged.

'Too dark?' I said.

She nodded again.

'I couldn't tell the colour. It was nighttime. He had many

bands. Some tight, some loose,' she said. She was finding it hard to keep her eyes open.

'It's okay, you rest. We will talk later, Suhana.'

'You will read *Matilda* to me later?'

'Sure.'

'Don't leave, okay?'

'I'll try. If I do, I will read to you tomorrow.'

'Why don't you stay at my house forever?'

I smiled and ruffled her hair.

'I have a room in a hotel.'

'But here you get to be with me,' she said. I didn't know about her mother yet, but I had definitely fallen in love with this girl.

'I can't. I have other work. But I will come every day.'

'Promise?' she said, pinkie finger out. I did the same to show her my commitment.

'He had some drawing on his hand.'

I squinted down at her.

'What drawing, Suhana? Where?'

She touched her right forearm with her left index finger.

'Like a tattoo?'

Oh, Suhana, please, please. It would be so helpful if you can describe that tattoo more, I said to myself.

'What kind of drawing? Can you tell me more?'

She shook her head.

'The friendship bands covered it.'

'Okay, no problem. Sleep.'

'Sleep gone now.'

'It will come.'

'I heard bad man talk.'

'Talk? What?'

'He asked Siya didi to go with him.'

'You remember the exact words?'

'Yes. He said, "No sound. Or I kill your brothers and sisters. Come with me quietly. I won't hurt you."'

'Anything else?'

'Yes, he kept saying "chalo, chalo" as they walked out of the room.'

'So English and Hindi mix?'

'Yes.'

'Do you remember what kind of clothes he wore?'

'Couldn't see.'

'Clean or dirty?'

'Clean.'

'Loose or tight?'

'Loose.'

'Anything else?'

'His hair had some oil. It was shining.'

'Oh really?'

'Yes. Didn't smell good though.'

'What kind of smell?'

'Kitchen smell.'

'You are too smart, Suhana. You remember so much.'

'Thank you. But I don't remember more.'

'May I ask you one last question?'

'Yeah.'

'Did his voice sound familiar?'

'Meaning?'

'Like had you heard it before somewhere? Or was it of a complete stranger?'

'Heard it before.'

'Oh,' I said, surprised. 'But you couldn't tell who?'

'No,' she said. Her eyes shut completely as she drifted off to sleep. Mine remained wide open as my mind worked at top speed thinking about everything Suhana had just told me.

Chapter 30

Of the fifteen follow requests I had sent, eight of the unknown accounts had accepted within a day.

I could now check more details on these eight accounts, including all their Instagram posts so far. Most of the accounts seemed to belong to young children. Their posts were about school or hanging out with their classmates. They were perhaps Siya's classmates, who wanted FakeInstas of their own.

'Hi there,' a message flashed on my Instagram. Someone had sent a DM, a direct message, to Daisy. The message came from an account called 'SaveAnimals100'.

'Thanks for the follow request. Accepted!' SaveAnimals100 sent another message.

I sat on the sofa in my room at Tower House. I opened the profile of the SaveAnimals100 account. The bio said: 'I save animals. Purer and more innocent than humans.'

The account's display picture had an image of a baby elephant in the jungle. I checked the posts in the account. It had posted pictures of rescued animals in animal shelters, expressed support for wildlife organisations like PETA and shared photos of cute puppies and kittens. The account holder had not put his or her own picture anywhere. I did see a couple of posts with a black and white silhouette of a man wearing a hat, his back always to the camera.

'Do you like animals, Daisy?' I had another message from the account.

'I do!' I typed back to engage in a conversation. I added emojis of a dog and an elephant as well.

'That's amazing. Do you have any pets?'

'No,' I sent back, along with a sad face.

'Why? Pets are so fun.'

'My parents don't allow it.'

'Oh. Parents don't understand sometimes. Isn't it?'

'Yes.'

'I have two pug puppies right now.'

He sent a picture of two puppies that resembled the dog in the Vodafone ad.

'OMG, so cute. What are their names?' I replied.

'Oreo and Coffee. Both a month old.'

'They are adorable. What's your name?' I replied.

The account answered after a pause.

'Would you like to play with them?'

'I wish! But you didn't tell me your name.'

'Why? Would you like to be friends with me?'

'Depends.'

'Depends on what?'

'If we click.'

'I think we will. You and I both love animals.'

'Yes,' I replied. I added a parrot and a kitten emoji.

'But how can I be friends without knowing your name?' I sent another message, along with a laughter emoji.

'How about we get to know each other better first?'

I decided not to push too much, to avoid suspicion.

'Sure.'

'Okay so you are Daisy. Thirteen years old?'

'Yes. It's in my bio. Ha ha.'

'Where are you?'

'Kochi. Okay, my turn to ask questions.'

'Sure.'

'Are you a guy or a girl? Lol. I don't even know that.'

'I am a guy.'

'How old?'

'Ask something else,' he said, along with the hands-covering-face emoji.

'Which city?'

'Delhi.'

'Oh, I keep coming to Delhi.'

'How come?'

'My grandparents live in Delhi.'

'Nice. Tell me when you are here next.'

'Why?'

'Don't you want to meet Oreo and Coffee?'

'I would love to!!!'

'When do you come next?'

'Next month maybe. When I have my school break.'

'Cool. Let's become good friends until then. What class are you in?'

'Grade VIII.'

'Oh, that's good. You know quite a lot then.'

'Am not that good in studies.'

'That's okay. Even I wasn't. But I am happy now.'

'What do you do?'

'I travel. To see wildlife all over the world is my dream.'

Okay, I had someone engaged in conversation. He did believe Daisy was real. He sounded like a grown-up man. He had also followed Siya from a fake account.

'That's so cool,' I replied.

'Thanks,' he said.

I decided to end the conversation for now to sound more realistic.

'Listen, SaveAnimals100, I have to go. My mom is shouting at me for being on the phone.'

'Parents = Pain,' he replied.

'Absolutely, ha ha.'

'When will you chat with me again?'

'At night. After my parents have slept. Works?'

'Yes. Will check if you are online then.'

'Bye, SaveAnimals100, my new friend who won't tell me his name,' I replied with a sad emoji. I was about to toss my phone aside when he replied.

'Ha ha. Don't be sad. Okay, I will tell you.'

'What?'

'My close friends call me Roy. Okay, bye for now, chat later.'

I jumped up from the sofa as I read his last message.

I sent a WhatsApp message to Saurabh.

'Roy and Daisy are now friends!'

Chapter 31

'Frustrating,' Alia said, 'this "go slow" strategy.'

'I can't escalate the pace with Roy too much. I have to follow his lead,' I said. I had briefed Alia about my chats with Roy on Instagram for the last couple of days.

'We have to wait. I have to build the relationship. Win his trust so he agrees to meet me.'

'For how long? You have been chatting with him for three days,' Alia said in an agitated voice. She was walking me back to my hotel after I had spent the afternoon at her house.

'I need some more time,' I said.

'Why? Let's just fix a place to meet and catch him. Shake him up and make him talk about Siya.'

I shook my head.

'If he senses even the slightest thing amiss, he will block me, rather Daisy, on Instagram. We can never get him after that.'

She didn't answer. We walked in silence until we reached Tower House.

'I am sorry to make you wait,' I said. 'A little more patience, please. A few more days.'

'I have waited 336 days, Keshav.'

'I understand. I'll go as fast as I can.

'Thanks.'

'Anything else I can do for you right now? You seem so stressed.'

'I'll be fine.'

'Coffee?'

'If you want me to feel less stressed, give me company for a real drink. I am sick of coffee.'

The waiter placed two tall glasses of vodka–tonic on our table, along with a bowl of cashew nuts spiced with chillies. We were at one of the corner tables in the lobby of Tower House, which served as a bar-cum-restaurant in the evening. Antique coffee tables and sofas facing the sea dotted the lounge.

I checked my phone. Roy had sent several messages. He wanted to chat. I replied I had homework to do and couldn't talk right then.

'Roy?' Alia said.

'Yeah,' I nodded.

'May I see your chats with him?' she said. She extended her hand.

'I'd rather you didn't. Could be disturbing for you,' I said. I handed her the glass of vodka–tonic instead.

She didn't insist. Both of us took a sip of our drinks. I looked outside the window. The sky had turned golden. A few more visitors, most of them foreigners, had come to the Tower House for their evening cocktails.

'Okay, so what is your exact strategy with Roy?' Alia said. 'How do we actually get him, physically?'

'Let him suggest meeting up.'

'And you will keep talking to the creep until then?'

'I have no choice.'

'What if he doesn't want to meet?'

'Oh, he will. They always push for more.'

'You sure?'

'Yes. He's already started flirting with me, I mean Daisy. Last night he dreamt about my eyes and beautiful hair.'

'Disgusting.'

'Yeah. But the point is, he is escalating it fast. If I play along, he will keep asking for more.'

'And you will just go along with him?'

'Not blindly. I will balance it out.'

'How?'

'Show some resistance. Like any child would. But ultimately, I will also comply a little. Don't worry, Alia, we will get him.'

Alia kept her drink down and looked into my eyes. Her face took on the colour of the pink sunset.

'You seem confident. Have you done this before?' she said.

'Pretended to be a thirteen-year-old and lured a paedophile? Definitely not,' I said.

The waiter came to ask if we needed anything. Alia ordered another round of drinks.

'It's on me,' Alia said as the waiter left.

I smiled.

'Not that I could ever repay you. Thanks, Keshav,' Alia said.

'For what?'

'Suhana. Roy. Coming to Kochi. You are doing so much.'

'I like solving cases. I'll do whatever it takes to catch the culprit. Plus, spending time with Suhana is actually fun. She is very sweet.'

Alia smiled for the first time that evening. I didn't want to discuss the case anymore, lest she became sad again.

'So, you grew up around here?' I said, pointing to the road outside.

'Yes. My school friends and I used to go to Vasco da Gama's church, not far from here.'

We spent the next hour talking about Fort Kochi's history and Alia's childhood. I learnt that Vasco da Gama, the guy who discovered India, had first landed in Fort Kochi.

I told Alia everything I knew about Vasco da Gama. Every Indian student mugs up the year he came, 1498, in history class. We don't discuss how Vasco da Gama organised the trip, without GPS or even knowing the final destination. In the Indian education system, mugging up the year he landed in India is far more important than discussing the explorer's sense of adventure, risk-taking ability or organisational skills. We don't care about all that. We just care about mugging up a pointless year.

'Speaking of the Indian education system,' Alia said, 'how's your Civil Services preparation going?'

'Oh, don't even remind me. I'm supposed to be studying in Kochi as well. I'd rather play with Suhana.'

'Well, you are studying Indian history and heritage right now,' Alia said. 'Look around you. History everywhere.'

I didn't want to look around. Two vodka–tonics down, I only wanted to keep looking at Alia. I should have realised the danger of drinking with her, especially after what had happened last time.

I should stop, I told myself.

'One more round, please. Yes, same, vodka–tonic,' Alia said to the waiter before I could say anything.

'Alia, we have already had two drinks,' I said in a meek voice after the waiter left.

'So?'

'Nothing,' I said. I saw raindrops splatter against the windows as it began to drizzle outside.

'Did you know the tonic water in vodka–tonic has quinine? The British consumed it as a precaution against malaria in India. Mixed it with alcohol, of course.'

'Oh, really?' I said.

'Yes. See, you are learning history. You are studying,' Alia said and laughed. Alcohol made her more cheerful, even if for a short time. I laughed along with her.

The sky outside turned dark. I lost count of the number of drinks we consumed.

'Oh damn,' Alia said, picking up her phone after a long time. 'I have so many missed calls.'

'Your mom?' I said.

'Two from Manish, five from Amma.'

I stood up to move away and give her privacy as she called them back.

She gestured to me to stay, phone to her ear.

'Amma? All okay? Sorry, had the phone on silent,' Alia said. She and her mother began speaking in Malayalam and I couldn't understand.

'Fine, Amma, I will. Yes, right now,' Alia said finally. I finished the last few cashew nuts in the bowl. The waiter came to ask if we needed more drinks. I declined even as Alia intervened.

'One second, Amma,' Alia said and turned to the waiter. 'Yes, one last round please.'

'I am at Tower House, Amma, five minutes away. I'll come in a while. Anyway it's raining right now. You and Suhana eat the attalam please.'

She ended the call and turned to me.

'I am sorry,' she said. 'Manish called me. When I didn't pick up, he called Amma a couple of times. She freaked out and called so many times.'

'Everything okay?'

'Of course. Amma is scared of my in-laws. She's like, "Call him back right now."'

'You should.'

'First time he has called me since I came. Why should I bother?'

'Must be something he wants to say.'

'I'm having a good time, Keshav. Must I spoil my evening?'

I didn't answer. The waiter returned with our drinks. I remained quiet until he had collected our old glasses, placed the new ones and left.

'Oh, okay, I'll call him back,' Alia said. 'He stays silent for two weeks, but I have to call back on the spot. You are like Amma only.'

'I didn't—' I began but she shushed me, pointing to her phone.

'Yes, sorry, I was outside,' she said on the phone. I heard Manish shout on the other end. I couldn't make out his words.

'Manish, calm down. You haven't bothered to check on me for two weeks. Don't pretend to care all of a sudden.'

I found it awkward to listen to a conversation between a husband and wife. Especially when I had started to care about the wife a little too much. I stood up again, to give her privacy, but Alia raised her hand, motioning to me to stay put.

'Fine, divorce me if you want to. You think that's a threat?' Alia said on the phone, her voice loud. Manish screamed something on the other side.

'What's the point of this marriage, anyway? Seriously, if you can't support ...' Alia said, her voice resonating through the entire bar. A waiter came up to us.

Before he could ask her to keep it low, she said, 'One sec, Manish.' She placed the call on mute.

'I am sorry. I will step outside,' Alia said.

'It's raining outside,' I said. I pointed to the window. The drizzle had turned into a downpour.

'Can you give me your room keys? I need to finish this call. Give him a piece of my mind,' Alia said. She extended her hand. I looked at the waiter and Alia in quick succession. I took out the card key from my pocket.

'Room called Moen. First floor,' I said.

'I will show you, madam,' the waiter said. He walked Alia out of the lounge towards the steps going up to the rooms.

I waited in the lobby for forty more minutes, sipping on my drink. I kept an eye on the staircase. Alia did not come down. Maybe they were having a really long fight, I thought.

I messaged her after an hour.

'Done?'

'Give me a few minutes,' she replied.

I kept my phone aside. The waiter asked me if I wanted to order dinner. I assumed Alia would eat with me before going home. I ordered a kadala curry, made with black chana, along with Malabar parottas for the both of us.

She messaged me after ten minutes.

'Finally. Done with the call. So sorry.'

'It's okay. Come, I ordered dinner,' I replied.

'Thanks. I feel so drained. Don't feel like eating.'

'Have something.'

'Fine. Can we eat in your room? I don't want to be with people right now.'

'Okay, I'll ask the waiter to send it up,' I said.

Chapter 32

'That's it. I'll get a good lawyer,' Alia said.

I didn't respond, just listened as she vented. Every two minutes, I'd point to her parotta and curry, urging her to eat. She didn't. She spoke about how Manish had called her an obsessive freak, a psycho and a crazy woman who needed help. He had told her to come back on the next flight with Suhana. She had refused. He wanted her to drop the investigation. Alia had told him she had made progress. Manish didn't want to listen to it anymore. He had threatened divorce instead.

'He thinks I can't fight back. I will. He calls Amma and says I am an irresponsible wife. How dare he!'

'Alia, your food is getting cold. Eat, please,' I said.

'I let his affairs pass. Now I'll bring it all up in court.'

I rolled up the parotta, dipped it in the kadala curry and handed it to her.

'Finish this quickly,' I said, like my mother does to me sometimes. She looked at me, surprised. She ate a couple of bites as she composed herself.

'Sorry I spoke too much,' she said.

'It's okay,' I said. 'You had a rough call.'

'I ruined the evening, didn't I?'

'No, the kadala curry is amazing, isn't it? Okay, finish whatever's left in your plate.'

She looked at me, amused by my instructions.

'C'mon, be a good girl. Don't waste,' I said. I repeated the same lines Alia often used to make Suhana finish her food. She laughed. I joined her as well.

'Why am I telling you my marriage problems? It's not your job to listen to all this,' she said, eating a spoonful of the spicy curry.

'It's not always about the job. Sometimes we have to be there for each other as people.'

She looked at me and smiled. Our eyes met. I wanted to look away from her. I couldn't. She had a little bindi on her forehead. It made her look delicate, or maybe I just felt protective of her in that way today. Her cream salwar kameez glowed in the soft yellow lights of my room. She finished the food and showed me her empty plate. I nodded my approval. She lifted the entire tray of food and kept it aside, in one corner of the room. She walked up to the window and looked outside. The rain had stopped. The streets outside had become calm. Moonlight fell over the sea, causing glittery waves.

'Another drink? she said.

'No way. We've had enough,' I said. I could still feel the buzz from the alcohol I had had earlier. I handed her a glass of water instead.

'Here, have this. Stay hydrated.'

'Are you always this caring?'

'What? It's just water.'

'It's the little things, Keshav. Little acts of caring, kindness and love that make a relationship work.'

Wait a minute, I thought. *Why did she mention the word 'relationship'? In what context?*

'Manish and I lost all this over time. Now, our relationship is broken.'

Ah, so she is saying this with respect to Manish, I said to myself.

'But you are nice, Keshav. You genuinely care. Any girl would be lucky to be with you.'

'Thanks,' I said. 'Let me know when you want to leave.'

'You want to kick me out?'

'No, I meant whenever you want to. It's dark outside. I will walk you home anyway.'

She looked at me and smiled.

'What's so funny?'

'See, you can't help but care.'

'But I just said—'

Before I could complete the sentence, our lips had already met. Only this time we didn't peck like two anxious birds. We kissed in what was the best kiss of my life by an enormous margin.

Lightning flashed outside, perhaps triggered by our planet-shifting, earth-shattering kiss. A few seconds later, the sound of thunder filled the room. However, we didn't stop kissing. Hell, a lightning bolt landing directly on our heads could not have stopped that kiss.

I didn't want to pause for a second. I was afraid that if I did, Uncle Conscience would come back, this time with Aunty Guilt. I was sick and tired of these sane voices in my head telling me to be good all the time. I had had to control myself every time I was near Alia. I had gone to Alia's house, read stories to Suhana and pretended I didn't want Alia more than anything else. I'd had to somehow make peace with the fact that I couldn't have her because she was married.

Her lips felt tender and moist as she continued to kiss me deeply. I held the back of her head with both my hands. Her hair felt soft to touch.

'We can take a second to breathe,' Alia said after five minutes. I took deep gulping breaths. My judgmental relatives, Uncle Conscience and Aunty Guilt, started to ring the doorbell in my head. Fortunately, Alia acted before they could enter the house.

Alia leaned forward to kiss me again. The rain resumed, and raindrops began pelting my window. As it poured outside, I held Alia and made her sit on the four-poster bed.

I kissed her again. I held her shoulders and looked at her beautiful face.

'What?' she said.

'Nothing.'

'Don't overthink it.'

'I am not.'

'So what are you thinking? Tell me.'

'That right now I am the luckiest man on earth.'

Maybe it was the historic hotel building, or the tastefully done up room, or the magnificent four-poster bed. It all seemed destined, right and wonderful. I kissed every part of her face—her eyebrows, cheeks, dimples, eyelids, forehead and lips. I slid off the bed. I went up to the window to draw the curtains.

'Leave them open. I like the moonlight,' she said.

She switched off the bedside lamps, so the soft moonshine was the only light in the room.

I took off Alia's clothes. Her skin literally glowed in the darkness. I could have simply sat there and admired her perfect body all night.

'Come here, Keshav,' she said. She held my hand and drew me closer.

'You are beautiful.'

'Thank you,' she said. 'You make me feel beautiful.'

The sheer fabric hanging from the four-poster bed enveloped us. The sound of rain, her breath and soft moans filled the room. Occasionally, a streak of lightning lit up the room brightly, allowing me to see her body and face clearly for a second.

She kept her fingers intertwined with mine and our eyes remained locked as we made love. Uncle Conscience and Aunty Guilt had been kicked out of my mind.

She kissed my neck and ears, making my entire body quiver.

Why does it have to be so good? Why does it feel like I am making love to my soulmate?

Her fingernails dug deep in my back as both of us finished at the same time.

I fell into her arms, my heart beating frantically. I could practically hear my heartbeat. Sheets of rain continued to beat against the windows. I lay next to her. She turned to my side and clasped my hand.

'Thank you,' she said in a soft voice.

Thank you? What the hell was that? Did I just provide a service or what?

I remained silent. I rolled over and switched on the bedside lamp.

'Say something,' she said.

'What am I supposed to say? You're welcome?'

'How about "my pleasure"?' she laughed.

'That is indeed true,' I said and smiled.

'You liked it?'

'Best I ever had,' I said.

'Ah, I didn't know I was in competition.'

'I didn't mean it like that.'

'Relax,' she said and laughed. 'I take it as a compliment. Thank you.'

I looked up at the sheer fabric over the four-poster bed.

'How did you like it?' I said after a pause.

'I can only compare with Manish,' she said and smiled.

Anger and jealousy bolted through me like the lightning outside. Why did she have to mention him? And why did it bother me so much?

'Forget it,' I said.

She kissed me on the cheek.

'There's no comparison. With Manish, it's a biological process. Something a husband and wife are supposed to do. Not that we do it much, or at all.'

'And with me?'

'You rocked my soul, mister.'

'You did too,' I said.

She spoke after a pause.

'Wow, this is so James Bond. This room, us, you being a detective.'

She kissed me again. I smiled happily at her.

A few minutes later, she sat up and picked up her clothes.

'Don't go,' I said.

'Amma will freak out if it gets too late.'

'Tell her it's raining.'

'But—'

Before she could say anything more, I pulled her back into bed. Tomorrow morning, I might have my annoying relatives back in my head. I had to make the most of tonight.

'I really should go,' she said.

'Leave after a coffee?' I said. I went up to the room kettle and returned with two cups of black coffee.

'Thank you,' she said as I handed her a cup. She used the cup to warm her hands as she took small sips. Both of us sat in silence, on opposite corners of the bed.

Words are unnecessary when everything in the world is perfect. I looked at her. She was lost in thought. I fell more in love with her with every passing second. I even loved the way she sipped her coffee, wrapping both palms around the cup.

'He insisted on a DNA test,' she said, her gaze away from me.

'What?'

'Manish did a DNA test for himself and Siya,' she said.

'Why?' I said.

She shrugged. Tears rolled down her cheeks. I gave her a hug. She buried her face in my chest.

'His mother said Siya didn't look like Manish,' she said.

'What the heck!' I said.

She nodded, her face still in my chest. I gently held her shoulders and pushed them back, to make her face me.

'When?' I said.

Alia leaned back on the huge headboard of the bed and sat facing me.

'Five years ago. Some neighbour saw Siya and Suhana together. Told my mother-in-law, "Suhana is a copy of Manish, but Siya doesn't look like him."'

'Damn. What happened then?'

'She filled Manish's head with all this. He started suspecting me as well.'

'Did he have a real reason to?' I said.

'As in?'

'Like, was there ...' I searched for the right words.

'Keshav? I just told you. The only person I've slept with before you is Manish.'

'Sorry, I didn't mean to ...'

'That's it, right? You see how these aspersions work? Once someone accuses you, it's hard to shake it off. Even you suspected me.'

'I didn't. It's just shocking your own husband would doubt you for no reason.'

'The whole neighbourhood did. Because my mother-in-law wouldn't shut up. There was only one way. Manish did a DNA test. He is Siya's father, and that's what the test said too.'

'I am sorry you had to go through all this.'

'He brought it up on the call today. He had the guts to bring that up again.'

I handed her the coffee cup again.

'You can say something, instead of giving me caffeine.'

'Like what?'

'Like call Manish a jerk. You always become silent when I discuss him.'

'I feel weird commenting on your issues with Manish.'

'Why?'

'He's your husband. It's personal.'

'Oh, you can't say "Fuck Manish", but you can fuck his wife?'

'What?' I said, shocked.

'I am sorry,' Alia said. 'I should go. Where are my clothes?'

She picked up her salwar kameez from the floor.

'Manish is an asshole. And the biggest fucking idiot on this planet,' I said.

'What?' Alia said and smiled, looking at me in surprise.

'Yes, and I hate him.'

'Elaborate?' she said.

'He's an asshole to make you go through what he did. He's

an idiot because he has an amazing woman like you and doesn't value you. And I hate him because ...' I said and became silent mid-sentence.

'Because?'

'... because if he wasn't in the picture, I could have been with you.'

Chapter 33

Is it inappropriate to fall in love with a client? Yes.

Is it wrong to have an affair with a married woman? Absolutely.

Could I have shown better self-control? Of course.

My 'mental' relatives, Uncle Conscience and Aunty Guilt, had returned in the morning in time for breakfast. I held my head to make their interrogation stop. The bedsheets still carried her fragrance. The pillow next to mine had a long strand of hair on it. Sunlight filtered through the windows, illuminating all the immorality that had happened in this room last night. I picked up the phone to check the time. It was 11 a.m. I had no messages from her. I did, however, have a couple of messages from Roy and a missed call from Saurabh. I wondered who to reply to first, Saurabh or Roy.

I chose Alia instead.

'Hey, slept okay?' I typed on my phone and deleted it before pressing send.

'Good morning,' I typed again and erased that as well.

'Last night was amazing,' I typed in as a third attempt.

I did not press send, and deleted this message too.

Don't be so eager, I told myself.

Why hasn't she messaged?

Did it not mean anything to her?

Is she regretting it?

The games had officially begun. This is what scares me about relationships—the games. The second-guessing and third-guessing and fourth-guessing.

Is she thinking something and not saying it?

What will she think if I message this?

Should I not message at all even though I really want to?

Why do male–female relationships get complicated so fast? Or is it just me? Maybe I am making this more complicated than it needs to be? I should just send her a message. But, technically, I took her out for drinks and dinner. She should send me a thank you message first, right? But perhaps she doesn't want to come across as clingy. So will I come across as clingy if I send her a message first? Okay, I am definitely over-complicating this.

Saurabh's call interrupted the slush of thoughts in my brain.

'You sound sleepy,' Saurabh said.

'Yeah, just woke up.'

'At 11? Seriously?

I saw two half-filled cups of coffee on my bedside table from last night. One of the cups had lipstick marks on it. I drank insipid, room temperature black coffee from both of the cups to wake myself up.

'Was up late,' I said.

'Studying?'

'Not really,' I said after a pause.

'Then?'

'Golu, Alia's mother-in-law and husband made her take a DNA test.'

'What!'

I repeated the story Alia had told me last night.

'Weird set of people, man. All the more reason to get access to the family. As soon as possible.'

'Alia is working on it. She is on the verge of divorce over it, in fact.'

'What!'

'Yes, she's in a terrible marriage. They have so many issues.'

'You are into marriage counselling too these days?'

'Very funny. I have to go. Roy is waiting for Daisy,' I said and ended the call.

I walked to the centre of my room in a daze. The plates from last night's dinner lay neatly arranged in the corner. I felt upset and confused. Neither had Alia messaged me nor had I a clue if I should message first.

C'mon, work, I told myself.

Keshav, the idiot who had fallen for a married woman, had to turn into a happy Daisy.

I opened Roy's latest message.

'Good morning. I dreamt of you again.'

'What did you dream?' I replied, yawning.

'Ah, finally. You answered,' he replied in an instant.

'Yes. Sorry, overslept.'

'I missed you.'

'What was your dream? Tell me.'

'I am shy to tell you,' he replied, along with a hands-covering-face emoji.

'Why?'

'It was naughty.'

I sat up straight and took a deep breath. He had escalated. I had to play this right.

'Naughty?' I replied.

'We were playing games.'

'What games?'

'We were in bed, all cuddled up.'

I took another deep breath.

'Really?' I replied.

'Yeah, with not many clothes on.'

Okay, so this was how paedophiles talked to thirteen-year-olds. Maybe it was the hangover or the spicy food from last night, but his words made me nauseous.

'Oh,' I replied.

'Would you like to do that with me?'

How would a thirteen-year old girl respond to this? I had no idea.

'I don't know,' I sent a message.

'Have you just chilled with anyone in bed?'

'No,' I said.

'If a boy and a girl love each other, they express their love by cuddling and kissing.'

'Okay, yes. I know.'

'Would you like that?'

'I am not sure. I am a bit young to do those things.'

'C'mon, you studied biology in school, right? The male–female stuff?'

'You mean reproduction?'

'Yes.'

'Yes, I know about sex. But it's what grown-ups do.'

'It's natural when you love someone.'

'Okay.'

'So that was my dream. You and I together.'

'I don't even know you that much.'

'What do you want to know?'

I paused to think. I had the chance to get something out of him. However, if I asked something too invasive, he would back off.

'How old are you?'

'Thirty-seven,' he replied, after a pause.

I did a silent 'what the fuck' as I typed back a response.

'Wow. You are so much older than me.'

'I am a kid at heart. Really, I connect with you better than anyone my age.'

'Okay.'

'Daisy, sweetheart, send me your picture.'

Damn, I should have seen this coming. What could I send him?

'You send me yours first,' I replied.

'I asked first.'

'I'll send you after you do.'

'Promise?'

'Yes.'

After one minute, he sent a selfie of himself. He had taken the selfie from the top. He had used his hand to cover most of his face. He had salt and pepper hair and a defined jawline. He did not wear a shirt and had a fit body.

'That's me,' he texted.

'Why did you cover your face?'

'Should save something for when we meet, right?'

'Are we meeting?' I said, as my heart beat fast.

'When are you in Delhi next?'

'Next month.'

'We will meet then.'

'Maybe.'

'Why maybe? Don't you want to meet me? Don't you want to see Oreo and Coffee?'

'I do!'

'Then come and see me soon.'

'Okay!'

'Fine, your turn. Send your picture.'

'Later. Mom around right now.'

'Just take a quick one.'

'Can't.'

'Fine. I'll wait. But send me a no-shirt selfie. Like I sent you.'

'No! Never taken a picture like that.'

'I'll buy you something online.'

'What?'

'If you send me a no-shirt selfie, I'll get you a nice gift.'

'What gift?'

'Whatever you want. Maybe I can buy you a pretty dress online.'

'Really?'

'Of course, sweetheart. I love you. Okay, bye for now. Send me the picture soon!'

I video-called Saurabh right after my chat with Roy.

'Why are you video-calling me? I am eating,' Saurabh said, sitting with a bowl of sprouts and clear soup. 'Let me enjoy the few calories I get.'

'I am impressed. Sticking to your diet!'

'I hate my life. How do people become thin? Don't they die in the process?'

'Nobody died eating sprouts. Listen, I need your help.'

'I already have so much Cybersafe work to do. What is it?'

'You have to scan pictures of young girls on the internet.'

'What!' he said, soup spoon in hand.

'Yes. Find one specific girl who is an adult in real life but could pass off as a thirteen-year-old. And her pictures are available.'

'Why?'

I updated Saurabh on my conversation with Roy.

'You want me to find a young teen in revealing poses? That's called child pornography. We will be in jail.'

'No, Golu. I said a girl who is an adult in real life but could pass off as a teen.'

'How?'

'Look for petite, small-framed girls. Go to Instagram for instance. Look for accounts that post photos of petite bikini-clad adult girls. Crop screenshots. Use your photoshop skills on their face. Make it all look natural. Hide most stuff. Reveal just a little.'

'Why?'

'I have to send them to Roy. He's escalating. I have to keep him hooked.'

'You want me to turn into a total pervert? Fiddle around with images of girls' bodies?'

'Come on, Golu. I have to keep Roy engaged. Make him desperate to meet me. You are way better than me at computer stuff.'

Saurabh clicked the keys on his office computer keyboard.

'I already found a site. They specialise in pictures of extra-petite girls on the beach. All adults though, so legal. Maybe I can filter Latina girls. They can pass off as Indian.'

'See, I told you. You're a natural.'

'Oh fuck!' he said.

'What happened?'

'My office computer flashed a warning that I'm visiting

inappropriate sites. Oh, damn. I have to get Jacob to unlock it now. So embarrassing.'

'Forgot you worked for a cyber-security company, didn't you?' I said and laughed.

'I'll work on this at home. On your computer,' he said, flustered, and ended the call.

I took a shower, cleaned up my room and opened my Civil Services textbook on the Indian Constitution. I could not read beyond one paragraph. My mind kept going back to my phone. It was 1 p.m. She hadn't messaged. *Maybe I should message, even if I come across as clingy*, I thought.

My phone pinged.

'You coming for lunch, right? Amma made steamed jackfruit,' Alia messaged me.

I let out a huge sigh of relief.

I waited five minutes to respond, to not come across as too keen.

'Sure. Just leaving my room,' I replied.

She replied with a smiley emoji.

I kept staring at the emoji. Did that smiley mean she liked what happened last night?

It was amazing how this one tiny yellow circular cartoon controlled my mental state.

'See you,' I replied with two smiley emojis.

Chapter 34

'We call this chakka puzhukku,' Manju said, serving some of the jackfruit dish and rice on my banana leaf.

Alia, Suhana, Manju and I were sitting for lunch in the courtyard. Suhana had already booked me to read *Alice in Wonderland* to her later.

'Take the vellarikka pachadi with it,' Alia said. She handed me a pot of what looked like cucumber raita. I looked at her properly while serving myself some pachadi. I wanted to see if last night had changed her, like it had changed me.

'So much pachadi?' Suhana laughed. I had taken too much and the liquid was running out of my leaf.

I read Suhana her naptime story after lunch. Alia remained busy with her mother in the kitchen.

I wanted to talk to her alone. Too much had happened. I couldn't pretend to be normal, eating pachadi and reading about Alice.

Suhana drifted off to sleep. I leaned against the wooden pillar in the courtyard and shut my eyes as well.

'Manish is calling you, Alia, take his call,' Manju's voice woke me up from my snooze.

'I'll call him later, Amma,' Alia said from her bedroom.

'Don't annoy him. He's making an effort,' Manju said.

'Good. He should, for a change.'

Alia walked out to the courtyard.

'Hey, Keshav, why are you sleeping here? You want to rest in Amma's room?' she said.

'Oh, no. I should leave. I'll go to the hotel.'

Offer to come out for a coffee, please, I thought. *Or at least walk me to the hotel. Let's get a moment together and discuss last night.*

Manju came out of the kitchen into the courtyard.

'Alia, he called thrice. What is this childish behaviour? Return his calls.'

'Stop taking his side, Amma.'

'I am not ...' Manju said and stopped mid-sentence as she realised I was there, listening to their internal family conflict.

'Okay, Alia, see you later,' I said and took rapid steps out of the house.

I finished three chapters on the Indian Constitution. I had to stop thinking about her, even if it meant studying the most boring topics in the world. I looked out of the window. Dusk had set in. It was already dark outside. The intercom in my room rang right then, startling me.

'There's a visitor for you, sir,' the receptionist said on the phone.

'Oh, who?'

'One Ms Alia, sir. If I have your permission, I will send her upstairs?'

'Sure,' I said as happiness bubbles burst inside me.

I scrambled to clean up my room before she reached upstairs.

'Do I have permission to come in, sir?' Alia said from the door.

She was wearing a western-style sleeveless black dress. Her fair skin glowed in contrast to her outfit. She wore a solitaire diamond necklace with matching earrings, which glittered in the yellow light of my room.

'Am I disturbing you?' she said, flipping through the Indian Constitution textbook.

'No, I finished my studies. You look ...' I started, searching for the right word, '... different.'

'You can say I look nice. "Different" is not a compliment.'

'No, I meant the dress.'

'This was how I used to dress before marriage. All the traditional dressing came after I moved into Manish's joint family.'

'Oh.'

'I'm meeting my school friends in Jew Town. Might even stay over with one of them. I dressed like this to celebrate old times.'

'Oh, so are you on your way there?'

She sat down on the antique wooden rocking chair.

'No, that's the story I told Amma. You believed it. It works, doesn't it?'

'But why did you tell her all this?'

'So I could come and be with you instead.'

'Oh,' I said.

'Are you really a detective, Mr Keshav?'

'No, I didn't realise ... wow!'

'Having a slow day? Or is it too much of the Indian Constitution?'

'Yeah, maybe.'

'Is it okay if I stay here tonight?'

'More than okay. It's great, actually. Thank you.'

'Welcome. Now, what does a girl have to do to get a drink around here?'

Lovemaking. Post-lovemaking conversations. Snooze. Repeat. I checked the time on my phone: 5 a.m. I stepped out of bed and opened the window. The gentle sounds of the sea filled the room.

'What?' Alia said in a sleepy voice. She was covered in a white sheet.

'Wanted some fresh air,' I said and came back to bed.

'I spoke to Manish finally. Amma insisted,' she said after a pause.

'And?'

'He apologised for the day before.'

'That's good.'

'He said he lost an order for three crores that day. Some employee's stupid mistake. He said he was stressed, which made him lose his temper.'

'All okay now?'

'On the surface, yes. He always has some justification for treating me like shit. Work stress. Mummyji stress.'

'But he's okay for now? To let you hire us?'

'Yes, he will be. I told him you guys are doing good work.'

'What did you say?'

'I told him about Roy. How you patiently became friends with Suhana to make her talk without pressure.'

'Wait. You told him about me being here?'

'Well, yeah. To meet Suhana in a free setting, like Amma's house. That's why you came here, right?'

'Yes, but you told Manish I've been in Kochi for the last two weeks?' I said, tense.

'Calm down. Breathe. No big deal. Yes, I did. Had to. Suhana would have eventually told him anyway.'

'And did he say anything?'

'About what?'

I pointed to her and me.

'Of course I didn't tell him about us. Have you really lost it today, Keshav? Does Civil Services prep destroy brain neurons?'

'Sorry,' I sighed. 'I'm a bit freaked out.'

'I told him that's how you guys do your job. That's it.'

I shrugged. 'As long as he is okay. Saurabh and I want to meet your in-laws at the soonest.'

'If Roy is your main suspect, chances of my in-laws being involved are low ...'

'Low, but not zero,' I said. 'Hope your husband gives us permission soon.'

'Don't talk like that.'

'Like what?'

'Saying "your husband" and all. I checked out of this marriage long ago.'

I remained silent and looked out of the window.

'What's the matter, Keshav?'

'Nothing,' I said.

'I may not be a detective, but I can tell when people have something on their mind.'

'What is this?' I said, pointing to her and me in quick succession.

'What?'

'Whatever we are doing, what does it all mean?'

'Do we have to analyse everything?'

'I'm sleeping with you, Alia. Your mother and daughter are a couple of streets away. Your husband, yes, "your husband", thinks I am working for you.'

'Yes, all true. So?'

'So? What am I to you? Just somebody you sleep with?'

'The stereotype is that girls talk like this. But this is sweet. Go on.'

'Is this a game for you? Some fun back in your hometown? Or am I just a way to get even with your husband?'

I clenched my lower lip. I didn't want her to see me overcome with emotion.

Alia sat up on the bed.

'Whoa, relax Keshav. Stop assuming things. Where is all this coming from?'

She placed a hand on my shoulder. I shrugged it off.

'Honestly, I've not had any time to process this,' she said.

'Neither have I. But ...'

'But what?'

'But I missed you all day yesterday. I really wanted to talk to you in private.'

'Why didn't you call or message me?'

'I didn't want to come across as clingy.'

'What? Who are we? Seventeen-year-old teenagers playing games? You feel like talking, you call me. Okay?'

'Am I even allowed to miss you?'

She leaned forward and gave me a peck on my lips.

'Yes, you are allowed. In fact, you are encouraged. I missed you too.'

'You did?'

'That's why I lied to Amma. To come and spend the night with you. Isn't it obvious?'

'And what after this? What happens when we go back to Gurugram?'

'Am I supposed to have all the answers right now?' Alia said. She leaned forward to kiss me again.

'I love you,' I said. I don't know why I said it.

She froze. She looked up at me.

'What, Keshav? Really?'

'I do. I'd like this to mean something, go somewhere ...' I said as she kept her hand on my mouth.

She removed her hand and got out of bed.

She walked up to the window. Outside, the dawn blushed in pretty pinks. 'Being with me is difficult. It isn't just sleeping with a woman in a four-poster bed, Keshav,' she said.

'As in?'

'I come with baggage. I have two daughters. One is missing. The other one is little. And for what it's worth, right now, I have a husband.'

'I know.'

'Even if I leave him, I will always have huge baggage from the past.'

'That's part of your attractiveness.'

'What?' Alia said and looked at me.

'Your scars. Your battles. You've seen life. You can deal with a crisis. You are not just a pretty girl. You are a fighter. That's why I want to be with you. To fight life together.'

She drew the curtains and came back to bed.

'Come here, let's fight,' she said, raining kisses all over my face.

Chapter 35

'This is insanely good work,' I said. I flipped through the images Saurabh had sent me.

'Thank you, bhai. Took me three days and three nights.'

Saurabh had created a portfolio of over fifty realistic images of a light-skinned girl. The pictures ranged in how risqué they were. In the first few, the girl wore a short tennis skirt and T-shirt. In some, she had shorts on. In others, she stood in provocative selfie poses, wearing nothing on top and covering herself with her arms. None of the photos revealed her face.

'These are made with images of eight different girls,' Saurabh said.

'Wow, they look like they belong to the same person.'

I ended the call with Saurabh and opened Daisy's Instagram.

Roy had sent a 'good morning'.

I sent a picture of Daisy, the one in the short tennis skirt. Sunlight hid her face.

'Amazing,' Roy replied.

'Thank you.'

'This is nice. But isn't like the one I sent.'

'As in?'

'#Shirtless. #Selfie. Where is that?'

'I am shy.'

'Come on. I have been waiting all these days.'

I selected a selfie from Saurabh's portfolio of pictures. The topless, skinny girl looked sideways and had her arm covering her chest.

I sent Roy the picture.

'Hot!' he replied, along with two flame emojis.

'Suhana, stop bothering Uncle,' Alia said.

'One more horsie ride, please,' Suhana said. The little girl climbed on my back for the fourth time, clasping her hands around my neck.

I jogged in circles along the perimeter of the courtyard. Suhana shrieked in delight.

Suhana and I were now 'best friends', as she put it, and did a lot of things together. We made mudpies, played hide and seek and bought candy from the little general store outside Alia's mother's house.

I was still a horsie when we heard the doorbell ring.

'Get the door, horsie, go,' Suhana said, pointing me to the door.

I opened the door, with Suhana still on my back.

'Daddy!' Suhana squealed. Manish stretched out his arms and Suhana leaped towards her father. My heart leaped outside my chest.

'Keshav uncle, this is my daddy,' Suhana said.

'Hi,' Manish said. 'Keshav, right? We met in the Icon garden briefly.'

'Yes. Yes, sir,' I stuttered. I don't know why I called him sir. Maybe the extra respect for him came from sleeping with his wife.

'Alia mentioned you are here,' he said.

'Manish?' Alia said, surprised.

'Ah, marumakan shri, welcome,' Alia's mother said as she came to door as well.

Manish leaned forward to touch his mother-in-law's feet.

'What a nice surprise to see you here. Isn't it, Alia?' Aunty said.

Alia glanced at me and didn't respond.

'Manish, how come you—' Alia said.

'I missed my family,' Manish said, interrupting her. He put Suhana down, went up to Alia and gave her a hug. Alia reciprocated in a cursory manner.

'Family is everything, makane,' Manju said.

'I was at work and then said, screw it, this will never stop. Went to the airport and took the next flight,' Manish said.

'Now that you are here, I hope you will stay for a while,' Manju said.

'Not too long. I came to take them back. Suhana's school starts soon,' Manish said.

'It's okay. She can skip a few days.'

'Let's see,' Manish said and smiled.

'Anyway, you wash up. You came right in time for lunch,' Manju said.

'I've missed your cooking. You are the best cook.'

'Stop buttering me up. I can't make rajma chawal like your mother.'

'Yeah, but you make perfect Kerala dishes.'

'If I knew you were coming, I would have made more items. I only made prawn theeyal today.'

'I love your prawn theeyal.'

'Ayyo, let me at least make some payasam.'

I felt out of place in this family reunion. Alia sensed my unease.

'Manish, you met Keshav? I told you on the phone.'

'Yeah,' he said, turning to me. 'Alia told me you have done good work.'

'Me and my partner Saurabh.'

'Tell me about it. I'd love to know more.'

'Sure. You have just arrived. I can come later and ...' I said, looking at the exit.

'Where are you going? Stay for lunch, no?' Alia said. When you are involved with someone, a layer of informality creeps in, no matter how hard you try to hide it.

Her 'where are you going' sounded too friendly. Fortunately, Manish's attention was on Suhana.

'Daddy, Keshav uncle reads me stories.'

'Oh, nice,' Manish said. He looked at me and smiled.

'Daddy, will you read me some too?' Suhana said, tugging at Manish's shirt.

'I'll let you guys have lunch together as a family. Let's meet separately to give Manish an update,' I said.

Before Alia could respond, I folded my hands in a namaste, smiled and walked out of the house.

'What are you eating?'

'A cheese sandwich.'

'Gosh, that melted cheese looks so good. Here's an existential life question for you.'

'What?'

'Why get thin when there is grilled cheese in this world?'

'Golu, I will change the video call to audio if the food is distracting you.'

'Oh, I see a drink too. Is that a shake?'

'Yes. Oreo milkshake.'

'This is not fair, bhai. I'm killing myself. All I do is graze on salad leaves like a goat. You are slurping Oreo milkshakes.'

I had come to Loafer's Corner, a few lanes away from Alia's mother's house. Having left the potentially awkward lunch at Alia's mother's house, I didn't want to eat alone in my room. Saurabh had video-called me as he wanted to talk about something.

I slid my food out of the frame so Saurabh could not see it.

'Sorry. Anyway, tell me what you called me for,' I said.

'Yesterday, I went and checked all the people Roy follows. It is in the hundreds.'

'The SaveAnimals100 account?' I said.

'Yes. And one of those accounts was Dharam9912. Guess who that is?'

'Who?' I said.

'Dharmesh, Siya's tutor.'

'What the fuck!' I said. The sandwich fell out of my hand.

'Yes. Roy and Dharmesh are connected,' Saurabh said. 'And that's what I thought I should call and tell you.'

'Unbelievable,' Manish said.

Manish, Alia and I had come to Kashi Art Café. I sat facing the two of them. Over multiple cups of filter kaapi, I'd updated him on Saurabh and my progress. I handed Manish my phone to show him the Roy–Daisy chats.

Manish scrolled through Daisy's fake selfies and Roy's responses to them. He shook his head in disbelief, my phone still in his hand.

'This paedophile was chatting with our Siya?' Manish said and looked at Alia. 'And we had no idea.'

'We could have both done a better job,' Alia said.

'I was busy with work,' Manish said.

'That absolves you, right?'

'Alia, stop, let's not fight over this. Let's focus,' Manish said and turned to me. 'So the police didn't find out about this Roy in their past investigations?'

'They handle a hundred cases at the same time. Sometimes they miss an angle.'

'They were only interested in attacking my family. They did whatever the media circus pressured them to do.'

'Roy hid his tracks well too. Saurabh is an excellent cyber expert. It is he who found him. He's also helped a lot in making Daisy look realistic,' I said.

'The guy who was with you that morning?'

'Yeah,' I said. 'He's really good.'

I missed Saurabh. I no longer wanted to be in Kochi, especially with Manish hovering over Alia.

Manish looked at the Roy–Daisy chats on my phone again. The same phone also had my WhatsApp chats with Alia.

'I will kill this guy,' Manish said.

Okay, he means Roy and not you, I told myself.

'For that, we have to get to him in person,' I said. I gently took my phone back from Manish.

'Yeah, how do we do that?' Manish said.

'I am working to arrange a meeting between Daisy and him. But we'll need the police's help too.'

'Police?' Manish said.

'Yes. We'll only get one chance to get him. Once he finds out that Daisy isn't real, he will try to escape. The police have to be present to catch him right then.'

'Fine,' Manish said. 'Chautala can at least do this for us. Anything else you need?'

'I need your support, sir. We'd like your family to cooperate with Saurabh and me.'

'Okay,' he said. 'As long as their name doesn't get dragged through the mud again.'

'It won't,' I said.

'That's fine then. Anyway, if you catch this Roy, it will remove the slur on my family.'

'We will do our best,' I said.

He clasped Alia's hand. I wanted to yank his hand away from hers. I concentrated hard on my filter kaapi to control my emotions.

'My wife has worked alone with you guys. Not anymore,' Manish said.

Alia smiled and wriggled her hand out of Manish's grip. Manish continued to speak.

'I was wrong. I thought this was a pointless exercise. It isn't.'

He placed his arm around Alia's shoulder. I had the strange urge to punch his face.

'Happy?' he said, looking at Alia.

'Yeah,' Alia said. 'I'll be happier when I find Siya.'

'Wait till Chautala throws Roy in lockup. He will talk, won't he, Keshav?' Manish said.

'I hope so, sir,' I said.

I shut my laptop and placed it in my backpack.

'Keshav, don't call me sir. Nobody calls me that even in my office. I am Manish. She's Alia. Okay?'

'Yes, sir, I mean, Manish.'

'Second, you must try the banana cream pie here. It's good. Alia recommended it to me first.'

Alia and I looked at each other.

I've had enough banana pies with Alia before you came to Kochi, I wanted to tell him, but didn't.

'I am quite full. Some other time,' I said and stood up to leave.

'Did you know, Alia and I used to come here before our marriage?'

I smiled.

'Those were the days. When we were just two young lovebirds,' Manish said before I left the café.

Chapter 36

'What are you doing?' Roy messaged me.

'Packing,' I replied.

'Going somewhere?'

'Yes.'

'Where?'

'Grandparents' house. Delhi.'

'Oh! You are coming to Delhi!' he sent a response, with a surprise emoji.

'Yeah, I told you I would be coming.'

'But you said next month.'

'Mom said let's go now only. She's got some cheap tickets.'

'When are you coming, sweetheart?'

Before I could respond, my phone rang. Alia had called me.

'I have no idea why Manish just landed up all of a sudden. I'm sorry,' she said.

'It's okay,' I replied.

'He's trying to make peace. He's realised how easily I could divorce him, possibly taking all his money,' she said.

'Okay,' I said, unsure of what to say to her.

'I'm still the same. My issues with him are still the same,' she said.

'Fine.'

'What's with the okay and fine? Say something else.'

'What do I say?'

'Nothing. I have to go. He's around. Listen, it's the same.'

'Same?'

'You and I. Still the same. I wish I could come over tonight.'

'But you can't.'

'Of course not. Okay, he is calling me. Bye.'

The call ended. Before I could go over what Alia had said, Roy had sent three more messages.

'When are you coming, baby?'

'Where are you staying?'

'How do we meet?'

'Our flight is on Friday,' I replied to Roy.

'Great. Which part of town will you be staying?'

'My grandparents live in Gurugram. Will be staying with them.'

'Great! I live in Gurugram too.'

'Awesome.'

'Oreo and Coffee too.'

'Aww! I want to meet them.'

'And me?'

'You as well. Yes.'

'I have so many gifts for you.'

'You do?'

'Yes, I'll give them to you when we meet.'

'Thank you!'

'I'll show you Delhi. In my car.'

'Yes. Can we take Oreo and Coffee along?'

'Sure. How will you meet me though? What will you say at home?'

'I'll figure something out.'

'Like?'

'I have a friend in Gurugram. My parents know her. They will allow me to go see her. I'll meet her first and then see you after that.'

'You are a gorgeous girl.'

'I have to go now. Mom is scolding me for using the phone.'

'Okay, baby, sure. Go. Where's my picture for the day?'

'I sent you so many.'

'Send one more. Naughty one, please.'

I flipped through Saurabh's photoshopped images. I found a selfie of a girl in a bathroom and forwarded it to him. It was the most explicit picture I had sent him so far.

'Baby,' Roy messaged.

'Yes?'

'I can't wait to see you.'

'Same here,' I replied and kept my phone aside.

I was back home after two weeks. My mother had made gatte ki sabzi, a Rajasthani delicacy, to celebrate my arrival. It felt good to eat my mother's cooking after so long. However, a part of me remained in Kochi. I missed having curd rice in the sunny courtyard of Alia's mother's house without getting cross-examined through my meal.

'That Alia Arora was there?' Ma said. 'Met her?'

I looked up at my mother.

'Yes,' I said. 'And yes.'

'Where?'

'At Alia's mother's house. So I could spend time with Suhana, her younger daughter.'

'Oh,' my mother said.

'You did some studies or only worked on the case?' Papa said, looking up from his plate.

'A bit of both. I couldn't study twenty-four hours, right?'

'How often did you meet her?' my mother said.

What did Ma want? Time tracker logs of all my meetings with Alia? I felt anger rise within me. I didn't want to shout at my parents on my first day back.

'Her husband Manish also came,' I said, to calm everyone down.

'Oh, Manish Arora?'

'Yes. Is your curiosity satisfied now, Ma?'

'What difference does it make to me?' Ma said. 'And stop sounding irritated all the time.'

'I am not irritated. Just tired of so many questions,' I said.

'Okay, I will stop. What is it to me? My fault for taking interest in your life.'

'Ma, stop it now,' I said. Emotional manipulation is as common at Indian dining tables as passing the salt.

'Here, take another roti. Must've been eating only rice in Kerala. Have proper food.'

I wanted to shout that even rice was proper food. However, my father spoke before me.

'Tell him about Gehlotji's daughter,' Papa said to my mother. Why did he have to route conversations through his wife?

'There is this girl. Sulochana Gehlot. Your father's shakha friend's daughter,' my mother said. 'She's twenty-seven. Done her Master's. Looks good. Works in a computer company in Jaipur.'

'So?'

'I saw her Instagram. She has posted photos of the dishes she made. Cooks well too.'

'Good for her. But why are you telling me this? Is there a case she wants me to solve?'

'No, you idiot. She is a proposed match for you,' my father said. 'We told her parents we would be interested.'

'What!' I said. 'How can you do this?'

'How can we do what? How can we think of settling our son down? Or how dare we think of being happy?' Ma said.

'I don't want to get married to Gehlot uncle's daughter,' I said.

'What is wrong with Gehlot's daughter? You haven't even met her,' my father said.

'Something's wrong with me, not her. Okay?' I said. I stood up and left the dining table. I heard them grumble about me from my bedroom. I put on my headphones and turned the music up loud.

Alia messaged me.

'Saturday afternoon. Tea at my in-laws' place. Confirmed. You and Saurabh can meet them there.'

'Great,' I replied.

She sent a hug smiley.

'I miss your Amma's house in Kochi,' I replied.

'I miss you,' Alia messaged back.

'Have some more.' Durga Arora offered Saurabh a plate of cashew nuts.

'No, thanks, ma'am,' Saurabh said with a tragic expression on his face.

We sat in the Navratna House garden with the entire family. A domestic help served us tea in expensive china cups, along with chilli cheese toast, besan barfi and a dry fruit platter.

'You won't even have one cheese toast?' Durga said.

Saurabh shook his head vigorously.

'At least you take some,' Durga said to me. She wore a purple salwar kameez with a golden print on it. Her ears, neck and wrists sported diamonds and precious stones of various sizes. She didn't look like the evil villain I had imagined her to be. She resembled an overweight aunt with a tacky, blingy dress sense who insisted on feeding people.

'He's on a diet,' I said. Saurabh sighed.

'Alia tells me you guys did a lot of good work,' Shamsher said. Alia's father-in-law, with his royal moustache and tweed jacket, resembled one of those distinguished elderly men in expensive watch advertisements.

I turned to look at Alia. She wore a black salwar kameez and a dupatta with black and white checks. She prepared a plate of snacks for her father-in-law.

'We made some progress. Still a lot to be done,' I said.

'We are happy to cooperate in any way,' Shamsher said. 'I never said no. Just didn't want the media drama like last time.'

'Don't put it softly, Papaji. The media didn't just do drama. They effectively killed our family's reputation,' Timmy said, his large frame making the snacks plate in his hand look extra small.

'That stain on our family is still not fully gone,' Durga said. 'That's why we stopped pursuing this.'

'We have nothing to do with the media,' I said. 'Saurabh and I won't speak to anyone.'

'Then I am here to help with whatever you need. I want to know what happened to my granddaughter. How did she disappear from my own house?' Shamsher said. 'And who is this Roy?'

I looked at Manish.

'I told them. They are family. Don't worry. Everyone here can be trusted,' Manish said.

Saurabh and I nodded. I spoke after a pause.

'We are laying a trap to catch Roy. I request you to not discuss him or any details with anyone.'

'Who will we discuss with?' Durga said.

'Neighbours. Relatives. Friends. Don't mention it to anyone. We have to catch him first,' I said.

'How do you plan to do that?' Manish said.

'I will get him to a location. The police will be ready to catch him,' I said.

'Police?' Durga said, throwing her hands up in the air. 'Oh God. Again the police?'

Shamsher signalled to his wife to calm down.

'Keshavji, the police can't be trusted. They planted the theory of family involvement in the media,' Shamsher said.

'I understand, sir. But we can only find the culprit. It is the police who have to catch him. We'll only get one chance.'

Shamsher and the others looked at each other. Durga stood up.

'I have to consult Panditji.'

'Sit down, Durga. You don't have to be superstitious,' Shamsher said.

'There's no harm,' she said. She went to the dining area, made a two-minute call and returned to sit on the sofa again.

'What?' Shamsher said.

'Panditji said no harm in going to the police again. He doesn't see any bad times for the family coming anytime soon.'

'See. You unnecessarily worry,' Shamsher said.

'What if this leaks out to the media? More news and more attacks on the family and brand? With great difficulty, we have brought back some business,' Timmy said.

'How can it harm the family, Timmy bhaiya?' Alia said. 'If anything, it will help clear our name.'

Durga turned to look at Alia with mistrustful eyes.

'She's absolutely right,' I said.

'How?' Timmy said.

'Even if news leaks out, it will be that of a paedophile being caught for Siya's abduction. It absolves the family,' I said.

'It will actually help fully clear the family name, Timmy bhaiya,' Manish said. 'That's why I agreed with Alia to hire these two.'

Everyone fell silent. Shamsher spoke after a pause.

'Fine, go ahead. Anything else you want from us?'

'We might talk to all of you over the next few days. Do tours of the house, take pictures,' I said before Durga interrupted me.

'Talk about what? What pictures?' Durga said as Shamsher shushed her.

'It's fine. Do your job. What else?' Shamsher said.

'Come with us when we go to Inspector Chautala. To ask for his help in catching Roy,' I said.

I was at my study table when Roy messaged me.

'Have you reached Delhi?'

I kept my textbook aside and picked up my phone.

'Yes, landed last night.'

'Oh! You are here? In Gurugram?'

'Yes.'

'When are you meeting me?'

'I dunno. When do you want to meet?'

'I am free. You tell me when.'

'Okay, wait. Let me check,' I replied and took a deep breath.

'Day after?' I texted him after a few minutes.

'Sure. When?'

'Afternoon is better. Driver is free.'

'Fine.'

'I will meet my friend afterwards.'

'Sure. Can you come to Ambience Mall?'

'What is that?'

'It's a huge mall near the Delhi-Gurugram toll booth.'

'Okay.'

'Everyone knows it. It has great shopping and eating places.'

'Okay. I will ask my friend to come there as well.'

'Only after you meet me, I hope.'

'Of course.'

'How about we meet at noon? We can have lunch.'

'Where?'

'Taco Bell. It's in the mall.'

'I will find it.'

'You are the smartest! After lunch we can go to Zara, so you can buy whatever you want.'

'Whatever I want?'

'Yes, my sweet little sweetheart. First time I'm meeting you. I have to get you some gifts.'

I rained him with heart emojis in response.

'Are those hearts for me?'

'Yes, who else? What time shall I tell my friends?'

'Five-ish?'

'That late?'

'Come home with me for a while.'

'Home?'

'I can't bring Oreo and Coffee to the mall, right?'

'Aww. I do want to see them.'

'Exactly. We will eat and shop. Then go to my place for a bit.'

'Sounds good.'

'I'll drop you back at the mall at 5.'

'Can't wait to see you. I have so much to tell you.'

'See you, love. No picture for me today?'

'Difficult in grandmother's house. People around.'

'Ah. It's fine. I am seeing you soon anyway.'

'Okay, have to go. Bye!'

He replied with several kiss, hug and heart emojis.

I called Alia right after my chat with Roy.

'The stage is set. The meeting with Roy,' I said.

'When, where, how?'

'I'll explain everything. Can you help fix a meeting with the police?'

Chapter 37

Inspector Chautala's office was so full, we needed extra chairs from the next room. Alia's entire family, Saurabh and I sat in a semi-circle around the inspector's desk. Viren and Rajan had joined us as well.

Chautala rubbed the stubble on his chin after I finished telling him about Roy.

'Viren, you had searched Siya's phone, right?' Chautala said.

'Yes, sir. I couldn't locate these Telegram chats,' Viren said.

'She had deleted them. I used special recovery software,' Saurabh said.

'Viren, you couldn't do that?'

Viren hung his head low.

'Mr Saurabh, how did you even get access to the information on Siya's phone? We had Siya's phone and the data in our possession,' Chautala said.

Saurabh had already thought of an excuse. We couldn't come out and say we had stolen the information from the police station.

'Long story, sir,' Saurabh said, and switched to techno gibberish. 'You see, I work in a cyber-security company. I used certain primary patch protocols along with a VPN server and—'

Chautala raised a hand to make him stop.

'Leave it. Let's focus on the suspect. You have any idea what this Roy looks like? Where does he live? Phone number?'

'No, sir,' I said. 'Even the name Roy might be fake.'

'And you say this idiot tutor Dharmesh is connected to him?' Chautala said.

'On Instagram, yes,' Saurabh said.

'Let's get Dharmesh at least then. Two nights in a lockup and he will tell us everything.'

'I am sorry, but that may not work,' I said.

'Why?' Chautala said.

'Roy is the guy we want. If we catch Dharmesh now, it will alert Roy. Roy will vanish,' I said.

'Keshav has a point, sir,' Viren said.

'Very smart, Viren. Now you have all the opinions?' Chautala said sarcastically. 'Couldn't even check Siya's phone properly.'

'Sorry, sir,' Viren said, his head bent down again.

'Dharmesh is a coward. We'll give him two slaps and he will spill. But fine. Whatever you say. I can send a team to Ambience to catch this Roy first. Shamsherji, you are okay with this?' Chautala said.

'The boys make sense. Let's catch Roy first. Then go nab Dharmesh immediately.'

'Not that, Shamsherji. Are you okay with reopening this? Didn't you say you wanted to bury all this? After that parcel with her belongings, you know that Siya bitiya is gone forever.'

Alia glared at Chautala.

'Sorry, madam, but it is true,' Chautala said.

Shamsher cleared his throat before speaking again.

'Chautalaji, even if that's true, if this helps us find out what exactly happened to Siya, it is worth it.'

'Durgaji?' Chautala said.

'If catching this Roy means finding the real culprit and clearing the stain on my family for good, it is definitely worth it,' Durga said.

Chautala gave a slow nod.

'Fine. Let's reopen this cold case.'

'One request—no media, sir, please,' Timmy said.

'Yes, Timmyji. Even I don't want to be made fun of again. You two detectives, no talking to the press. Okay?'

'Never, sir,' Saurabh said.

Chautala turned to Viren.

'Arrange a six-member team of cops for day after. Plain clothes. Let's all go shopping to Ambience Mall,' Chautala said.

Ambience Mall in Gurugram claims to be one of the biggest malls in India, with corridors that add up to more than a kilometre across the floors. I reached the shopping mall at 10 a.m. to familiarise myself with the location.

Taco Bell, a Mexican fast food restaurant, is located on the second floor, right next to PVR Cinemas.

I stood on the third floor, the one above Taco Bell, on the opposite side. This allowed me to see the restaurant diagonally below me through the atrium quadrangle. This early in the morning, the restaurant had no customers.

'Good morning, baby,' Roy sent me a message.

'Good morning,' I replied.

'I am so excited for today.'

'Same here.'

'What are you doing?'

'Getting ready.'

'What are you going to wear?'

'Dunno. Will decide. Why?'

'How will I recognise you?'

'Ha ha. Of course you will.'

'Still. Tell me.'

'I think I'll wear my red dress.'

'Cool. I like red.'

'It's, like, my favourite colour.'

'I'll buy you some more red dresses then.'

'Thank you!'

'I may reach the mall early,' Roy said.

'Oh, okay,' I replied. *Could he already be here?* My heart started to beat fast.

'I can roam around before you come.'

'Okay, or wait in Taco Bell. I will come there,' I said.

Not me, but six strong Haryanvi cops will, I thought.

'No. You message me when you reach Taco Bell. I will come only then,' Roy sent a message.

'What?' I said. My heartbeat grew faster. That wasn't how I had planned it.

'I'll come once you reach Taco Bell. I will look for a pretty little girl in a red dress.'

'Oh, okay. Fine,' I replied, even though my mind was racing.

I ended the chat and put my phone back in my pocket. I didn't want to lurk around in the mall corridors. I found a Van Heusen store next to me and went inside.

'Some formal shirts for you, sir? We have nice Egyptian cotton ones,' a salesperson said.

'Do I look like a guy who wears formal shirts?' I said.

'Pardon, sir?'

'Nothing. Do you have casual shirts?'

'Yes, sir, over there,' he said and pointed me to the casual section.

I picked out three shirts from a shelf and went to the trial room.

I called Saurabh from inside the trial room.

'We have a problem,' I said.

'What? Don't tell me he cancelled!'

'Listen to me—I think he might be in the mall already. Roaming around.'

'Fuck. I will be there soon,' Saurabh said.

'That's okay. You don't have to come. Chautala's team will be here by 11.'

'What's the issue?'

'He told me to message him once I reach Taco Bell. He will only come after he sees Daisy.'

'Oh!'

'He asked the colour of my dress. I said red.'

'Okay.'

'He said he'd come to Taco Bell and look for a girl in a red dress.'

'What's the problem then?'

'This place is like an open café, Golu. I can see inside the restaurant from the opposite side, from the floor above and below.'

'Hmmm. He may not enter until he sees a young girl in a red dress sitting in there.'

'Exactly. He is here already. He'd be keeping a watch.'

'Can't Chautala's team scan the mall and catch him anyway?'

'Not possible. We don't know what he looks like. It's a huge mall. He could literally be in any of the five hundred different shops.'

A knock on the trial room door made me jump.

'Everything okay, sir?' the salesperson said from outside.

'I am fine,' I said, opening the trial room door.

'Perfect fit, sir,' the salesperson said, seeing me in one of the new shirts.

'I need more time,' I said and shut the trial room door again.

'What's happening, bhai?' Saurabh said.

'Nothing. Golu, we need an actual girl. A thirteen-year-old in a red dress,' I said to Saurabh.

'Are you crazy, bhai? How can we involve a child in this? And where do we get one right now?'

'It's just to get him into the restaurant. Then Chautala's team will pounce on him.'

'You have to arrange for a girl around that age. Not photoshopped pictures, an actual girl, in two hours. Do you realise that?'

'One-and-a-half hours now, actually.'

'Crazy. How?'

'I'll call Alia.'

'Why?'

'Do you know any thirteen-year-old girls, Saurabh?'

'What? No.'

'Exactly. So let me call Alia,' I said and ended the call.

I came out of the trial room. I handed the salesperson a blue-and-white checked shirt.

'I'll buy this.'

'Thank you, sir. I'll pack it. Anything else?' the salesperson said.

'Do you mind if I roam around the store for a while?'

'No problem, sir,' he said.

I went up to the entrance of the shop. I could see Taco Bell downstairs. Two young couples sat in the small restaurant, which only had a total of ten tables.

I called up Alia.

'I need your help. It's urgent,' I said. I explained the situation to her.

'Now? You need someone who can stand in for Daisy in an hour?'

'I'm sorry. This complication just came up. Damn. I don't want to miss catching him after so much effort.'

'What do you suggest?'

'How about Suhana?'

'Are you serious, Keshav?'

'Six cops will be around her at all times. She will be safe.'

'Isn't Daisy supposed to be thirteen?'

'Yes.'

'There's a huge difference in size between a seven-year-old and a thirteen-year-old. One can tell, even from a distance.'

'Fuck,' I said out loud. The salesperson looked at me, puzzled.

'Classmates,' Alia said, after a pause.

'What?'

'That's the only thing I can think of right now. One of Siya's classmates from school.'

'Yes, that could work. Please ask someone.'

'What will she have to do?'

'She just has to sit in the restaurant, her back to the entrance. Roy comes in, says hi and the Haryana Police greets him with handcuffs. That's it.'

Alia remained quiet for a few seconds.

'We don't have time, Alia. Tell me fast. Can you arrange for someone?'

'Everyone is in school though. Oh, Keshav, this is stressful.'

'If Roy escapes today, we will never be able to catch him.'

'I'll ask Vaibhavi,' Alia said.

'Who's that?'

'Parvathy's mom. Siya's best friend. I'll request her to send Parvathy.'

'Fine. She has to be here in the next thirty minutes.'

'What? She'll be in school.'

'Fine, get her here soonest. Will she have a red dress?'

'Red dress? Why? She'll be in school uniform.'

'I'll arrange for the dress. You bring Parvathy here fast,' I said and ended the call.

I walked up to the salesperson.

'Yes, sir?' he said with a smile.

'Where can I get a red dress for a young girl in this mall?'

'Fits fine,' I said.

Alia, Parvathy and Vaibhavi had met me at the Gini & Jony store on the ground floor of the mall. We only had thirty minutes until noon. After several trials, Parvathy had found a red dress that fit her.

'I think it looks lovely on you,' Alia said.

'Whatever,' Parvathy said, shrugging and chewing gum. She remained glued to her phone as she checked her friends' Instagram stories.

'Pay attention, Parva,' Vaibhavi said. I went to the cash counter to pay for the dress, but Alia had already settled the bill.

'This better work,' Alia said.

I blinked at the tension in her voice. 'I'll need to go up now and meet the police team. They are already there.'

'Sure,' Alia said.

Parvathy and Vaibhavi came up to us.

'What do we do now?' Vaibhavi said. 'And is there a way I can keep Parvathy in my sight through all this?'

'Yes, you can see Taco Bell from the Van Heusen store.'

'Vaibhavi and I will go there,' Alia said.

'Fine. Once I give the signal, Parvathy needs to take the lift to the second floor. Once there, she needs to walk in a normal manner to Taco Bell and take a seat.'

Parvathy took a boomerang selfie of herself for her Insta story, swirling the camera around her.

'Pay attention-aa,' Vaibhavi said.

Parvathy shut her phone and turned to me.

'Sorry, what?' Parvathy said.

'Walk to Taco Bell. Take a seat facing the counter. Your back to the entrance. Clear?' I said.

'Yes. What is really going on? Why did you get me out of school? Why this new dress?'

'This is for Siya,' Alia said. 'Parvathy, we really need your help. Be focused.'

'Siya? But how ...?'

'Shh, I will explain later. Keshav, you go ahead,' Alia said.

Chapter 38

Chautala's six cops sat down as customers in groups of two each at Taco Bell. I met Chautala at Red Mango, a frozen yogurt shop, right next to Taco Bell. We sat facing each other.

'Parvathy's ready in the red dress,' I said.

'Getting this girl involved is something new you sprang on us,' Chautala said.

'I had no choice. Came up suddenly.'

'Fine. Want to eat anything while we wait? They are selling a cup of frozen dahi for three hundred rupees,' Chautala said.

I shook my head.

'We are the police. We will get it for free.'

'No, sir, thanks,' I said.

'Why are you so tense?' Chautala said.

'Only fifteen minutes left,' I said, looking at my phone.

'Don't worry, my men are already there.'

I leaned forward to take a look inside Taco Bell. The six hefty Haryana cops, in shirts and jeans, were sipping cold drinks and eating tacos at their respective tables.

'Thanks, Chautala sir,' I said, letting out a deep breath.

'You focus on your guy.'

I nodded and opened my phone. I had a message from Roy.

'Where have you reached?'

'Just reached Ambience. Walking towards Taco Bell.'

'Cool, let me know when you are there.'

'Okay.'

I closed Instagram and sent a WhatsApp to Alia.

'Send Parvathy.'

Two minutes later, a girl in a red dress came out of the lift on the second floor of the mall. Parvathy looked calm as she chewed gum and looked around for Taco Bell. She saw balloons outside one of the shops and took a picture. She spotted the restaurant and walked towards it.

She reached Taco Bell and went in. She took a seat, her back to the restaurant entrance, exactly as instructed.

I took out my phone.

'This place looks cool,' I sent a message to Roy.

'Hey, you are there?' Roy replied.

'Yes, where are you?'

'Coming, coming. Walking towards Taco Bell.'

I looked up at Chautala and gestured to him. Chautala nodded and sent his cops a WhatsApp group message to be alert.

'Come soon. I am hungry,' I replied.

I waited for Roy to walk into Taco Bell. Every second felt like a minute, every minute like an hour.

I checked the time: 12.05 p.m.

Should I send a message? I decided to wait some more. No thirteen-year old girl would be so desperate.

12.20 p.m. He hadn't shown up yet. I had a sinking feeling.

'Where are you? I am waiting,' I sent him a message, along with a cute puppy emoji.

'Fuck you bitch,' was the response.

'What the hell!' I blurted out.

'What happened?' Chautala said.

'I don't know,' I said. 'Something doesn't seem right.'

'Where is he? Did he become suspicious?'

'Yes, I think so. He must be trying to leave the mall.'

Chautala whipped out his walkie-talkie.

'Leave Taco Bell. Seal mall exits. Run out and catch him. Now,' Chautala said.

I checked my Instagram. The chats with Roy had been deleted. I checked the SaveAnimals100 account. It didn't exist anymore.

'North exit for you Verma. South for you Kripal. He's in the mall,' Chautala shouted instructions on his walkie-talkie, and turned to me. 'What's happening?'

'I am sorry, sir. He's gone,' I said as I threw my phone on the table.

Failure sucks. Public failure sucks even more. Saurabh and I sat with our heads down in Chautala's office. Alia's family and Chautala stared at us in silence.

'I am sorry,' I said for the fifth time.

Chautala smirked.

'Apologising so many times isn't needed,' he said. 'I want to know what the hell happened?'

'I'm trying to figure it out. Somehow Roy found out about our plan,' I said.

'How?' Chautala said.

'Someone leaked the information, clearly. He was on board just minutes before the scheduled meeting,' Saurabh said.

'Are you suggesting the police leaked it?' Chautala said in an angry tone.

'Not really,' Saurabh said.

'That's what you are implying,' Chautala said.

'Not at all, sir,' Saurabh said.

Chautala banged a fist on his desk. He turned to Shamsher.

'See, Aroraji, this is why I didn't want to reopen the cold case. You came to us. Out of respect for you, I decided to help you.'

'Yes, sir,' Shamsher said meekly.

'I sent six men dressed as customers. Did I not?'

'You did, sir,' Shamsher said.

'These so-called detectives make a mess of their own plan. Suspect runs away. The police get blamed. Is that fair?'

Nobody said a word. Saurabh and I kept our gaze down. Alia broke the silence.

'Nobody is blaming you, Chautala sir. We thank you for your help,' Alia said.

'I am not looking for a thank you, Alia madam. I want to

know this. Why does the blame for a leak only come to my people? My cops are like my family. What if I said someone in your family, one of you guys here, leaked the information?'

'What!' Timmy said.

'See, this is what I was afraid of, Timmy. They will again end up smearing the family reputation,' Durga said. 'Let's go home. This was a useless exercise. I don't know who these strange detectives are that Alia hired.'

Durga stood up, her large frame looming over everyone. Alia looked at me, embarrassed.

I apologised to her with my eyes. I could see her pain. I had let her down. That mattered more to me than any of this drama around us.

'Sit, Mummyji, please,' Manish said.

'What's the point?' Durga said even as she sat down again. The old wooden chair creaked under her weight.

'See how it feels to be unfairly targeted?' Chautala said.

'We know, sir,' Manish said and folded his hands. 'My family has been through this. No more of that, please.'

'We are not blaming you or your team, Chautala sir,' Saurabh said. 'We will try to figure out what happened. Maybe we messed it up somewhere.'

'You did. You said there is a Dharmesh–Roy link. I wanted to catch that tutor first. Make him talk. You didn't let me,' Chautala said.

'He could alert Roy if the police contacted him,' Saurabh said. 'That was our fear.'

'I would have tossed him in the lock-up before he could alert his own ass,' Chautala said.

'Even him being in a lock-up could have raised doubts ...' Saurabh said.

'Shut up and let me think,' Chautala said, interrupting Saurabh.

'Sorry, sir,' I said. 'Saurabh, it's okay. Sir is right. It's our fault.'

'You know the problem, Keshav? You think you are the only smart one,' Chautala said.

'No, sir,' I said as Chautala raised his hand and gestured to me to be quiet.

'Viren,' he shouted. Sub-inspector Viren came to his office from the adjoining room.

'Sir?' Viren said.

'Contact that Bihari tutor. Tell him to drop everything and come see me immediately.'

'Yes, sir,' Viren said and left.

Chautala stood up to signal the end of the meeting.

'Thank you, sir,' Manish said.

'I might reach further this way. Better than buying red dresses,' Chautala said.

I inhaled deeply to withstand the humiliation.

Viren re-entered Chautala's office.

'Dharmesh's phone is not reachable, sir. Switched off.'

Chautala looked at Viren, surprised.

'Send a Gypsy to his house and get him here,' Chautala said.

Viren nodded and left.

'Don't worry, Shamsherji. I may be old. I may not know all this Instagram business, but I have my own ways that work too,' Chautala said and folded his hands to bid the Arora family goodbye.

'Sleeping?' Alia sent me a message well past midnight.

'No,' I replied. I sat up in bed.

'Did they get Dharmesh?'

'He's not at home. They are trying to find him.'

'Okay, I hope they do.'

'Same here.'

'How are you?'

'Miserable.'

'We almost had Roy.'

'Almost means nothing. We don't have him. He's gone.'

'You had a solid plan. Someone must have leaked it.'

'I am sorry I messed up. Let you down.'

'It's not your fault.'

'Who else then? This is entirely on me.'

'Keshav.'

'Yes?'

'Thank you.'

'Please don't humiliate me further. I don't deserve your thanks.'

'Thank you for trying. You got further than anyone else.'

'But I didn't get there in the end. I hate myself. Like my love life, like my Civil Services preparation, I fucked this up as well.'

'You didn't. I feel terrible too that we lost Roy. But I will feel worse if you take all the blame.'

'Thanks.'

'For what?'

'For messaging and trying to make me feel better.'

'You mean something to me.'

'Do I?'

'Yes.'

'Okay, good to know.'

'Why did you include your love life in your list of fucked-up things?'

'My love life is actually fucked up.'

'Really?'

'Yeah, it involves a married client with kids and a huge joint family. I sit and eat chilli cheese toast with her in-laws, pretending everything is normal, while deep inside it kills me.'

'What kills you?'

'To not be with you. To see you as Manish's wife and the Arora family's daughter-in-law.'

'I am all that too, Keshav. At least right now.'

'Exactly. Now you know why my love life is fucked up?'

'What do you want from me?'

'Nothing. It's all my fault. I fuck everything up. Including my relationships.'

'Don't say that.'

'The woman I love chats with me every night while her husband sleeps next to her. Isn't that fucked up enough for you?'

Chapter 39

'He's not at home,' Chautala said. 'Neither in Manesar nor in Patna.'

Chautala had called Saurabh, Alia and me to his office. Viren joined the meeting.

'Checked with his students?' Alia said.

'Did not show up for tuitions at any of his students' places for the last two days,' Viren said.

'What about his friends?' Saurabh said. 'The ones he went to Goa with?'

'Nobody has any idea,' Viren said.

'Get his call records,' Chautala said.

'Already did, sir,' Viren said. He passed a file to Chautala.

'Last call at 12.15 p.m. Two days ago,' Chautala said, running his finger down the call records printout.

'To an Ola driver,' Viren said.

'You called the driver?' Chautala said.

'Yes. Obtained the ride details too,' Viren said.

Viren leaned forward and turned the pages of the file in Chautala's hand.

'Here,' Viren said, 'that's the ride summary, sir.'

'12.15 at Manesar. Then he went along the highway. Ends at T3. Airport, right?'

'International airport, sir,' Viren said. 'Switched off his phone after that.'

Chautala shook his head.

'Like Roy, he's gone too,' Chautala said.

I wanted to cry. Chautala continued.

'You were right about one thing, Keshav. Roy and Dharmesh are linked. Both went missing at the same time. If only you had let us catch one of them,' Chautala said.

I said nothing. I did not trust myself to speak.

'Viren sir, did your team check his Manesar house? Any clues there?' Saurabh said.

'We did. His landlord had a spare key. Clothes, appliances and utensils, they are all there. He just left. Didn't even pack.'

'Fine. It's over then. Unless he emerges somewhere, we can't do anything. Alia ma'am, we'll file this back as a case cold again.'

'But, sir—' Alia began, but Chautala interrupted her.

'We tried, no? Now your suspect and his associate ran away. What to do? You want me to put a lookout alert for them in the media?'

'No, no media, please,' Alia said.

'Exactly. Last thing your in-laws want. If you hear anything from this Dharmesh or Roy again, do tell us. Until then, let's move on.'

'You move on, sir. I can't, ever,' Alia said as she stood up, turned around and left Chautala's office.

Saurabh, Alia and I came out of the Sushant Lok Police Station after our meeting with Chautala.

'Saurabh, my driver can drop you to the office after he drops us at the Icon,' Alia said.

'I can call a cab,' Saurabh said.

'I insist. Please,' Alia said as her driver arrived with the car.

The three of us sat in Alia's black S-class Mercedes, Saurabh in the front and Alia and me in the backseat. The driver left the Sushant Lok complex and drove us towards the Icon.

None of us had anything to say. Alia looked out of the window, her hand next to mine on the seat. I controlled my urge to hold it.

I opened Instagram on my phone. Once again, I tried to search for Roy, even though I knew there was no point. His account didn't exist anymore. I went to Dharmesh's Instagram account. He had a profile picture of a math problem. The rest of his account was private.

Alia's phone rang. She had a call from Vaibhavi.

'Yeah, see you at school, Vaibhavi. I'll come at 3.30 to pick up Suhana. You are coming to pick up Parvathy, right? Yes, see you,' Alia said and ended the call.

'Oh, damn. I figured out what went wrong with Roy,' I said.

Alia and Saurabh turned to look at me.

'What?' Saurabh said.

'Did Dharmesh teach Parvathy?' I said.

'Not anymore. But he did teach her last year. He taught many students in Siya's class.'

'Is he following Parvathy on Instagram?

'Maybe. I can ask her mother. Why?'

'Vaibhavi lives nearby?' I said.

'Yeah, at Pinnacle. Right next to the Icon.'

'Could we meet her for a minute?'

'Sure,' Alia said. 'I'll ask her to come down.'

Alia messaged Vaibhavi and instructed her driver to take the car to Pinnacle.

Vaibhavi was waiting for us in the long driveway of her posh building.

'Come upstairs, guys, have a cup of tea at least,' she said.

'Another time, Vaibhavi. Keshav wanted to check Parvathy's Instagram on your phone,' Alia said, still in the car.

Vaibhavi handed me her mobile. I opened Instagram on her device. I went to Parvathy's account. Dharmesh did follow her.

I saw Parvathy's posts. Two days ago, at 11.34 a.m., Parvathy had posted a selfie of herself in the red dress. I read the caption for the post.

When mom drags you out of school to shop. Who's complaining? #LittleRedDress #ShoppingOverSchoolAnyday

She had also tagged the location as Ambience Mall, Gurugram.

'Damn,' Saurabh said as I handed him the phone.

Vaibhavi and Alia looked at Saurabh, puzzled.

'Parvathy posted this. Dharmesh saw it and shared it with Roy, since he probably knows Roy likes pictures of young girls.'

'The red dress and location would have alerted Roy. Vanished,' I said.

I returned the phone to Vaibhavi. Alia told her driver to leave.

'I am so sorry,' Vaibhavi said. 'Parvathy is an idiot. Posting everything.'

'I'll see you later, Vaibhavi,' Alia said. As we drove out of the Pinnacle compound, I spied a teardrop at the corner of her eye.

'Drop Saurabh sir to his office,' Alia said to her driver.

'Thanks again,' Saurabh said as he pushed back the front seat to get more legroom and waved us goodbye.

Alia and I remained at the Icon gate.

'I don't want to go home,' she said. 'Can we go somewhere? Where we can talk undisturbed.'

'The pedicure place?'

'No, somewhere more private.'

'Where?'

'For God's sake, don't you get it, Keshav? Book a hotel room or something.'

'Huh? Okay.'

I opened a hotel booking app. I found Hotel Anya, a five-star property located six hundred metres from us.

'Done,' I said, after making the booking.

'You start walking there. I'll enter separately, a few minutes after you,' Alia said.

Chapter 40

'He offered ten per cent,' Alia said.

This was the first time she'd spoken since entering the room at Hotel Anya. She'd arrived ten minutes after I had checked in and gone straight to the minibar. She drank three mini bottles of vodka, one after the other, like shots.

I didn't react. I wanted to let her deal with her feelings the way she wanted. She came and held me. She wanted to make love, if only to feel better and lessen her pain. I wanted her as well. Every bit of me had missed her since we had come back from Kochi.

We lay in bed afterwards, staring at the ceiling.

'Ten per cent,' she repeated. 'The settlement for our divorce. Ten per cent of his assets. That's Manish's offer.'

I sat up on bed. I felt a warm happy river flow through me. She was actually leaving him so she could be with me. She continued to talk.

'He said let's avoid a big battle in court. Let's do it with mutual consent. Agree to the terms and sign the agreement.'

I nodded as she spoke again.

'We won't even need two separate lawyers. A common lawyer can submit our mutual settlement in court.'

She looked at me. I had to say something.

'How do you feel?' I said, careful not to let my happiness show.

Alia shrugged. She bent and picked up my shirt from the floor and wore it. I loved when she did that. She spoke again.

'In a way I am grateful to him. Our marriage hasn't been working for a while. I'm glad he started the process to end it.'

'And you are okay with his terms?'

Alia shook her head.

'I don't care about the money. My big issue is he wants full custody of Suhana, which is totally unacceptable to me.'

'He'll keep her?'.

'Yes, he says he has more means to educate and bring her up well. He said she will also have her grandparents. He wants to move back to Navratna House with her.'

'Where will you stay? At the Icon?'

'Maybe, if I negotiate well and get it as part of the settlement.'

'Where else could you go? Kochi?' I said.

'Not without Suhana. I can't be away from her.'

'He'll agree to let you keep Suhana?'

'If he doesn't, I will fight him in court.'

'Mothers usually get custody,' I said.

'Yes, but I can't afford big lawyers like he can. Anything can happen in court.'

'I hope it doesn't get to that.'

'I don't want to lose another child.' She began to cry.

I went up to hold her.

'I am sorry about Parvathy,' Alia sobbed into my chest. 'I chose her.'

'Alia it's not your fault. It's nobody's fault. Sometimes it is just bad luck.'

'Why does my Siya get all the bad luck? What did she even do to anyone?' Alia said.

I had no answer.

'I'll beg Manish. Give me Suhana. I don't want any money. I can't deal with a drama in court. I'll accept my defeat.'

'What defeat, Alia?' I said. 'You are strong. That's what's special about you.'

'I am tired of being strong. I'll take Suhana and go live with Amma. He can keep the Icon flat too.'

'Then I will come with you.'

'What?'

'I can't live without you.'

She went up to the bay window and looked outside.

'What happened?' I said.

She turned around to face me.

'Keshav.'

'Yes?'

'A single woman may find your unrealistic sweet nothings cute. When you say something to a married, broken woman, be careful.'

'Unrealistic?'

'Don't say things you don't mean, even if it is to make her feel better.'

'I am not just saying it. I mean it. I will move to Kochi if you go there,' I said in a firm voice.

I bent down on one knee.

'Keshav, don't, please,' she said, fighting back tears.

'Shh,' I said. 'Listen carefully, Alia. These aren't sweet nothings. This is what I truly want.'

She looked at me.

'I am Keshav Rajpurohit. I am thirty years old. I am tired of living my life alone. But I don't want to be with just anyone. Not some random Gehlot uncle's daughter or some girl I find suitable. I like you. I love you.'

'Keshav, I love you too but look at my state. I am not some bright and chirpy girl ...'

'Shh, I am not done. I don't want to be with someone who is always bright and chirpy. I want to be with someone real. Someone who has also seen the dark side of life, so she can support me in my darkest moments. I love you because you are that. I want to be with you.'

I kissed her hand. I stood up and lightly kissed her lips.

'That's sweet, Keshav, but I told you before, I have way too much baggage.'

'I will help carry your bags then. Don't worry, together we will have enough baggage allowance.'

'Are you sure?

'Yes.'

'What about your parents?'

'We'll invite them to our wedding for sure,' I said.

'What!' She giggled.

'My parents will have to eventually accept our relationship. They have no choice.'

'What about Suhana?'

'She will be my daughter too. I already see her as that.'

'She misses you a lot. Keeps asking me when she can meet you.'

'What do you tell her?'

'I tell her let your mommy get some time with him first.'

'What!'

'Kidding. I tell her you will meet her soon.'

'I hope so too.'

'You'll wait for me until my divorce mess is cleared? It may take a while.'

'Of course. This is about the rest of my life.'

She came forward and kissed me.

'I will talk to Manish. End this as soon as possible.'

'I hope he is fair to you.'

'Don't worry. I'll get my due, and Suhana.'

'That sounds like the strong Alia I know.'

'You are my strength,' she said.

My phone rang in my pocket.

'Want to take that?' she said, as I continued to hold her.

'No,' I said.

The phone continued to ring.

'Take the call. I am here only.' Alia let go of me.

I took out my phone. The call was from Saurabh.

'You read the article I sent you, bhai?'

'No.'

'Check your WhatsApp.'

'What is it?'

'It leaked. The whole thing about Roy and Dharmesh. Our failed operation.'

'What the hell! Really?' I said. I put the call on speaker mode to access WhatsApp on my phone. I clicked the news link Saurabh had sent me. I read the headline.

Siya Arora kidnapping case: Child predator 'Roy' and tutor Dharmesh identified as prime suspects, manage to abscond

'What the hell is this!' I said.

Alia looked on curiously. I kept a finger on her lips, asking her to remain silent.

'Read the whole article. They screwed us too. Fortunately, they didn't use our names,' Saurabh said.

'Fine, I'll read it. Bye then,' I said, to end the call.

'Okay, bhai. By the way, where are you? Not at home?'

Alia watched me with a concerned expression.

'Why?' I said.

'Aunty called. She said you hadn't come home yet. She wanted to know about your lunch plans.'

'I am busy. Don't worry. I will message her. I will be back in the evening.'

'Okay. Where are you anyway?'

'I came to get a haircut.'

'You need until evening for that?'

'I am getting other treatments.'

'What treatments?'

'Golu, let me read this stupid article. I'll talk to you later.'

I disconnected the call.

'You could have made up a better excuse,' Alia said.

'Whatever. Let's go through this,' I said.

Alia and I read the article together on my phone.

The Siya Arora case, which involved the abduction of the twelve-year-old girl from her grandparents' Gurugram house last year, was recently reopened. The Gurugram police released the names of two suspects—Siya's

> tutor Dharmesh Kumar and another unknown person with the alias 'Roy'—who the police describe as 'a middle-aged child predator'. According to our sources, a Gurugram police team led by Inspector Chautala almost caught both suspects in a trap laid at the Ambience Mall. But both of them managed to escape and remain untraceable. The police did not reveal the exact reason for the failure of that operation. However, our sources suggest two amateur private detectives appointed by the Arora family caused the bungling up of the entire operation.

'What is this nonsense!' Alia said. I continued to read.

> Talking about the case, Inspector Chautala said, 'I feel bad that the suspects got away. However, the current development does finally remove any doubt cast on the Arora family, who were vilified in certain sections of the media. Siya Arora was the unfortunate victim of a paedophile ring, and that's the sad truth of the case.'

'Aren't you upset?' Alia said. 'The police has leaked this to the media. And they are blaming you even though you did all the work.'

'They didn't leak it. They released it. It's official. Chautala gave his quotes,' I said.

'It's false, Keshav,' Alia said. 'They can't entirely blame you.'

'Doesn't matter. I deserve it. I did screw up, after all.'

Chapter 41

368 days missing

'No, Uncle, I'm fine,' I said.

'Take a small one. It's good for health,' Shamsher said.

He handed me a glass of Scotch on the rocks. A small peg for Punjabis is an extra-large one for the rest of mankind. Saurabh and I had been invited for dinner at Navratna House. They had also invited Chautala and Viren.

All of us were waiting for Manish and Alia in the living room. Shamsher told us they were running late and would reach in about twenty minutes.

Viren and Chautala looked far less threatening in civilian clothes and holding whisky glasses. Chautala wore a kurta pyjama and a sleeveless jacket. He could pass off as a local politician. Viren was in jeans.

Chautala addressed everyone in the room as he shared his wisdom.

'In high-profile cases, you have to handle the media well. They will provoke you. You have to keep your cool. Experience teaches you.'

Viren, Shamsher and Timmy nodded in response. Durga sipped her drink. She kept one eye on the maid who was bringing in the snacks. Rachna was with the kids upstairs. Chautala continued to speak.

'That's why when this reporter called me, I gave proper quotes on Roy and Dharmesh. If I had avoided the journalist or yelled at him, asking how he had found out about our operation, he would have written all sorts of nonsense.'

'Absolutely, sir,' Viren said enthusiastically. 'Your quotes were excellent. Pure class, sir.'

I didn't see any excellence or class in Chautala's quotes, on a story he had definitely leaked and planted himself. I kept quiet and sipped my whisky. Chautala continued.

'Thanks. You also learn all this, Viren. The police doesn't exist in isolation these days.'

'Yes, sir. One loose comment from our side and social media will roast the police all week,' Viren said.

'Yes, don't you remember last time?' Shamsher said. 'They twisted what we said at the press conference and blamed our family. Bloody rascals.'

'Horrible!' Durga said as she shuddered. 'The very worst time of my life. One year of hell. Never want that to happen again.'

'It won't, Durgaji,' Chautala said. 'Even social media is completely sympathetic to you now. Right, Viren?'

'Yes, now they are talking about paedophile rings. Your family is being seen as a victim of cyber predators. Dharmesh and Roy—all the anger is directed at them,' Viren said.

The maid came and placed plates loaded with chicken kebabs and paneer tikka on the coffee table. Durga picked up the plate of kebabs and offered it to the cops.

'Pure veg, madam. That's the one difference between Haryana and Punjab, even though we are neighbours,' Chautala guffawed.

'Oh, sorry,' Durga said. She switched to the paneer tikka plate instead.

'But in this golden poison, we are same,' Chautala said, displaying his drink to Shamsher.

'Cheers,' Shamsher said. They clinked their glasses.

'We didn't catch the criminals, but at the least your family name was cleared. That gives me peace,' Chautala said.

'That's the best thing that happened,' Durga said. 'I can't thank you enough for that.'

'All Chautala sir's idea,' Viren said and immediately realised Saurabh and I were also present. He spoke again, 'As in, once the media somehow got to know of it, sir said why not we set the narrative this time.'

'Thank you, Chautalaji,' Timmy said, topping up the inspector's drink.

'Welcome. This is good whisky,' Chautala said.

'Glenlivet, twelve years old,' Timmy said. 'I'll send a couple of bottles to you. Actually, I will send a case.'

'Oh no, sir. Not necessary,' Chautala said and grinned.

'Sir, if it's not for anything in return, it's not wrong. I will send it as a friend. I'll send a case to you as well, Viren sir,' Timmy said.

Viren beamed back.

'Thank you,' Viren said and lifted his glass. 'Twelve-year-old whisky? Amazing to think how long ago it was kept in a cask.'

I wanted to say it was around the same time Siya was born. The same Siya they had forgotten about. Instead, Viren and Chautala listened to Timmy explain about the Scotch bottling process, which he had personally witnessed on a tour in Scotland.

'Scotch has its own class,' Chautala said. 'Totally amazing how they manage to maintain the quality in every bottle.'

'What do we do next about Dharmesh?' I attempted to change the topic.

Everyone looked at me like I was the uncle who had suddenly entered the party and shut down the music.

Timmy, Shamsher and Durga remained quiet. Chautala spoke to me.

'I sent lookout alerts to all stations. What else to do now but wait until he surfaces?' Chautala said.

'Is it possible to get flight data for all flights taking off from Terminal 3 that afternoon?' I said.

Viren kept his glass down and said, 'Not a bad idea, actually. We will need DGCA permissions but—' Chautala interrupted him.

'We would actually have Dharmesh in custody if you hadn't stopped us from catching him that day,' Chautala said.

Saurabh and I silently studied the floor.

The doorbell rang, breaking the uncomfortable silence in the room.

'Ah, Manish and Alia are here,' Durga said and stood up. 'They are so late. Come, let's move to the dining table. It's time for dinner.'

'The family is super happy, bhai,' Saurabh said. He sat on the Icon gym floor with his legs stretched out, holding a medicine ball between his hands. He angled his round body in opposite directions as he moved the ball from side to side.

'I'm shocked,' I said. 'I thought the Aroras would put more pressure on the police to find Dharmesh and Roy. They are sending them liquor bottles instead. Like they are celebrating some victory.'

'Their name is cleared. Public sympathy is back with them. Diamonds are selling again. It's what they wanted most,' Saurabh said.

'Yeah. Anyway, now lift your legs in the air while you do the same twists,' I said.

'What!' Saurabh said, aghast at my suggestion.

'Of course. That's the real abdominal exercise,' I said.

He lifted his legs in the air for two seconds before they came crashing down.

My phone rang. The same call had come four times that day.

'+8475 calling' it said on my phone screen.

'Why don't you pick up?' Saurabh said, huffing and puffing in the middle of his twists.

'It's a weird number,' I said. I showed him my phone.

'Oh, I had two missed calls from the same number too. Seems like a scam.'

'Yeah. I'll ignore it,' I said. I handed him a five-kilo dumbbell.

'What's this for?'

'Bicep curls. You need to build muscle.'

'Bhai?'

'Yes?'

'When will I get a six-pack?'

I lay in Saurabh's bed in his room late at night.

Alia messaged me.

'I miss you.'

'Miss you too. What's happening with Manish?'

'He said let's decide when to tell the parents about the divorce. And how to break it to Suhana.'

'Custody?'

'He agreed to joint custody. I want full.'

'Okay.'

'Sorry it's taking time.'

'I understand,' I messaged her.

'Who are you chatting with?' Saurabh said.

'Alia. Just discussing some bills and other routine stuff,' I said to Saurabh and looked at my phone again.

'Manish and I both felt it's better if we inform his parents after October 17,' Alia had sent me another message.

'Why that date?'

'Siya's birthday.'

'Oh. Sorry.'

'My in-laws and Manish are thinking of doing something that day.'

'Doing what?'

'Like a function. We do a puja and donate to charity. Maybe call some underprivileged kids and distribute some gifts. Have to figure out details.'

'That's nice.'

My phone rang. The strange number was calling me again.

'Golu, what the hell is this!' I said, showing him my phone screen.

Saurabh and I looked at each other.

'Pick it up once,' Saurabh said. 'What's the worst that can happen?'

I took the call on speaker mode.

'Hello?' I heard a young male voice on the other side.

'Yes,' I said in a soft voice.

'Keshav sir?'

Saurabh and I looked at each other in astonishment.

'Yes,' I said.

'It's Dharmesh.'

I literally sprang up.

Saurabh gestured to me to keep talking to him.

'Hi, Dharmesh, where are you?' I said.

'I've been trying to reach you since yesterday.'

'I don't pick up calls from suspicious numbers.'

'I'm using an encryption app to call. It hides the number.'

'Why? Where are you?'

'I can't tell you my exact location. All I can say is I am not in India.'

'You ran away.'

'It's not what you think, Keshav sir.'

'What isn't?'

'I saw the media stories. My parents saw them too. It's not true.'

'You ran away, Dharmesh.'

'No, sir.'

'You saw Parvathy's post, alerted Roy and made him escape too.'

'You know about Parvathy's post?'

'Yes. What you are doing is wrong, Dharmesh. You can't hide forever.'

'I didn't want to run away. He told me to.'

'Who?'

'My sir.'

'Who's your sir?'

'This person you call Roy. That's the name he uses on the net.'

'What's your sir's real name?'

'I honestly don't know his real name. Even if I did, I couldn't tell you, Keshav sir.'

'Why not?'

'He's very powerful. He will harm me.'

'He is a paedophile. You helped him kidnap Siya. You are already in big trouble, Dharmesh. Don't make it worse for yourself.'

'I didn't help kidnap Siya, I swear.'

'You had so many of her pictures on your phone. Why?'

He remained silent. Saurabh signalled to me to stay calm.

'Listen, Dharmesh, the real culprit is Roy. We want him. Tell me what happened, please,' I said in a gentle voice.

'He told me to fly out immediately. No luggage. Just my passport. He sent the ticket and visa on my phone.'

'Roy did? When?'

'Minutes after I sent him a screenshot of Parvathy's post in a red dress.'

'Why did you send him Parvathy's picture? She's a child.'

'For five hundred rupees.'

'What!'

'He set a rate. Five hundred rupees per picture. One thousand for a video. Ten thousand if I connect the student to him on social media.'

'He paid you to supply pictures of your students?'

'Yes.'

I slapped my forehead in disbelief. 'Why did you agree to do that?' I said.

'I thought it was harmless. The pictures didn't have anything revealing in them. He just wanted normal pictures of real kids. Maybe chat with them a bit through social media.'

'It's wrong,' I said.

'I now realise it was wrong. I needed the money. I had no

business in the lockdown. Been trying to recover ever since. For one tiny video I earned the same as two hours of tuitions.'

'He asks little children for their nudes. Wants to meet them and take them home.'

'I swear, sir, I never knew all this. I thought he's some lonely, rich man.'

'How did you get to know him?'

'He contacted me on Instagram.'

'Have you met him?'

'A couple of times. He would meet and hand over cash to me.'

'How old is he?'

'Around fifty.'

'Fuck. Dharmesh, you helped a fifty-year-old perv meet young girls?'

'I swear, sir, I didn't know. I am sorry, sir. Please, sir, help me, sir. The police and the media are painting me as this kidnapper.'

'You introduced him to Siya?'

'Yes, sir. But that's it.'

'Did Roy kidnap Siya?'

'He didn't. At least that's what he has told me several times. Said he had nothing to do with the abduction. He wanted you and the police to know that. But I honestly don't know, sir.'

In the background, I could hear the sound of the azaan.

'Which country are you in? Is that Arabic?' I said as I tried to recognise the language.

He did not respond.

'I can find out. Flight records will tell me eventually anyway.'

'Keshav sir, I am in Dubai. Clear my name, sir, please.'

'And Roy?'

'He travels all over the world. Not sure where he is now.'

'Dharmesh, help us get Roy.'

'I have to go, sir. I'll talk later.'

'When? I don't have your number …'

But he had cut the call.

Saurabh and I looked at each other, perplexed. I shrugged.

I stepped off the bed to go to my room. Saurabh spoke from behind me.

'Tell Chautala about this call?' Saurabh said.

'Never. He'll blurt it out to the media. It'll ensure Roy and Dharmesh vanish forever,' I said as I left his room.

Chapter 42

'Hello, Mr Arora? Keshav Rajpurohit here,' I said on the phone.

'Oh, how are you, Keshav?' Shamsher said.

Saurabh's head swerved towards me in surprise.

We were at the Reebok store in Ambience Mall. Saurabh wanted to buy new fitness clothes. He was trying on a shiny red T-shirt with a matching pair of red and white shorts.

'Why are you calling Shamsher?' Saurabh whispered.

'One second, Mr Arora,' I said and placed the call on mute. 'To fix a meeting with him,' I said to Saurabh.

'Why?'

'I'll tell you. Listen, you look like a tomato in this all-red outfit. Please get something else.'

Saurabh made a face as he went back to the trial room. I unmuted the call.

'Sorry, to keep you holding, Mr Arora. It is just that Saurabh and I would like to meet you.'

'Sure, come anytime in the evening. Actually, I have to give your invitation card to you.'

'Invitation?'

'We are doing a small function to commemorate Siya's birthday.'

'Oh, yes. Alia mentioned it.'

'Yes, we have tied up with an NGO called Raasta, they work with underprivileged children. If we are meeting, I can give it to you personally.'

'Sure. Mr Arora, I have one request though.'

'Tell me.'

'We would like to talk to you alone. Not with your wife present.'

'Wait, let me see,' he said and paused. I waited until he spoke again.

'Saturday afternoon Durga will be out. She has to meet the priest and make other arrangements for Siya's function. Timmy and Rachna also usually take the kids out on Saturday afternoons.'

'Thank you. I'll see you then,' I said and ended the call.

Saurabh emerged from the trial room again. This time he was wearing a neon T-shirt and shorts. He looked like a glowing lemon and I had to squint to prevent too much light from hitting my retina.

'This is fine, right?' he said and twirled around. 'Bright and cheery?'

'You sure? No tea, coffee, nimbu pani?'

'No, sir, thank you.'

'Whisky?'

'Of course not, sir,' I said. Saurabh and I had arrived at Navratna House at two in the afternoon. Shamsher had met us alone in the living room.

'Snacks?' Shamsher said.

'Which snacks exactly, sir?' Saurabh said. I stared at him.

'Nothing, sir, please sit. Don't be formal. We are fine,' I said.

Shamsher handed us a cream envelope. I opened it and read the invitation card inside.

More than one year ago she was taken from us. While she is never out of our thoughts for a single moment, we wanted to remember her with our family and friends on her special day.

We, Durga and Shamsher Arora, request you to join us on the birthday of our granddaughter
Siya Arora
(d/o Manish and Alia Arora)
On 17 October 2021
Time: 6.00 p.m.

At Serene Villa Neighbourhood Park
(opposite Navratna House)
Programme:
Ganesh Puja, havan and bhajans: 10.00 a.m. – 11.00 a.m.
Charitable distributions to underprivileged: 11.00 a.m. – 12.00 p.m.
Lunch for underprivileged children: 12.00 p.m. – 1.00 p.m.
No gifts or flowers please.
Please donate to the NGOs we support instead.

I kept the card back in the envelope.

'What did you want to talk about?' Shamsher said.

'About Siya.'

'Oh. Any news of Dharmesh or Roy?'

I shook my head.

'I wanted to discuss another possibility with you. What if Roy and Dharmesh didn't do it?'

'What do you mean?' Shamsher said, sitting up straight on the sofa. 'Roy is your suspect. Dharmesh helped him. Both escaped. Isn't it?'

'Yes,' I said.

'Then why are you second-guessing your own theory? Has anything happened?'

Saurabh and I looked at each other. We didn't want to tell him about Dharmesh's call.

'No, sir,' Saurabh said. 'But while we try to locate them, we thought why not explore other angles?'

'Angles? What angles?' Shamsher appeared perplexed.

'Let me be direct with you, Mr Arora. Do you trust your wife completely?' I said.

'As in?' said Shamsher, his eyebrows peaking.

'We know she does not have a good relationship with Alia,' I said.

'But that is common, saas-bahu not getting along. Durga has a loose tongue, makes it worse.'

'But do you feel ...' I said as Shamsher interrupted me.

'You think I haven't answered this to the police a million times already?'

'You have, sir. But we are not the police. We aren't talking to the media. And we will never implicate anyone without evidence.'

'Then what are you doing right now? You want to check my home, do it. You want to interview everyone in this house or every other house on the street, do it. It's all been done multiple times.'

'We know, sir, we checked all testimonies,' I said.

'Durga has issues. She is mean, petty and I would say, even horrible to Alia sometimes. But she can't kidnap or be involved in kidnapping her own granddaughter. It's just not her,' Shamsher said.

'Did she insist on a paternity test for Siya?' I said in a plain voice.

The colour evaporated from Shamsher's face.

'You know about this?'

'We are just doing our job, sir,' I said. 'Nothing personal.'

Shamsher let out a sigh.

'Yes,' he said. 'She had Manish and Siya tested. A low point for our family.'

Saurabh and I nodded. An awkward silence followed.

Shamsher came out of his reverie.

'I thought of the possibility too. Did Durga make Siya disappear ... ?' Shamsher said emotionally.

He looked away from me.

'What made you think that?' I said.

'Durga never liked Siya much. Alia came into our house because of her, after all.'

'Okay,' I said. 'So there is a possibility.'

Shamsher shook his head.

'No. The more I thought about it, the more implausible it all looked.'

'Why?'

'Durga and I were in the same room that night. If she had planned a kidnapping, some stress would show on her. I didn't see any such sign.'

'That does not mean—' Saurabh began, but Shamsher interrupted him.

'She's impulsive and emotional. She can't hide her feelings like a smooth criminal. Something would have cracked in the past year. Nothing.'

'The intruder took the side gate. She could have arranged for the keys,' I said.

'A saas giving taunts is one thing. Plotting a child's abduction is quite another. Too far-fetched.'

'I understand, sir, but ...'

'And why would she arrange the kidnapping from her own house? She could have arranged it outside. She knew what Siya was up to, where she went. Why risk incriminating people living in the house?'

'Point,' Saurabh said.

I looked warningly at Saurabh.

Shamsher continued.

'No phone calls. No messages. Nothing. The police checked everyone's call records. They called all the numbers Durga spoke to in the past few months. They never found anything fishy,' Shamsher said.

'Maybe you are right,' I said.

'Keshav beta, I like you. You have a never-give-up attitude, which is great. But if you go about this case like this, you will be in endless loops forever. I have seen life. Sometimes, painful as it is, you have to let things go.'

I nodded. He took out a chequebook. He signed a cheque for two lakh rupees.

'I know Alia is paying you separately. But here's a bit extra from my side. For all your hard work.'

Saurabh extended his hand to take the cheque. I pulled his arm away.

'No, sir, we can't,' I said. 'We've been paid enough. We didn't even solve the case.'

'You did. Dharmesh and Roy are behind this. As a detective, your job was to find the criminals. Catching them is the job of the police.'

Shamsher tried to hand the cheque to me again. I took it and gave it back to him.

'Thanks for the gesture, sir, but we can't accept it,' I said and stood up to leave.

'I insist,' Shamsher said.

'Sir, if you want, please add this amount to the charity distributions at Siya's function,' I said.

Chapter 43

395 days missing

'We could have taken the two lakh rupees. We could have used it for a car. We wouldn't have to be in this polluting machine,' Saurabh said.

We were in an autorickshaw headed for the commemorative function for Siya. Saurabh and I had dressed up in kurta-pyjamas for the solemn occasion.

'Golu, Alia paid us five lakh rupees already. How can I take more?'

'We didn't ask Shamsher uncle. He was giving it himself. He liked our work.'

'Alia gave us more than enough,' I said.

'Whatever. Is she okay?'

'Meaning?'

'I am sure today is hard for her. Siya's birthday.'

'Yes.'

'You chatted with her about how she was feeling?'

'As in?'

'You do, right? You chat with her every night at eleven.'

I looked at Saurabh.

'I am a detective, bhai,' he said. 'I notice things.'

I turned away from Saurabh to look outside. I felt the mid-morning breeze on my face.

'Golu, I have a question for you. Don't freak out.'

'What?'

'If Alia wasn't married, would you be okay with me dating her?' I said.

'Huh?' Saurabh said. 'Why are you asking me that?'

'Hypothetically. I am checking what is the bigger issue. Her being married or her being a client?'

'If she wasn't married it would be okay after the assignment is over. She isn't a client for life, after all.'

'Good to know I have your approval on that.'

'But why did you ask me that?'

'Nothing. See that big tent in the park. That's for Siya's function. We've reached.'

'Okay, great. Listen, I am going to eat today. You said I am allowed a cheat meal occasionally.'

'Within limits.'

'Whose limits? Yours or mine?' Saurabh said as the auto came to a stop.

A hundred children, between six and fourteen years, sat in neat rows on red and black striped floor rugs in the tent. An NGO called Raasta had arranged for these underprivileged children to attend.

Pandit Shastri, with two of his assistants and the Arora family, sat around a havan kund with burning firewood. Idols of Hindu gods and a large framed picture of Siya were placed near the holy fire.

Alia sat next to Manish, her hands folded and eyes closed in prayer. She had not seen me yet. I noticed the white salwar kameez and white dupatta on her head. After removing our shoes outside the puja area, Saurabh and I sat down in the third row, behind Alia and her family.

The priest chanted mantras. Sometimes he would ask members of the family to repeat a few phrases. As he reached the final prayers, he addressed the entire gathering.

'For Siya Arora and her entire family's peace, let us end today's puja with everyone repeating the Gayatri mantra twenty-one times. During the chant, everybody come up here, one at a time, for prasad and blessings.

'Everyone knows the Gayatri mantra?' one of the supervisors from Raasta said to the children.

The kids nodded.

'Okay, one by one go for prasad. With discipline. Understood? Else, no gifts later,' the supervisor said.

The children nodded their heads vigorously.

'Okay, let's all begin ...' he said, and a hundred children joined in.

Oṃ bhūr bhuvaḥ svaḥ
Tat savitur vareṇyaṃ
Bhargo devasya dhīmahi
Dhiyo yo naḥ prachodayāt

The tent resonated with the chanting. I saw each tear that rolled down Alia's cheeks.

The children went up to the havan kund one at a time and bowed to the idols of the various gods. Panditji and his assistants applied tilak, gave prasad and tied a thread on each of their wrists.

The heavy chants in the air slowly rendered Alia inconsolable. Rachna put an arm around her shoulders, which were shaking visibly. Suhana glanced worriedly at her mother from time to time. The Gayatri mantra continued to reverberate in the background.

'Fold your hands and chant, bhai,' Saurabh said as he noticed me looking at Alia, before going back to reciting the mantra.

After collecting prasad, the children moved to the lunch area towards one corner of the tent. Each child received a set of textbooks, three sets of clothes, a blanket and a bag of chocolates. In addition, each underprivileged child's parent received five thousand rupees through a direct bank transfer. The Aroras also gave an additional donation of two lakh rupees to Raasta, probably the cheque I had declined.

Durga came up to me a little later.

'Come, Keshav and Saurabh. Get your prasad. The children are done,' she said.

I nodded and stood up.

'After that, come to the house for lunch. Family and friends will be eating there,' Durga said.

I guess I belonged to the 'family and friends' category now. I wondered how that would change after their daughter-in-law divorced their son and came to live with me.

Saurabh and I reached the holy fire. We too bowed to the various deities. I spread my palms above the fire to take in the warmth. Pandit Shastri asked me to extend my arm so he could tie the mouli, or the holy thread.

He chanted mantras as he tied a red and white cotton thread around my wrist. Like an expert who had done this a million times, he tied the knots without looking at my hand. I saw his deft fingers move. I also noticed he had several mouli threads tied around his own wrist as well. The ends of the threads hung loose. Behind those threads was a tattoo, comprising of some Sanskrit words.

I froze, my gaze transfixed on his wrist.

'Done, beta, take the prasad,' he said, offering me a spoonful of halwa.

'Huh?' I said, eyes still on his wrist.

'Fast-fast, chalo, keep moving. There are more people waiting.' He made an impatient clicking sound with his mouth at my slowness.

I noticed his perfectly combed hair glistening with oil. I leaned forward and sniffed as deeply as I could.

The smell of mustard oil, one often used in cooking, hit my nose.

'Keshav, so happy you came,' Alia said and smiled, even as she wiped her tears.

'Definitely. I am so happy I came too,' I said, with my heart beating like a drum.

'Let me eat,' Saurabh said. 'It's my cheat meal.'

'No, you come with me now,' I said.

Saurabh was holding a plate with four pooris and a bowl of aloo sabzi.

'I need to talk,' I whispered in a concerned and urgent manner. Milling around us were the many guests of the Aroras in their living room.

'So talk,' Saurabh said. He took a bite of a poori. He went into semi-ecstasy as he tasted fried dough after months.

'Alone,' I said. He noticed my serious expression. I yanked the plate out of his hand.

'Bhai?'

'Later,' I said. 'Come with me.'

I grabbed his hand and dragged him towards the garden.

'Where are you going? Eat something,' Rachna said as she saw me pulling Saurabh like a bull through muddy slush.

'Yes,' I said, 'in a minute.'

'What's the matter?' Saurabh said once we reached the garden.

I pointed to the recently tied thread around his wrist.

'What's this, Saurabh?'

'Mouli.'

'Pandit Shastri has many moulis on his wrist. Some hang loose.'

'So?'

'What did Suhana say she saw in the darkness? Friendship bands. Many of them loose.'

'Oh my God. You sure?'

'He has a tattoo with Sanskrit lettering too. Behind the moulis.'

'Same as what Suhana said. Oh God, what do we do?' Saurabh said.

'Still want to eat your pooris?'

Saurabh shook his head. 'Bhai, I didn't know. But Shastri? Are you sure?'

'Suhana also said the bad man had a pungent smell that she associated with the kitchen. She told me all this in Kochi.'

'And?'

'Shastri's hair reeks of mustard oil. Suhana also said the bad man had a familiar voice. C'mon, Saurabh.'

'Damn.'

'We still need to confirm it ourselves. Can't tell the family until we are absolutely sure. He is their priest.'

'Yes, for decades. What do we do?'

'We have to follow him.'

We walked out of the house to the lane outside. Multiple cars of visitors were parked on the street. As we scanned the various vehicles, Pandit Shastri and his two assistants passed us on their way to Navratna House.

'Let's find out Shastri's vehicle. When he leaves, we'll follow him,' I said.

'He'll probably go home. We can ask the family for his address.'

'No. I don't want them to get even a whiff of us looking around. As far as the Aroras are concerned, our assignment is over. I remember Alia telling me his home and office are in Hauz Khas Village.'

'How about I ask Shastri for his card?'

'Don't alert anyone, Golu. No talking to him at all. Let's just follow him.'

'How? We don't even have a car. Plus, he or his assistants might figure out someone is following them.'

What next? I scratched my two-day stubble.

'Wait, I have a better idea than us following him,' Saurabh said.

'What?'

'I have a spare phone and a power bank at home.'

'And?'

'I'll go get them. You find out which is his vehicle. We'll hide that phone in his car.'

'Oh, track his location through GPS?'

'Exactly. Come on, bhai, better than us chasing him through the city.'

'Superb, Golu,' I said. 'You are too good.'

'I know. Anyway, I better find an auto. I'll be back in half an hour. Meanwhile, you do two important things.'

'What?'

'One, find Shastri's car and figure out a way to hide the phone and power bank inside it.'

'Okay. What's the second thing?'

'Keep six pooris and lots of aloo sabzi for me.'

It took me ten minutes to find Pandit Shastri's Innova amidst the fifty-plus cars parked outside Navratna House. The car had a little saffron flag on the bumper and 'Om' stickers on the rear and front windows. I waited a few steps away, keeping an eye on the vehicle. Five minutes later, one of Shastri's assistants walked towards the Innova. He was carrying three idols. I noticed him struggle to take out the Innova keys from his kurta pocket. I walked up to him.

'Let me help you,' I said.

'God bless you,' the assistant said.

I took the keys from his hand and opened the rear door. It opened upwards, allowing access to the entire back of the car. The assistant folded one of the rear seats to make more space. One by one, he placed the three idols in the back of the vehicle. He touched the feet of each idol and wrapped them in a blanket already kept in the car. After the idols were secure, he stepped back to allow me to shut the rear door again. I brought the door down and it closed with a thud.

'The Gayatri mantra chants by the children were amazing,' I said.

'Thank you,' he said.

As I spoke to him, I pulled out the Innova key from the rear door. However, before I pulled it out, I flicked the key to the right once to ensure the rear door remained unlocked.

'All those vibrations from children chanting together, so soothing. Made me feel so peaceful,' I said and returned the key to him.

'I am glad you found it beneficial,' the assistant said and smiled. 'May Krishna bless you.'

'He just did,' I whispered to myself as I folded my hands to the idols inside the car.

Saurabh met me outside Navratna House. He handed me a washcloth with two hard rectangular objects wrapped inside.

'My spare phone, on silent mode. Connected to a big power bank. Should keep going on standby for a week.'

'Okay,' I said.

'Did you find his car?'

I pointed to the Innova.

'How do we put in this contraption? Stick it at the bottom?'

'Not necessary,' I said and smiled. I walked up with him to Shastri's vehicle. I looked around to ensure nobody was watching us and opened the rear door with a simple press of the latch. Saurabh looked at me gobsmacked as I smiled at him.

I lifted the rubber mat on the floor. A spare tyre lay underneath. I hid the phone and power bank under the spare wheel and replaced the rubber mats. I slammed the Innova door shut.

'There, done. Come, it's time to eat. As many pooris as you want.'

Saurabh walked back with me to Navratna House with a stunned expression.

'Bhai,' Saurabh said. 'How did you open the Innova so easily?'

'You saw the idols of gods wrapped in the blanket in the car?'

'Yes. What about them?'

'Let's just say the gods themselves decided to help me today.'

Chapter 44

'He's been at this Hauz Khas Village location all afternoon. Boring,' I said.

Saurabh had enabled location tracking of Shastri's Innova on both our phones. I sat on his bed late at night, staring at my mobile phone.

'See, better to track him like this than sit in a car and wait all day ... Oww!' Saurabh winced in pain.

He lay in bed next to me, holding his stomach.

'Are you okay?' I said.

'Stomach hurts like hell. Too many pooris,' Saurabh said.

'I told you to stop at six.'

'You don't understand. I don't get cheat meals every day. I had to make the most of it.'

I shook my head and smirked.

'I will have Eno,' he said. He walked towards his closet to take out the medicine.

He mixed a packet of Eno in a glass of water and drank up the bubbling solution.

'Golu, he moved.'

'What?' Saurabh said.

'The car moved,' I said. I showed him my phone.

'Where's he going at midnight?' Saurabh said.

'Let's see,' I said.

The special purpose GPS app displayed a red dot, indicating the location of Shastri's Innova. It moved out of Hauz Khas towards Aurobindo Marg. Saurabh lay in bed next to me, one eye on the phone.

'He's getting on to the Delhi–Meerut Expressway,' Saurabh said.

'We should have been behind him. How will we know what he's up to?'

'Let's wait and watch first. If we followed him at midnight on empty roads, you think he won't notice our car behind him?'

'What's up?' Alia's WhatsApp notification flashed on my screen. Fortunately, she hadn't sent anything more affectionate, with Saurabh's hawk eyes on my phone.

She sent another message.

'Sorry I couldn't attend to you today. Too many guests.'

'Alia Arora sends you messages at midnight?' Saurabh said.

I shrugged.

'Bhai? Want to say something?'

'She's divorcing Manish.'

'What? How do you know that?'

'She told me. They are negotiating custody and assets.'

'I was so overwhelmed today,' Alia sent another message.

'She shares all this personal stuff with you?' Saurabh said.

'What's the big deal?' I said. I angled my phone away from Saurabh and sent a reply.

'Can understand. With Saurabh now. Catch you later. Good night.'

'What did you reply?' Saurabh said.

'Nothing. Should we focus on Shastri? Or let him vanish?'

'He won't. The red dot is always going to be visible,' Saurabh said, taking out his own phone. 'Anyway, I will keep an eye on him here. You can use your phone to keep chatting with her.'

'I already said good night to her. Where's Shastri?'

'He crossed the Delhi border and left the highway in Ghaziabad. Going towards some villages,' Saurabh said, eyes on his phone.

I opened my phone to the tracking app as well. The red dot followed the thin rural roads of Ghaziabad.

'You told Alia we are tracking the priest?' Saurabh said.

'No, I am not telling anyone this time.'

'Good,' Saurabh said

'Golu, you said it's fine, right?'

'What?'

'If Alia is divorced and no longer a client I can date her?'

Saurabh sprang up to sit on the bed.

'Are you serious?' Saurabh said.

'Don't freak out. It's a possibility.'

'So, you do like her,' he said and lay back again.

I looked at Saurabh.

'You are my best friend. I don't want to hide things from you.'

'Meaning?'

'If Alia is single and available, I want to be with her.'

'She's a mother.'

'So? Any woman I marry will eventually be one, isn't it?' I said.

'Marry? You must like her a lot.'

'I meant in general. Anyway, I'll need your support. With the parental tsunami I will have to deal with, even if I date her.'

Saurabh looked at me and smiled.

'I am always with you, bhai.'

'Thanks. Oh, the red dot stopped,' I said.

Saurabh and I looked at our phones. Saurabh switched on the satellite view in his map.

'He's parked off the main road. Inside some field. All green around him.'

'It's an area called Morta,' I said.

The red dot remained there for over ninety minutes. At 1.30 a.m., it finally moved again. The car retraced its path. Forty minutes later it came back to the same spot in Hauz Khas Village.

'We should go check this place. Why did the Innova go there so late?' I said.

'Yes, I will save the GPS coordinates,' Saurabh said and yawned.

'Good. Anyway, let's sleep now,' I said.

'Bhai, I'll ask you something?'

'Yes.'

'Do you love her?' Saurabh said.

'Good night, Saurabh.'

'Just sugarcane fields. That's all people grow here,' Bansi said to me.

Shastri's Innova had done the midnight trip from Hauz Khas to the same spot in Morta for three consecutive nights. I had come to visit the spot in the afternoon. Located between Ghaziabad and Modi Nagar, Morta is a collection of several small villages. The spot's GPS coordinates, accurate within a twenty-metre radius, brought me to the middle of a sugarcane field.

I found Bansi, a local farmer, riding a bicycle in the fields.

'What are those sheds?' I said, pointing to a building that resembled a warehouse.

'They make jaggery there. Most of the sugarcane is sold to a government agency. Some is used to make jaggery,' Bansi said. 'Why?'

'I am an agriculture student. I have to make a report on crops grown around Delhi.'

'What is there to report? Sugarcane grows, they sell it. Or they take out the juice and boil it. Whatever is left is jaggery. Centuries-old method.'

I smiled at Bansi, a thin man in his sixties with wrinkled skin and muscular legs.

'Are you from this area?' I said.

'Born here. Will die here.'

'Who owns all these fields?'

'Different people,' Bansi said. 'See that boundary? Beyond that is my field. The ones to the left belong to Raghu Singh. The one we are standing on belongs to the Shastri family.'

'That jaggery unit also belongs to the Shastris?'

'Yes, although they don't come here much. They hire labour in season, that's it.'

I walked towards the jaggery shed. I saw a dirt track with tyre marks. The Innova could have followed this path at night.

'Their fields are neglected. I have been asking them to sell me the land, but they won't,' Bansi said.

I nodded.

'Does all that go in your report too? Who owns the farms?' Bansi said.

'No, just curious,' I said and smiled.

'Okay, what's your name?'

'Krishna,' I said.

'I'll leave now. Nice meeting you, Krishna.'

'Same here. Bansiji, so this jaggery unit is operational?'

'It's a jaggery unit plus a sugarcane storage godown. I've not seen smoke come out of the chimney for a while though. I don't think they use it. All are busy with their jobs in the big city. That's the trend these days,' Bansi said as he pedalled off.

I walked out of Shastri's farm to the main road where my hired car waited for me. I sat in the car and we headed back to Delhi. I dialled a number.

'Viren sir? I need your help with something. But Chautala sir can't know about it,' I said.

Chapter 45

'Why are we here? I feel like I am in a horror movie,' Saurabh said.

We had reached Shastri's farm at ten in the night. We sat in our hired car, parked on the main road, fifty metres ahead of the farm.

'We have to wait until he arrives,' I said.

Saurabh jumped as my phone rang.

'Sorry, I need to put this on silent as well,' I said.

The call was from sub-inspector Viren.

'Why is he calling you?' Saurabh said as I shushed him.

'Viren sir, have you decided?'

'Yes. I will help you.'

'Thank you so much, sir. We don't have much time. You need to send the two men right now.'

'You only told me you need two men. You didn't tell me why,' Viren said.

'I need two strong guys. To help if the situation I am in gets violent.'

Saurabh looked at me, panic written on his face.

'What situation? Where are you? What's going on?' Viren said.

'I can't tell you, Viren sir. I just want you to trust me. Send two men. Without telling anyone. Not even Chautala sir.'

'Keshav, you know I can't do this. You have to tell me more. We are the police, not a bodyguard service.'

'Sir, can you come too, then? Bring at least one tough cop with you. Normal vehicle. No lights, no sound.'

'Where?'

'Morta, UP. After Ghaziabad. I'll drop the location pin. Come within an hour.'

'What is this about? At least tell me that.'

'Will you keep it to yourself?'

'Yes, Keshav. You have my word. Tell me, what is this about?'

'Siya Arora,' I said and ended the call.

2 hours later

'He moved,' I said.

Like every other night in the past week, the red dot left Hauz Khas and came towards Aurobindo Marg.

'Who?' Viren said. 'Shastri moved?'

Sub-inspector Viren had arrived one hour ago with Billu, a six-foot-tall broad-chested constable. They sat on the front seat of our hired Maruti Suzuki Dzire. Saurabh and I sat in the back. We had asked our driver to shift to Viren's car, parked a hundred metres away. Viren had come in a rented car as well, and not in the usual police Gypsy, to avoid attention.

'Yes, sir,' I said, looking at the red dot on my phone. 'Car leaving Hauz Khas.'

'Chautala sir has no idea,' Viren said. 'Don't get me into trouble.'

'Never, sir,' I said. 'Our man's on the Delhi–Meerut Highway.'

'Shastri is not just the Aroras' family priest. He also has connections with top families of Delhi. If you get this wrong, and Shastri finds out I helped you, he can ruin my career.'

'Won't happen, sir,' I said. 'Relax. You will stay here until I really need you.'

'What do you want to do anyway when he arrives?'

'For now, only I'll go out,' I said.

'Go where, bhai?' Saurabh said in a concerned voice.

'To the jaggery shed. I'll tail him if he goes in. See what he is up to.'

'Alone?' Saurabh said.

'Yes. One person can hide behind him. All of us can't. If I am in danger, I will call you guys to come save me.'

Viren nodded. We remained quiet for the next twenty minutes. The only sound we heard came from the chilly breeze rustling through the sugarcane. All I saw was the red dot.

'He is five minutes away. I will leave now.'

I opened the car door. Viren turned to look at me.

'Are you sure this a good idea, Keshav? What if there's nothing there?' Viren said.

'Whatever it is, we will find out in a few minutes,' I said as I left the car.

Chapter 46

There was a heavy wooden door at the entrance of the shed, with a thick brass lock on it. I found discarded pieces of broken furniture strewn around the door. I hid under a broken table and switched off my phone light.

I waited in the darkness, crickets chirping in the eerie silence. Seconds moved slowly as the red dot inched towards my own location, towards me.

A few minutes later, I saw bright headlights as a vehicle rustled through the dirt track and stopped outside the jaggery shed. It was Shastri's Innova.

The car's engine was switched off, the headlights faded and it became pitch black again. I heard the Innova door open and shut.

I saw the silhouette of a man walk towards the shed. He came and stood outside the main door, three feet away from me.

I remained absolutely still under the broken table.

The man took out his phone and a bunch of keys from his pocket. He turned on his phone flashlight. I could see Shastri's face. He wore a white kurta pyjama. His oily hair shone in his phone's light. A plastic bag hung from his wrist.

The door opened with a loud creak as Shastri unlocked it and pushed it in with some effort.

He went inside the jaggery unit and switched on a light, which lit up the windows. To have a better look inside, I had to come out from under the table. I tiptoed to the main door.

I saw him through the windows. He still held the bunch of keys in his hand. He switched off the main light inside. After a few seconds, I saw another faint light come from the windows.

I went closer to the window. I saw heavy machinery and a pile of plastic gunny bags inside the unit. I could not see Shastri.

I also saw stairs going down within the unit, probably towards a basement. This faint light came from below the staircase.

I went to the main door and pushed it firmly and slowly, leaving it slightly ajar. I waited for a few seconds and went into the unit. My heart was in my mouth as I walked towards the staircase.

My foot hit a piece of floor machinery hard. I felt blood trickle through my toes. I bit my lip to avoid making any sound from the pain and grabbed my foot for a few seconds as I regained my composure. I heard the jangling of keys from the basement level. I hobbled over to the staircase.

I saw him down below, at the bottom of this inner staircase, his back towards me. He turned a key inside a keyhole to open another basement door, which had multiple locks. He spent thirty seconds unlocking all of them one by one. Once this basement door opened, it revealed another iron mesh door. As Shastri searched for the right key for this door, he spoke for the first time.

'I have a gift for you today,' he said.

My heart jumped out of my mouth. Had he spotted me? I placed one foot in front of me and tensed up my arms, ready for a fight. I waited for him to turn around. However, he didn't.

'You wanted a new notepad, right?' he said, turning the key in the mesh door.

My mouth fell open as I understood the situation. I called Saurabh.

'Yeah? Shall we come?' Saurabh said as he picked up the call in an instant.

'Immediately,' I whispered and cut the call.

Shastri heard my voice. He turned with a jerk and looked up, surprised. Due to the low light, he couldn't make out my face.

'Who is it?' he said in Hindi.

'Shastri?' I said. 'Stay where you are.'

'Kaun hai, behenchod?' he screamed, running up the steps. I stepped back as he charged towards me.

He reached upstairs and looked around. He located me in a

corner of the unit. He pulled out a large, nine-inch switchblade knife from his pocket.

'Who is it? From the village?' he said. 'What are you doing here?'

'It's over, Shastri. Stay where you are and keep the knife down.'

From my words, he understood I wasn't a local villager from Morta. He switched on the main shed light. We could both see each other clearly. He tried to place me but couldn't. I saw the panic on his face. He ran towards me, knife in hand. I dodged him a few times, moving right and left, and hid behind the jaggery-processing machinery.

He kept stabbing the air with his knife. My injured foot twisted and hurt me as I darted around. He caught up with me soon. He took his arm back and aimed the knife at me with full force. I picked up a gunny bag and placed it between us. The knife struck the jaggery-filled bag and went in.

Shastri screamed curses as he tried to yank out the knife. I pushed the gunny bag hard against him. He walked backwards, not letting go of the knife. We reached the end of the shed in this manner, his back against the wall.

'Don't move,' I said, gunny bag pressed against his chest.

He managed to yank out the knife. He struck at me again.

A shooting pain went through my entire arm as the knife struck my shoulder. The gunny bag fell from my hand. He came close to me. He lifted his arm again to stab me, this time in my chest.

However, Shastri's arm froze mid-air.

'Enough, Panditji!' Viren shouted.

Shastri couldn't move. Billu held him from behind in an arm-lock around his neck. Shastri groaned as Billu's heavy biceps suffocated him. Billu used his other hand to twist Shastri's wrist until the knife fell down.

I held my injured shoulder with my other arm. Saurabh ran up to me.

'Are you okay, bhai? There's so much blood on your shirt,' he said.

'I am fine,' I said, catching my breath. Shastri glared at me even as he remained in Billu's tight grip.

I walked to the staircase to go to the basement.

'Where are you going?' Saurabh said, as he saw me stumble down the steps.

'Wait,' I said, pressing my shoulder.

I found Shastri's bunch of keys at the bottom of the stairs. I tried them one by one, until one of them worked. I opened the iron mesh door.

I stepped into the basement, which felt like a dark dungeon. I switched on my phone flashlight.

It revealed a large godown-like room. I saw several dusty rugs on the floor. Along one wall, I saw a wash basin in a tiny kitchen counter. I moved my phone light around. I saw a small Indian-style toilet.

'What was that noise upstairs, ji?' A soft female voice startled me. I turned around. The phone light fell on a folding bed in front of me. A girl sat on the bed, partially covered in a quilt. She had long, unkempt and curly hair that reached down to her knees. I pointed the phone flashlight on her face.

Her hazel eyes glittered back at me.

'Siya?' I said.

She didn't recognise my unfamiliar voice.

'Who is it?' she said, her voice terrified.

I moved towards her.

'No, no, please no. Don't come close.'

She began to shiver. I sat down next to her.

'Siya, it's okay. I have come to rescue you.'

She shook her head.

'No. Please, don't. Please leave. Who are you? Where's Shastriji?'

I realised she had not seen my face. I turned the phone flashlight towards me.

'Relax, Siya. I am Keshav. Your mother sent me.'

She blinked at me.

'Alia asked me to find you. You are free now. Come, let's go.'

I offered my hand to her. She didn't take it. Instead, she began to sob uncontrollably.

'Please trust me, Siya. Your mother asked me to find you. Your sister Suhana saw you get kidnapped. That night when Shastri came with a knife.'

She looked up at me. I continued.

'It's okay. The police caught Shastri. Let's get out of here. I'll take you home. The Icon,' I said. I extended my hand again.

She held my hand. Her thin fingers trembled. They felt weak and malnourished.

'May I carry you?' I said.

She nodded. I lifted her along with the quilt. My shoulder hurt even more with the extra weight. She continued to cry as I took her past the mesh door. Saurabh came running down the steps.

'Bhai?' he said and froze, his mouth open, when he saw Siya in my arms.

'Hold her, please,' I said. 'My shoulder is killing me.'

Chapter 47

Siya speaks

'Good night, Siya didi,' Suhana said.

'Good night, my little baby Suhana. Love you,' I said.

Suhana smiled. She loved it when I called her a little baby, like when she was a toddler. I shut my eyes and tried to sleep. I couldn't. I kept thinking of Aryan. Last week he liked and commented on all of Parvathy's posts. She'd done the same for his pictures too. Is something going on between them? Doesn't Parvathy know Aryan is my crush? She is my best friend. She should leave him alone. Did she offer to kiss him or what? I would never do that. It's not right at our age. Parvathy says she's my best friend, but always wants what I want.

Why isn't sleep coming? Hope Mommy and Dad are okay and don't fight again. Mommy agreed to spend the weekend at Daadu–Daadi's house, but it always leads to some argument.

I tossed and turned in bed. My mind went to Roy. I need to stop chatting with him. He is not a good person. I finally felt drowsy. I drifted off to sleep.

'Wake up. Utho.' I heard a voice. Someone shook my shoulder. A man. Not Dad. Is it Timmy uncle? Daadu? No, it's a different voice.

'Hmmm?' I said. I felt sharp, cold metal on my neck. It's a huge knife. He pressed it harder and it hurt a little. Is this a bad dream? No, I can see Suhana lying next to me. My eyes are open. There's someone in the room.

'Shh. Ekdum chup. Stay absolutely quiet, or I will kill you and all these children,' he said.

I want to scream but my throat won't cooperate. I can't speak. He will kill me. He will kill Suhana, Rohit and Sanjay too. Who is he? A robber? He's come to rob Daadu–Daadi's house?

'Come with me quietly. Chalo,' he said.

Where does he want me to go? My legs began to tremble. He pressed the knife harder into my neck.

'No sound. I'll push this knife deep inside you and your little sister.'

Suhana moved a little in her sleep. I don't know what to do. He could finish us all in a minute. What does he want?

'Be quiet and come with me. Nothing will happen. I won't hurt you,' he said.

I've heard his voice before. Who is he? I try to make out his face in the darkness. I can't.

We came out of the room and walked down the steps. Everyone is asleep. All of the bedroom doors are shut. He made me walk out of the living room and through the front door. We came out into the garden. It was dark and quiet outside. He kept me in front of him, knife at my back.

We reached the side gate. It's unlocked. He pushed the side gate open and we came out into the street. He took me to the lane behind Navratna House. He poked the knife in my back, nudging me forward.

We reached a large car. He gestured to me to step inside. He made me sit in the backseat and handed me a quilt.

'Where are you taking me?' I spoke finally.

'Shh,' he said, showing me the knife.

'Cover yourself completely with this quilt. And no sound,' he said again.

He sat in the driver's seat. The dim streetlight hit his face.

'Panditji?' I said.

He turned around and slapped me hard across my face.

'I said no sound. My people are still inside your house. If you make a sound or do any tricks, they will kill your entire family.'

Fear gripped me. My body froze. I couldn't scream even if I wanted to. He pulled the quilt over my face and told me to keep my eyes shut. I complied. The car began to move. We kept driving for an hour. I didn't think about what was happening to me. My only thought was that Suhana and my cousins would now be safe.

2 days missing

'Eat,' he said. He pushed a plate with rotis and dal in front of me.

'I want to go home,' I said.

'This is your home now.'

'This is hell. Take off these chains, please. I beg you,' I said and cried.

I sat on the folding bed with several old quilts. I looked around the dark windowless room. A tiny ventilation slit near the ceiling let a bit of light in, telling me it was daytime outside. Two lightbulbs tried hard to keep this basement room illuminated. Stacks of sugarcane lay in one corner. Dirty rugs covered the muddy floor. He had tied me up with long steel chains, hooked up to the ceiling. The chain lengths just about allowed me to reach the toilet and the water tap.

He sat next to me on the folding bed.

'Look, crying won't help,' he said in a sympathetic voice, as if he was on my side. 'I don't like it when you cry. And please eat. Otherwise you will feel worse.'

'Why have you brought me here?'

'You don't understand. This is God's will. God instructed me. You see, I had a dream. You are to be my wife. That's my destiny.'

'Destiny?' I said in a faint voice.

'Of course. I helped your mother get married to your father so you could come into this world. If I wasn't there, who knows, they would have aborted you.'

'Aborted?'

He ignored me and continued.

'I also did the vaastu of Navratna House, so I knew about the side entrance and the location of the key rack. It was God helping me. I came so often to Navratna House, I could take the side-gate key during one visit, make a duplicate, and hang it back on another visit. If all this is not destiny then what else is it?'

'Are you crazy?'

'No. I am in touch with God. Four days later is an auspicious day. That's when we will get married.'

'Married ... ?'

'I won't touch you until then,' he said.

'Please just take me back home.'

'Ever since I saw your mother and placed my hand on her head, I felt something. But she was meant for Manishji. I kept wondering what it was that made me feel that way. That desire a priest is not supposed to feel. Later I realised, it was you. You were inside her then. And grew up to be just like your mother.'

I cried. But I could not shut out his words. They entered my ears smoothly like acid.

'I wondered what would be the right moment to take you. And then I saw the pictures of your dance performance in school. You were Menaka, I was the rishi. Menaka came to break Vishwamitra's meditation. You came to break mine. You were dancing for me ... '

'No,' I said and shook my head violently.

'It's okay, you wouldn't realise all that. But this is what I have been instructed to do.'

'By whom?'

'By God.'

'I am twelve.'

'Do you know how old Mahatma Gandhi was when he got married? Thirteen.'

'What?'

He stepped off the bed. He walked up to the sink. He pointed to a cardboard box kept on the counter.

'There's soap, toothpaste, shampoo, everything you need. I even brought some clothes. I'll get your wedding dress later.'

'Panditji, you have kidnapped me. Take me home. My Daadu and Dad will catch you.'

Panditji smiled.

'Nobody can find you here. Anyway, your grandmother doesn't like you. They won't look for you. But I will care for you, provide for you. That's why I am telling you to eat. Don't make trouble.'

'The police will find you.'

'Not here. See, if you trouble me, I will have to kill you and bury you right here. Nobody will know.'

He walked up to the mesh door.

'Where are you going?' I said.

'I have work. As your husband, I have to go earn a living for both of us, right? I'll be back tomorrow.'

'Please take off these chains.'

'I will. When you behave yourself. Eat, shower and take care of yourself.'

'My grandparents hold you in such high regard.'

'I hold them in very high regard too,' he said as he left.

I heard the sound of two doors being shut and four locks being locked. The basement fell silent after he left. I cried alone for another hour.

I realised that if I ever wanted to get out of here alive, I had to survive.

I pulled the plate with rotis and dal towards me.

6 days missing

'Wear it,' he said. He thrust a red lehenga at me.

I shook my head and instinctively ducked as he raised his hand. 'Don't make me slap you.'

I shook my head again. He grabbed my hair and tugged at it hard.

'I know how to tame you, you cat-eyed kameeni,' he said.

He took out his switchblade knife and flicked it open.

'Okay, okay, fine. I'll wear it,' I said.

'Good,' he said as he unchained me. 'And this is for your good behaviour. No more chains from now on. See, I am a good man.'

I dragged myself out of bed and went to a corner of the room with the lehenga.

'Can you look away?' I said.

'I am going to be your husband soon ... ' He laughed and turned around. I changed into the garish red outfit.

'Beautiful,' he said. 'Your eyes have done magic on me. They attracted me for years. I knew there was something. That's why I had that dream to make you my wife.'

He made me sit on the floor. After lighting a small fire in a small iron utensil, he began to recite some mantras. He pulled me up by my hand and made me take several rounds around the fire with him. Smoke choked the entire basement, as the ventilation slit could not get rid of it fast enough. I coughed non-stop.

After the ceremony, he made me sit on the bed again.

'You and I are now husband and wife.'

'No,' I said, 'we are not.'

He slapped me.

'As a wife you are not to answer me back.'

My ear was hurting from the blow.

'It's time now to do your wifely duties,' he said.

I gave him a blank look.

'Take off your clothes.'

His eyes told me what was about to happen.

'No. Please, no, I beg you,' I said. 'This is wrong.'

He grabbed my shoulder.

'I have married you. You are with your husband. How is it wrong?'

The next hour of my life is an hour I would rather forget. Or at least I try to. For those sixty minutes I ceased to be. I became numb, to whatever was happening, to the fear, to the intense pain.

I contemplated taking his knife and killing myself. But would my parents be looking for me? Won't Suhana be missing me? Should I live for a few more days so they find me?

'I'm leaving. I'll be back tomorrow,' I heard him say through the door as he locked it from the outside.

30 days missing

He caught me trying to escape today. He beat me up with a stick. My legs hurt from being chained. I can't move. I can't reach the tap for water. I can't even get to the toilet. No food or water for two days. That is my punishment for trying to escape.

I had figured out a way to reach the ventilator. I made the folding bed stand upright. I brought it near the wall. I climbed up on the upright bed to reach the ventilator. I couldn't get out through the six-inch gap though. But I could see outside. I saw a muddy ground and a boundary wall, with fields beyond it. I also saw sugarcane stacks and piles of gunny bags.

By now I knew Shastri's routine. He only came at night. In the daytime, I could reach the ventilator and scream out loud. Maybe someone would hear me.

'Help me, I am trapped,' I shouted into the ventilator slit for several hours every day. Nobody heard me, but I didn't give up. Every afternoon I shouted for help till my throat gave up.

However, he came in the daytime today. He heard me scream for help. He saw me precariously balanced on the upright bed.

'You ask to be punished,' he said, bringing the stick.

The chains were back, this time fastening me tighter to the bed. I didn't say a word. I didn't cry through his beatings or whatever else he did to me. I had to survive.

67 days missing

'Come here,' he said.

I began to remove my clothes. I knew the ritual well. The sooner it began, the sooner it ended and the sooner he left. Living a solitary life seemed infinitely better than having him around.

'No, not for that,' he said. He sat next to me, flicked open his switchblade knife and cut a lock of my hair.

'This is for your parents. They just won't stop looking for you.'

Hope lit up inside me.

'Where's the dress you had on that night I brought you here?' he said.

'In that cardboard box. Why?'

He took out my night suit from the box and put it in a plastic bag. Next he poked the knife into my forearm. Blood spurted out.

'Why? I didn't misbehave today,' I cried.

He took my soiled night suit and rubbed it on the fresh blood.

'You didn't. I just need them to think you are dead. So they stop looking for you, forever,' he said before he left.

I fainted. Along with blood, I had also lost any last bit of hope.

395 days missing

'Here, special food today,' he said. He had brought a four-tier steel tiffin with him.

He spread an old newspaper on the bed. He took out pooris, aloo sabzi, halwa and an assortment of mithai from the tiffin.

I ate the food in silence. He walked around the basement and turned to me.

'You never say thanks,' he said.

'For?' I said.

'I do so much for you. Give you food, shelter, clothes. You should be grateful.'

'Thank you,' I said. I didn't want a slap while I ate.

'Welcome. How is the food?'

'Nice,' I said, trying to keep my voice friendly.

'It's from your grandparents' house.'

I looked at him in confusion.

'I conducted a puja there today. The food is from your house.'

I felt nauseous. I didn't feel like eating anymore. Why did he do this to me? Does he enjoy seeing me in pain?

'The puja was for you,' he said. 'It's your birthday today. Happy birthday.'

Sadness ambushed me as tears streamed down my eyes. I didn't even know how long I had been here. He had kidnapped me a month before my birthday. I had spent an infinite amount of time here since then. How old was I? Thirteen? Fourteen? I remembered the last birthday I'd celebrated. We had a party with all my classmates at the Icon club house.

'Why are you crying so much?' he said.

I tried to gulp down my tears. I didn't want to be beaten up on my birthday.

'Eat,' he said.

I nodded.

'What gift can I get you for your birthday?' he said.

I looked up at him.

'Can I step outside?' I said. 'I'd like to see the sky above me.'

'That will never happen. Your entire life is now here forever. Anything else?'

I kept quiet.

'Tell me, my pretty little wife?'

'Could you get me some notepads and pens?'

Chapter 48

400 days

Siya sat huddled in the backseat next to me. Saurabh sat next to the driver who was taking us all back to Gurugram. Viren and Billu had separately taken Shastri to the Sushant Lok Police Station in their own car.

Our car zipped through the empty roads at night and reached Gurugram much faster than usual. Siya kept looking outside the car with a blank expression. She turned to look at me once. I smiled at her. She did not respond.

I took out my phone and made a call.

'Keshav?' Alia whispered in a sleepy voice as she picked up the phone.

'Hi. Sorry to wake you up.'

I could hear her make her way out to the living room. She spoke again.

'Why are you calling me so late? It's two in the morning.'

'I am coming to your place.'

'What?'

'Yes. Can you tell the watchman downstairs you are expecting me so that he lets me into your tower?'

'What? Now? Are you crazy? Why?'

'Have to tell you something.'

'Are you drunk? Manish is sleeping in the other room.'

'Wake him up too.'

'What?'

'We'll be there in ten minutes,' I said.

'We? There's more than just you?'

'Yes, don't worry. See you soon,' I said and ended the call.

I turned towards Siya.

'Are you okay? Want anything?'

She nodded.

'What?'

'Home.'

I rang the doorbell of Alia's house with one hand and held Siya's hand in the other. Saurabh and the tower watchman stood behind me. Three rings later, Alia opened the door.

'Yes, Keshav,' she said. Manish stood behind her. He rubbed his eyes, just awakened from sleep.

I didn't answer. I simply nudged Siya forward. Alia's mouth and eyes opened wide. She lifted her right hand to cover her mouth. Alia's body trembled as she bent lower on her knees to come level with her daughter.

'Siya? My Siya,' she said, still in shock. She kept her hands on her daughter's thin shoulders very delicately.

'Mommy,' Siya said and began to cry softly.

'Oh my God. Siya,' Alia said. She hugged her daughter tight, their bodies shaking as one as they wept. Manish seemed to be in a daze as he bent to touch his daughter's hair.

'Siya?' he said in a broken voice.

Manish looked at me.

'How… ? How did this happen? How did you find her?' he said.

'It's late. Siya needs to rest. I'll share everything tomorrow,' I said.

I gestured to Alia to take her daughter inside. She and Siya left. Manish remained with us.

Saurabh pressed the lift button.

'There is so much blood on your shirt, Keshav. Are you okay?' Manish said as Saurabh, the watchman and I entered the lift.

'Don't worry about me,' I said. 'Just take care of Siya.'

'Your picture is on TV, on the local news channel,' my father said.

'Really?' I said. I stretched my arms as I sat up in my bed. Despite my late night hospital visit, my shoulder still hurt.

'You found their girl?' Papa said.

'We did,' I said.

'Congratulations!'

'Thank you, Papa.'

'There is a bandage on your shoulder. What happened?' he said.

'Minor injury. I am fine,' I said, getting off the bed.

I followed my father to the living room.

I read the flashing headlines.

Siya Arora found.

Family priest arrested.

Girl held captive for 400 horrific days.

The local anchor spoke on screen.

'In a miracle of sorts, thirteen- or rather fourteen-year-old Siya Arora has been found 400 days after her disappearance. In a dramatic and clandestine midnight operation, a special team raided and found her imprisoned at a jaggery-processing unit owned by Pandit Shastri, the Aroras' family priest. The special team comprised private detectives Keshav Rajpurohit and Saurabh Maheshwari. Accompanying them were sub-inspector Viren Hooda and constable Billu Tomar from the Gurugram Police.'

I looked at my phone. I had messages from Inspector Chautala, Saurabh and Alia. I read Chautala's message first.

'Amazing job, Keshavji. You only took Viren. But, bro, don't forget my contribution. Taking good care of Shastri. Don't worry, we will get him the death penalty, no less. Will see you soon, bro.'

I had become Chautala's 'bro' overnight.

'Thank you, sir,' I replied to him. He called me back immediately.

'I should thank you, Keshav bro. By the way, we checked

flight records. Dharmesh went to Dubai. This Roy should also be there. We have contacted Dubai Police. Don't worry, we won't leave this stalker Roy either.'

'That's great,' I said. We spoke for some time and made a plan to meet up soon.

I opened Saurabh's message.

'Bhai, we are stars. That girl Jyoti who rejected me saw my name on TV and messaged. She wants to meet! Okay, bhai, call me when you wake up.'

I finally opened Alia's message.

'Keshav, you are like God to me. I love you.'

1 week later

'I am sorry, one more minute and I will release you,' she said.

'It's okay, Alia, I love your long hugs,' I said.

I had booked a room at Anya again. Alia and I had barely spoken all week. She told me that the plethora of media requests for interviews had not stopped. She had declined them all. Countless friends, curious neighbours and classmates wanted to come over and visit as well. Alia had said no to most of them. Finally, seven days after Siya had returned, she messaged saying she wanted to see me.

'How's Siya?'

Her face was still buried in my chest and her voice was muffled.

'It will take her a long time to be completely okay, but she's better. Started therapy.'

I stroked Alia's hair.

'She started talking to me. She is telling me in bits and pieces what happened to her. It's just the worst ... horrible.' I could feel the front of my shirt grow damp with her tears.

Alia sat up and wiped her eyes.

'Keshav, is it okay if we don't do anything today? You know what I mean? I am not in that frame of mind.'

'Of course. I just wanted to meet you. More than anything else.'

'Yes, I did too. Sorry, I have had no time.'

'I understand ... it's okay,' I said.

'You are the sweetest. You are the best. You truly are God for me, Keshav,' she said.

'Stop saying that,' I said.

'No, really. And I don't like that we have to keep meeting in secret.'

'Me neither,' I said.

'I've finalised everything with Manish. After the puja, we had decided to tell his parents. And work out the asset split. But right now I have to ensure Siya gets okay. She's top priority, Keshav.'

'I understand,' I said. 'You and I can wait for a while.'

'Will you give me one month? What date is it today? 29 October, right? Let's meet here at Anya again after exactly one month, on 29 November. We'll finalise our plans then, I promise. Will you be okay with that?'

'I will be okay if you smile,' I said. 'Just focus on healing Siya.'

She smiled as we embraced each other again.

1 more week later

'Alia's father-in-law and husband are here,' my mother said, standing at my bedroom door.

'Huh?' I said, surprised. I leapt off the bed. It was mid-morning on a Monday. I changed out of my nightclothes into a shirt and pants and went to the living room.

Shamsher and Manish stood up to greet me. 'We wanted to come and thank you properly,' Shamsher said. 'Thank you.'

'Welcome, uncle. Hello, Manish. How is Siya doing?'

'Good,' Manish said. 'Her physical health is fine. Counselling going on too. Her therapist said she will take a little while to be ready to meet other people apart from family. But she's better.'

'Great. Please sit,' I said. All of us sat down on the sofas. My mother offered tea. They declined.

'We won't take much of your time. We have to go to work anyway,' Manish said.

'Your son is a gem,' Shamsher said to my father. Papa smiled, not used to hearing things like that about me.

'Keshav, what you have done for us is priceless, but we wanted to give you something,' Shamsher said.

He took out a jewellery box from his jacket pocket.

'This is for your mother. I made a necklace similar to this for my own mother when I opened my jewellery business.'

He handed my mother the box. Ma opened it and almost toppled over.

'What is this, Aroraji?' she said, displaying the diamond necklace in the box to all of us.

'From our side. Please ...' Manish said and folded his hands to my mother.

Before my mother could react, Shamsher spoke again.

'That's not all. Keshav, last time you returned my cheque. I am not going to give you that option today. Check your messages. I sent something by bank transfer.'

I opened my phone and checked my email. I had a message from my bank, saying I had received a payment of a number that began with one and had several zeros.

'Uncle, but—' I began.

'It is the least we can do,' Shamsher said. 'And this was Durga's idea. To send you a wire transfer, to ensure that you get the money.'

I nodded.

'This is just a small thank you from us, Keshav,' Manish said. 'You gave my family a new life. We can never repay you for that.'

'My wife would have come and thanked you personally too. She just feels too ashamed,' Shamsher said.

I nodded.

'She'll change. We all have to make sure she does,' Shamsher said. 'Shastri being the culprit has shaken her very badly. She trusted him with her life.'

'I haven't been there for Alia. I let her be mistreated. I promise it won't happen again,' Manish said.

My father looked at Shamsher and Manish, stupefied.

'You must have lunch. How can you leave without lunch?' my mother said, necklace box still in hand.

'Some other time,' Shamsher said as he and Manish stood up to leave. 'Thank you once again.'

I messaged Saurabh right after they left.

'Shamsher gave me more money.'

'And you returned the cheque again?'

'He wired it. I can't.'

'How much?'

'Ten lakh rupees, I think.'

'Wow. Send me the message.'

I went to my email, copied the bank's message and pasted it into my WhatsApp chat with Saurabh.

'Bhai, that's not ten lakhs.'

'Then?'

'It's one crore. You missed one zero.'

Another week later

I dropped the barbell hard on the ground. I had finished my fifth and final set of hundred-kilo deadlifts. I still had two more weeks before 29 November, when I would meet Alia again. To make time go faster, I stayed longer and worked harder at the gym. I picked up my phone after the workout.

An unknown number had sent me a message.

'Hi. This is Siya.'

I wiped my face with a hand towel and replied.

'Hi, Siya, how are you?'

'I am well. Mom gave me your number. Am I disturbing you?'

'Not at all. I am glad you are doing well.'

'You are the first person I am sending a message to since the therapist allowed me to use the phone again.'

'Oh, that's great.'

'I never got a chance to thank you.'

'It's okay. You had been through a lot.'

'Thank you for finding me and saving my life. Thank you for not giving up on me.'

'It's your mother. She is the one who never gave up. She told me to find you.'

'Yes. I love my mother the most.'

I could have replied with an 'I do too', but didn't.

'That's so nice,' I responded.

'I love Dad and Suhana a lot too.'

'Yes, of course.'

'Suhana told me how you used to play with her.'

'Yes, say hello to the little Uno champion.'

'I will.'

'Listen, Siya. If there's anything I can do for you or anything you want, let me know, okay?'

'I only wanted one thing. And you already gave it to me.'

'What?'

'My family.'

Chapter 49

2 more weeks later
Anya Hotel, Gurugram

'I can't tell you how much Siya has improved,' Alia said, looking rested and truly happy for the first time since I had met her. 'The therapy, family time, it is all working.'

'I am so glad,' I said.

She came close to me on the bed in the hotel room and started to put her arms around me. I stopped her.

'What?' she said.

'Let's talk first.'

'Yes, of course.'

'It's 29 November. The date to make plans.'

'Yes,' she said, with a slight hesitation in her voice.

I remained silent. She spoke again.

'What do you think we should do, Keshav?'

Before I could respond, her phone rang. Siya had called her from home.

'Yes, beta, I will be home soon …' Alia said. 'An hour or two, is that okay? Okay, sure, I will come sooner. No, I won't go out anywhere today after that. Take rest, beta.' Alia ended the call and turned to me.

'Sorry, it was Siya. Had to take it.'

'Of course, is everything okay?'

'Yes. She just needs to talk to me frequently, or she gets a little anxious. Anyway, where were we? The plan, right?'

I didn't say anything. I watched her face as she continued to talk, mostly to herself.

'We had to meet today to discuss the plan, right? We had to discuss us.'

I remained quiet. She continued to ramble.

'Should I go to Kochi again? Take the girls with me for Christmas break? Should I communicate with Manish from there? What do I tell him?'

In her sky-blue chikan salwar kameez with her long hair left open in soft curls, she looked beautiful, even if a little tense. Her mentioning Kochi brought a rush of memories of our nights at Tower House.

No, I couldn't allow myself to think of all that. No, Keshav, no. Be strong.

'Are you even listening?' she said.

I shook my head. I had to be strong through this.

'Alia, you know it and I know it.'

'What?' Alia said, confused.

'There's no us. There's no us anymore. We both know it.'

Alia's face froze, as if surprised that I had sensed what was on her mind.

'We can't do this,' I said.

Tears streamed down Alia's face as she gave the tiniest nod.

'Alia, I love you. More than anything else in the world.'

'I know,' she said. 'So how can I say we can't. I had promised you.'

'Shh, Alia. Listen to me, I love you, I want you, but,' I said and paused.

'But what?'

'But Siya needs her family more,' I said.

Alia looked into my eyes. She remained silent for a minute before she spoke again.

'And what about you and me?' she said. I shook my head again.

'It can't be about you and me. It's about Siya. I met Manish. He is trying to make things better, right?'

'Yes,' Alia said in a soft voice.

'Alia, Siya needs this. Suhana needs this. You need your family together. You and me, well, no. We aren't above all this.'

I could no longer restrain my tears. I walked up to the window to look outside, so she wouldn't see me cry.

She came up and held me from behind.

'I had similar thoughts. That Siya needs to have her family. Unlike you, I didn't have the courage to bring it up. I feel so bad.'

'Why?'

'Because what about you?' she said. 'It would be so selfish if I just leave you after this.'

'I'll be fine. I know you are not being selfish. You are being selfless.'

'I love you, Keshav.'

'I'll always love you too, Alia,' I said, 'for the rest of my life. But sometimes love means letting go, for the happiness of others.'

I turned around to face her and we embraced one last time.

'Alia,' I said, fighting back tears.

'Yes?' she said.

'Tell Suhana I miss her. Keshav uncle misses his little Uno champion.'

Chapter 50

I ate my dinner in silence. Saurabh and my parents could sense my sombre mood. They left me alone. Papa spoke to Saurabh.

'What's the point of your Cybersafe job now?'

'What do you mean, Uncle?' Saurabh said, eating his dietary allowance of two small chapatis as slowly as possible.

'The Aroras gave you so much money. You have start-up capital now. Many of my Marwari friends' children have started their own business,' Papa said.

'Actually, I did have an idea. Something Keshav and I could do.'

'What?' I said, speaking for the first time that evening.

'Combine the detective agency with a child security software company.'

'Child security?' Papa said.

'Parents are worried about what their kids are doing on their phones. We can make apps that keep children's phones safe. Alert parents if something seems wrong.'

'That's good, actually,' I said. 'It will have a lot of demand. Behind every kid with a phone, there are worried parents.'

'Do it then,' Papa said.

'What about my IPS preparation?' I said.

'What's the point of it? Less than 0.1% chance of selection. Even then, they will shunt you around remote corners of India. Make you suck up to politicians. Do your own thing. You have the capital to open your own office and even hire a small team.'

'We do,' Saurabh said in an excited voice. 'What say, bhai?'

'We could,' I said.

'Why is your mood so off these days?' Ma said. She added more baingan bharta to my plate.

'I am okay,' I said.

'How's Alia Arora and her family?' Ma said.

I looked up at my mother at the mention of Alia's name.

'Must be fine. Their daughter is doing better last I heard.'

'Not in touch?' Ma said.

'Work done, have to move on, right?' I said.

My mother nodded. She spoke after a pause.

'I heard from a neighbour downstairs her marriage isn't going well. They are looking at a divorce. Is that true?' Ma said.

'When did you hear this?' I said.

'A couple of months ago. Do you know?'

'Firstly, Ma, I don't gossip about my clients. Second, no. Her marriage is fine. Siya coming back has brought the whole family back together. They cherish it like nothing else. So stop this loose talk.'

'Okay, fine. Why are you being so grumpy?' my mother said. She stood up with her plate and went to the kitchen in a huff.

'Keshav,' my father said.

'Yes, Papa?' I said.

'I am so proud of you,' he said.

I sat in my balcony, staring at her apartment in the opposite tower. Like every night, her lights went off at 11 p.m. Unlike before, she no longer messaged me around this time.

I could evade thoughts about her in the daytime, but the nights were difficult. Somehow, every night I ended up in my balcony, hoping to get a glimpse of her.

I continued to look at her dark apartment for over an hour after the lights went off.

'Bhai?' Saurabh said, coming into the balcony.

'Hey, Saurabh, haven't slept yet?'

'No, couldn't sleep. How come you are here?'

'Just wanted some air.'

'She's gone to sleep?' Saurabh said, looking at her apartment.

I looked at him, surprised. He smiled at me. Both of us burst into laughter. I couldn't hide anything from this idiot even if I tried.

'Sometimes true love means sacrificing your own happiness. So that others can be happy. Isn't it?' Saurabh said.

I nodded and smiled.

Saurabh patted my shoulder.

'I can't be her, bhai. But I will always be there for you.'

'I know. And thank you for that,' I said and gave my best friend a hug.

'Want to step out for coffee?' Saurabh said.

'It's midnight. What place would even be open?'

'There's Anya Hotel nearby. They have a twenty-four-hour café.'

The mention of Anya made me freeze.

'What? Isn't Anya okay?' Saurabh said.

I remained silent.

'You don't want to? I know the coffee is expensive. But, hey, we have money now,' Saurabh said.

'Huh? No, Anya is fine. Let's go,' I said and took out my phone. 'Wait, let me call a cab.'

'No, let's walk. Burns more calories that way,' Saurabh said and smiled.

About the Author

Chetan Bhagat is one of India's most acclaimed contemporary authors, with fourteen bestselling books to his credit. He is the author of ten blockbuster novels—*Five Point Someone, One Night @ the Call Center, The 3 Mistakes of My Life, 2 States, Revolution 2020, Half Girlfriend, One Indian Girl, The Girl in Room 105, One Arranged Murder* and *400 Days*, and most recently, *12 Years: My Messed-Up Love Story*—and four successful non-fiction titles—*What Young India Wants, Making India Awesome, India Positive* and *11 Rules for Life*. Chetan's books have remained bestsellers since their release. Many of his novels have been adapted into successful Bollywood films such as *3 Idiots, 2 States, Kai Po Che* and *Half Girlfriend*.

The New York Times called him the 'the biggest-selling English-language novelist in India's history'. *Time* magazine recognized him amongst the '100 most influential people in the world', while Fast Company, USA, listed him as one of the world's '100 most creative people in business'. Chetan writes columns for leading English and Hindi newspapers, focusing on youth and national development issues. He is also a motivational speaker, screenplay writer, YouTuber and podcaster.

Chetan quit his international investment-banking career in 2009 to dedicate his time entirely to writing and driving positive change in the country.

Chetan studied at IIT Delhi and IIM Ahmedabad. He is married to Anusha, an ex-classmate from IIMA, and they have twin boys, Shyam and Ishaan.

BESTSELLERS BY CHETAN BHAGAT

FICTION

400 Days

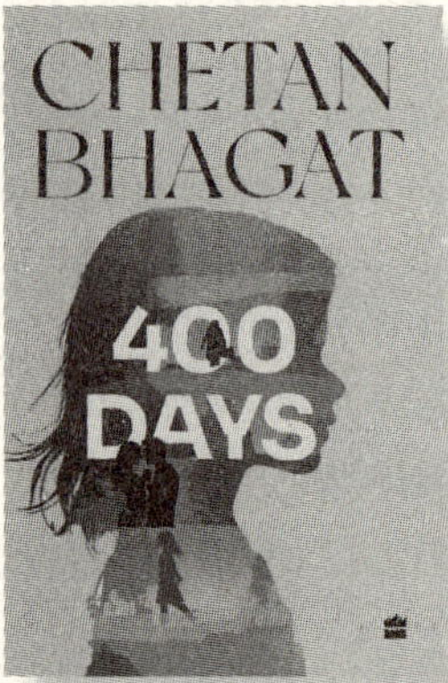

Hi, I am Keshav Raj Purohit and I am a disappointment to everyone around me.

I live with my parents, who keep telling me how I should:

a) get married,

b) focus on my IPS exams,

c) meet more people, and

d) close my detective agency.

But Alia Arora, neighbour and ex-model, wanted my help. And I couldn't take my eyes off her face ... I mean ... her case.

'My daughter Siya was kidnapped. Nine months ago,' Alia said. The police had given up. They called it a cold case. Even the rest of her family had stopped searching. Alia wouldn't stop looking, though. She wanted to know if I could help her.

Welcome to *400 Days*. A mystery and romance story like no other. An unputdownable tale of suspense, human relationships, love, friendship, the crazy world we live in and, above all, a mother's determination to never give up. From India's highest-selling author comes a page-turner that will not only keep you glued to the story but also touch you deeply.

One Arranged Murder

'Ever since you found Prerna, I lost my best friend ...'

Hi, this is Keshav, and Saurabh, my best friend, flatmate, colleague and business partner, won't talk to me. Because I made fun of him and his fiancé.

Saurabh and Prerna will be getting married soon. It is an arranged marriage. However, there is more cheesy romance between them than any love-marriage couple.

On Karva Chauth, she fasted for him. She didn't eat all day. In the evening, she called him and waited on the terrace for the moon and for Saurabh to return to break her fast. Excited, Saurabh ran up the steps of her three-storey house. But when he reached ...

Keshav has set up an investigation agency with his best friend, Saurabh. Can the two amateur detectives successfully solve another murder case that affects them personally? And where will it leave their friendship?

Welcome to *One Arranged Murder*, an unputdownable thriller from India's highest-selling author. A story about love, friendship, family and crime. It will keep you entertained and hooked right till the end.

The Girl in Room 105: An Unlove Story

Hi, I'm Keshav, and my life is screwed.

I hate my job and my girlfriend left me. Ah, the beautiful Zara. Zara is from Kashmir. She is Muslim. And did I tell you that my family is a bit, well, traditional? Anyway, leave that aside.

Zara and I broke up four years ago. She moved on in life. I didn't. I drank every night to forget her. I called, messaged, and stalked her on social media. She just ignored me.

However, that night, on the eve of her birthday, Zara messaged me. She called me over, like old times, to her hostel room 105. I shouldn't have gone, but I did … and my life changed forever.

This is not a love story. It is an unlove story. From the author of *Five Point Someone* and *2 States*, comes a fast-paced, funny and unputdownable thriller about obsessive love and finding purpose in life against the backdrop of contemporary India.

12 Years: My Messed-Up Love Story

He's 33. She's 21.

He's a struggling stand-up comic. She's a rising star in private equity.

He's divorced. She's never had a boyfriend.

He's Punjabi. She's from a conservative Jain family.

They shouldn't be together. But they can't stay apart.

Welcome to *12 Years: My Messed-Up Love Story.*

Saket and Payal couldn't be more different—age, background, beliefs. Yet, they're drawn to each other in ways they can't explain. Is it just chemistry, or something deeper? Is it madness and lust, or is it love?

Unputdownable and thoroughly entertaining, *12 Years* tries to answer the eternal question: How do you know if someone is *the one*—especially when everything says they're not?

From India's top-selling writer Chetan Bhagat comes a powerful new love story that will make you laugh, cry and rethink everything you know about love.

NON-FICTION

India Positive: Simple Takes on India's Burning Issues

Does it make any difference to the ordinary citizen which party is in power? Whether it's a majority or a coalition?

What can we do to better job prospects for India's youth?

How can we create a more equal society?

How do we create more world-class educational institutes?

What can we do about social media warriors and trolls?

In *India Positive*, bestselling author and columnist Chetan Bhagat brings together essays that work as a manifesto for change. Examining a gamut of subjects—from education to employment, from GST to infrastructure, from corruption to casteism—Bhagat reflects on what we can do right in order to move forward and become a truly modern, progressive country. He expresses in these pages his belief that, if we want to see reform, we—as citizens—need to be the solution. If our country is to shine, Bhagat says, we need to stand up and be 'India Positive Citizens'.

In a world ridden with negativity, these simply written, perceptive and solution-driven essays are a must-read for anyone invested in the present and future of India.

11 Rules for Life: Secrets to Level Up

MANDATORY READING FOR ALL INDIANS

One summer afternoon, Viraj, a food delivery guy, brings lunch for an author named Chetan. He is late and appears to be in distress. When Chetan asks him what the matter is, Viraj breaks down.

'I hate my life. My career is going nowhere. My girlfriend left me. I have no future,' he says.

The author offers Viraj a deal. 'I can fix this for you. Come back every day, when I order lunch. Each day, I will tell you one secret I've learnt about life.'

Welcome to *11 Rules for Life*, a no-holds-barred book that will transform your life.

In his most personal book yet, Chetan draws on his failures and triumphs, his many conversations with high achievers from all walks of life and over two decades as a celebrated motivational speaker.

Written in the inimitable style that has made Chetan one of India's top-selling writers, this inspiring, easy-to-read and straight-talking guide will help you rewire your brain for success in today's ultra-competitive and unfair world.

Ready to live your best life? If one book can change your life, this is it.

All these titles are also available in Hindi.